COLD STEEL, HOT LEAD

Another five minutes and they would be as dead as King Sol, Smoke Jensen thought as the fresh wave of bandits rolled toward them. He took time to aim carefully and knocked another outlaw from the saddle. Still they came. Around him, the *vaqueros* from Rancho de la Gloria pumped round after round into the advancing gang members.

Little more than two dozen yards separated the contending forces. Smoke and the *vaqueros* would have to break and run or be annihilated.

The outlaw leader sensed it also. With a triumphant whoop, he urged his men on. They closed the gap by five yards. Suddenly a stutter of shots erupted behind them. It rapidly grew to a ragged volley. Confused, fully half of the bandits turned about. Smoke Jensen seized the moment to charge.

"At them! *¡Cuchillos y machetes!"* he yelled, calling for knives and the deadly long blades used for chopping jungle and high grass.

"Yiiiiiiii!" several *vaqueros* shouted in unison.

With bared blades in one hand, revolvers in the other, reins between their teeth or looped over the large, flat pommels of their saddles, the Mexican cowboys broke clear and thundered down on the astonished Anglo outlaws. The appearance of keen-edged steel unnerved many among the gang. They would gladly face down four or more blazing six-guns, but the thought of deep, gaping wounds, of severed limbs, or decapitation filled them with dread. Pressed from both sides, they abandoned all effort at resistance and fled in panicked disarray.

In no time, the posse led by Sheriff Banner and the *vaqueros* joined up. The field had been abandoned by Quinn's rogues so swiftly that the wounded had been left behind. Smoke and the sheriff rode among them. None of them appeared capable of further fight.

"It's over," the sheriff opined.

Smoke did not share Banner's confidence. "For now."

<u>BOOK YOUR PLACE ON OUR WEBSITE</u> AND MAKE THE <u>READING CONNECTION!</u>

We've created a customized website just for our very special readers, where you can get the inside scoop on everything that's going on with Zebra, Pinnacle and Kensington books.

When you come online, you'll have the exciting opportunity to:

- View covers of upcoming books

- Read sample chapters

- Learn about our future publishing schedule (listed by publication month *and author*)

- Find out when your favorite authors will be visiting a city near you

- Search for and order backlist books from our online catalog

- Check out author bios and background information

- Send e-mail to your favorite authors

- Meet the Kensington staff online

- Join us in weekly chats with authors, readers and other guests

- Get writing guidelines

- AND MUCH MORE!

Visit our website at
http://www.kensingtonbooks.com

TRIUMPH OF THE MOUNTAIN MAN

William W. Johnstone

PINNACLE BOOKS
Kensington Publishing Corp.

http://www.kensingtonbooks.com

One

Once a week, a Sugarloaf hand rode into Big Rock, Colorado to pick up the mail. Lost Ranger Peak brooded over the town, its 11,940 foot summit covered by a mantle of white year round. Often the journey proved to be nothing more than an excuse to spend an hour or two in the Bright Lights saloon. With the exception of Sally Jensen's sporadic correspondence with a few old school friends, scant mail ever came to the home of the fabled gunfighter, Smoke Jensen. On a fine morning in late April, then, Ike Mitchell, the Sugarloaf foreman, expressed his surprise when Smoke Jensen announced that he reckoned he would be the one to ride into Big Rock.

Ike hastened to relieve his employer of the burden. "No need to trouble yourself, Mr. Jensen. One of the boys can make the mail run."

"No trouble, Ike. I really feel like I ought to go." Smoke brushed at his reddish blond hair and gazed across the pastures of the Sugarloaf with his oddly gold-cast eyes. "There's some little——something——nagging me to make the ride into town."

Ike chuckled behind a big, work-hardened hand. The wings of gray hair at his temples waved in a light breeze. "Needin' a little time away from Miz Sally, eh?"

"Not exactly, Ike. Though I'll admit I would enjoy a good card game and a few schooners of beer with friends."

With a knowing wink, Ike encouraged Smoke. "You'll

have time enough for that, like as not. Not many people know where the Sugarloaf is, let alone how to reach it by mail. Enjoy your day, Mr. Jensen."

"I will Ike. Anything I can bring you from town?"

Ike removed his black, low-crowned Stetson and scratched his head. "The missus could use a bottle of sulphur elixir to treat the young'uns for spring."

Smoke involuntarily made a face at the memory of that medical treatment. It had not been one of the things he missed when separated from his family and taken in by Preacher. "I'll get it, then. Only, don't tell your brood who it was brought it."

Amorous meadow larks whistled to prospective mates as Smoke Jensen rode over the wooden bridge that spanned the Elk River. and entered Big Rock. He kept his 'Palouse stallion, Cougar, at a gentle walk. In spite of the chill in the air, the sun felt warm on his shoulders. He had left his working chaps behind, and wore a rust-colored pair of whipcord trousers, a green, yoke shirt and buckskin vest. Around his narrow waist he carried his famous—or infamous according to some—pair of .45 Colt Peacemakers. The right-hand one was slung low on his leg, the left in a pouch holster high on the cartridge belt, the butt pointed forward. Several writers of dime novels, Ned Buntline included, had made such a getup known to millions as a "gunfighter's rig."

Smoke looked on it as a practical necessity. The same as the .45-70-500 Winchester Express rifle in the saddle scabbard. While not expecting trouble, Smoke had learned long ago that it paid to come prepared at all times. As his legendary mentor, Preacher, had said, "It tends to increase a feller's life span."

* * *

"Morning," Smoke greeted a teamster who struggled with the ten-up team hauling a precarious-looking load of logs on a bedless, cradle wagon. The man gave a wave as Smoke rode on.

Farther into town, the streets became more populous. Women in gingham dresses and bonnets, their shopping baskets clutched in gloved hands, clicked the heels of their black, high-button shoes on the boardwalk of the main street. Horses stood, hip-shot, outside the saddle maker's, the bank, three saloons and the general store. A couple of empty buckboards rattled in from another direction, while one was being loaded by a harassed-looking teenager in a white apron. A typical Saturday in Big Rock, Smoke allowed. He nosed Cougar toward the hitch rail in front of the general mercantile. There he dismounted and climbed to the plank walk.

Inside the store, Nate Barber, the owner, greeted Smoke warmly. "Not often enough we see you, Mr. Jensen. You sure picked a day for it. Got near a whole mail bag full for you."

Smoke raised a yellow-brown eyebrow. "That so? I wonder what the occasion might be?"

"Catalogue time again," the postmaster/merchant advised, then added a familiar complaint. "Those mail order outfits are going to be the ruin of stores like mine."

Smoke nodded and went to the caged counter, behind which ran a ceiling-high rank of pigeon-hole boxes to hold the mail. His, he noted, bulged with envelopes. Barber went into his small post office and bent to retrieve a stack of bound, soft-cover volumes. "Here you are, Mr. Jensen. I'll get those letters for you, too."

Smoke went quickly through the catalogues. He found the latest *Sears* issue for Sally, another for musical instruments by mail order, and one for himself, from a saddle and tack manufacturer. That might prove useful, he reasoned. Anything made of leather eventually wore out, and no manner of patching could salvage it in the end. Some of the breaking saddles used on the Sugarloaf had begun to look rather shabby. If the prices were lower for this outfit in San Angelo, Texas, than in Denver, he might order four new ones. Among the correspondence he found a creamy, thick envelope of obvious high quality, addressed to him in a rich, flowery script that denoted that the writer had learned his letters in a language other than English. The return was Rancho de la Gloria, Taos, New Mexico Territory. Don Diego Alvarado, Smoke recognized at once.

Smoke had come to know Diego Alvarado several years ago, when he had been in New Mexico briefly on a cattle-buying trip. The gentlemanly, reserved Don Diego was the grandson of an original Spanish grandee, who had the patent of the King of Spain for roughly a thousand acres of high, mountainous desert to the west of Taos. His father had retained title to the land through service to the Mexican government after independence and had added to the family holdings. Steeped in the traditions of his ancestors' culture, Alvarado was a superb host who loved to entertain. Smoke had soon discovered that Diego's facade of reserve quickly vanished with a glass of tequila in one hand and a slice of lime in the other. The "little feast" put on for Smoke and his hands had turned out to be a three-day extravaganza of food and drink. They had paid for their lavish keep before leaving, however. Smoke and his men had joined the *vaqueros* of Rancho de la Gloria in fighting off a band of renegade Comanches who swarmed up out of the Texas panhandle.

Barber interrupted his speculation. "Need any supplies today, Mr. Jensen?"

"No, Nate, I didn't bring a wagon along. Say, do you happen to have any of that sulphur elixir?"

Nate Barber nodded. "Just happens I do, now that I bought out old Doc Phillips's stock from the apothecary shop. How many bottles?"

Smoke chuckled. "Ike's got six youngsters out there. Might as well make it two bottles."

"Sure thing."

The merchant produced the corked, seamless glass bottles and wrapped each in paper. Smoke noticed that the packaging material appeared to be printed pages. "Advertising your place now, Nate?"

Nate glanced down, then smiled as he cut his eyes to Smoke. "Nope. Discarded catalogues Some folks find 'em a bother and toss 'em away."

Smoke nodded his understanding, paid for his purchase and took his mail and the medicine along. Outside, he stowed it all in his saddlebags, swung into the saddle, and directed Cougar toward his next stop. Monte Carson would no doubt be downing his twelfth cup of coffee about now.

"Smoke! How'er you doin'?" Monte Carson bellowed as Smoke entered the office portion of the jail. Smoke and the sheriff had been friends for many long years, ever since the time when Smoke foreswore the dangerous life of a gunfighter-for-hire and stood back-to-back with Monte to rid the streets of Big Rock of some mighty nasty gunhawks and saddle trash. They had done a fair job of cleaning up all of Routt County for that matter. Smoke Jensen wore a badge for the first time in his life then, and had done so often since. Not that Smoke had been an outlaw in the truest sense of the word. He had never stolen anything, nor had he taken money for killing a man. Yet, it was always a close thing for a gunfighter to prove self-defense in a shoot-out. Being fully and permanently on the side of the law had a good feeling. Smoke had Monte to thank for that.

He poured coffee for himself and used the toe of one boot to hook a captain's chair over by a rung. Seated, he faced Monte. "Well, Monte, I came in on the mail run."

"You expectin' somethin' important?"

"No, but it appears I got it anyway." He went on to tell Monte about the letter from Don Diego Alvarado.

"Why don't you open it up and find out what it is?" Monte asked. "Might be an invite to the wedding of one of his sons."

Smoke shook his head. "I doubt that. Last I heard, Alejandro was already married. Xavier is down in Mexico at some seminary, studying to become a priest. Pablo would be a mere boy in his teens. Lupe could be only eight or so, and Miguel was born not three years ago."

Always curious, Monte prompted his friend. "So? Open the dang thing up and get a look."

"I will. But, being it's near noon, I thought you'd like to join me for a schooner or two of beer and some of Hank's free lunch over at the Bright Lights."

Monte grinned and, coming to his boots, nodded his head in eagerness. "You buyin'?"

"Of course. Although I wouldn't want it to be considered bribing an officer of the law. I don't want to be a guest of the county for even half an hour."

Monte reached for a drawer. "Well, then, hang a deputy's badge on yer vest and we'll call it a treat among brother lawmen. You know I'll bend heaven and earth to get a free beer."

They laughed together as they left the office. It was a short enough walk, only across the street, Smoke left Cougar tied off in front of the jail. The bar of the Bright Lights was crowded when they entered, so they took a table near the back of the room. The resinous odor of fresh sawdust perfumed the saloon. Smoke and Monte ordered beer and then built sandwiches of thick-sliced country ham, Swiss cheese, and boiled buffalo tongue, all on home-baked bread. They added fat dill pickles and hard-boiled eggs to their plates and carried them to where they would sit.

After taking a bite and chewing thoroughly, Smoke asked Monte about the town. The lawman responded eagerly.

"Let me tell you about these two drifters who tried to rob Nate's general mercantile," Monte began around a bite of his huge sandwich. "This happened about a week ago. They went in with bandannas pulled up over their noses and six-guns out. Well, Nate had no mind to try to stop them. One of the saddle trash growled at him about giving up all the money. Nate did, and put it in a paper bag, like they asked. The one who took the bag must have had a sweet tooth, 'cause right then he spied a jar of rock candy on the counter. Like a kid who only gets to town once in six months, he set the bag full of money aside and made for that jar. He stuffed his shirt pockets full of candy, and the ones in his vest, too. Then he grabbed up the cash and started to back out the door with his partner.

"What he didn't know," Monte went on, fighting back laughter, "is that he set that paper sack on top of the pickle barrel. It was a new, unopened one, but the lid had sprung. The bottom of the bag got soaked, and the weight of the money caused it to fall through. Coins went ever which a way. Right then, Nate grabbed up his shotgun while the robbers gaped at the fluttering bills that still fell from the sack. He had 'em disarmed and hands in the air when a passerby saw what was happenin' and came over to get me."

Smoke joined Monte's chuckles. "They don't make desperados like they used to. That all the excitement you've had?"

"Nope. Mrs. Granger had another baby, her eighth. Her husband swore he thought they were both too old for that to happen. A boy. That makes five boys and three girls."

"And all living?" Smoke inquired.

"Yep. By some miracle. Oh, yeah, how'd you fare out at the Sugarloaf in that thunderstorm middle of last week?"

"Not bad. Barely a shower there."

Monte frowned. "Might lot more around here. A regular goose-drowner. The Elk River went over its banks all along the valley. We had tree trunks and driftwood floating down Tom Longley Street for two days."

Smoke bit, chewed, and swallowed before remarking, "I thought it looked a mite damp along there."

" 'Damp' don't get it by about three feet, Smoke. Had some of the merchants writin' to the governor to ask for help in cleanup and repair. Hell, any fool knows the government ain't got any money. Only that they take from the people in taxes."

Smoke nodded agreement. "And I remember the time when a decent man wouldn't ask for a handout when he could make do for himself."

Monte put on a poker face. "But I reckon times they are a-changin'. It's gettin' too civilized around here."

Smoke slapped a big palm on one thigh. "Don't get me started on that. Any other urgent news?"

"Only that my chief deputy, Sam Barnes, was sparking the young widow Phillips last Sunday at the church box supper social."

"You mean the pretty young thing that some gossips are saying put old Doc Phillips in an early grave?"

"The same. A man's shy some gravy for his grits when he brings one home that's not half his age. Mind, I don't know about their home life and have no desire to speculate. She's a looker, though."

"That she is, Monte." In silence, they returned to their food.

Ace Banning paused to extinguish a quirley before he entered the bank in Big Rock. Few people remained in the lobby this close to noon. The bank would close in five minutes, according to the oak-cased wall clock that hung on the far wall. He waited behind a weighty dowager at one teller cage, and when his turn came, he asked for change for a twenty-dollar gold double-eagle. All the while, his eyes shifted, taking note of the layout of the establishment. Would they shut the vault at noon? He doubted it. There were two armed guards. That made Ace think of his friends waiting outside.

Shem Turnbull and George Cash lounged in front of the Bucket O' Suds saloon, two doors down from the bank. As noon neared, the street began to clear of people. Most of the shops closed over the dinner hour. Carefully they eyed passersby. Many of the men were armed. Those who were going home would be no trouble. Already a line had formed outside the eatery on the corner, and those would have to be closely watched. Shem turned to George.

"We shoulda brought another gun. Three fellers is not enough to carry this off."

"Oh, I don't know, Shem. They won't be expectin' anything, and their minds will be on their dinners. Ace can handle it real good."

"Not without a little help from you," Ace Banning declared as he walked up to his friends. "Shem, I want you inside with me. There's two armed guards. We've got only a minute, so let's move."

Smoke Jensen downed the last of his second schooner of beer, pushed back his chair, and dug in his pocket for a cartwheel dollar. "I'll walk over to the office with you, but then I have to head right back. I've got three mares who are due to foal at any time."

"You never opened that letter from Alvarado," Monte complained good-naturedly.

"That's right. I'll have to read it when I get home." Then reading his friend's expression, he added, "I'll let you know what Don Diego wrote about."

They had reached the tall, double doors with the painted glass inserts when the sound of a gunshot came from the direction of the bank. A woman's scream followed. Smoke turned that way at once, to be stopped when Monte laid a hand on his shoulder.

"I'll take care of this, Smoke. No need for you to stick your neck out."

Smoke cut his eyes to his friend and growled, "Even if I want to?"

Monte shook his head. "Not this time."

He set off for the bank. Monte made it halfway down the block before the outside man saw him coming and fired his six-gun from the lawman's blind side. The bullet struck Monte in the chest. Deflected as it punched through a rib, the slug cut a path through his lung from front to rear and buried itself in the thick muscle of his back. Shock took Monte off his boots. At once, Smoke started for him.

"Watch it, there's one over there somewhere." A pink froth formed on Monte's lips, and his voice came out far weaker than he expected.

Smoke reached his friend, his .45 Colt in hand, and glanced in the direction Monte pointed before the sheriff lost consciousness. Smoke saw his man instantly. A cruel grimace distorted the outlaw's mouth as he raised his revolver for another shot at the lawman. Smoke fired first. His round pinwheeled the man, punched through his sternum and tore apart his aorta. Charged up on adrenaline and action, he bled to death before he hit the boardwalk.

Kneeling, Smoke examined his fallen friend. Monte's face had grown pale, with a tinge of green around his lips, his breathing shallow and rapid. Smoke could hear a faint gurgle. If that bastard's killed him . . . he thought in a flash of anger. The thought came to him then. The first shot had been muffled; it had to have come from inside the bank. At once, he started that way.

It began going wrong the moment they entered the bank with bandannas tied over their faces. The employees and customers of the bank had no doubt what the masked men intended. Shem Turnbull headed for the teller cages, and

Ace Banner shoved through the low swinging gate in the wall that divided the lobby from the working area. At once, the tellers raised their hands. Shem gestured with his gun barrel.

"That's right, keep 'em up until I tell you otherwise. You, get a money bag and start filling it," he told the nearest teller.

Ace concentrated on the portly, balding man in a glassed-in cubicle. "Step out here and come over to the vault. We want all the hard money and all the greenbacks you can load in those sacks."

Rosemont Faulkner knew better than to make vain protests about the robbers not getting away with it. He left his desk and hastened across the floor to the door of the vault. There, instead of stooping to load the bank's precious capital into a canvas money sack, he swiftly grabbed the heavy door and gave it a hefty swing. It clanged shut, and he spun the dead bolt wheel. Defiantly he put hands on his hips and spoke with relish.

"That's a time lock. It won't open again until eight o'clock tomorrow morning."

That's when Ace Banning, already strained beyond control by the presence of two armed guards who were presently out of his sight, lost it.

"You bastard!" he screamed as the hammer fell on a cartridge, and Ace shot the bank president through the heart. A woman behind him began to scream. He spun on one boot heel and strode to the tellers.

"All right, Shem, grab everything they have and let's get out of here."

Two minutes went by with the outlaws holding bags in one hand and tellers stuffing them. Then a loud report came from outside. Ace nodded to the door. "That's George, let's go."

Quickly they reached the door, and Shem Turnbull flung

it open. They stepped out into the presence of an angry Smoke Jensen.

"Hold it right there," Smoke growled.

Two men stood before him, crowded into the open double doors of the bank. Each held three bulging canvas bags. They also gripped identical Smith and Wesson .44 Americans. Smoke followed his command with sizzling lead. Ace Banner dropped flat as the Colt in Jensen's hand bucked. The slug slammed into the pane of the bank door, and it shattered; shards flew inward to the chorus of screams from the three women inside. Ace fired wildly as the musical tinkle of glass sounded behind him.

His slug flew between Smoke's outspread legs. Already the last mountain man had moved his point of aim and triggered a shot that took Shem Turnbull in the thick meat of his side. He clapped a hand against it and discharged his Smith and Wesson The .44 bullet cracked past Smoke's left ear and struck the bannister post of the balcony across the street. Smoke moved then, as Ace fired again. His third shot struck the prone Ace Banner in his shoulder, snapped the collarbone and bored down into his lung.

At once, Ace began to gag and fight for air. His hand went slack on the revolver, and it dropped from his fingers. Smoke Jensen changed position again and fired a safety shot. Due to the small target, it gouged the back of Ace Banner. He cried out as the slug plowed along his spine and entered his right buttock. Beside him, Shem fired again.

A hot crease burned along the outer point of Smoke's left shoulder. Twisting with the impact, Smoke lined up on the bank robber and fired again. His bullet ripped into Shem's middle and punched a hole in his liver. As massive shock stole over him, he sagged back against the wall and released his hold on the money bags and six-gun. Slowly, he slid down to a sitting position. Peacemaker leading the way,

Smoke Jensen walked up to them and kicked the gun away from Ace, then Shem. Years of experience told him that both would die within an hour. One of the bank guards came to the door.

"Go get Doc Simpson," Smoke commanded the astonished man.

Ace groaned and looked up at Smoke. "Th-thank you, mister. Ah—who—who are you?"

Smoke kept it cold. "I didn't send for the doctor to treat you. You'll be dead before an hour's gone by. And, I'm known as Smoke Jensen."

Greater misery washed over the pale face of Ace Banner. "We—ah—we didn't think you were still alive. And a law-man at that."

His last sentence did not make much sense to Smoke, so he ignored it and replied to the first. "Your mistake."

Dr. Hiram Simpson entered the outer treatment room of his office wiping his hands on a towel. "Let's take a look at you, Mr. Jensen."

"First tell me, how is Monte?"

Doc Simpson sighed tiredly "It was close. I had to clean the wound channel first off. Then, when I got the bullet hole plugged, and closed the two holes in his lung, the Almighty musta smiled on me, 'cause the lung reinflated. He's healthy. he should heal that up in good time. I've given him enough laudanum that he will sleep through to evening. That should aid the healing process. But, the bullet is lodged in the thick muscle only a fraction of an inch from his spine. After having to open his chest to work on his lung, no one can go in there after it right now."

"When can you?"

Doc Simpson read the strain in Smoke's voice. "Provided the sheriff heals as expected, I'd say someone could operate within six weeks, if that lead don't shift and paralyze him in the meantime."

"That could happen?"

With a hesitant nod Simpson replied, "I'm not a master surgeon, but right or wrong, it is taught in medical school that foreign objects in the body can shift under certain circumstances. That's why I don't want to operate on him. I'll send for a special surgeon from Denver."

That information did not sit well with Smoke. While Dr. Simpson worked on him, he kept at the physician to give a more accurate description of what damage had been done to Monte Carson. He remained dissatisfied when the doctor cut the last piece of tape and handed him two laudanum pills.

"Take half of one of these now. If the pain persists, take another half every six hours."

"I don't think I'll be needing them, Doctor," Smoke informed him, handing back the medicine. "How much do I owe you?"

"The county will pay for it. You were working as a deputy at the time."

With that settled, Smoke shrugged into his bloodied shirt, put on his vest and hat and headed to the door. It would be a long, uncomfortable ride back to the Sugarloaf.

Two

Halfway back to the Sugarloaf, Smoke started to regret his rash decision to reject the opium-based medicine. He also thought darkly about the morning's events. Why did it have to be Monte Carson who caught that bullet? Although Monte had the constitution of an ox, he was nearing sixty. People didn't heal so quickly then. Smoke knew from experience that a lung shot often led to pneumonia which more often killed the victim than the bullet itself. In his moody thoughts, Smoke castigated himself for not having gone along with Monte. Better still, gone in his place.

No, Smoke admitted to himself, Monte had too much pride. It would have robbed him of his self-respect to acknowledge that age might be slowing his gunhand, delaying the proper read of a situation. Yet, the results spoke for themselves. Monte lay unconscious in the small infirmary off Doc Simpson's office. Smoke had a slight bullet burn on his shoulder. They had both gone about it wrong. Admitting it did not mollify Smoke in the least.

Once he had turned Cougar into the corral, in the hands of Bobby Jensen to cool him out, Smoke took the mail to the main house. Sally greeted him with a spoon dripping melted lard in one hand. "Hello, handsome. I'm fixing a batch of doughnuts. My, what a lot of mail."

"Yep. There's a *Sears* catalogue for you."

Sally clapped her hands. "Oh, goody, I get to buy things."

Smoke answered her with a sidelong glance. "No, you

don't. And a letter from a woman named Mary-Beth Gittings."

"Who?"

"That's what it says. I'll give it to you inside."

Seated at the kitchen table, Smoke distributed the mail into neat piles. While Sally chattered on and added more lard to the heated deep skillet for the doughnuts, he turned his attention to the intriguing letter from New Mexico. He opened it to find a disturbing difference in his old friend. Instead of the usual bubbling enthusiasm of this jovial grandee, who so loved to entertain, it was a gloomy account of growing difficulties. High in the Sangre de Cristo range of the Rocky Mountains, things were not right, Don Diego Alvarado informed Smoke Jensen. He went on to illustrate:

"There is an Anglo named Clifton Satterlee, who covets all of the land around Taos. He is powerful and wealthy. He has a hacienda outside Santa Fe and is believed to have the ear of many of his fellow Anglos in the territorial government. It is also said that he has many interests and much influence in the East. He has surrounded himself with some most unsavory men, who aid him in achieving his goals by any means necessary. Amigo," the letter went on, "there have been some incidents of violence. Men have been driven out, Anglos as well as Mejicanos."

Absently Smoke reached to the plate holding the doughnuts. He let go of one quickly enough the moment he touched it. "They're hot," Sally reminded him with a laugh.

Smoke went back to the letter for the final paragraph. "No one here seems capable of dealing with the man. So, forgive my presumption in asking this, old friend, but I feel that I must appeal to you to come out here and get the feel of what is going on." Only reluctantly, it seemed to Smoke, did Don Diego add his personal difficulties. "I, myself, have lost some cattle and the lives of some of my vaqueros." His missive concluded with some of his usual flourish. Smoke put it aside in thoughtful silence.

* * *

They rode up quietly, five beefy, hard-faced, tough men, and tied off their horses to a stone-posted tie rail outside the high-walled hacienda on Calle Jesus Salvador in Taos, New Mexico Territory. Beyond the wall they could see the red tile roof of a Spanish colonial style, two-story house. Nestled in a large valley, surrounded by the Sangre de Cristo range, the residence had an air of peacefulness. That was quickly broken when the leader, Whitewater Paddy Quinn, spoke to his henchmen.

"Remember, we ain't here to break him up, just to get him to sign."

One of the thugs, a man named Rucker, responded with a snigger. "Right, boss."

"Sure, I mean that, Rucker. Not a bruise. Now, let's get in there."

Quinn stepped up to a human-sized doorway inset in the tall, double gate, and raised a large brass knocker. The striker plate bolted to the portal gave off a hollow boom as he rapped it. He kept at it until a short, swarthy servant in a white cotton pullover shirt and trousers opened the door. *"¿Sí, señores?"*

"We're here to see Mr. Figueroa."

"¿Que? Lo siento, no hablo Ingles."

Paddy Quinn struggled to put his request into Spanish. *"Es necesario a hablamós con Señor Figueroa."* His grammar might not be perfect, but he conveyed the idea.

Figueroa's major domo brightened. *"Ay, sí! Vengan."* His leather sandals made soft, scraping noises as he led the visitors across the cobbled courtyard to the main entrance.

Through a wrought-iron gate and a pair of tall double doors, a tunnellike passageway led to a lushly planted open square. A large saguaro cactus filled one corner. In the center, a fountain splashed musically. Standing beside it was a slim gentleman of medium height, his white hair combed straight back in two large wings from his temples. He wore the costume of another age, tight, black trousers, trimmed with gray stripes along the outer seams, matching cut-away coat with gray lapels. His shirt was snowy, with a blizzard of lace and a wing collar. Calf-length boots had been burnished until they shone like polished onyx. From beyond him, practice scales on a piano tinkled from an open, curtained window. He turned at their entrance, and a dark scowl quickly replaced the smile of welcome he had prepared.

"You are not welcome in this house," he declared.

Paddy Quinn put a wide smile on his Irish face. "Sure, I'm sorry you see it that way, Mr. Figueroa. We will try to be brief, we will. I have come to arrange for the sale of this property to Mr. Satterlee."

Figueroa glowered at him. "Then you have come on a mistaken mission, señor. I have no intention of selling."

Beaming happily, Quinn ventured to disagree. "Oh, yes, you do."

"No, I do not. I have told you that five times before. I have not changed my mind. Now, leave or I shall send for some of my retainers."

At that, Paddy Quinn gave a signal to two of his henchmen. They crossed the space separating them from Ernesto Figueroa and grabbed the elderly gentleman by the arms. Quinn gestured toward the open window. With little effort, they frog-marched him to the lace-curtained window from which the music came. Quinn came up behind and shoved Figueroa's head through the opening. The scales had given over to a piece by Mozart now, played by a sweet-faced little girl.

"A nice girl, your granddaughter, she is," Quinn observed. "Lovely, innocent, vulnerable. You'd not be wanting anything to happen to her, now would you?"

A shudder of revulsion passed through Figueroa a moment before the thugs abruptly swung him around to face their leader. He fought for the words. "You wouldn't dare."

Quinn gave him a smile. "You're right, I would not. But I cannot account for every minute of my men's time. Come, señor. You will be more than generously compensated, an' that's a fact. You can take your lovely, expensive furniture and possessions elsewhere, anywhere you wish, and live to see her grow to womanhood. And a lovely figure she will make, it is."

Wincing from the painful grip on his arms, Ernesto Figueroa remained defiant. "What will happen if I still refuse?"

Paddy Quinn's face changed from beaming benignity to harsh evil. "Then I will let my men have their way with her and kill her before your eyes. But not you," he went on. "We'll be leaving you to live with what your stubbornness caused. Think about it, bucko."

Ernesto Figueroa hesitated only a scant two seconds before his head sagged in resignation and he made a hesitant gesture to indicate he would accept. Paddy Quinn handed him the papers and even produced a travel pen and brass ink well so the defeated man could sign.

After due consideration, Smoke Jensen decided to go to Taos. His reasoning was simple. The foaling season, from February through April, was over and the first of May not far away. Besides, he owed Diego Alvarado. He left the hands busy with the new colts and went to talk it over with Sally.

"I expected this since you first told me what the letter contained. I'll not beg you to stay here, Smoke. I know better, and you would be disappointed in me if I did. How long do you expect to be gone?"

Smoke considered it. "Ten days. Two weeks at the most."

Sally's chuckle held a hint of irony. "I've heard that before. How are you going to travel, Smoke?"

"I'll take the Denver and Rio Grande south to Raton, then go by horseback through the Palo Flechado Pass to Taos."

A light of mischief glowed in Sally's eyes as though she particularly liked the thought that burst on her. "That sounds easy enough. I think I'll come with you; it will be nice to see Don Diego again."

Smoke shook his head rejecting the idea. "Who'll run the ranch and look out for Bobby?"

"Ike can run the ranch, and Bobby is grown enough to bunk with the hands and take care of himself."

Smoke remained unconvinced. "Think about what you just said."

"About Ike running the ranch?"

"No. About Bobby. He's thirteen, Sally. Do you remember what our others were like at that age?"

Fresh worry lines formed on Sally's forehead. "Yes . . . unfortunately I do."

"I think you should reconsider."

Sally stood in silence a long two minutes, leaning shoulder-to-shoulder with Smoke. "All right, you win this one. I'll be realistic and not start to worry until three weeks have gone by."

"Nice of you," Smoke jested, giving her a swift hug. "I will write you when I reach Taos."

"Send a telegram instead. It will get here sooner."

"All right."

"Now, let me ask only one thing. What are you going to do when you have to keep your promise to that boy about taking him along on one of these trips?"

Smoke affected a groan. "I'll figure that out when the time comes. Now, dear wife, will you pack me something suitable to wear at Diego Alvarado's?"

With an impatient twist to his lips, Clifton Satterlee gazed from the narrow window of the mud wagon stagecoach that rattled and swayed along the narrow dirt roadway that led from Santa Fe to Taos. "One would think," he muttered under his breath, "that since our nation has conquered this country, the government would put down proper paving stones." If they did not reach the relay station soon, he swore he would leave his breakfast on the floor of the coach. Across from him, his chief partner in C. S. Enterprises, Brice Noble, sat beside Satterlee's bodyguard, Cole Granger. To the increase of his discomfort, Satterlee realized that Granger actually liked this trip. He seemed to thrive on the discomfort. Suddenly Clifton's stomach lurched, and a fiery gorge rushed up his throat. He turned sideways and hastily flung aside the leather curtain.

"Oh, God," Satterlee groaned as he thrust his head out the window. With explosive force, he vomited into the rising plume of dust that came from under the iron-tired right front wheel. He could feel Granger's amused gaze resting on him. Damn the man!

When he recovered himself, Clifton Satterlee crawled limply back inside. Cole Granger held out a canteen for him, which he took eagerly and rinsed his mouth. Then Granger extended a silver flask. "Here you go, Mr. Satterlee. It's some of your fine, French brandy."

Irritation crackled in Satterlee's voice. "It's cognac, Cole. C-O-G-N-A-C."

Hastily, Satterlee seized the container and swallowed down a long gulp. Immediately his stomach spun like a carousel. Then the warm, soothing property of the liquor kicked in, and his nausea subsided somewhat. From outside, above on the box, came a welcome cry.

"Whoa, Tucker, whoa, Benny, whoa-up, Nell. Wheel right." He called out the rest of the team, and the momentum of the stagecoach slackened.

Satterlee addressed the rest of the occupants. "About damned time. You know, that little upset of mine has left me ravenously hungry. Or maybe it is the cognac." He took another swig.

Cole Granger checked the stage itinerary. "There'll be a meal stop here, Mr. Satterlee."

Brice Nobel looked balefully out the window. "I certainly hope the food will be better than we had this morning. That must have been what caused your discomfort, Cliff."

Satterlee nodded his gratitude for his partner's cover-up of his motion sickness. He hated any sign of weakness, as did Noble. Clifton Satterlee studied his partner. A man in his late forties, ten years senior to himself, Brice Noble had a bulldog face with heavy jowls. For all his youth, Noble was completely gray, his hair worn in long, greasy strands. Shorter by three inches, Noble weighed around one hundred seventy pounds and had the hard hands of a working cowboy, although Satterlee knew he had been a wealthy man for a long time. Brice had never given up his habit of carrying a brace of revolvers, in this instance, Merwin and Hulbert .44s. Satterlee knew only too well how good he could be with them. His pale blue eyes had a hard, silver glint when angered.

For his own part, Clifton made certain he never infuriated Brice. Even at six feet, two inches with longer, once stronger, arms and barrel chest, Satterlee readily acknowledged that he was no match for Noble. He sighed as he glanced down at the beginnings of a potbelly. He would have to get out and do more riding, Satterlee admonished himself. Although a lean man, Satterlee's left armpit felt chafed by the shoulder holster he wore there, and more so from the weight of the .44 Colt Lightning double-action that fitted it. Recalling its presence brought a laugh to the lips of Clifton Satterlee. He had not had occasion to draw it in anger or even self-defense in the three years since he bought it.

"What's funny, Cliff?"

"I was thinking about my gun, Brice. Do you realize I have not used it, except for practice, in the past three years?"

Noble nodded to Granger. "That's what Cole is here for. But, I can tell you I'm looking forward to whatever food they have for us."

With a shriek of sand caught between brake shoe and wheel, the stage jolted to a stop. The station agent brought out a four step platform with which the passengers could dismount. "Welcome to Española, folks. We've got some red chili, chicken enchilada and beans inside for you."

"Sounds good," Cole Granger told him with a big smile.

Clifton Satterlee saw it differently. "By all that's holy, don't you have any white man's food?"

"Nope. Not with a big, fat Mexican cooking for me. She cooks what she knows how to."

Satterlee appealed to his partner. "Do you know what that will do to my stomach, Brice?"

"Fill it, no doubt." Then, to the agent, "Do you have any flour tortillas?"

"Yep. An' some sopapillas with honey to finish off with."

Stifling a groan, Clifton Satterlee instructed, "I'll start with those."

Inside, over savory bowls of beef stewed with onions, garlic, and red chili peppers, corn tortillas stuffed with chicken, onions, black olives, cheese, sauce, the driver and guard joined in demolishing the ample food laid out for the occupants of the coach. Satterlee morosely doused the fried dough in an amber pool of honey. After devouring four of the sopapillas, he spoke lowly to Noble.

"I want you to stay a few days, up to a week, in Taos. Look around, make contact with our people. Make certain they are getting things done. My wife and I will return to Santa Fe two days from now."

Brice Noble chewed on the flavorful cubes of meat. He washed them down with beer that had been cooled in the well. "What do you propose doing next?"

"Our people have to accelerate their efforts. We need that

timber and damned soon. Our whole lumber business depends upon it. Go after those blasted savages."

Smoke Jensen stopped in on Monte Carson the next day, before he took the afternoon train south to Denver, where he would change for the run to Raton. He could have taken the AT&SF to Santa Fe, but he wanted to catch what word there might be running up and down the trail. Monte was awake when Smoke entered the infirmary. His skin held a pallor, and his response when he turned his head and saw Smoke was weak.

"Smoke, good you came. Maybe you can talk sense to the man."

"What's that about?"

"That croaker, Simpson, says I have to stay here for two, maybe three weeks. Then some kind of operation by a doctor from Denver."

Smoke nodded. "You've got a bullet in you, Monte. I'll tell you what he probably won't. It's near your spine. There's the chance . . . for permanent injury."

Monte cut his eyes away from Smoke. "Damn. If that happens, I won't be fit for anything. Old before my time and stove up. Not a fittin' end."

"No," Smoke agreed. "At least you would be alive."

"You call that *alive?* Ask me, it'd be nothin' more than livin' hell."

Smoke decided on a change of subject. "I came to tell you what was in that letter from Don Diego."

That brightened the lawman somewhat. "Really? What did the old grandee have to say?"

Smoke's fleeting frown framed his words. "There's trouble brewing out in the Sangre de Cristo. Some feller named Satterlee has it in mind to build himself a little empire. According to Don Diego, he's not shy about the sort of persuasion his men use to get what he wants. Alvarado's lost some stock and some cowboys. He asked if I'd come take a look."

"And are you?"

Smoke nodded. "Leavin' today, Monte. Train to Raton, then trail it from there. But, I feel bad about leaving you here all bunged up."

Monte tried to make little of it. "Not much happens in Big Rock anymore. My deputies can handle it."

"After that list you gave me yesterday, and what we ran into, I'd say your 'not much' is a bit of an exaggeration." Smoke tipped back the brim of his Stetson. "Well, I have to get to the depot. Look out for yourself, Monte. And do what the doctor says."

Monte scowled, then gave a feeble wave. "Watch yer back trail."

Smoke turned for the door. "I have a feelin' I'm going to have to."

Three

On the train south, Smoke Jensen settled into his Pullman car with a copy of the Denver *Dispatch* and sat in the plush seat that would become part of his sleeping berth. The editorial page contained the usual harangue about the lawlessness of the miners and smelter workers. Someone named Wilbert Clampton had a piece on the subject of temperance. According to him, Demon Rum was soaking the brains and inflaming the passions of the lower classes. Until Denver banned liquor, the depredations chronicled elsewhere in the newspaper would only continue and increase. A moderate man in his drinking habits, Smoke could not find the energy to get worked up over Clampton's cry for abstinence. After twenty minutes and a dozen miles had gone by, Smoke put the paper aside. Immediately he noticed an attractive young woman seated in the same car.

She smiled in his direction with her eyes as well as her lips, then dabbed at her mouth with a dainty square of white linen. Her heart-shaped face was framed by a nest of small, blond curls. That and her expensive clothes added to her allure. Fiercely loyal to his beloved Sally, Smoke made only the lightest of passing acknowledgment to her discreet flirtation. The rail carriage swayed gently as the train rolled through the high mountains. Up ahead, Smoke knew, his two horses, a sturdy pack animal and Cougar, would be comfortable in padded stalls in a special car. The expense of such travel conveniences had grown steeply over the past few years. Yet, he could afford it. Blooded horses brought good money. Far more so than cattle. Smoke went back to his newspaper.

There was talk again of building a canal across Central America to speed ship passage. More for cargo, Smoke knew, than passengers. With the nation linked from coast to coast with steel rails, the hazards of a sea voyage could be easily abandoned for the more secure railroads. At least with the James gang out of business, there seemed little possibility of robberies like those of the past. After completing the speculations on a canal, Smoke reached into an inner coat pocket and removed a twisted tip Marsh Wheeling cigar and came to his boots.

When he walked past the young woman, on his way to the vestibule for his smoke, she spoke in a melodic, honeyed voice. "Good day."

Smoke touched fingertips to the brim of his hat. "Yes, it is."

He had barely gotten in four satisfactory puffs when she appeared in the doorway to their car. With a hesitant smile, she came forward. "Excuse me. My name is Winnefred Larkin. Forgive me if this sounds too brazen. But, I'm traveling alone, you see, and I wish to ask you if you would be so kind as to escort me to the dining car later this evening."

Smoke hid his smile behind his cigar. "Not at all, Miss Larkin. My name is Jensen, Smoke Jensen. I would be delighted to be your escort."

"Thank you. I am so relieved. Smoke . . . Jensen. What an odd name."

"It's sort of a handle other folks hung on me. My given name is Kirby." *Now why did he say that?* Smoke wondered. He hated that name.

Winnefred made a small moue of her pretty lips. "Then I shall call you Smoke. First call for dinner is at five. Or is that too early for your liking?"

"Yes, it is, a bit," Smoke allowed.

"Would seven be better?" Without conscious intent, Winnefred appeared coy.

"Perfect. I'll present myself to you then," Smoke replied, working out of himself a gallantry he rarely had cause to display.

"Then, I shall leave you to your cigar. And again, my sincerest thanks."

When Smoke Jensen entered the dining car with Winnefred Larkin on his arm, it turned heads all up and down both sides of the aisle. They made a striking couple. Smoke led her to a vacant table and seated her, then drew up his own chair opposite. A rather recent addition, these rolling restaurants had been designed, like the sleeping cars, by George Mortimer Pullman. They had proven quite successful, much to the chagrin of the Harvey House chain of depot-based eating establishments. Smoke examined the menu, printed in flamboyant style, bold black on snowy white.

"What sounds good to you?" Winnefred asked after a few silent moments of study. "Everything seems so strange to me."

Smoke nodded understanding. "I gather you are from the East, Miss Larkin? When one gets this far west, the larder on these dining cars is stocked from locally available food for the most part. See? There's rainbow trout listed, though I don't know what *amandine* means. Bison tongue, elk steak, and beef stew."

"Please, make it Winnie. And, amandine means the fish is done with an almond and lemon sauce. Quite the rage in Philadelphia. Perhaps you would choose for the both of us, Smoke?"

Never a fancy eater, it took some concentration for Smoke Jensen to select something that he believed would please Winnie and yet not be too out of his ordinary fare. He selected cold, sliced bison tongue in a mildly hot sauce for an appetizer, then followed with elk steak, new potatoes and peas, cold pickled lettuce and hot bread. Winnie Larkin seemed enchanted with the choices. Their waiter, a large, smiling, colored man in a short, white jacket and black trousers, suggested a bottle of wine. At Smoke's insistence, Winnie made the selection.

For once it all turned out right, and even Smoke enjoyed the meal. Cut from the rib eye, the elk steak was juicy and tender. The California claret went well with it. Fortuitously, Smoke had asked that the cook withhold the green peppercorn sauce from the meat. It was rich and thick, and to the way Smoke thought, if a piece of meat was poor in quality, one could dump all the sauce in the world on it and not make it the least bit better. This time it was decidedly not needed.

While they ate, Winnie kept up a light, fanciful banter about her travels in the West. She found New Orleans charming, Texas rough and exhilarating, Denver a cultural oasis in the midst of near-barbarism. Now she looked forward to Santa Fe. She had heard somewhere that the territorial governor had written a most popular book.

"Yes," Smoke informed her. "It's called *Ben Hur.* Surely you have read it?"

"Oh! Then General Lew Wallace is *Governor* Wallace? And, yes, I have read that book. It is so . . . uplifting."

When she learned Smoke was involved in breeding blooded horses, she waxed ecstatic over her childhood desire to have a papered horse. All her parents had, Winnie lamented, were a pair of plodding dray horses. She spoke of riding lessons as a girl in her teens and how she still longed to own a Thoroughbred of her own.

Smoke quickly disabused her of that ambition. "I don't raise Thoroughbreds. They are for racing and fancy shows back east. Mine are 'Palouse and Morgans and Arabians. Those of lower quality I sell to the army as remounts. Arabians are show horses, but a lot of military officers want, and can afford, them for parade horses. The Morgans are great for carriages as well as saddle stock. Since the Nez Perce have been forced onto a reservation, their breed, the 'Palouse, has all but died out. I am trying to recover it."

Winnie looked entirely helpless. "Oh, dear, that sounds incredibly complicated. It must be rewarding to see all those horses thriving, though."

"Yes, it is, Winnie. I used to raise cattle. They are stupid, intractable animals. They also eat a lot and are vulnerable to the harsh winters in the mountains. Horses aren't much brighter, but they survive better and do useful work. Did you know that wolves are the smartest animals in the wild?"

Winnie shuddered. "Wolves? How awful. They're killers."

"No. Not how you mean. A wolf will not attack a human, even a child, unless cornered or they believe their young to be threatened. They have a structured society, with strict rules and a pecking order. They care for their pups until they are able to fend for themselves. They even have intricate tactics for hunting."

"See, that's what I mean. They are relentless killers."

Masking a flare of impatience with a straight face, Smoke tried to explain. "Wolves prey on the weakest animals of a herd. By doing so, they improve the breed. You might say that what I do for horses by record keeping and selective breeding, they do by instinct."

Tiny frown lines appeared on Winnie's high, smooth brow. "I've never heard anything like that before."

"Not likely that you will. People have been bad-mouthing wolves since the Middle Ages. Wolves are the most misunderstood animals on the frontier. I have counted up to eight in one pack running on my ranch, and I have never lost a foal." He paused, then produced a rueful grin. "Of course, I wouldn't want one living under the same roof with me. They are still wild animals."

Winnie's eyes grew wide. They went on talking amiably

through dessert and coffee. Gradually the car emptied of occupants. The waiters began to clear the tables and turn down kerosene lamps. Only a balding, portly man and his buxom wife remained when Smoke stood and went around the table to help Winnie from her chair. Smoke had noticed earlier that the fusty busybody had been giving them a jaundiced eye throughout the meal and had even restrained her husband when he made to leave earlier. With a silent snigger at those with nothing better to do, he pushed the incident out of his mind, took Winnie by the elbow and escorted her to the door.

They found their Pullman bunks made up and ready. Smoke and Winnie said their good nights, and Smoke went on back to the smoking car for a cigar. He struck up a conversation with a man near his own age about the severe storms of the previous winter. When their stogies had burned down to short stubs with long, white ash, Smoke excused himself and went on back to his bed.

A shrill scream punctured the peaceful silence of the sleeping car.

It seemed to Smoke Jensen that he had only just laid down his head, yet light streamed around the pull-down shade as he opened his eyes to the continued wailing that came from up the aisle.

"She's dead! She's dead! My God, it's horrible. Blood everywhere."

Smoke swiftly pulled on his trousers and boots, shrugged into a shirt and slipped a .45 Colt Peacemaker into his waist band. A middle-aged woman stood in the aisle, hands to her pasty white cheeks as she continued to shriek. Smoke reached her in four long strides. He took her by one shoulder and shook her gently.

"Who is dead? What do you mean?"

She pointed with a suddenly palsied hand, and her voice

quavered. "In—in there. Th—the y-y-y-young woman you took to dinner last night. W-w-we h-had an arrange—arrangement for breakfast this morning. Only her Pullman was still closed. I called out, then looked in." This time she covered her face and spoke through broken sobs. "Her—her eyes were staring right at me, but I could tell they held no life. Sh-sh-she's covered with blood." Suddenly she broke off and stared with horror at the hands of Smoke Jensen, as though expecting to see splashes of crimson.

Speaking firmly to maintain control, Smoke directed, "Sit down over there. I will go get the conductor."

He returned three minutes later with a worried man in a dark blue uniform trimmed with silver braid. At Smoke's urging, the conductor looked in the closed Pullman. He recoiled in aversion. "Lordy, what a sight. When did this happen?"

Smoke shook his head. "I don't know. The woman over there found her about . . ." He plucked his watch from the small pocket in his trousers. "Four minutes ago. Her screaming woke me up."

By then, a crowd had gathered, and Smoke noted five heads poking out of curtained bunks. The conductor examined them with disapproval. Then he waved the people away with small shooing motions as though dispersing a flock of chickens.

"There has been an unfortunate accident. Everyone who does not have a seat in this car, please leave. Those who belong here, take your seats and remain there." Then he turned to Smoke. "You'll likely want to get into your coat. Then I would like to talk to you at length. I'll send for the train crew to take care of the body."

Wise in the ways of trail crafts, Smoke knew how many bits of information could be gained from a study of all sign. "No, I don't think that's a good idea. I want to get a thorough look in there before anything is moved, including Miss Larkin."

Face twisted with distaste, the conductor responded indignantly. "We can't just leave a—a *dead body* lying here. People will blame the line."

Smoke spoke firmly, convincingly. "You can leave it until a peace officer examines the area around her."

"But that won't be until Walsenburg. And, oh, dear, everyone on the train will have to be questioned."

"As to your first observation, that is not necessarily so. Come with me, I have something to show you."

Still dithering, the conductor followed along in the wake of Smoke Jensen. At Smoke's bunk, he reached in and retrieved a small leather wallet from his valise. He used his back to block view of it from the rest of the car and opened the fold. The silver shield of a deputy U.S. marshal shined up at the conductor.

"I have jurisdiction in Colorado. In as much as you have a mail car on this train, I also have jurisdiction over any crime that occurs on it, if I choose to exercise it. What I would like you to do is lock the doors to each car and contain the occupants while you put this train on a siding somewhere along the line, close to here, then have your express agent use his key to send ahead to Walsenburg that you have an emergency and are on the siding and identify which one. That's when we can conduct our own investigation."

Testily, the conductor removed his visored cap and scratched at a balding spot on the crown of his head. "That's a tall order, Marshal—ah—"

"Jensen. Smoke Jensen."

"Jesus, Mary and Joseph! You're *the* Smoke Jensen?" At Smoke's nod, he went on in a rush. "I'm Martin Stoddard, folks call me Marsh. I'll try to do everything I can to see that you get what you want. We'll put men out once we've stopped to watch and make sure no one tries to get away from the train."

"Good thinking, Mr. Stoddard—er—Marsh. I'll naturally come with you. We will need to set up a place to question everyone. Say the smoking and bar car? But first, I want to take a look at the body."

Rail coaches squealed and jolted to a stop beyond the southernmost switch of a siding. The switchman threw the tall cast-iron lever that opened the switch and signaled to the engineer. Huge gouts of black smoke billowed from the fat stack as the engineer reversed the drive and the big wheels spun backward. Slowly the observation platform on the smoking car angled onto the parallel rails of the siding and swayed through the fog. With creeping progress, the other carriages followed. When the cowcatcher cleared, the mobile rails slid back to the normal position. The train braked.

At once, members of the crew dismounted. Armed with rifles and shotguns taken from the conductor's compartment, they took position to observe the entire length of both sides of the train. From the express car came a short, slender, balding man with a green eyeshade fitted to his brow. He carried a portable telegraph key with a length of wire attached. Smoke Jensen and Marsh Stoddard joined him at the base of a pole. The express agent nodded toward the upright shaft.

"I ain't gonna try climbin' that. Not a man of sixty, fixin' to retire."

Smoke turned to him. "Do you have climbing spikes and a belt in the express car?"

"Sure do."

"Fetch them for me, will you, please," Smoke requested.

Quizzically, the grizzled older man cut his eyes to Smoke. "D'ya mean you can do Morse code?"

Smoke nodded. "Among my lesser accomplishments I did happen to learn it. I may be a bit rusty, but I can manage. If need be, I'll have you write the message out for me in dots and dashes and simply follow along."

"Now that's a good ida. 'Sides, you'll need the identity code for Walsenburg."

"It is WLS, isn't it?" Smoke asked.

Surprise registered on the old-timer's face. "Wall I'll be danged, you do know something about it after all." Then he cut Smoke a shrewd look. "What about the train signal?"

"I'll bet it's DLX."

"Right as rain; Daylight Express." Nodding eagerly, the express agent started for the car. "Be jist a minute."

While Smoke Jensen fitted himself with the climbing gear, the agent wrote out the message, as dictated by Marsh Stoddard, in plain English and handed it and the key to the last mountain man. Smoke ascended the pole with ease. He settled himself comfortably at a level with the wires and fastened the bare ends of the lead to the proper one. Then he tightened the wing nut that fed power from the battery pack slung over one shoulder and freed the striker. Eyes fixed on the message form, Smoke tapped out the words.

After two long minutes acknowledgment came back along with a question. "DLX whose fist is that(q) It is not Eb(x)"

Smoke sent back, "No(x) Eb did not want to climb the pole(x) This is US Marshal Smoke Jensen(x)"

That brought a flurry of questions. "What is a marshal doing on the train(q) What is the nature of your emergency(q) How long will you be delayed(q)"

Smoke's reply must have electrified them. "There has been a murder(x) Notify the law in WLS(x) We will be at least two hours(x)"

With that Smoke detached the lead and descended the pole. "Now, Marsh, I suggest we set up to question the good folks on this train."

Naturally enough, Smoke Jensen began by questioning the people from the car where the murder had occurred. He had passed through ten of them, including the still upset woman who had found the body, when he came face-to-face with the nosey dowager from the dining car. Mrs. Darlington Struthers—Hermione—proved to be a woman of strong opinions and downright regal condescension to those she considered her inferiors. With small, gloved fists on her ample hips she stood before the table where Smoke interrogated the passengers.

"I will tell you nothing, young man. The very idea that an upstart the likes of you can commandeer this train, halt it on a siding and pry into the affairs of its passengers is a matter I shall have my husband take up with the directors of the line. Darlington Struthers has considerable influence, as I am sure you shall learn to your regret."

Smoke eyed her with ice glinting off the gold flecks in his eyes. "Are you quite through? This is a murder investigation. You will please answer my questions, or you will spend a few days at the tender mercies of the sheriff in Walsenburg."

Hermione's face grew bright red. "The nerve . . ."

"I assure you it is not nerve. Now, where are you seated in relation to the dead woman?"

"You are not the law, and I do not have to answer your questions."

Smiling, Smoke produced his badge folder. "Oh, but I am. Deputy U.S. Marshal. First, let me say that your evasions and bluster make you sound more like the guilty party than a mere fellow passenger. With that in mind, let me ask again: Where are you seated?"

Testily, Hermione Struthers answered. Smoke asked if she had seen or heard anything unusual during the night. Her face took on the expression of a dog passing a peach pit when she snapped her answer in the negative. Smoke tried another tack.

"Well, now, I might be just a hick lawman from the High Lonesome, but I do have some smarts about me. From where you would have been in your bunk, it is impossible not to have heard any sounds of struggle. And believe me, from the looks of that Pullman berth, there was considerable struggle. Even the window shade is torn."

"I am a sound sleeper."

Smoke could not resist the barb. "A little too much claret, eh?"

Indignation rose to balloon the face of Hermione Struthers. "I am a tea-totaler, I'll have you know."

Smoke considered her stubbornness. She knew something, of that he was sure. Yet, he could not use force to learn it. And right now, his guile was wearing thin. "So, you heard nothing. Did you see anything, anyone around there?"

"I am not in the habit of spying on others."

I'll bet you're not, Smoke thought silently. "Hmm. We'll let that pass for the moment. If you heard nothing and saw nothing during the night, what about early this morning, when people began to rise for the day?"

"Again, nothing. Not the least thing."

"Very well. You may go, ma'am. But I may want to talk to you again."

Hermione turned to the door and spoke over her shoulder. "Do as you will. You will get nothing from me." With a smug, tight expression she opened the portal and stepped across the threshold.

That's when Smoke Jensen launched his final arrow. "Oh, so there is . . . something?"

Outside in the vestibule between the smoking car and the rearmost Pullman, Hermione Struthers unloaded her bile on Marsh Stoddard, her voice loud and cawing. "Mr. Conductor, there is something you should know about that so-called marshal in there. To my certain knowledge, he is the last person to have seen the late Miss Larkin alive. They were carrying on scandalously in the dining car."

Four

For two blistering minutes, Hermione Struthers belabored Marsh Stoddard with a highly fanciful account of an imagined torrid liaison between Smoke Jensen and Winnefred Larkin. What she lacked in imagination, she made up for in viciousness. She concluded with a demand, hot with vehemence.

"I insist that you put this train in motion at once and proceed on our way. I'll have you know that my husband is an associate of the president of the line and well known to the board of directors. I intend to bring your dereliction to the attention of Mr. Struthers. Your future employment may depend upon your prompt obedience."

Stoddard tipped the billed cap to her and spoke softly. "Somehow I doubt that."

"What did you say?" Hermione demanded.

"I said, I don't doubt that."

"As well you shouldn't. I shall return to my car, and I want immediate entrance." She started for the vestibule steps.

Stoddard hurried to intervene. "I wouldn't do that, ma'am. One of the crew might take a potshot at you."

"What do you mean?"

"Marshal's orders, ma'am. All vestibule doors are to be kept locked, and no one is to leave the train until the killer is unmasked."

Hermione's face drained of color. "But I have already told you. *He* is the murderer. That false marshal in there."

Stoddard kept a tight rein on his expression. "Very well, ma'am, I'll take care of it right away. First, come with me and I will see you to your car."

Stoddard came back and entered the smoking car. "That damned woman. Claims you are the killer. Once she's got her steam up, she'll blow it off to everyone who will listen, and a good many who won't."

Smoke considered that a moment. "That could complicate matters a little."

"D'you have any more of an idea of who it might be?"

"None, so far. But I am convinced that officious old hen knows something she's not telling. I think I'll have her back in here after I've gone through all the others. Bring the next one, if you will, please."

During the next three-quarters of an hour, Smoke interviewed the train's porters and every one of the passengers, with the exception of four people. Those who had come from the car that housed Hermione Struthers cast nervous, suspicious glances at Smoke when they thought he was not watching them. So much for the old bag. Finally, one of that group blurted out his apprehension.

"Mrs. Struthers says she has positive proof that you are the killer."

"Well, Mr. Paddington, tell me this. When's the last time you saw a Poland China sail past overhead?"

Paddington looked confused a moment, then angry. "That's all stuff and nonsense. Ain't never been a Poland China that could fly."

"That's my point. You can believe whatever that woman says the day pigs start to fly. Now, would you tell me if you saw or heard anything out of the ordinary during the night?"

"Uh—uh well, nothing you'd call unusual, all considered."

"Meaning what?"

"Ain't unusual for young folks to do some sparkin' on a train at night. They think it's romantic."

That grabbed Smoke's attention at once. "And you saw something like that?"

"Yes, I did. I didn't see 'em actually clingin' to one another like soul mates, but I reckon that had come right before." Again, Paddington paused irritatingly.

"Before what?" Smoke pressed.

"Jist before I saw this young man leave our car. He come from down the direction of that poor young woman's berth."

"Could you recognize him?"

For once, Paddington did not hesitate. "Not for certain. His head was all in shadows. An' he seemed in a hurry. I was gettin' up to visit the slop jar an' he like to knocked me back into my bunk."

Smoke listed physical characteristics in an attempt to spark memory. "Was he tall? Short? Heavy? Thin? What did he wear?"

Paddington mused on it. "He was about my height, five-nine, slightly built, I'd say, and had a suit on. Seemed to me the shirt was of two colors, dark and light."

"Could that have been black and white?"

Surprise wrathed Paddington's face. "Say, yer right, marshal. It sure could have been."

"Are you aware that in very low lamplight, or moonlight, blood looks black?" There had been a lot of blood.

"Ohmygod! If only I'd seen his face."

Yes, if only, Smoke thought with disappointment.

That had been fifteen minutes earlier, and Smoke was now ready to start on the last four. He ruled out the first to enter at sight of the man. He was short, fat and wore spectacles that would rival the bottom of a wine bottle. Smoke questioned him anyway.

No. No one had passed through the chair car where he had been trying to sleep. He had heard nothing. At least not until some woman screamed bloody murder early in the morning. Could hear her clear up in his coach. Smoke excused him and asked Stoddard to bring in the next.

A slender man in his early twenties entered the smoking car. He had shifty eyes, and his palms were notably wet and unexpectedly cold when Smoke shook his hand. Smoke let him sweat in silence for two minutes after giving his name.

"Now, Mr. Reierson, in order to save time, we'll start this off the hard way. I am a deputy U.S. marshal, empowered to investigate the murder that happened on this train last night. I'm going to ask you some questions and I expect truthful answers."

"Why, of course. Any——" Reierson's voice caught. "Anything I can do to help."

While Smoke went through his routine questions, Reierson developed a nervous tic at the corner of his left eye. His trepidation increased the harder Smoke probed. More so when Smoke pointed out that his answers did not hold up with the observations of others.

Reierson tried bluster. "That's preposterous. I know where I was and what I did. They must be mistaken."

Smoke rounded on him suddenly, his voice a soft purr. "No they aren't. You did it, all right. What I don't know is why. What made you kill that lovely young woman?"

"I didn't! Y-you're falsely ac-accusing an innocent man."

"No, I'm not, Reierson. You did it, right enough. How did it happen? Did she resist your demands? Struggle? Maybe claw at you with those long fingernails?"

Face alabaster with fright, Reierson made to bolt for the door. Smoke Jensen reached him in two swift strides. He grabbed Reierson by one shoulder, spun him around and shoved him into a chair. Panicked, the pathetic specimen of a craven killer groped under his coat and whipped out a small, four-shot, "clover-leaf" pocket revolver.

"Yes, I killed her, goddamn you. And I'll kill you, too." Sobbing in frustration, he fired wildly.

Smoke Jensen was a lot faster and much more accurate.

Stoddard burst through the vestibule door. "What happened?"

"He confessed. After he drew a gun on me. I'll write up a complete report and you can give it—and the bodies—to the law in Walsenburg."

Soft music floated through the huge dining room of a hilltop mansion outside Taos, New Mexico Territory. A string quartet in formal black sawed away at an opus by Brahms. Clifton Satterlee sat at the head of a long, shining, cherrywood table that would easily seat eighteen. A wide strip of white linen ran the length of the ruddy, glowing surface. Brice Nobel sat to Clifton Satterlee's right, to his left, Clifton's wife, Emma. Noble's wife, Mildred, sat to her husband's right. At the far end were Patrick Quinn and a young woman of his acquaintance, Lettie Kincade. The other women at the table would have been scandalized and highly offended if they knew that until ensnaring the attentions of Quinn, Lettie had been the inmate of a deluxe Santa Fe bordello.

Soft, yellow light from three silver candelabra flattered the complexions of the older women, smoothing out wrinkles, while it put a light of naughty mischief into the pale blue eyes of Lettie Kincade. Cole Granger stood in front of the high double doors that gave into a high-ceilinged, vaulted corridor. Dinner had concluded and the last of the dishes cleared away. At a sign from her husband, Emma stood and addressed the other women.

"Ladies, I suggest that we retire to my sitting room for coffee and sweets. If you gentlemen will excuse us?"

Clifton nodded blandly, and all of the men came to their boots as the women left the room. When the side door closed behind them, Satterlee turned to the butler. "Pour cognac around, if you will, Ramon, then you are excused."

Soft clinking followed while Ramon Estavez poured from a crystal decanter into three glasses. When he finished his task and lighted cigars for all three, he soundlessly departed from the room. Satterlee lifted his glass in a toast and mockingly paraphrased Shakespeare.

"We grow . . . we prosper. Now, gods, stand up for bastards." They all laughed and drank; then Satterlee continued. "First, let me announce that my lovely Emma will be returning to Santa Fe with me the day after tomorrow. Now, Mr. Quinn, we would appreciate a report of your progress."

Rising, Quinn set aside his cigar. "The Bar-Four now belongs to C.S. Enterprises, it does. So does the Obrigon ranch. We completed papers on the Suarez ranch this morning. Two stores on the Plaza de Armas now belong to your development company, with three others likely to fall in line within two days more, an' that's a fact."

"Thank you, Paddy, my friend." Satterlee beamed.

"Ah, but there's more. The title on the Figueroa hacienda cleared the territorial land office late this afternoon."

Satterlee shot to his feet in enthusiasm. "Splendid."

"Here-here!" Brice Noble chimed in. "Though I must say, it was a blasted expensive undertaking. It cost a fortune to buy that mansion. Why not simply kill the old man? After all, the granddaughter could not inherit. The territorial government would appoint an executor to manage it until she reached her majority. And then"—he gestured widely—"through our connections in Santa Fe we could have gotten it for a song."

Satterlee countered that at once. "To use our bought politicians on so trivial a matter would have unduly compromised them. The time might come when we need their influence much more. Now, let us move on to the next phase of our agenda."

* * *

Railroad workers rolled a movable loading chute in place at the door to the stock car that held the horses Smoke Jensen had brought along. The last mountain man stood by patiently as a man led Cougar down the ramp onto solid ground. Smoke had been surprised by how much Raton had grown since he had last been in the northern New Mexico town. Low adobe houses now sprawled out for a good mile from the more settled part of the community near the depot, each with its familiar picket fence of ocotillo cactus rods. Smoke abandoned his reflections when Cougar let out a shrill squall and swayed drunkenly, unaccustomed to not having the surface below his hooves in constant motion. Smoke hurried to the heaving side of the big 'Palouse stallion.

"Easy, boy. Whoa, Cougar." To the depot worker he added, "He'll get his legs back in a bit. Don't try to walk him around right now."

When both animals had recovered, Smoke saddled them, then strapped the large panniers on the packsaddle. The sudden thought hit Smoke that in the years past, he had never needed a packhorse to accompany him. Nor had he dragged along all the comforts that the pouches of the panniers now contained. He would have laughed at the wrought-iron trestle, cast-iron skillet and Dutch oven, three-legged grill and cooking utensils. A coffeepot and a small, lidded skillet had been all he had ever needed. *Yet, when the years go by,* he mused with regret, *one's needs change.* Mounted on Cougar, Smoke walked his way toward the main intersection, where he would take the east-west trail toward Taos. With the Santa Fe and Denver and Rio Grande both passing through Raton, the usual entrepreneurs and hustlers had flocked into the burgeoning city. Hawkers with carts stood on street corners, touting their wares. Hundreds of people thronged the streets. A low haze of red-brown dust hovered at first-floor level throughout. Stray dogs yapped at the hooves of his packhorse, and the animal snorted its irritation and flicked one iron shoe. A yellow bitch yelped and slunk off. As he passed a saloon, a loud shout attracted Smoke's attention.

"Hey, let me go!" A young man stumbled out onto the street, as though propelled by eager hands.

Following him came three scraggly ruffians who spread out across the thoroughfare. To Smoke they had the seedy look of low-grade wanna-bes. The one in the middle raised an arm and pointed in a taunting manner. "Yer wearin' a gun, you little shit. Now yer gonna have to use it."

With a start, Smoke Jensen recognized the speaker as Tully Banning, a two-bit gunfighter more renowned for the number of his back shootings than he was for face-to-face shoot-outs. In the next instant, as he reined in, Smoke realized that the challenged youth could not be more than fifteen. A beardless, frightened boy. Smoke quickly sized up the two louts with Banning. What his read gave him he did not like. The boy did not have a chance. Smoke stepped right in the middle of it.

"Banning! Tully Banning."

Banning turned only his head. "Who th' hell wants to know?"

"That's not important. What I want to know is why you don't pick on someone your own age or older?"

Banning uttered a string of curses, and concluded with, "Maybe you'd be interested in taking this punk kid's place. If so, I'll deal with you first, then kill Momma's little boy anyway."

Smoke pulled a face. "I don't think so. Keep your stray curs off me while I step down so I can accommodate you."

"You've got that, old man."

Old man? Smoke never thought of himself as old. He climbed from the saddle and tied off Cougar and his packhorse, Hardy. Then he walked out to stand beside the youth who had been challenged. "Step out of the street, son. You didn't ask for this, and there's no reason you take any harm for it."

With an expression of mingled relief and frustration, the sandy-haired boy angled off the street to stand by Smoke's horses. Then Smoke looked up at Banning. "I'm ready any time you are."

Tully Banning's shoulders hunched, and his right hand twitched; but he did not go for his six-gun at once. It had been a signal, one old and familiar, to his companions. The challenged individual could be expected to focus his attention and anticipation upon the challenger. That's the way it had worked for Tully Banning time and again. So, when the cheat and sneak made the little jerk and arrest movement, his henchmen immediately drew their revolvers.

One small miscalculation marred their perfect ambush. Although the trio had often heard of the exploits of Smoke Jensen, none of them had ever met with him face-to-face. Now that they had, it was entirely too late. Smoke expected some sort of dirty work, so he readied himself accordingly. When all three louts drew, Banning last of all, Smoke already had their demise planned.

Drawing with his usual blinding speed, Smoke killed the one on the left first. Then he swung past Banning in the middle to take on the right-hand gunhawk. The poor soul never had a chance. He did get off one wild shot that split the air high above the head of Smoke Jensen. Then the hammer of Smoke's .45 Peacemaker fell, and a hot slug ripped into the ruffian's gut. It burned a trail of agony through his liver before it ripped out a piece of his spine and tore a hole in his back. Rapidly dying, he went to his knees as Tully Banning attempted to level his six-gun.

To his horror, Tully Banning saw the calm expression and faint smile of the man facing him an instant before flame and smoke spewed from the muzzle of the Colt and a wrenching agony exploded in his chest. Staggered, he took two feeble, uncertain steps to the right and triggered his piece. Banning's slug kicked up dirt between the widespread legs of Smoke Jensen.

Then Smoke shot again. Another terrible hammer blow smashed into the chest of Tully Banning. His legs went out from under him, and he dropped on his backside in the dusty street. Dimly he heard the shouts of amazement from the onlookers who had assembled well out of the line of fire. This couldn't be happening. The trap had always worked before. It would take the best gunfighter in the world to best the three of them, Banning's spinning mind fought to reject his mortality.

Blood bubbled on his lips as he asked weakly, "Who are you?"

Smiling that ghost of a smile again, Smoke Jensen told Tully Banning, who turned even whiter before he died. Suddenly, the freckle-faced, sandy-haired boy appeared at Smoke's side. "I didn't recognize you, Mr. Jensen."

"Don't reckon they did, either."

"You sure saved my life. Uh—my name's Ian MacGreggor. Most folks call me Mac. It's an honor to meet you. And, thank you, thank you for getting me out of that fix. They never gave me a chance to say no."

Smoke nodded understanding. "Their kind never do. And, they never, ever pick on anyone capable of defending themselves. Remember that."

"Yes, sir, I will. Thank you again."

It took Smoke Jensen an uncomfortable fifteen minutes with the town constable to explain what he had accomplished in two seconds. Given the assurance it would be recorded as self-defense, Smoke at last got on the trail to Taos.

Thick-foliaged palo verde trees made silver-green smoke clouds against the horizon of red earth and cobalt sky. Cattle grazed on the sparse grass of Rancho de la Gloria. Throughout the prairie lands, from Texas to Montana, cattlemen talked of cows per acre. Not so here. Don Diego Alvarado had learned at his father's knee to think in terms of acres per cow. In future times, the elegant Diego Alvarado often told himself, irrigation would make this harsh desert into a veritable garden place. Not in his lifetime, though. So he did not share his dream with his friends and fellow ranchers. His vaqueros knew of it, and believed him. Three of them had been given the assignment of tending a herd of two hundred that grazed through a high meadow on the north end of the ranch property.

They found their work peaceful and pleasing. Not far off lay a connected chain of *tanques* where the beasts would water and they could take their *almuerzo*. Each had a cloth bag in his saddlebag, provided that morning by his wife, that contained a burrito—beans and onion rolled in a flour tortilla—a savory tamale, and fresh, piquant chile peppers to add flavor and spice. Arturo had even brought along some cornmeal sugar cookies baked by his wife. Arturo Gomez and Hector Blanco had promised their younger sons they could bring lunches and join the men at the tanks, the lads taking a noontime swim. That would get them out from under their mothers' feet. The older boys all tended goat herds during the day and could always find ways to get cool and wet. As a newlywed, Umberto Mascarenas, the third vaquero, only dreamed of the day when he would have sturdy sons like his companions. He looked up at the sound of pounding hooves. Could it be the *niños* already?

Caught unaware, Umberto Mascarenas did not hear the first gunshot, or any of those that followed. A bullet struck him in the right side of his head, an inch above his ear, and blew out the other hemisphere. He pitched from his horse in a welter of gore.

"Git them other greasers," a harsh voice shouted.

More gunfire sounded across the plateau. Arturo Gomez returned fire with his Obregon copy of a .45 Colt and had the satisfaction of watching an Anglo *ladrón* spill from his saddle at the third round. Then pain burned the life from him as three bullets struck him in half a second. To his right, Hector Blanco dismounted and drew his rifle. The Marlin cracked sharply, and the hat flew from another rustler's head. Hector shot again, and the thief threw up his hands and fell backward off his mount.

By that time, the reports of the weapons had registered on the dim brains of the cattle. They reacted at once and broke into a shambling run. Controlling the cattle became the primary objective of the rustlers, yet one took the time to ride down on Hector Blanco and steal his life with a bullet through the brain. Then the killer galloped ahead to join the others in a V-shaped formation in front of the stampeded herd and direct it off Alvarado land toward a waiting holding pen in a blind canyon.

Twenty minutes later, the horrified and grief-stricken sons of Arturo and Hector found the bodies of all three vaqueros. The Whitewater Paddy Quinn gang had struck again.

Five

An hour short of sundown, with long, golden and carmine shafts of light spilling through the canyons, Smoke Jensen made night camp on a bluff above the Canadian River. He staked out his horses to graze and prepared a fire ring. Then he gathered dry windfall and laid a fire. With seemingly calm indifference to his surroundings, he went about setting up his cooking equipment. Constantly, though, he kept his ears tuned to the sound of soft footfalls that grew steadily nearer. Smoke's surprise registered on his face when the source of that noise came up within thirty feet of the campsite and hailed him.

"Hello, Mr. Jensen. It's me, Mac."

Smoke looked up from the task of slicing potatoes into a skillet to study the gangly youth. Mac's shoulders were broad and his arms long, the promise of a fair-sized man when he got his growth. He was slim, though, and narrow-hipped, and with that boyish face, he looked a long way from reaching that maturity. Smoke motioned him in.

"Howdy, Mac. What brings you along?"

"Well, Mr. Jensen, I wanted to thank you again for saving my life. Really, though, I sort of got to thinking. I wondered if—if you'd welcome me to ride along with you. Seein' we're headed the same direction, that is."

So much earnestness shone from his freckled face that Smoke had to turn away to keep control of his laughter. He fished an onion from a pan of water and began to slice it onto a tin plate to add to the potatoes. "Now, what direction would that be?"

"Why, to Taos, of course."

Smoke feigned doubtfulness. "I'll have to think on that one. But, step down. Least you can do now is share my eats. I've got some fatback, taters, and I'll make some biscuits."

Memory of the boiled oatmeal, twice a day, that had sustained him between his home and Raton prodded Ian MacGreggor. "Gosh, you sure eat well, Mr. Jensen."

"Call me Smoke, Mac."

Caught off balance by this, Mac gulped his words. "Yes, sir, ah, Smoke."

"Now, to eatin' well, it's only common sense. In this climate, a man has to use up his fresh stuff right at the start. By the time we reach Taos it'll be spare enough." Smoke turned his attention to the food for a while, then asked, "You have family in Taos?"

"No, sir, I'm leavin' home for good. I'm my pap's third son, so there's nothin' for me around the farm. We have a little dirt-scrabble place over in Texas. Whole lot of Scots folks around Amarillo. The farm'll go to my oldest brother, Caleb. Dirk is hot for workin' on the railroad. Wants to be an engineer. The apprenticeship and schoolin' costs money, so there was not much left for me."

"Then, I gather you are looking for work in Taos?"

"That's right, Smoke. I heard there was plenty work being offered out Taos way. There was even a notice in the Amarillo paper. A man named Satterlee. He's lookin' for cowhands, timber fallers, all sorts of jobs."

Smoke's frown surprised Mac. "Ah—Mac, I don't want to disappoint you, but do you know anything about this Satterlee?"

"No, no I don't. What's the matter?"

Smoke did not want the boy to go bad. He seemed to have some promise. So, he told Mac what he knew of Clifton Satterlee from the letter sent by Diego Alvarado. As he spoke, the youngster's eyes grew big, and he produced an angry expression. When Smoke concluded, Mac shook his head.

"I sure don't want anything to do with someone like that. Sounds like he's puredee crook." Then he took on a sad expression. "But now I've burned my bridges, what am I gonna do to make a livin'?"

"Taos is growing. And I have a friend. A man who owns a large ranch. Do you happen to speak Spanish? His name is Diego Alvarado; he's a real Spanish gentleman."

Mac nodded enthusiastically. "Sure do. Learned it from the sons of our hired hand. I growed up with them."

"Then, if Don Diego takes you on, you'll have lots of use for it. All of his ranch hands are Mexican."

Mac frowned. "I don't know much about cows. We planted mostly hay, sold it to the ranchers, put in some wheat, corn. Pap wanted to try watermelons. They grow real good in Texas."

"As I recall, Diego has some fields down by a creek that runs behind his house which he uses to irrigate them. He grows several kinds of melons, as well as corn, onions, beans, chile peppers, and a little cotton. He provides nearly all the needs for the entire ranch."

"How—how big is this place?"

"Three or four thousand acres, I'm not sure which."

Mac looked at Smoke in awe. "That's the biggest spread I ever heard of. All we have is a quarter section."

Smoke took pity on Mac, though not much. "Diego has more land under irrigated cultivation than that. I'm willin' to bet he could use an experienced farmer."

Over their meal, Smoke worried around another idea in his head. When Mac offered to wash up after supper, Smoke poured a cup of coffee and spoke his mind. "If Diego has no need for a farmer, there might be something else you can do. Something for me. Though it might prove risky."

New hope bloomed on Mac's face. "Anything, so long as it's legal, Smoke."

"I assure you it's that. Don Diego asked me to come out and take a look at this Satterlee's operation. I could use some help in doing that."

"How can you poke into something crooked? That's a job for the law."

Smiling, Smoke produced his badge and showed it to Mac. "So happens, I'm a deputy U.S. marshal. What I have in mind is that if Diego does not take you on, you go ahead and take that job with Satterlee. Only, don't break the law yourself. Look around, keep your ears open. See what kind of sign you cut on his operation. Then, make arrangements to report anything you learn to me. You'd get regular deputy marshal pay, provided by the U.S. Marshal's Office. That should give you a good stake after the job is over."

"What about the risk you mentioned?" Mac asked soberly.

No fool this one, Smoke reflected. "If you are caught, Satterlee or one of his henchmen will try to kill you. Or at least hurt you pretty bad."

Mac cut his eyes to the six-gun in the holster on his hip. "I ain't as fast or accurate as you, Smoke. An' I never caught on to the trap of those three in Raton. But I am good with a gun."

"You'll have to be. What d'you say?"

"Okay. I'll do it."

Smoke looked Mac levelly in the clear, blue eyes. "Done, then. But you may not live to regret it," he told the boy ominously.

A refreshing spring shower had brightened the yellow bonnets of the jonquils and purple-red tulip globes in the wide beds planted at the front of the main house on the Sugarloaf. A rainbow hung on the breast of the Medicine

Bow Mountains to the northeast. Sally Jensen gave up on her industrious dusting program at the clatter of narrow, steel-tired wheels on the ranch yard. She removed the kerchief which covered her raven locks, abandoned her smudged rag and straightened the apron as she walked to the door. She opened the portal to an astonishing sight.

A woman, vaguely familiar, and four children sat on the spring-mounted seats of a sparkling, brightly lacquered carriage. The three boys, their soft, brown hair cut in bang-fringed pageboy style, wore manly little suits of royal blue, Moorish maroon and emerald green, with identical flat-crowned, wide-brimmed hats. The small girl sat primly beside her mother, in a matching crushed velvet cape and gown of a puce hue, feathered bonnets to match. The young males quarreled loudly and steadily among themselves.

Sally took three small steps to the edge of the porch. She paused then as she put a name to the face, remembering the letter she had received three days earlier. Mary-Beth Whipple. No, Sally corrected herself, her married name was Gittings. Obviously when Mary-Beth had written asking to make a brief visit, she had taken for granted that the answer would be yes. How typical of Mary-Beth, Sally thought ruefully.

"Sally, dearest," Mary-Beth burbled happily as she reined in.

"Mary-Beth?" Sally responded hesitantly. "I—didn't expect you so soon."

Mary-Beth simply ignored that and gushed. "It's so good to see you again. You have no idea how much I've missed my dear schoolmate." She raised her arms and flung them wide to encompass the whole of the Sugarloaf. "We're here at last."

"Uh—yes, so you are. Won't you come in?"

"Of course. Right away. Can you get someone to take care of these dreadfully stubborn animals?"

For a moment Sally wondered if she meant the snorting,

lathered horses or her three sons. The volume of their altercation had risen to the shouting stage. Sally recalled her school chum only too well. The daughter of a wealthy New England mill owner, she had always been a petulant, spoiled young woman. One who proved woefully empty-headed. Sally had been compelled to drag Mary-Beth's grades upward at the Teachers' Seminary. Worse, she absolutely, positively refused to eat meat. Yet those were not her only eccentricities, Sally recalled as Mary-Beth spoke again.

"These abominable horses, of course. They have made our journey from Denver absolutely miserable. So tedious. Well," she declared, releasing the reins and standing upright in the carriage. "We're here now. And we can look forward to not having to deal with these fractious creatures for a whole month."

A month? Sally thought sinkingly. *That* was Mary-Beth's idea of a brief stay? "I'm afraid we're not . . . prepared for such a long stay."

Mary-Beth's face clouded up, and she produced a girlish pout. "But, we simply must. My husband is doing businessey things in Denver, and it is frightfully boring."

"But . . . my husband is not here. He has been called away."

"Oh, bother the men. They are all alike. Born to neglect. I sometimes regret that I gave birth to even a single male. Little Francine here is all my life."

Her words chilled Sally, who instantly saw the confusion and hurt in the expressions and suddenly flat eyes of the boys. For all of that, Sally's inborn hospitality compelled her to welcome them. She opened her arms in an inviting gesture. "Come on in, then. I'll fix coffee. And I have a sponge cake. Your boys will like that, I'm sure."

Three bright, happy faces shined out on her. "Cake, yah!" they chorused.

Inside, with the boys gulping down slice after slice of the cake Sally had planned to have for herself and Bobby for supper, Mary-Beth returned to her earlier topic. "Ever since you described this heavenly place to me, I've dreamed of visiting. And we simply must stay the whole month. Grantland will be tied up in dull meetings every day for a full thirty days. Lawyers have such a dreary life. Besides, Denver is so depressing, with its heavy pall of smelter smoke hanging over everything. And, such rough, unlettered people swarming everywhere, with absolutely no control over them." Mary-Beth paused and looked at her cup.

"Actually, I prefer tea. Could you arrange to have tea from now on?"

Sally curbed her temper. "I have some tea. When it's gone, it's gone."

Mary-Beth reached over and patted Sally's forearm. "Fine, dear, I understand." She looked over to where her sons had started to squabble noisily over the last slice of cake. "Boys, you go outside with that. You've eaten quite enough. It will spoil your supper."

Grumbling, the three little louts jumped from the table and trudged outside. Mary-Beth picked up again. "At what hour do you serve dinner? We are accustomed to eight."

"Well, Mary-Beth, we are accustomed to six. If you'll pardon me, we will stick to that schedule." Gloomy images of a month of this flashed through Sally's mind.

Bobby Jensen first encountered the newcomers when he came up to the main house from the foaling barn where he had been mucking out stalls. He went directly to the wash house, where he had laid out clean clothes before beginning his task, to clean himself of the stink of blood, manure and horse urine. Bobby had barely eased himself into the big, brass bathtub and shuddered in pleasure at the feel of the warm water when he heard a sound like rats in the rafters. He looked around and saw nothing, so he went to his ablutions. The sound came again.

Bobby paused in the vigorous scrubbing of his hands and arms and let his gaze slide from corner to corner. Again he could find no source. He ducked his head of white-blond hair below the surface and began to lather it when he came up. The rustling persisted. Bobby rinsed his hair and pushed up on one arm.

"Who's there?" When no reply came to his demand, he gave careful examination to the interior for a third time, then returned to his bath. When he was satisfied with his degree of cleanliness—he had not washed behind his ears—Bobby climbed from the tub and stepped under the sprinkler can nozzle attached to a length of lead pipe. Lukewarm water cascaded down on the crown of his head and his thin shoulders when he pulled a chain attached to a spring valve. While he rinsed, he caught sight of furtive movement over by the chair where he had laid his fresh clothing.

A small, pale white hand reached slowly around the obstruction of the chair and headed for the parrot bill grip of Bobby's .38 Colt Lightning. Bobby took three quick steps toward the hidden person and called out in as hard a voice as he could muster.

"Get your hand off my gun."

Suddenly, a boy somewhat smaller than Bobby popped up behind the chair. His appearance would have made Bobby laugh if he were not so angry. He wore a funny blue suit, with a big old flowery tie done in a bow under his chin, and had hair only a few shades more yellow than Bobby's, done in a sissy cut. Ribbons tied the bottoms of his trouser legs just below the knees. Full, bee-stung lips that were made for pouting formed a soft, Cupid's mouth. He screwed those lips up now and spoke in a snotty, superior tone.

"You can't have a gun. You're only a kid. Besides, nobody has a right to have a gun, except a policeman. And even they shouldn't have them. My mother says."

Although naked as a jaybird, Bobby immediately snapped

out his verbal defense. "The hell I can't. Smoke Jensen gave me this six-gun himself I've got a rifle, too."

"Liar. My mother says no one has the right to a gun. That they are the most evil things on earth."

Bobby bristled further. "You're the liar. You ever hear of the Constitution? Smoke taught me real good. There's a part of it that says, ' . . . the right of the people to keep and bear arms shall not be infringed.' So there."

Mary-Beth's eldest, Billy, narrowed his eyes and balled his small fists. "Think you're one of those dirty, back-shootin', coward gunfighters like Smoke Jensen?"

That proved too much for Bobby. He swiftly closed the distance between himself and the other boy and gave his antagonist a two-handed shove to the chest. Rocked off his heels, twelve-year-old Billy stumbled backward. Bobby came right after him. Another push and Billy went sprawling out of the wash house. Bobby watched the other boy flail in the dirt a moment, then turned back and shrugged into his trousers. He came out of the building as Billy scrambled to his feet.

Billy made the mistake of swinging the moment he saw Bobby. Young Jensen ducked and threw a punch of his own. It smacked Billy under the left eye. He cried out at the pain and then rushed Bobby. Bobby side-stepped and tripped Billy. At once, the older boy dropped down on his knees, astraddle the small of Billy's back. Bobby began to drub his opponent on the shoulders. Billy made squealing, yelping sounds and kicked the toes of his boots against the ground. At last he found purchase enough to thrust upward and throw Bobby off of him.

"Damn you, you don't fight fair," Billy sobbed, his dirt-smeared cheeks streaked with tears. He dived on Bobby before the older boy could get up.

From there their fight degenerated into a lot of rolling around in the dirt. Bobby got a couple of good punches to Billy's ribs. Then he clouted his opponent on the ear, which brought a howl of agony from Billy. Bobby wrestled himself around on top and began to drive work-hardened fists into Billy's midriff. All pretense of toughness deserted Billy, and he began to wail in a pitiful voice.

"Help me! Momma, help me! Get him off, get him off."

The sudden commotion reached the ears of Sally Jensen and Mary-Beth Gittings where they sat on the porch, sipping at cups of jasmine tea. Mary-Beth's face went blank, then white a moment, and she clutched at her heart. Half rising, she put her cup aside.

"I think that's Billy. Whatever could be happening?"

Sally listened to the uproar a moment and picked out Bobby's voice. "Yer a liar and a trespasser. Git the hell outta here."

Dryly she remarked to Mary-Beth, "I think he has met our youngest. We had better go see."

Together they headed in the direction of the wash house. The sight they saw made Sally Jensen ache, though inwardly she burned with pride for her adopted son. Bobby Jensen remained astride Billy Gittings, pounding him rhythmically. Billy was getting his tail kicked right properly. One eye showed the beginnings of a splendid mouse, and his nose had been bloodied. He sobbed wretchedly with each punch Bobby delivered. She could not let that go on, Sally realized at once. She hurried to the boys.

"Bobby, you stop that at once. Get off Billy this instant." Embarrassment filled Sally Jensen as she dragged Bobby Jensen off Billy Gittings.

Mary-Beth Gittings harbored entirely different emotions. Her voice became accusative and filled with indignation. Her son and Bobby each gave his version of what had started the fight. Her face red, she turned with hands on hips to lash out at Sally.

"Billy is correct. No one has the right to own a gun except the police. I would certainly never allow a child of mine to have one."

Bobby remained defiant. "Then why did he try to steal mine?"

Surly, though in control of his sobs and tears, Billy answered truculently. "I was gonna take it away from you and do what's right and give it to Mother."

Sally stepped in. "Bobby is correct. Taking another person's property, whether you think he has a right to it or not, is stealing. There will be no more of that around here. Now, both of you go in there and get yourselves washed up. You're a couple of mud balls. And shake hands and try to be nice."

Thoroughly mollified, Bobby put out a hand. "My name's Bobby, what's yours?"

"Billy," the other boy answered, still offended. Then he drew himself up. "William Durstan Gittings. But you can call me Billy."

They released their grip and turned away from the adults. With an arm around each other's shoulders, they walked toward the bath that awaited them. Sally breathed a sigh of relief, only to learn that Mary-Beth had not finished.

"One thing you must accept, dear Sally. My son was right in what he did. He certainly did not deserve anything like the beating he got."

Sally groaned inwardly at the thought of the ensuing month, saddled with this now former friend.

In a large, adobe mansion outside of Santa Fe, Clifton Satterlee and four of his associates from back east sat in a sumptuous study, two walls lined floor to ceiling with books in neat rows on their shelves. Long, thick, maroon brocade drapes covered the leaded glass windows, with the usual wrought-iron bars covering them from outside. A small, horseshoe-shaped desk occupied the open space directly in front of the limestone casement. That was where Satterlee held court. The tall back of a large, horsehair-stuffed chair loomed over his six-foot-plus height. He wore a blue velvet smoking jacket and open front shirt of snowy perfection, riding trousers and calf-length boots. His guests clothed themselves with all the formality of eastern evening wear. Brass lamps provided illumination, and the yellow rays of the kerosene flames struck highlights off the cut crystal decanter and five glasses on a low table around which the visitors sat. The topic of conversation had turned to their plans for the conquest of Taos and its environs.

"We already have a good foothold," Satterlee reminded his associates. "C.S. Enterprises has the timber rights to a thousand acres on the eastern slopes of the Sangre de Cristo range. By selective cutting, we can clear a way to allow passage of the logs we harvest from the land currently held by those Tua vermin. We can pass them off as coming from our legally held property."

Durwood Pringle cocked an eyebrow. "Do you think that will fool any inspectors the Interior Department sends out here?"

"Of course, they are the same kind of trees. We will continue to log off the eastern slopes so that an inspector will see cutting activity. And, we will have ample advance warning of any surprise visit. Besides, when it comes to the local officials, we have already bought them."

Pringle still lacked assurance. "Yes, but are they *honest* politicians?"

Satterlee snorted in impatience. "What do you mean? We paid them off, didn't we?"

"I understand that, Clifton old fellow, what I mean is that an *honest* politician is one that once he's been bought, he stays bought."

They shared a good laugh at this levity. Then Satterlee moved on to the next subject. "The merchants and residents of Taos remain stubborn for some reason. Although we have added to our cattle holdings recently with two hundred head from the Alvarado ranch."

A frown creased the forehead of Durwood Pringle.

"That's excellent, Clifton. But what we want to know is what is being done to encourage these reticent merchants in Taos to sell out?"

Clifton Satterlee took a long pull on his cognac and produced a warm smile. "Have no fear, Durwood. That is being taken care of as we speak."

Six

Bright orange tendrils of flame coiled through the black night sky over Taos, New Mexico. The intensity of the inferno paled the thin crescent of moon and dampened the starshine. A horse-drawn fire wagon, its bell clanging frantically, sped through the streets. Men in light blue cotton shirts tugged at the suspenders of their bright yellow, waterproof, oil-skin trousers. A cold hand clutched their minds as one. The worst possible disaster had actually happened.

"Where's the blaze, Cap?" a late arrival volunteer fireman asked of his captain.

Captain Taylor pointed to the south. "Couldn't be worse, Clem. The lumberyard is on fire."

Seconds later, their red-and-black lacquered fire engine stormed down the street toward the lumberyard, which had become an orange ball. The chief of the volunteer fire department, Zeke Crowder, directed them to the south side of the block-square enterprise. Flames and showers of sparks shot fifty feet into the air. Zeke Crowder studied this condition with a grim expression. After several seconds, he called his captains together.

"We've got to keep this from spreading to other buildings. Remember what happened in Albuquerque last year. Three blocks in a row wiped out by what started as a small fire in a restaurant kitchen."

"How do we go about it, Chief?" Fire Captain Taylor asked.

Chief Crowder produced a thoughtful expression. "Even though most of these buildings are made of adobe, they all have palm thatch roofs. Dry as it is, if sparks land in that, fire can sweep through as fast as the scorpions and other critters that live there. We have to knock down the flames now to keep that from happening. If we don't, we'll lose half of Taos."

"How we gonna git it done?" another captain persisted.

Chief Crowder did not hesitate. He gestured to the twelve-foot adobe walls that surrounded the lumberyard. "We need to knock down these walls, make 'em fall inward and blow out the flames. Parker, go to the general store. That's the only other source of dynamite in town. Oh, and you might send someone out to the mines. They'll have some. But hurry."

Captain Taylor stated the obvious. "Don't we have to get Mike Sommers' permission to blow up his walls?"

"Yeah, if we can find him. I haven't seen him at all." Chief Crowder paused a second, then directed Taylor. "Find Hub Yates, Mike's foreman. I need to talk to him anyway."

Five minutes later, Capt. Don Taylor returned with Hubbard Yates. "Hub's not seen Mike, either, Chief."

Quickly, Captain Crowder explained the situation to Yates. He concluded with an appeal. "We have to get someone's permission to knock down these walls."

Yates shook his head. "I don't know if I can do that or not."

"If you can't, I do have the authority to do it anyway. Only thing is the city could be charged with the cost of rebuilding. But, if we don't do it, like I said, we can lose half of the town."

Hub Yates looked at the towering column of sparks. "Go ahead, then. I'll take the chance and speak for Mike."

"All right. Don, come with me. We're going to set charges on both sides of the walls. The stronger ones on the inside. You take a crew that knows explosives and put them to it.

And tamp them solid. We want to upend those adobe blocks and drop them inward. The blast should help blow out the flames, too."

While volunteers and onlookers alike labored at the long pumper rails, other fire fighters directed inadequate streams of water onto the burning stacks of raw pine and fir. Steam rose in gouts. The core of the fire glowed a dark magenta. Don Taylor and his men took cases of dynamite as they arrived and prepared charges. A shout of alarm rose when the roof of the building nearest the blaze caught from sparks and began to burn lustily.

At once, Chief Crowder directed the three hoses of one company onto the new hot spot. Hissing in protest, the flames slowly died. "Keep on wetting that one down," Crowder directed. He sent two runners to instruct the other fire rigs to do the same.

"Why are you giving up?" a bystander demanded.

"We're gonna lose the whole she-bang, that's for certain. All we can hope for is to keep it from spreading."

"I still say you oughtta keep on fighting."

Crowder eyed him coldly. "You're not wearing this coal scuttle on yer head, either. Hell, you're not even helping. I'd keep that mouth buttoned up tight, if I were you.

After half an hour, Captain Taylor reported to the chief. "We're all set."

"Then let her rip!"

At a signal from Taylor, fuses were ignited. The solid thump of explosions rippled along the walls, working outward from the center. Thick clouds of dust billowed and obscured the fire. With a muffled rumble, the tiers of adobe blocks leaned inward and began to fall. The initial blasts had dampened the flames considerably. Now, the four-sided curtains of disturbed air from the falling walls snuffed much more. The feeble streams from the hoses began to gain ground. From the far side a cheer went up.

Chief Crowder began an inspection tour of the fire site.

He found that through some fluke, the building front had only been slightly charred. Taking two firemen with him, he picked his way gingerly through the smoldering coals and mounds of ash. Near the rear of the store portion, where the fire had been far hotter, he came upon a huddled mound. Crowder brushed at accumulated ash with a gloved hand and revealed a human shoulder.

"Give me a hand here," he commanded.

His firemen bent to the task. Shortly, they recovered and revealed the severely burned corpse of the owner. A sickeningly sweet odor wafted up from the seared flesh. One of the fire fighters, who had eaten mutton for supper, turned away and abruptly lost his supper. Fighting back his own rush of nausea, Chief Crowder issued yet another command.

"Get Doc Walters over here right away."

In midmorning of the next day, a visibly troubled Dr. Adam Walters found Zeke Crowder in his saddlery shop. The volunteer fire chief sat at a bench, shaping strips of leather into the skirt of yet another of his excellent saddles. A steaming coffee cup rested to one side. He looked up as the bell over the door jingled and the doctor entered.

" 'Morning, Doc. What news on Mike Sommers?"

"Nothing good, I'm afraid, Zeke. That's why I'm here. I also asked Hank Banner to join us. He should be along shortly."

"The sheriff? What for? Mike died in an accident, didn't he?"

"No. The fire was not an accident and Mike did not die from it."

Right then the bell jingled again, and Sheriff Hank Banner entered. "Howdy, Adam, Zeke. Now, what was so all-fired important, Doc?"

Dr. Walters sighed heavily. "Maybe we should all have a

cup of coffee at hand. I brought along some medicinal brandy."

He remained silent while Crowder poured. Then the physician added brandy to all three mugs. He sighed heavily again before he made his revelation. "Mike Sommers was murdered. He had been shot twice. Once in the chest and once in the head. Whoever started that fire figured he would be too badly burned for us to find that out."

"Any idea who might have done it?" the sheriff asked.

Dr. Walters hesitated. "I think you could guess the name I'd give you. Mike told me only last week that he had been approached with an offer to buy him out. He refused. Then three of the ruffians who have been moving into town of late roughed him up some on Saturday night. Now, this fire, and Mike is dead, killed by someone working for Clifton Satterlee, or I'll eat my medical bag."

With a grunt, the sheriff raised a restraining hand. "Be careful about unsubstantiated accusations, Doc. You know that particular gentleman would not hesitate to haul you into court on a slander suit."

"But dang-bust it. What can we do about this? About everything?"

Again Hank Banner urged caution. "I must admit I share your suspicions that Satterlee is behind all that has happened, including the fire and the murder of Mike Sommers. But, I have no proof. Get me something positive and I'll fling him in jail so fast his boots will take a week to catch up. You know, every day I see more hard cases moving into town. I've a feeling this is about to come to a head."

Beyond the first line of trees that screened a small clearing beside the steep, winding grade that formed the eastern up-slope to Palo Flechado Pass, Moose Redaker, Gabe Tucker, Buell Ormsley and Abe Voss watched two riders walk their mounts past their observation point. When the pair, a young wet-behind-the-ears kid and an older man, had ridden well out of hearing range, Moose Redaker elbowed Buell Ormsley in the ribs.

"Didn't I tell you? When I first seed them, I knew that bigger feller was Smoke Jensen. We're lookin' at better than five thousand dollars re-ward on the hoof."

"You sure those flyers are still in force?" Abe Voss, the cautious one, asked.

Moose had a ready reply. "They ain't been tooken up, have they?"

"That don't mean someone will pay up after all this time."

"Sure they will. And even if they don't, killin' that holier-than-thou gunfighter will be pure satisfaction in itself." Moose Redaker beamed at his companions. "He's done collected too many bounties that should have been ours by rights. 'Sides, it'll do a whole lot for our reputation, now ain't that so, Gabe?"

Gabe Tucker showed a grin of crooked, green-fringed, yellow teeth. "Right as rain, Moose. Hey, how'er we goin' about this?"

A shrewd light glowed in the eyes of Moose Redaker. "These flyers all say he's wanted dead or alive, right?" He paused and put a hand to his wide chin, which hung below a lantern jaw. "Do any of you hanker to manhandle a live and kickin' Smoke Jensen?"

Buell Ormsley scratched at his fringe of ginger hair that surrounded his bald crown. "Not this lad. My momma never raised no idiots."

"She come mighty close," Moose Redaker jibed. "Yep, I reckon we'd do best to jist shoot him in the back and haul his body up north, Montana way."

Buell Ormsley squeezed his bulbous nose. "Won't he get to stinkin' a lot, we do that?" He had a valid point.

In his usual manner, Moose had an answer. "Not if we go by train and ice him down."

Abe Voss rubbed his gloved hands together. "Then, let's get at it."

"Don't be in such a hurry. We gotta do up a plan first."

"What about the boy?" Gabe Tucker inquired.

"Kill him an' leave him for the buzzards," advised Moose.

Ian MacGreggor had dropped back to tighten a loose cinch and relieve a swollen bladder. His horse stood stubbornly sideways in the trail as he tried to mount it. When he swung aboard, he got a quick glimpse of four grim-faced men riding toward him at a fast pace. Swiftly, he turned the animal's head and put spurs to its flanks. Behind him, the evil quartet put their mounts into a gallop. Rapid reaction by Moose Redaker prevented Abe Voss from firing a shot at the boy and revealing their presence for certain. As it happened, they might as well have shot anyway.

When Mac came within hailing distance of Smoke, he called out a warning. "Look out, Smoke. Four hard-looking guys headed our way." Then he reigned smartly to the side and disappeared behind a large boulder.

Redaker and his crew of ne'er-do-well bounty hunters crested a rise that had separated them from their quarry and found the boy gone from sight. The four of them faced a lone Smoke Jensen. Had their combined intelligence been anywhere near average, that fact might have given them more than a little pause to consider. Since it was not, they blundered on, drawing their six-guns as they came. Smoke waited patiently. The moment the first cager lout came within range, Smoke cut him down with a round from his Winchester Express rifle.

Abe Voss flew from the saddle, while still far out of revolver range. His companions could only curse. The deadly accurate rifle spoke again and a 500 grain .45 slug sped downrange. Moose Redaker had accurately gauged Smoke Jensen's intentions and ducked low at the precise moment.

A fraction of a second later, the bullet cracked past in the space formerly occupied by his head. The distance had decreased, which lent encouragement to the bounty hunters. Gabe Tucker jinked to the left and rode into the meadow to that side. He sought to flank Smoke Jensen and get in a good shot. He made it half the distance to his goal when an invisible fist slammed into his right side and knocked him out of the saddle. He hit in a shower of broken turf and rolled to a halt faced away from Smoke Jensen. The burning pain began to fade to the numbness of shock.

On the other side of Moose Redaker, Buell Ormsley angled toward the cluster of boulders. He watched as Smoke Jensen swung the muzzle of the Winchester toward Moose Redaker. When the express rifle bucked in Smoke's grip, Buell swung the nose of his mount back toward the last mountain man and let fly with two fast rounds.

At first, he thought he had hit his target. Smoke Jensen reared back in his saddle and then bent forward. With a start, Buell realized that Smoke had merely put the rifle back in its scabbard. Jensen came up with a six-gun that looked right at him. A wild cry of denial and fright blew from Buell Ormsley's thick lips as Smoke Jensen fired.

At a range of some thirty feet, the bullet had not the power to kill, but it did hurt like hell when it punched through the leather vest Ormsley wore and broke a rib. Reflex action sent him out of the saddle and onto the ground. He landed hard. More pain shot up his spine when his rump made contact with the soil. Temporarily out of the fight, he fought a wave of dizziness. Dimly he saw Moose Redaker close within killing distance of Smoke Jensen.

Smoke remained calm as he waited out his opponent. The only one still astride a horse, the scruffy-looking hill trash presented the only challenge Smoke could see. Both men fired at the same time, and their slugs missed. Smoke's by so narrow a margin that a hot line burned along the rib cage of Moose Redaker. Moose yowled and fired again. The slug punched through the side panel of Smoke's vest. That brought an instant response.

Another .45 round spat from the Pacemaker in Smoke's hand. This one struck Moose in the chest with stunning force. Redaker reeled in the saddle and tried to put his own six-gun into action. A dark red curtain seemed to descend behind his eyes, and the world grew hazy. At last he triggered his Smith American. The .44 slug screamed off a rock and disappeared in the direction of Taos. Then the ground seemed to leap up and smack Moose in the face. He died wondering how that could happen.

Buell Ormsley scooted over the ground toward his dropped six-gun. He had quickly discovered that he had sprained an ankle in his fall from the horse. Buell reached the weapon while Smoke scanned the other three for any sign of continued resistance. Carefully he raised it, and sighted in on the broad back of Smoke Jensen. He eared back the hammer of the Merwin and Hulbert .44 and sighted again. Buell heard the beginning of a loud report from a revolver close by an instant before an intense light washed through his brain, as the off side of his skull flew apart in gory shards.

Ian MacGreggor rode out onto the trail, smoke still curling from the barrel of the old Schoffield Smith .44 in his left hand. "He was gonna back-shoot you, Smoke."

Smoke masked his surprise and produced a grateful grin. "You done good, Mac. Saved my life, that's for sure. I'm beholdin' to you."

With sincere modesty, Mac made small of it. "You'd a done the same for me."

"Thanks all the same. I wonder if it's worth the effort to take this trash along and see if there's a bounty on any of them?"

"D'you think there might be?" Mac had not considered such a possibility.

"Never know." Smoke searched the body of Moose Redaker and found the aged, out-of-date posters depicting his own face. Also a letter signed six years earlier giving a commission to one Albert Redaker to seek out wanted miscreants under the auspice of the sheriff of Denton County, Texas. "Still don't mean they're free of any head money."

"I—ah—if it's all the same, I'd just as soon not have them along for company." Smoke noticed that Mac looked a little gray-green around the mouth.

"First time you killed a man?"

"First time I ever shot at one," Mac admitted.

"Take it from me, Mac, it don't get any easier. Only your reaction to it changes. We'd best cover them with rocks and mark 'em so the nearest law can find them."

Back at the Sugarloaf, little Seth Gittings, Mary-Beth's middle boy, had become a particular burden for Sally Jensen. Every bit as much a brat as his elder brother, he chose this afternoon to leave off the severe biting of his fingernails long enough to bite Bobby. His little jaws proved exceptionally strong as he crunched down on Bobby's left forearm. Bobby instantly felt a jolt of hot pain run up his arm and spread in his chest. He wanted to cry out, to even shed a few tears of agony. Yet he shut his mind to such childish things and sought to remedy the situation.

His hard right fist cracked into the side of his tormentor's head. Seth let go with a yowl and an instant flood of tears. "Ow! Owie! Billy, Billy, he hit me. He hit me," quickly followed.

Bobby immediately pursued his advantage. Chin on his chest, shoulders rolled like Smoke had shown him, he waded in. Fast, solid rights and lefts rained on the chest and exposed belly of Seth Gittings. The ten-year-old back pedaled and flailed uselessly with his stubby arms. Bobby changed his target and felt a flood of satisfaction as blood gushed from Seth's nose. He continued to whale away on Seth until

Billy arrived. At once the twelve-year-old took up for his brother and joined the fray in the form of an attack on Bobby Jensen's turned back.

It staggered Bobby for a moment. Then, determined not to be deterred until he had taught them a lasting lesson, Bobby put his back to the outer wall of the bunkhouse and forced them to come at him from the front. His superior size and strength soon began to tell. First Seth, the cause of the altercation, gave up. He ran off, whining and crying, to find their mother. Billy battled on. The pain of his bite had been forgotten. Bobby never gave it thought until droplets of his own blood splashed in his face. Then he shook his arm in the astonished face of Billy.

"See this? See what that brat little brother of yours did to me?"

Stunned by this evidence, Billy gave off fighting with Bobby. "Yeah, he does get sorta wild at times. Bit the hell outta me once."

Bobby, too, stopped exchanging blows. "What did you do?"

"I whipped his butt."

"What do you think I was doin'?"

"Yeah, but he's my brother."

"So? It's me he bit this time."

"Yep, I guess so. Uh—you oughtta get that fixed, Bobby."

Quickly as that, the two boys dissolved their animosity. They had their differences amicably ironed out when Mary-Beth Gittings, led by a wailing Seth, and Sally Jensen descended upon them.

"What is the meaning of this, you monstrous, vicious little wretch?" she snarled at Bobby Jensen. Even her son looked shocked at her vehemence. Then she rounded on Sally Jensen. "Sally, you simply must punish that unruly boy."

Mutely, Bobby held up his arm to show the tooth marks and the blood that ran from them. Always slow to anger,

Sally suppressed a hot outburst and spoke sweetly. "Since it was two on one, and Seth obviously bit Bobby, perhaps your little darlings share some of the blame."

To the surprise of the Jensens, it was Billy Gittings who came to the defense of Bobby. "He bit me, too, Mother. Remember?"

Mary-Beth pulled an expression of horror. "The very idea!" Thus dismissing her son's revelation, she turned on Sally and snapped, "Seth would never do a thing like that. My precious children are learning such terrible, ruffian ways out here on the frontier. This—this cast-off child of yours is nothing short of a savage. If it weren't so intolerable in Denver, I would return at once."

Oh, do, please do, Sally thought to herself.

Seven

On a hill overlooking Taos, New Mexico Territory, Smoke Jensen halted to consider their course of action from this point on. He turned to Ian MacGreggor. "We'll enter town from different directions. Remember, Mac, when you see me, you don't know me. Later, when this is over, I will definitely introduce you to Diego Alvarado."

Somewhat sobered by the shoot-out on the trail, Mac nodded thoughtfully. "I can understand that, Smoke. Only, how do I make contact when I learn anything important?"

"If there is time, send a letter to Paul Jones, care of general delivery in Taos, giving a time and place. If not, break off from Satterlee's men and ride like the wind for town."

Mac pulled a dubious expression, but answered easily. "Sounds simple enough. Why Paul Jones?"

"More likely to slip past anyone Satterlee might have watching the mail."

Mac pursed his lips. "Yeah—yeah, that makes sense. Did you learn all of this to be a marshal?"

Smoke had to chuckle over that. "No. A lot I figured out on my own, some Preacher taught me, and the rest I got from lawmen like our sheriff back in the High Lonesome. Monte Carson is mighty savvy about such things." For a moment, recollection of Monte brought a tightness to Smoke's chest. "Now, get on your way. I'll give you twenty minutes and then ride in."

Smoke watched Mac ride away and could not help but

reflect on himself at that age. He had been rough-edged, a bit wild and woolly, and had lived about a year with Preacher. The old mountain man—some people called Preacher the *first* mountain man—had proven to be incredibly knowledgeable about every aspect of life in the High Lonesome. He could lecture for hours on the habits, love life, construction skills and market price of the beaver. Add in religion and fighting techniques and he could do the same for a good seven Indian tribes. A complete fascination with such subjects soon smoothed the rough edges, calmed the wildness and trimmed the wool of young Kirby Jensen.

At fifteen, Mac's age, Smoke had received a special present from Preacher. It was a Colt, Model '51 Navy revolver in .36 caliber. With it came grueling hours of drill and instructions in how to load and accurately fire the weapon. He had also learned the speed draw that had made Preacher famous as the first gunfighter. That had not come without a price. More than a dozen times Smoke had discharged blank loads with the revolver still in the pocket. The accidental discharges had burned like hellfire and scarred his leg. Preacher had found it amusing.

Chuckling each time it happened, he had reminded young Kirby, "Boy, you've gotta be quicker on the draw before you work on quick on the trigger."

It had embarrassed the youth, but it made him work harder and become better. In later years, his speed and accuracy with a six-gun would excel even that of his mentor. If Mac was only a quarter as good as Smoke had become, he could for sure hold his own.

Pablo Alvarado, third son of Diego Alvarado, strolled into the cool interior of the Bajo el Cielo de Mexico cantina in Taos during the busy noon hour. The ever-present muslin sheeting dropped white bellies from the rafters, placed there to prevent unwelcome visits by the scorpions and other insects that inhabited the palm thatch roofing. Men lined the bar, gustily drinking down their cellar-cooled beer, while they munched industriously on plates of *taquitos*—rolled corn tortillas filled with roast, shredded goat meat and crisp fried. Others consumed small clay cups of *caldo de camarón*, a thick dark red chile-shrimp soup made of tiny dried shrimp, onions, garlic, tomato paste and hot chiles. All of them frequently dipped tortilla chips into bowls of fresh-made *pico de gallo* salsa, redolent with the aroma of chopped chiles, garlic, and fresh coriander. Nearly half of the patrons were Anglos. Pablo joined three vaqueros from his father's *estancia*, Rancho de la Gloria. He soon had a tall, slender glass of beer, called a *tubo*, in one hand. With his other, Pablo lifted a *taquito* from a plate.

His presence was immediately noted by a trio of scruffy saddle trash seated at a corner table. They bent their heads together and the leader, Garth Thompson, spoke in a low voice. "That's one of that stubborn greaser's sons. I think you two ought to arrange a little entertainment for him outside this place."

"That shines, Garth. What sort of party should we figger to throw?" Norm Oppler responded.

Thompson pursed his lips, then spread them in a nasty grin. "One that will leave him definitely hurting."

Hicky Drago, the third hard case, flashed a toothy smile. "Now that sounds like fun. Do we leave him alive and hurtin'?"

Garth showed his own teeth. "That's entirely up to you."

Both downed their drinks and came to their boots. They left the busy saloon without attracting any attention. Over at the bar, Pablo gestured to an old woman in a plain polka dot dress, her head swathed in a black rebozo. *"Una copa de caldo de camarón, por favor."*

Bearing a large, blue granite kettle, the seam-faced woman attendant came over and ladled out a cup of shrimp soup for the young *caballero*. Pablo took it and nodded his appreciation. *"Gracias."* Then he turned to the ranch hands.

"We will have to start back to the ranch after we've eaten. There seems not to be enough hours in the day."

"Especially to get the work done and for you to see Juanita, eh, *patrón?"* one of the cowboys remarked with a smile.

Pablo's eyes twinkled as he thought of his current favorite. "Juanita is . . . worth making time for. We are going to be married. She doesn't know that yet, but I do."

"¡Que romantico!"

Pablo chided him in jest. "Do not mock true love, Arturo. Some day it will overwhelm you."

"What, me? With a fat wife and three little ones?"

Garth Thompson watched them darkly as they laughed over that sally. He had been given his orders by Whitewater Paddy Quinn as to what to do about the family of the stubborn old fool, Diego Alvarado. The rancher refused to sell out, and his Mexican cowboys had already killed three and wounded eight of those sent to harass him. It was time to turn up the heat, Paddy had said. *So be it,* Garth mused. He watched while Pablo and the vaqueros downed a prodigious quantity of food and two glasses each of beer. Then they hitched up their belts and walked toward the door. Silver conchos along the outer seams of their pant legs sparkled even in the low light.

When they stepped outside, Garth strained to hear over the low rumble of conversation and laughter the challenge he expected. It came a moment later in an angry growl from Norm Oppler.

"Hey, watch where you're goin', greaser."

Smoke Jensen walked Cougar and Hardy down the broad eastern avenue that led to the Plaza de Armas in the center of Taos. Palo verde trees had been planted in circular basins all along the residential section. Their pale, wispy, smokey green leaves fluttered in a light breeze, like the fine hair of a young woman. Most houses sat well back from the Spanish tile sidewalks, presenting high, blank walls to the passersby. Some had built-in niches where flowers had been planted or religious figures installed. Red tile roofs peeked over the blue and green shards of broken bottles plastered into the tops of these ramparts. The last block before the central square had been overtaken by shops, restaurants and cantinas. Smoke reached the midpoint when a harsh voice called out insultingly.

"Hey, watch where you're goin', greaser."

A handsome, light-complexioned young man of Spanish/Mexican descent took a step back and spoke soft words of apology. Then the import of the insult sank in. His eyes narrowed, and his full lips twisted in offense. "What did you call me?"

"I called you a bean-slurpin', chile-chompin' greaser."

Smoke Jensen reined in to watch the exchange. The youth had a familiar appearance, though Smoke could not place a name with the face. Both men were armed, though the well-dressed Spanish youth chose to use his hands. With a suddenness that spoke well of his ability, he swung a balled fist that smashed into the jaw of the loud-mouthed saddle trash with enough force to knock him off his boots.

He hit the tile walk with a flat smack. At once the youth stepped over him. "I'll accept your apology for that insult and there will be no harm done."

"Like hell you will!" shouted the thug as he whipped out his six-gun and fired point-blank into the young man's belly.

At once the other Anglo cleared leather. His bullet cut a searing path across the small of Pablo's back. Smoke Jensen had time only for a hasty shout before his own hand filled with a .45 Colt. "Don't!"

Three dark-complexioned vaqueros with the youth only then reacted, spreading apart with shock and surprise on their faces. One drew a knife. The Colt in the hand of the seated hard case roared again. He missed his attempt to shoot the knife wielder through the chest. His slug bit flesh out of the vaquero's side.

"Drop the guns, both of you," Smoke demanded.

When the Anglo opponents refused to comply, Smoke tripped the trigger of his Peacemaker and shot the seated one through the shoulder, breaking his scapula. The smoking revolver in his hand flew from his grasp. His companion spun on one boot heel to face Smoke Jensen. He raised his six-gun to shoulder height and took aim as Smoke cocked and fired his .45 a second time. His bullet took the gunman in the center of his chest. Behind Smoke, Hardy whinnied in irritation. Shouts came from inside the saloon. The man Smoke had shot looked down at his chest with a dumb expression of disbelief as he staggered forward. Slowly he released his grip on his weapon. The revolver thudded in the dirt of the street a moment before the body of the dead assailant.

By then, the wounded one seated on the tile walk had recovered his Colt and threw a shot at Smoke that cracked past the head of the last mountain man to bury itself deep in an adobe wall across the street. Without a flinch, Smoke returned fire. Hot lead punched a neat hole in the upper lip of the shooter, exposing crooked, yellowed teeth. He went over backward and twitched violently for a few seconds.

During that time, the three vaqueros recovered their composure and rushed to the side of their fallen companion. "Pablo, Pablo, can you hear me?" one spoke urgently.

Pablo? Keeping his Colt handy, Smoke Jensen dismounted and crossed to where two of the Mexican cowboys kneeled beside their employer's son. *"¿Con permiso?"* Smoke addressed them in his rusty Spanish. "Is this Pablo Alvarado?"

Dark, angry faces turned toward him. "Why do you ask, *gringo?"*

Smoke answered simply. "I am a friend of his father."

The surly one produced a sneer. *"Ay, sí.* And I am the pope in Rome. What is your name, *gringo?"*

"I am called Smoke Jensen."

Surprise registered on the three faces. Embarrassment warred with it. At last, the angry vaquero spoke in an amiable tone. *"Tengo mucho vergüenza,* Señor Jensen. I should have known. No one else could have handled two gunmen so fast and so effectively. It is only that Don Pablo has been shot, and Ricardo, *tambien.* And it is forbidden us to carry our *pistólas* into town. We could do nothing."

"And naturally that bothered you. That I can understand. One of you had better go for a doctor." Smoke examined the wounded men. "Ricardo has only a scratch. Pablo is still breathing and he has a strong heartbeat," Smoke observed as he examined the young man. "But he still needs help right away, *inmediatamente, comprende?"*

The embarrassed one spoke up. "I am called Miguel Armillita. I will go."

"Good, Miguel. Another of you should ride to the ranch and tell Don Diego."

"Uh—there is a wagon with supplies," a young vaquero blurted.

Smoke spoke decisively. "Ricardo can drive that, after he is patched up. The other take a fast horse and head for Rancho de la Gloria."

The town marshal and the sheriff of Taos County arrived at the same time. Pablo Alvarado remained unconscious, and two of the vaqueros had sped off on their assigned tasks. An angry and shaken Garth Thompson, who had only now come out of the saloon, leaned against the outside adobe wall of Bajo el Cielo de Mexico scowling at Smoke Jensen. When the lawmen pushed through a crowd of the cantina's patrons, he spoke up in angry accusation.

"This stranger came along and shot two of my men for no reason at all. Shot the Mexican kid as well."

"I'll take that iron," the marshal demanded as he and the sheriff drew their weapons. "You've got some tall explaining to do, mister. Since this involves folks from outside town, I'll let you handle it, Hank. I'd better see to a doctor for young Alvarado."

Smoke looked up at them. "I've already sent for a doctor."

Hank Banner, the sheriff, spoke up then. "I'll take that gun, feller, seein' as how you've not handed it over.

Smoke complied, giving the sheriff both of his Colts, but insisted on waiting until a physician arrived. Miguel Armillita came with him and stood back, silent and respectful in the presence of such awesome authority as the marshal and sheriff. After the doctor had arranged to move Pablo to his office and bandaged Ricardo, and Hank Banner had taken Smoke Jensen off to jail, Miguel went to his horse and rode hastily off toward Rancho de la Gloria to inform Don Diego of this turn of events.

"Sit down and tell me something about yourself," Sheriff Banner invited as he gestured to a chair beside his desk. "Do you regularly go around shooting men without the least provocation?"

Smoke Jensen declined the chair for the moment. Being uncertain as to which side the lawman happened to be on, he did not use his real name nor did he show his U.S. marshal's badge, nor did he use the cover name he had given to Ian MacGreggor.

"Let's get one thing straight first, Sheriff. I did not shoot Pablo Alvarado. My name is Frank Hickman, and I do go around shooting people who shoot friends of mine."

Banner looked skeptical. "You are a friend of the Alvarados?"

"I am."

Now the sheriff leaned forward, his expression turned hard. "Why is it I don't believe you?"

Smoke gave him a cool, indifferent look. "I could give you a couple of reasons."

Banner did not give in. "Try me."

A frown momentarily creased Smoke's forehead. "You could be one of those folks who dislikes people of Spanish or Mexican origin and is unwilling to believe any white man could be friends with them. Or, you could be one of those lawmen who has taken some consideration from a powerful man."

Banner clenched his fists and made to swing on Smoke. Smoke raised a staying hand. "Sit down, Sheriff I apologize for baiting you that way. What is it you want to know?"

"Everything that happened out there. Start from the first."

"I was riding into town when those two provoked a quarrel with Pablo Alvarado. At that time, I didn't recognize Pablo, it has been quite a while since I last saw him."

Banner still had not lost his suspicion. "People don't often change that much."

"They do if they were ten the last time someone saw them."

"Ah—yes, yes, that makes sense. Go on."

Smoke Jensen related the events surrounding the shooting of Pablo Alvarado. Then he described what he did. When he concluded, the two men sat a long while in silence. At last the sheriff spoke up.

"So you intervened in defense of Pablo Alvarado? He was armed, I saw that."

"The one who shot him first didn't even call him out, he just drew and fired away. The other one tried to back-shoot Pablo."

"Yes, you said that. I think I understand. What I don't follow is why you stepped in at all."

Smoke sighed out his irritation. "Because I have a big

problem with sneaks and back-shooters. Both of them drew on the boy. Pablo's men were unarmed. I could do something about it, so I did."

"Sheriff?" a squeaky voice called from the open doorway.

Smoke looked over to see a boy of ten or eleven standing there, his head crowned with a thick thatch of sandy brown hair. His gray-green eyes sparkled with intelligence above speckled cheeks and a wide, generous mouth. Oblivious of Smoke's scrutiny, the lad concentrated on the lawman.

"What is it, Wally?"

"Doc Walters says Pablo Alvarado is con—con—awake now. He's ready to make a statement. But you have to come over to Doc's office."

"Thank you, Wally." Banner flipped a nickel to the boy and cut his eyes to Smoke. "I think you should come along. If Pablo can identify you, I'll be satisfied with your account of what happened."

Well, the Frank Hickman name was out of the barn with this, Smoke thought with irritation. He smiled evenly at Banner. "Whatever you say, Sheriff"

Dr. Adam Walters had his office and infirmary on the entire second floor above a men's haberdashery and a women's clothier. Smoke Jensen followed Sheriff Hank Banner up the steep flight of stairs and through a white-painted door. The odor of ether and carbolic acid hung heavily in the still air of the interior. Dr. Walters greeted the men with surgical tools in hand, which he scrubbed at energetically.

"Pablo got lucky this time, Hank. It was a clean, through-and-through shot to the side. Missed his intestines and liver. He got just a scratch across his back. I cleaned the wounds, closed and sutured them. I'd say he's a sure bet to recover. He's awake now and asking for you. Oh, who is this?" The last accompanied a nod toward Smoke Jensen.

"Says he's a friend of the Alvarados."

"He can come in, then."

They found Pablo Alvarado propped up on pillows, the

sheet and quilt folded down to his waist. His bare middle was swathed in bandages. He looked up as they entered and broke out a big smile. "Smoke! You came like Poppa said you would. Sheriff, it's good to see you."

Smoke Jensen cut his eyes to the lawman and saw genuine affection for Pablo shining in his. Banner gave him a puzzled expression. "Smoke?"

"I'm afraid I wasn't entirely truthful with you, Sheriff. My name is Smoke Jensen.

"The hell. *The* Smoke Jensen?"

"The only one I know. I needed to find out whose side you are on before letting out too much."

Banner nodded. "Everything I've heard about you argues to that. It's a pleasure to meet you. Now, excuse me. What do you have for me, Pablo?"

"I know those *ladrónes* who shot me, Sheriff. They run with the gang led by Paddy Quinn. They didn't give me a chance. They just drew and fired on me."

"How did Smoke Jensen get involved?"

Pablo frowned. "I'm not sure. I was down by then. What's certain is he saved my life. Smoke is an old friend of my father."

Banner remained skeptical. "That may well be, but not every card is on the table as yet. I'll keep Smoke around until everything is straightened out."

"In jail?" Pablo demanded.

With a shrug, Banner replied. "Where else?"

Eight

Late in the afternoon, Don Diego Alvarado, accompanied by Miguel Armillita, arrived at the jail. He stormed in and confronted Hank Banner at his desk. The pencil line of black mustache on Diego's upper lip writhed with his agitation.

"What is this that you have my good friend, Smoke Jensen, in jail? I insist that you release him at once."

Banner remained obstinate. "Now, why should I do that? Two men have been killed. Your son has been shot."

"First, because Smoke is a valued friend. I will vouch for him. And because I sent for him to look into the matters we have discussed. Clifton Satterlee owns the judges, half of the legislature and nearly as many lawmen. If not for you and Marshal Gates, there would be no one opposing him."

Hank Banner came to his boots. "Then he's as free as a bird, *amigo*." Taking his keys, the sheriff went to release Smoke Jensen.

Diego greeted Smoke with an energetic *abrazo*, then turned to Banner. "His *pistolas?* I am sure he will have need of them."

His weapons restored, and with the assurances of Diego Alvarado as to the honesty of Hank Banner, Smoke Jensen at last showed his badge and covered the reason for being in Taos. "I have to ask you to keep this an absolute secret between us, Sheriff."

"You have my word on it. And I wish you luck. Whatever

happens, let me advise that you had better not operate outside the law."

"Sheriff, in my world, I've found it wise to always shoot the bear before the critter could wrap arms around me."

Banner eyed him narrowly. "What does that mean?"

Smoke cheerfully mixed his metaphors in his reply. "When a feller is dealing with a rattler, he doesn't pay much attention to any rules that protect the snake."

"I . . . see."

"I hope you do, Sheriff. Now, Don Diego and I have a lot of catching up to do."

Diego went first to see his son. Then he directed Smoke around the town to proudly show off the improvements that had taken place in the absence of the last mountain man. He waved an arm expansively at an adobe building with a second story of clapboard siding. A large bell stood in the bare yard outside.

"We have a new school now. A *secondary* school, amigo. In my modest way I contributed to its construction and established an account in the bank, to which others contribute, to provide pay for the teachers." Diego frowned slightly. "There are only four qualified ones now. The other three are volunteers from among the merchants. Alejandro teaches Spanish when he can get away from the *rancho*. It is all very exciting, no?"

"Of course it is. How is Alejandro and all your other children?"

"Healthy, thanks be to God. To my way of thinking, living in town robs a man of vigor and his years. My next to youngest, Lupe, who is eight, still breaks the thin spring ice from the *riachuelo* to swim, like her brothers before her. *Gracias a Dios,* she will live a long life. I, myself, have fifty-two years."

"I don't believe it, Don Diego," Smoke spoke truthfully.

Diego Alvarado looked far from fifty-two, more like a young forty. His full mane of longish, black hair showed only thin streaks of gray at the temples, and his face remained unlined, save for the effects of sun, wind and cold. Trim and fit, he could not weigh more than a hundred fifty pounds, Smoke estimated. He wore his *traje corto* on a five-foot-nine frame with an elegance that made others appear common and shabby.

Dressed all in brown today, his cordovan sombrero sat his head at a rakish angle. The bolero jacket, adorned with small, silver conchos, rode the midline of a scarlet sash around his waist, above flared-cuff trousers, with wide gussets of satin in matching color to his girdle. A snowy shirt, with lace-trimmed pleats, appeared above his vest. His string tie stood out in starched erectness, rather than the usual limp droop. All together he represented a fine rendering of the man Smoke had known ten years earlier.

"I saw all the new houses to the east," Smoke remarked.

Diego looked unhappy. "Yes. So many children being born and so few jobs on the ranches. They come to town to work in the fine homes of the rich *gringos* and Mexicans, and to make more babies."

Smoke shrugged. "Nature has a way of doing such things. What else is new since my last visit?"

"Come, I will show you. We have a *teatro,* an opera house. Opened last year. At last I can hear my beloved music. Handel, Mozart, Bach. And, of course, the classic Spanish composers. We will stop by the theater first. Then we shall stop at La Comida Buena for something to eat before heading to the ranch."

Seated at a rickety table in the Bloody Hills road ranch outside Taos, Whitewater Paddy Quinn listened in stony silence to the report of his lieutenant, Garth Thompson. Two men killed. Gunned down, according to Garth, by a saddle tramp who looked to be about forty or so. Impossible. He said as much to Garth.

"No. Norm Oppler and Hicky Drago weren't exactly the fastest and best," Garth advised. "I didn't see the shooting myself. I came out of the saloon after it was over. Like to have knocked me out of my boots. He must have called them out with a gun already in his hand. Don't see any other way."

Quinn's eyes narrowed in curious speculation. "Now I'm wonderin', what was it they were doin' to get themselves killed?"

Garth Thompson studied the toes of his boots, uncomfortable with that question. "Young Pablo Alvarado came into the cantina and joined with some of his vaqueros. That Miguel Armillita was amongst them. You know the one?"

Paddy Quinn nodded. "Him that gives those disgusting bullfight demonstrations, is it?" At Garth's nod, he went on. "Bloody damn barbarian, says I. Sure an' cows is for givin' milk and eatin', not for bloody sport."

"You've got to kill a cow to eat it, don't you?" Garth brazened out.

Quinn sighed and cut his eyes to the ceiling. "An' that's a fact, Garth me boy.

"When this Armillita kills a bull, he gives the meat to the sisters at the mission to distribute to the poor. So it's not a waste."

Quinn cocked an eyebrow, and anger lines formed around his mouth. "Yer talkin' like you approve of that deviltry, is it now?"

Thompson hastened to regain the respect of his superior. "No-no, it's only the man's courage that I admire. It takes a lot to stand out on the sand, with nothing but a cloth in yer hands, in front of a half a ton of raging animal that has two-foot-long horns."

A twinkle in the eyes of Paddy Quinn betrayed his true

opinion, contrary to that which he spoke. "Cowards the lot of them greasers."

Secure in his position once more, Garth Thompson hazarded a barb. "Would you do it?"

Quinn did not hesitate. "Hell no! D'ye think me a bloody fool?" Of a sudden, his mood grew serious again. "Still, I want to know what those two were up to."

Garth swallowed. "You said to put pressure on Alvarado. So I sent Oppler and Drago to pick a fight with Pablo. They did, and they shot him, but he didn't die."

"Something has to be done about the shooting of our boys. This stranger has to be taught a lesson, made an example of, don't ye see?"

"I'll send Luke and Grasser to keep an eye on him. I heard before I left town that the sheriff let him out of jail. Seems he's a friend of the Alvarados."

Fire and ice warred in the black eyes of Paddy Quinn. "Sure an' I'd not lose any sleep if something happened to old man Alvarado. Maybe you oughtta get together enough of our lads to have a go at the both of them."

Garth Thompson gave a steady look at his boss. Paddy Quinn had a deceptively cherubic Irish face. He was always smiling, even when he killed a man. He was big for a victim of the potato famine, standing 5'10", with about 158 pounds behind his belt. He had small ears and nose, his mouth wide only when he smiled. A shock of glistening black hair hung over a high forehead. Without his brace of .45 Colt Peacemakers and the .38 Smith and Wesson he carried for a hideout, he could easily pass for a shopkeeper. Garth knew better, though.

When on the prod, the fit, trim, hard-muscled Quinn virtually exploded into violent mania, calmed only by a frenzy of blood-letting. Odd, Garth speculated, that Quinn of all people would object to the violence and spectacle of bullfighting. But, then, the man who had hired the gang had a fondness for pussy cats. No telling, Garth thought in dismissal of his reflections.

"Where do we wait for them?"

"Here to begin with. Then it depends on what Luke and Grasser report. Get on it, then, bucko."

Smoke Jensen recognized the type the moment Luke Horner and Charlie Grasser tied off their horses at the tie rail outside the saloon across the street from La Comida Buena. As always, Diego Alvarado had shown impeccable taste in his choice of a place to eat. Contrary to usual Mexican custom, the thinly sliced steak turned out to be remarkably tender. It had been marinated and then quickly grilled over charcoal. The *carne asada* had come to their table on platters that held beans and rice, along with a bowl of freshly made *pico de gallo*. The salsa of tomato, onion, garlic, chile peppers and chopped cilantro was hot enough to blister the mouth of anyone of lesser fortitude than possessed by Smoke Jensen. He heaped it on everything and chewed with obvious enjoyment. Formal dinner, Smoke knew from experience, would come at around nine-thirty that night at the ranch. It would be preceded by a steady flow of tequila and beer, and served with fine wines from Pedro Domecq, a winery located in the high central valley in the Mexican state of Aquas Calientes. His pleasure diminished when the two hard cases arrived. He nodded to the street, and Diego paused in his mastication to look over his shoulder.

"See that pair? That's more trouble on the hoof, or I miss my guess."

"De veras. That's true, my friend. Though they are obviously—how you say?—small fry."

Smoke produced a wry expression. "Where the fingerlings swim, the bigger fishes are close behind."

Worry clouded the face of Diego Alvarado. "Do you think they came to finish with Pablo?"

With a negative shake of his head, Smoke gave his surmise. "No. I think whoever sent the first two has someone else in mind."

"Meaning you?" Diego prompted.

"Yes. And perhaps you. Well, old friend, let's finish up. We don't want to disappoint them."

Smoke Jensen would have liked to follow, and perhaps question, the two hard cases. Proddy, and eager to impress his boss, Luke Horner didn't give them the chance. He leaned against an upright four-by-four post that supported the canopy over the saloon front across from the restaurant where Smoke and Diego had eaten an early supper. Luke swiveled his head constantly, alert for a sight of the familiar figure of Diego Alvarado. When the subject of their surveillance appeared suddenly outside the restaurant, Luke turned his head away and alerted his companion.

"Grasser, there they are. Right across from us. I say we can take them right now. You game?"

Charlie Grasser came upright in the chair made from a small barrel and peered across at the two men. "I'm not so sure, Luke. Didn't Garth say that feller was faster than greased lightning?"

Luke remained unimpressed. "So what? He caught the boys unaware. There's two of us, an' he can't be all that fast. That old greaser won't be able to shoot very well. I think we oughtta do it."

So saying, he pushed away from the post and stepped out into the street. Not nearly so eager, Charlie Grasser separated from his companion and did the same. Luke jabbed an extended left forefinger toward Smoke Jensen, his right hand already on the butt of his six-gun. "Hey, Mister, you killed two friends of mine. I don't take kindly to that. I'm here to make you pay for it."

With that, Luke Horner pulled his Colt.

Smoke Jensen bested him anyway. The .45 Peacemaker appeared in his hand as if by magic, the hammer fully cocked. As the muzzle leveled on the center of Luke's body, Smoke triggered a round. The bullet struck Luke at the tip of his breast bone. He jolted backward and bent double. The barrel of his Colt had not yet cleared the holster. To the surprise of Charlie Grasser, Diego Alvarado had drawn with nearly equal speed.

Don Diego's Obrigon cracked sharply, and the slug chewed a nasty trough across Grasser's left shoulder, after breaking the collarbone. Charlie howled at the pain. To his right, Luke struggled feebly to free his six-gun and get off a shot. Alvarado's .45 spat another chunk of hot lead, which missed Grasser only because he had spun to his left to distance himself from the fight. Diego cocked the Mexican-made weapon again as Grasser made his first long stride toward the welcome void of an alley.

Dying on his feet, Luke Horner managed to draw at last and distracted Diego Alvarado momentarily when he sent a bullet speeding toward the fastidious rancher. It missed, and the air filled with the hiss and crack of hot lead. Smoke Jensen fired a safety shot into the top of Luke Horner's head, which blasted the second-rate gunfighter off this earth for all eternity. By then, Charlie Grasser had found the safety of the alley and sped off to inform Garth Thompson.

A scant minute later, Sheriff Banner arrived and took in the body of Luke Horner. "Shootin' snakes again, Jensen?"

Smoke tipped back his Stetson. "You might say that. One got away."

Diego Alvarado stepped forward, replacing his three expended cartridge casings. "I wounded him. Too bad he could run faster than I could shoot."

"Do either of you think you could identify him?"

Both men nodded, and Diego spoke. "Oh, yes. He'll have his left arm in a sling. I am positive I got him in the collar bone."

Hank Banner listened to their account of how the shootout had begun and left them with another admonition. "Remember, you make good and sure that they force the action every time. I'd not like to lock up a friend . . . friends," he amended.

On the road to Rancho de la Gloria, Smoke Jensen and Diego Alvarado discussed the possibility that there would be another personal attack upon them. Diego weighed all Smoke said about these sort of gunhawks and offered a prophesy.

"You are probably right. But, Satterlee has so far kept it rather quiet. He does not seem ready to force the issue. I think it will be some time before any more of his *ladrónes* come after you or I."

Five minutes farther down the trail proved how wrong he had been.

A fine Andalusian, the horse ridden by Don Diego Alvarado shied a fraction of a second before a plume of white powder smoke spurted upward in a thicket of mesquite that had been cut and stacked for burning. In the next fraction of a second, a bullet cracked past so close to the rancher that it clipped the sombrero from his head. Half a dozen more rounds came from the ambush site.

To Diego's right, Smoke had already fisted his .45 Colt and returned fire. He drubbed Cougar's flanks with his round knob spurs and started away from the hidden gunmen, only to find the way blocked by more of their kind. In a swirl of dust, Smoke Jensen released his packhorse, Hardy, and charged the obstruction.

Nine

Men cursed and fired blindly at where Smoke Jensen had been only moments before. They next saw him as he burst through the fog of dust and powder smoke and blazed away at point-blank range. Two men left their saddles in rapid succession. A third yelped a second later and clutched at his suddenly useless right arm. The rifle he had been holding dropped from his grasp, the small of its stock shattered by the bullet that had smashed his shoulder socket.

Smoke did not stop there. He whirled and disappeared into the miasma, to pop out on the flank of the mesquite barricade, flanking the ambush. One hard case sensed the presence of Smoke Jensen and whirled to fire his weapon. That way, he took the bullet from Smoke's Colt full in the face. He went over backward with a soft grunt. Beyond the dying man, Smoke saw Diego at the opposite end of the hiding place. Alvarado placed his shots carefully, wounding three men. As soon as they could recover enough of their difficulties, they hastily abandoned the fight. With their desertion, the ambush began to quickly dissolve.

But not before Garth Thompson snapped off a round that nicked Diego Alvarado in the fleshy part of his left upper arm. Diego squinted with the pain that shot through him and coolly pumped a round into another of the outlaws. Garth's hammer dropped on an expended cartridge, and he rose in his stirrups.

"Break off! Pull back, boys. Scatter," he bellowed.

Garth's head spun in confusion over the ferocity and speed of the reaction of their targets. It had not been a fluke, or a sucker call, that had downed Oppler and Drago. Whoever this master gun happened to be, he was fast and mean as a hell hound. The man beside Garth fired again at Diego Alvarado and put spurs to his mount. Garth quickly joined him.

At once, Smoke and Diego joined up and went in pursuit of two of the hard cases who had chosen the roadway as the easiest route of escape. Diego hailed Smoke with a big smile on his face. "We have them trapped between us and the ranch. They will not get far, *amigo*."

"Might be, but will anyone be expecting them?"

"We are close enough that the shots will have been heard. Someone will be watching. It is too bad the others got away."

Smoke thought on that. "Not for long if we get to question these two."

They picked up the pace then. Within ten minutes they rode through the low scud of red dust stirred up by the hooves of the horses ridden by the fleeing men. Moments later, the sound of gunfire came from ahead, and the pursuers urged their mounts into a gallop. At that ground-eating pace, Smoke and Diego soon saw the backs of the two outlaws. One was on the ground, drawn up in a fetal position. The other, his horse shot out from under him, used the fallen animal as a breastwork.

Although wounded, he fired over the saddle at unseen adversaries as Smoke Jensen closed the gap between himself and the member of the Quinn gang. When Smoke and Diego came into clear view, whoever kept the outlaw pinned down ceased fire. In the silence that followed, the hard case heard the hoofbeats behind him and turned to see Smoke and Diego less than twenty feet away. All resistance left him, and he laid down his revolver and raised his hands.

"I'm givin' up. Don't shoot me."

"Seems as how you tried like hell to do just that to us," Smoke growled.

His feeble protest would echo down the halls of the future. "I was jist followin' orders. Nothin' personal, you understand?"

Smoke snorted in contempt. "When someone throws lead at me, I take it right personal, y'hear?" Smoke dismounted as Alejandro Alvarado showed himself, along with three of the vaqueros.

Beaming, Alejandro extended a hand. "It is good to see you again. Poppa said you would come."

"He made it sound irresistible. Let's take a look at the fish you caught."

Roughly they searched the outlaw, supervised by Smoke Jensen. Two knives, a stubby-barreled Hopkins and Allen .38 Bulldog revolver and a .41 rimfire derringer appeared from the voluminous clothing of the miscreant. For reasons known only to himself, Smoke found that amusing.

"Looks like whatever you lack in skill, you make up for in sneaky armament."

"Who are you, mister? You tore through our ambush like a bull through a corral of steers."

"Folks call me Smoke. Smoke Jensen."

"Awh . . . dog pucky. That ain't fair. It jist ain't fair. How was we to know you were around here anywhere?"

"Chalk it up to bad luck. Now, my good friend here, Don Diego, and I would like to know who you work for?"

Defiance flared in his eyes. "You'll never hear it from me."

Smiling, Smoke Jensen taunted the injured man. "I'll hear it when I want to. Although I don't think I really need to. Don Diego has told me all about your boss, Whitewater Paddy Quinn."

Ever so slightly, the gunman's eyes narrowed and tension lines sprang up that did not come from the bullet wound in his thigh. He pressed his lips tightly together. Smoke shattered the man's new-found resolve with one terse, ominous sentence.

"If he won't confirm that, Alejandro, kill him."

That broke the last of his bravado. "Yes—yes, you're right, goddamn you, Jensen. And when Paddy Quinn finds out what you done to us, he'll be down on you like stink on a skunk."

Dryly, Smoke answered him. "I can hardly wait."

"Amigo, we still have a league to ride to the *estancia,*" Diego reminded Smoke.

"Then, we'd best be going. I trust you can deal with this mess, Alejandro?"

"*Si.* Any day, Smoke."

They left Alejandro to clean up after the ambushers and to send vaqueros to town to deliver the dead and living one to the sheriff.

Smoke Jensen was met by the entire Alvarado flock. The youngest, a totally naked toddler of two, crawled up on Smoke's knee and patted him on the cheek. Horrified by the overly familiar conduct of her infant son, Señora Alvarado, Lidia rushed forward to pluck the squealing boy from his perch and apologized effusively to Smoke for the social gaffe. Smoke laughed about it and patted the youngster on the top of his head.

"But, you are a *caballero,*" Lidia protested. "You should not be bothered by the prattling of children."

Smoke smiled to show his sincerity. "He's no burden, Doña Lidia. I remember my own at that age."

Lidia Alvarado gave him a surprised look. "But they are all grown, yes?"

"All but one my Sally and I adopted not long ago. He has thirteen years."

"A burdensome age. I will leave you gentlemen to your

tequila and old campaigns." With that, Lidia exited, her giggling youngster on her hip.

Diego took up the subject of most interest to both men. "Let me tell you what I believe is behind Clifton Satterlee's determination to secure all of the land for twenty miles around Taos. It is greed, plain and simple. Somehow he has found a way to make a profit out of land that sells for twenty-five cents an acre, due to its poor quality of soil. In its natural state, nothing much grows here, except for cactus and mesquite. Perhaps he has learned, as I have, of the value of irrigation. I do not believe that is the case. He means to plunder the land and leave it desolate.

"There is gold in the mountains. Not much, but enough to attract a greedy man. There is also the cattle that I and others raise. The price of beef is going up, now that it has been made more tender and palatable to the eastern taste. Satterlee's entire assets, at least those I have been able to discover, are not worth more than one hundred thousand dollars. The sale of our cattle would increase his holdings by ten fold. There is five times that value in the timber on the Tua reservation. Although the land is protected by your government in Washington, treaties have been broken in the past and will be again, given enough money changes hands."

Smoke smiled warmly. "You don't put much trust in the United States government, amigo."

"No more than I did that in that of Ciudad Mexico. Politicians are . . . politicians. It is the nature of government to become more intrusive, more controlling of people's lives and their property. Yours, ours now, perhaps less than many others. But who knows what the future may hold? Satterlee is a law unto himself. Therefore, I believe that he is not so much empire building as empire looting."

Smoke gave that some thought. "That's a strong accusation. Why would he want to acquire the town of Taos?"

"It is the seat of power in this part of New Mexico. We are far removed, by mountains as well as distance, from the government in Santa Fe. Our governor is a good man. I regret that I cannot say the same for some of those around him. Recently there was an affair that is being called the Lincoln County War. Governor Wallace offered amnesty to those of both sides. Secretly, some of those in power put out the word that certain among the combatants were to be killed upon their surrender. It seems that their continued existence would prove an embarrassment to some of our politicians.

"But, I digress, old friend. You are here to determine exactly what it is Satterlee intends, and if it is illegal or harmful to the best interests of the people, to put an end to it." Diego paused to refill his clay cup with tequila. He prefaced his next words with a low, self-deprecating chuckle. "That sounds remarkably like a politician, does it not? Forgive me, you came here of your own accord. If I have burdened you with too great a load, it is only because of my great concern."

Smoke shrugged. "If you'd put too much on my plate, I'd be riding out now."

"It's the people I am concerned about. Many of those who live around Taos work for me, or have sons and daughters who do. And Alejandro has business interests in the town. Then there are the Indians. Did you know that they rose up one time and slaughtered all the Spanish living around here? They are capable of doing so again. Now, let us go in to dinner. Fernando has roasted us a whole small pig. It will make excellent *carnitas de puerco.*" Diego added in explanation, "One of those traditional dishes that happened by accident the first time. Someone accidentally dropped chunks of pork into boiling oil. By the time they were fished out, the meat was crispy on the outside, juicy and tender inside. I'm sure you will enjoy it."

Smiling, Smoke emptied his cup of the maguey cactus liquor. "Anything Fernando cooks is an equal to my Sally's best efforts. I'm sure I'll like it."

Later, after the sumptuous meal, Smoke retired to a guest room for the night. As he lay on the comfortable bed, his thoughts strayed to the High Lonesome and to Sally. He fell asleep with visions of her in his mind.

Around noon the next day, Sheriff Monte Carson rode up to the main house on the Sugarloaf. He brought with him two dispirited, hang-dog youngsters atop a mule he led by a long rope. Seth and Sammy Gittings, although looking contrite, to Sally Jensen's expert eye managed to reveal their confidence that they would escape punishment. Monte reined in and greeted the two women who were picking spring flowers to brighten the interior of the house.

"Mornin', Miz Sally. Mornin', ma'am. These two belong to someone out here? Least they say they do."

Mary-Beth looked up with apprehension and surprise. "Why, they are my sons. Where did you find them?"

"In town, ma'am."

A fleeting frown spread on Mary-Beth's forehead. "Seth, Sammy, didn't I tell you not to leave this place? It is wild and dangerous out there."

"There's more to it than that, ma'am."

"Why, what do you mean—ah—Sheriff?"

"I caught them in the general store, stealin' horehound drops from a jar."

Predictably, Mary-Beth sprang to the defense of her sons. "That's not possible. My sons never steal."

Monte nodded to the boys. "Unlike these two, I never lie, ma'am."

"They don't lie, either."

"Oh? Then they are the sons of Johnny Ringo, and he and his gang will come get me if I don't let them go?" Monte maintained a straight face as he related the wild tale the boys had spun.

Shocked, her shoulders slumped with defeat, Mary-Beth

Gittings resorted to a woman's best defense—tears. She dropped her bouquet and covered her eyes with both hands. Her body shook with sobs.

"Whatever am I to do? My hus-husband is nearly always away on business. And when he is home, he spoils the children abominably. I feel so helpless. Someone tell me how to deal with these things?"

Unconvinced by her performance, Monte snorted in disgust. Sally, equally dubious, smiled sweetly. "It's simple," she spelled out for her guest. "First, you talk to them and explain that what they did was wrong. That such behavior by children or adults is not tolerated by society."

"What do I do then?"

"Excuse me. I'll be right back and tell you."

Sally went into the house and directly to one corner of her kitchen. Then she returned, one hand held behind her. "Now comes the part that has the most positive effect. You yank down their britches and smack the hell out of them," she concluded, revealing the thin willow switch she had held behind her back.

Monte Carson whooped with laughter. "Now, that sounds like jist the thing. I'll haul them down and you do that, ma'am. You do that right now."

Dohatsa tugged at his forelock and looked down at his moccasin-clad feet in the manner his people had been taught since the Spanish first came. He was not conscious of his hand extended with palm up. The small bag of coins that dropped into it felt heavy indeed. It made Dohatsa glow inwardly.

"That's me good lad, Dohatsa. Now you go back to yer mud houses and stir up some mischief for me, won't ye now?" Paddy Quinn grinned at the young Tua warrior.

With another nod, Dohatsa tucked the money behind the wide, yellow sash that he wore over his shirttail and loincloth. Then he turned and trotted off toward the distant Tua pueblo located north and a bit west of Taos. Whitewater Paddy Quinn turned his horse and walked away in the opposite direction. He had other errands to perform.

There was that fat, stupid policeman in Taos who must be paid his monthly stipend, who reminded Paddy of another lawman he'd known, the reason Paddy had decided to come to America. Dead policemen, even a white pudding of a bobby in Dublin town, raised quite a row. In Boston he had quickly learned that the fine art of bribery got one far more benefit than did muscle. Not a copper, it had seemed, that wasn't on the take. Inevitably, Paddy had encountered the exception to the rule. A lad from the old sod at that. John Preston Sullivan. Which was what had brought Patrick Michael Quinn to the West. No doubt Sullivan still searched the alleyways of Boston for him. Ten years to the day and Quinn was now the boss of the largest gang of cutthroats, highwaymen and robbers on the frontier. Which reminded him that Garth Thompson and some of the lads had something on for later that afternoon. Sure ought to stir things up a mite.

Smoke Jensen rode at ease alongside Diego Alvarado. The hacienda had put out flankers and two men on point for protection even here on his own huge ranch. Those visible rode with their rifles across their thighs, and were in sight of others farther out. It had been so, Don Diego had explained, since the first raid by the rustlers. More likely, Smoke reckoned, it had been so since the first Alvarados came here in the fifteen hundreds. He suggested the possibility.

"It was like this the last time I visited, if I recall correctly."

"Yes, *los Indios* were raiding."

Cougar whuffled softly, and Smoke popped his next question. "And in your father's time?"

Diego chuckled, a low, throaty sound. "There was a war. We had you gringos to combat, if you recall."

"And your grandfather?"

"The revolution against the Spanish. My family fought for Mexico."

Smoke waved at the vaquero bodyguards. "So this arrangement is nothing new?"

"I thought not to make you uncomfortable. This is a cruel, wild land. Most unforgiving. Not all of the danger comes from two-legged foes. Tell me, my friend, did you come to any conclusion as to how to deal with Satterlee?"

A smile crinkled Smoke's lips. "I slept too soundly. Too much tequila, I suppose. I'm not accustomed to much strong drink. Beer is more my style."

Diego appeared intrigued by this. "For a man who does not drink much, you show a lot of machismo, amigo."

Smoke avoided a response by a study of the distance. Up ahead, he saw a flock of sheep, herded by half a dozen small boys ranging from ten to twelve. It made him think of Ian MacGreggor. "Diego, I have a friend who is looking for work. He speaks Spanish and rides well. But . . . he's a farmer's son. I promised him I'd ask you if you had need of anyone like that on the ranch."

Diego considered that a moment. "Enrique Toledo is growing old. His bones ache him. Perhaps he would welcome a younger assistant. When would this young man want to start?"

"After I've taken care of this business with Satterlee."

Diego cocked an eyebrow. "He is secretly involved in this?"

Smoke pulled a droll face. "In a manner of speaking. He is looking into some things for me. I haven't seen him in a couple of days."

Drawing a deep breath, Diego made his decision. "I will suggest something to Enrique. I am sure he will welcome the idea of help."

Ten

A large mesquite bush toppled down a rocky slope to block the road, located twenty miles outside of Taos. Its sudden appearance did not rattle the driver of the Butterfield stage that ground its way along the narrow, rutted trace. He hauled in on the reins and worked the brake with his booted foot, the long wooden lever operated by an angle iron that jutted from the underside. Too late, he realized the purpose of the fallen bush.

Swarming out of defiles and crevasses, a dozen men in the colorful, loose clothing and braided headbands of the Pueblo Indians closed around the coach. They wore high-top moccasins and long, black hair. All of them carried rifles or revolvers at the ready. With eyes keen and knowledgeable, the driver sized up these Indian highwaymen and reached a quick conclusion. He shared it in a whisper with the express guard.

"Injuns don't rob coaches."

At once, the shotgun rider brought up his short-barreled L.C. Smith 10-gauge and discharged a round. The shot splattered the shoulder of one pseudo-Indian, who howled involuntarily and cursed in English.

"I tol' you so," the driver hollered as he reached for his six-gun. "Ain't one of them's an Injun."

An arrow thudded into his chest and skewered his heart. He folded sideways as the six-up team came to a halt before the prickly branches. Two revolvers cracked, and the guard dropped his shotgun. Blood spurted from his shattered shoulder. "I don't believe a thing he said," he babbled.

They killed him anyway. While two of the Quinn gang held the headstalls of the lead team, another ambled his horse over to the coach and grunted in his best imitation of an Indian. "You get out. Put up hands. Give money. Much money."

"Make fast, squaw," another demanded of a hefty dowager who whimpered and jiggled as she climbed from the stage.

Quickly the outlaws gathered the valuables from the passengers while others released the draft team. After securing the strongbox, the members of the Quinn gang rode off, scattering the stage horses ahead of them. That left the frightened, demoralized passengers to fend for themselves. One of them, a portly man in a green checkered suit, expressed the astonishment of them all.

"Well, I never. Indians actually robbing a stagecoach. We have to get to the way station and find help."

Her cheeks ashen, the dowager suggested, "Someone should go on to Taos."

"Lady, we're on foot. It's too far to Taos. We'll find someone at the relay post with a horse. Then we'll report these Indians to the law."

On a low knoll, beyond his palatial hacienda outside Santa Fe, shaded by an ancient cottonwood, Clifton Satterlee watched the convolutions of an attractive young woman. Martha Estes was his house guest, the daughter of one of his business associates. That did not serve as a deterrent for Satterlee, whose lust guided him. His wife had decided to return east and visit her family, so he knew himself to be free to pursue and conquer the lovely Martha. To do so, he had set forth on a subtle seduction.

From her position, where she exercised her horse, Martha

Estes studied Clifton Satterlee from under the brim of a rakishly cocked, feminine version of a man's top hat. The bright green, crushed-velvet head adornment with its scarlet feather contrasted nicely with the red cape and riding skirt of the same material. She had become well aware that Satterlee was engaged in a skillful seduction, and it amused her. But why all the elaborate preamble, when all he need do was ask?

He needn't have given her pearls, or the promise of a luxurious house in Taos. She would have happily fallen into bed with him on the afternoon of her arrival. Her loins ached and throbbed with desire. Clifton represented power, raw, naked strength, and the willingness to employ it. Martha had hungered for him since her eleventh year, when he and her father had become associated in some slightly shady enterprises. Now, eight years later, her craving had not diminished. If anything, it had grown to unbearable dimension. She abandoned her musings to give Clifton a cheery wave and rode up to join him.

"You are a magnificent horsewoman, Martha."

"Thank you, Clifton. It is one of my . . . lesser accomplishments." She lowered long, silver-blond lashes over cobalt eyes in a coy invitation.

"Let's proceed on, shall we? There is a charming little place I want to show you."

"We'll picnic there?"

"Yes, my dear Martha. And while away the hotter part of the afternoon. The natives call it *siesta,* and I heartily recommend it."

Half an hour's ride brought them to the reverse slope of a larger knob. There stately, ancient palo duro trees shaded a trio of deep tanks which had formed in depressions of solid rock. Martha clapped her hands in delight. Clifton Satterlee dismounted and helped her from the cumbersome sidesaddle. He held the heavy picnic basket while Martha spread a blanket. He came to kneel beside her then, and put out their repast. Martha's eyes sparkled as she took in the elaborate fare.

"Is that really a *paté de fois en brochet?*"

"Yes, it is, Martha. Goose liver at that. And we have sliced ham, roast beef, pickled tongue. Oh, so many things."

Martha Estes affected an insincere pout. "You'll make me fat and unattractive."

Clifton patted one gloved hand. "Never, my dear. Many men are strongly enamored of full-figured women. I am, myself, I have to admit. Though I will say that you wear svelteness to perfection."

A trill of pleased laughter came from Martha. "You flatter me shamelessly. Um, I am hungry. A morning's ride always stimulates my appetite."

"I brought wine," Clifton offered.

"How thoughtful. I hope you brought a corkscrew."

Clifton produced the tool with a flourish. "I thought of everything."

Martha began filling her plate while Clifton opened the bottle. Then he availed himself of the splendid viands and poured wine for both of them. Sunlight sparkled off the clear water of the tanks. Overhead, cactus wrens twittered in domestic harmony while they sought grubs to feed their young. After some thoughtful chewing, Martha brought up the subject of the house in Taos.

"When do I get to see my house in Taos?"

"Soon. Within three days, I should think."

"Wasn't it once owned by a Mexican family?"

"Yes, it was. A family named Figueroa. They named a price I could hardly refuse."

Affecting a jaunty swagger he did not recognize as his own, Ian MacGreggor pushed through the glass-beaded curtain that formed the entryway of Cantina Jalisco, in Taos. Half a dozen hard-faced men had gathered at one end of the bar. They drank beer from glazed clay pots. Even to Mac's untutored eyes, they all appeared to pay deference to a burly, barrel-chested man at the center of the group. Mac walked up near them and ordered a beer. The bartender took in the six-gun at Mac's hip and served him without question. Mac lifted the foam-capped container in salute to the Irish-looking, beefy man and pulled off a long swallow.

It nearly choked him, but he did not let on since he felt all eyes turned to him. After another swallow, he walked closer to the hard cases and addressed the man in the bowler. "Might you be a gentleman known as Paddy Quinn?"

Eyes narrowed, Whitewater Paddy Quinn fired a question of his own. "Who might it be that is askin', is it now?"

"I'm known as Mac. Ian MacGreggor."

Quinn smiled. "A fellow celt, as I live and breathe. It is said that the clan MacGreggor defended Queen Mary and the faith. Would ye be of those MacGreggors?"

Mac tilted his beer pot to Quinn. "Aye."

"And for what is it ye'd be wantin' Paddy Quinn?"

"I hear you are hiring gunhands for a man named Satterlee."

Paddy held up a cautionary hand. "Sure an' we don't be mentionin' certain names in so public a place. Say, rather, that I be hirin' for mesel', ye should."

"Well, then, for yourself?"

"What if I be? You don't look dry behind the ears."

Mac eyed Quinn levely. "You have heard of Billy Bonney?"

That gave Quinn a good laugh. "Sure an' its a lot of horse dung if yer tryin' to pass yerself off as Billy the Kid."

"No, I'm not. But, Billy was not yet dry behind his ears when he killed his sixth man. I'm not in his class, but I'm good with a gun."

"Are you now? Suppose we go out behind this place and you show me."

"I'm not calling you out, Mr. Quinn. All I say is that I am fast and I hit what I shoot at."

Quinn stepped forward, away from the bar, and patted Mac on one shoulder. "Nah—nah, don't fash yerself, lad. I was thinkin' of whiskey bottles, or better still beer bottles. They make smaller targets. One o' me boys could throw them up, say two at a time, and you draw and break them both before one hits the ground."

When there had been money enough for powder and lead to make reloads, Mac had practiced at that often enough to feel confident. "I think I can do that."

"Come along, then." Quinn turned to the bartender. *"Oye,* Paco. We're gonna take some of your empties out and make little pieces of glass out of them."

Paco shrugged. "Whatever you say, Señor Quinn."

Behind the saloon, the gunmen stood to one side, except for one, who reached to a stack of wooden cartons and extracted two beer bottles. He faced quarter front to Ian MacGreggor. Paddy Quinn gave his instructions at Mac's side. "When I nod, Huber there will throw the bottles in the air. You draw and fire at will."

With that, Quinn stepped behind Mac, so the youth could not see him give the signal. Not hesitating for a second, Paddy nodded to Huber. Two beer bottles sailed into the air. The moment they came into Mac's line of sight, he made his move. Before the two containers reached the apex of their arc, he had his six-gun halfway out of the holster. His first shot blasted a bottle to fragments a heartbeat later. The second clear glass cylinder seemed to hover at the peak, then turned to a bright shower of slivers as a second bullet struck. The gun was back in Mac's holster before Quinn could recover from his involuntary blink.

Quinn scowled, unconvinced. "Try that again."

Mac did, with the same results.

"One more time, lad."

Both bottles broke this time before either had reached the

apex. "B'God, it's fast ye are. Only one little thing, there is. I wonder how you would perform if the target was shootin' back at ye?"

Mac considered that a moment, then decided to answer with a cleaned-up version of the truth. "A friend of mine and I were jumped on the way here to Taos. Four men. I killed one of them, and Joe took care of the others."

Quinn cocked an eyebrow. "Who'd you say that was?"

"You wouldn't know him. Joe Evans, from over Texas way, where I come from."

"He your age?"

Mac kept his gaze cool and level. "No, sir. He's older. Around twenty-five."

"Would he be lookin' for the same thing you came after?"

"No, sir, Mr. Quinn. He rode on to Santa Fe."

"Well, then," Quinn boomed with a hearty clap on Mac's shoulder. "It looks like we got us only one more good gunhand. You'll do, young MacGreggor. At first, I'll be puttin' you with someone more experienced. At least until ye get yer feet wet, so's to speak. You'll be paid sixty dollars a month. Ammunition bought for you. Later, there'll be a share of any spoils we bring in. Now, then, go settle up with wherever ye've been stayin' an' meet us ten miles out on the road to Questa."

Their rumps sore from unaccustomed hours in the saddle, two frightened and wounded survivors of the Butterfield Stage Line robbery trotted their borrowed mounts into Taos in late afternoon. They asked for directions to the sheriff's office and for water to drink in that order. Next the two men stopped at a public horse trough and refreshed their flagging animals, industriously working the pump to bring up fresh for themselves. The sheriffs office came next.

"Sheriff," one blurted as they stumbled through the door. "The stage from Albuquerque got robbed outside town about twenty miles. We were on it. Owens here took a nick in the shoulder. All I got's a scratch. But the guard and driver are both dead. It was Injuns done it, sure's you're born."

Sheriff Banner had strong doubts that the Tua, or any of the Pueblo Indians, had taken to robbing stages. "You got a good look at these highwaymen?"

"That's what we just told you, Sheriff. Long black hair, head bands, floppy clothing. Swarthy skin and mean as hell. Oh, they was Injuns right enough."

Banner remained unconvinced. "What way did they ride when they left?"

"To the west."

"Toward San Vincente?"

"What's that? We don't know the area."

"It's a pueblo and mission out that way. But the San Vincente Pueblos are even more peaceful than the Tuas."

"They talked funny English and rode bareback," Owens added helpfully.

"Anyone can talk funny and ride bareback. Did they speak any Spanish or Indian tongue?"

Owens cut his eyes to his companion. "Nope. Come to think, all they did speak was English."

Banner rubbed his hands together in satisfaction. "Well, gentlemen, I think you have been had. Sounds to me like white road agents done up to look like Indians. At last, that's the way I'm going to look into it." Banner turned to the door and called out. "Wally, come in here."

Wally Gower, who had been lurking outside the door to learn any gems of news he could sell to the editor of the Taos *Clarion,* popped around the door frame and darted to the sheriffs desk. "Yes, sir?"

"Dang you for a rascal, Wally. But this time you can be of some good use. I want you to ride out to Rancho de la Gloria. Ask for Smoke Jensen and tell him to please come in. Say I have something interesting for him to look into."

"Yes, sir. I'll do it right now."

"Good. There'll be two bits in it for you."

"Gosh. That much? I never get more than a nickel."

"You will this time. There's a lot of trouble brewin' out there. Now, get along."

Wally Gower led an ideal life for a kid. He was footloose and, for the most part, unsupervised. His father had been injured in a mining accident several years ago in Colorado. While his father remained unable to work and stayed at home to care for the seven children, his mother did custom alterations and general sewing for Señora Montez, the fashionable Spanish lady who owned a large women's clothing store in Taos. When school let out for the summer, Wally gleefully abandoned studies, shoes, and often shirt, to hang around town doing odd jobs for the money it brought in for the family. A lot of his time went to swimming with friends at the many *tanques* outside the town, or in pulling slippery rainbow trout from the icy creeks fed by snowmelt in the Sangre de Cristo range. He liked it most when the sheriff had something for him to do. The lawman paid better than anyone else. Wally was glad he had a pony he could use for this present assignment.

It was a small, shaggy mustang and only partly broken to saddle. But Wally loved Spuds with all his heart. He went to the small stable house behind their adobe home and saddled Spuds. He led the snorting half-wild animal from its stall, plucked a parsnip from last winter's garden and fed it to Spuds. Chomping pleasurably, the pony ground the pungent root vegetable into a mash which it swallowed. Wally put one bare foot in the stirrup and swung aboard. He angled Spuds toward the alleyway behind the Gower home. Had it been anyone else atop the little horse, it would have exploded into crow hops and sunfishing that would have unseated any but the most expert horse breakers.

Wally trotted toward the western edge of town and the

trail southwest to the Alvarado ranch. He reached the scattered fringe of small, poor Mexican adobe homes when he found out that life in Taos had drastically changed for the foreseeable future.

Three hard cases leaned against a low adobe wall, with two split rails atop. When Wally approached, the lean, tallest one eased upright and stepped into the road. He raised a hand and spoke in a low, menacing voice.

"Whoa-up, sonny. Where do you think yer goin'?"

A quick thinker, Wally invented something he hoped would be believed. "Out to where my paw works."

"Where's that?"

"Uh——the Bradfords' B-Bar-X."

Eyes narrowed in accusation, the clipped words challenged Wally. "He ain't come through here since we've been here."

"Oh, no. He goes out before dawn."

"Well, there ain't nobody goin' out of town from now on without our say-so."

Wally pulled another appeal from his ingenuity. "Bu—but my paw will beat my tail if I don't bring him his coat. He's got night guard tonight."

A nasty sneer answered him. "That's your problem, kid. If you're smart, you'll do what you are told. You go on back now, get lost and tell that sheriff friend of yours nothing."

"Yes, sir. I suppose you're right, sir."

Being a plucky lad, Wally turned on the first side street, cut his way through several blocks and went directly to Hank Banner's office. He made his report with wide-eyed excitement. Hank listened to him with a growing frown. Then he made a suggestion that appealed to the adventurous nature of the boy.

"Well, then, why don't you ride out the other side of town?"

"Sure enough, Sheriff. Right away."

Wally dusted out the door and swung into the saddle. He

drubbed bare heels into the flanks of Spuds and started for the east end of town. He made it half a mile out of Taos this time. Four of the biggest, meanest-looking men Wally had ever seen in his eleven years blocked the entire road. A line of people on foot, in wagons and on horseback had formed in front of them. The surly fellows allowed free entry to town, but denied departure to all except for the poorest *campesinos* and mission Indians. Patiently, though with mounting apprehension, Wally waited his turn. He tried his "taking a coat to Paw" story again and was again turned back.

On his own, Wally tried the south road out of town. This time he believe he had it all figured out. When he saw an angry-looking farmer and his family headed back for town in a wagon, Wally hailed them and asked if the road was closed.

"Why, yes, son, how did you know?" the wife asked.

Wally worked his shoulders up and down. "I got turned back two places already. What is goin' on?"

"Some bad folks up there, boy," the farmer told Wally. "Best thing for you to do is turn around and go back now."

Wally scrunched his freckle-speckled button nose. "How far to where they are?"

Scratching his head, the farmer figured on that. "Quarter mile, maybe a little more. Beyond that bend yonder."

"Thank you, sir," Wally replied politely.

He turned Spuds' nose to the west and cut across a field in the direction of Pacheca Creek. Keeping constantly alert, Wally looked to the threat on his left as he progressed through a corn field and into a pasture beyond. He did not see the men who he now knew to be nothing more than outlaws, so he felt confident they could not see him. A line of cottonwoods and aspen marked the course of the creek. He pulled up inside the screen and leaned down to pat Spuds on the neck.

"You're gonna get cold, Spuds. So am I. We gotta swim

our way around those fellers. When we git outta the crick, I'll rub you down and dry off, then we'll cut to the southwest and head for the Alvarado spread." Wally reached in his hip pocket and produced another parsnip, which he fed to Spuds.

Dismounting, Wally led his pony to the creek bank and stepped gingerly out on the sand and pebble-strewn streambed. They stayed in the shallows for a while, the water frigid and hip-high on Wally. When he gauged they had come close to being opposite the hard cases, he urged Spuds out into the current, and they both swam past, gooseflesh forming under Wally's shirt.

When he reached a spot he considered safe, Wally swam cross-current until he gained footing. Spuds reached solid underpinning first and surged forward past the boy's slim shoulders. Wally stumbled behind. On the bank at last, boy and beast stood shivering.

"That was colder than I thought, boy," Wally admitted through chartering teeth. "Gotta strip and warm up."

With that he pulled off his wet clothes and threw himself down on a sun-warmed rock. Before long, the chill subsided, Wally's eyelids drooped and he fell into a light sleep.

Eleven

Nearing the end of the first week's visit by the Gittings, tension hung over the Sugarloaf. Normally a direct, outspoken person, Sally Jensen repressed her instinctive reaction to Mary-Beth's feather-headedness and the constant misbehavior of her undisciplined brood. As a result, Sally's old friendship with Mary-Beth was in conflict with her good sense. Put simply, Sally knew she should firmly demand that they leave.

Especially when Seth and Sammy had escaped their deserved spanking for stealing the candy. Oh, Mary-Beth had switched them—two half-hearted whacks on buttocks that had not even been bared. Both boys shot sneers at Sally and laughed openly over the lightness of their punishment as they walked away. That had been two days ago, and the situation seemed to worsen by the hour. From the direction of the corral, a boy's voice, raised in anger, reminded her of that.

"Stop that! Stop it, damn you, Seth, Sammy. Those foals can be hurt real easy."

It was Bobby's voice. Sally wondered what devilment the Gittings boys had gotten up to this time. If it was serious enough, she would find out right soon. She had asked their foreman, Ike Mitchell, keep an eye on the rebellious boys, and to take matters into his own hands if need be. Since he had been successful on earlier occasions, she also implied the same to Bobby.

The boy was more than capable of taking responsibility for himself. He could act in a responsible manner toward others as well, Sally reasoned. Bobby's voice once more cut through her self-examination. "Hey, what are you doin'? Quit that."

Then came a long silence. Sally's apprehension rose.

Bobby Jensen came upon Seth and Sammy Gittings at the small corral outside the foaling barn. There the mares and their newborn could exercise away from the rest of the herd. Both of the younger boys had taken it in mind that it would be funny to watch the reactions of the small horses when they pelted them with rocks. Bobby looked on in shock and anger as two missiles struck a stalky-legged foal and it ran off squealing in terror to find its mother. The building rage pushed out the disgust Bobby felt. He stepped in at once, voice raised to a strident shout.

"Stop that."

Seth and Sammy looked blankly over their shoulders at Bobby, and the younger boy stuck out his tongue. As one, they hefted fresh rocks and hurled them at another colt. Bobby's voice deepened with his outrage.

"Stop it, damn you, Seth, Sammy. Those foals can be hurt real easy."

"Oh, yeah?" Seth challenged in a quiet voice. "Says who?"

Sammy added his opinion. "Yeah. 'Sides, it's funny when they make that noise and run around."

Bobby's voice grew low and menacing. "You stop that or I'll make you hurt like you've never hurt before."

Seth sneered. "No you won't. Mother won't let you."

With that, both Gittings boys turned and chucked stones at Bobby Jensen. One struck his left shoulder with enough force to hurt, though it merely angered him more. He tried once again to end their assault. "Hey, what are you doin'. Quit that."

Laughing, the boys threw more rocks. For a moment, while he dodged the fresh onslaught, Bobby thought of pulling his six-gun and blasting the both of them to oblivion. A satisfying, warm rush washed through him. Then he remembered what Smoke had taught him. Only a coward settles something with a gun that he can handle with his fists. Accordingly, Bobby rushed the smaller boys and threw Sammy to the ground. Seth leaped at him and swung a fist that contained a healthy-sized stone. It struck Bobby on the forehead and split the skin.

Blood began to run down through one white-blond eyebrow and into Bobby's left eye. He ignored the discomfort and shot a fist to the nose of Seth Gittings, who dropped the rock, screeching his agony. Bobby grabbed the front of Seth's shirt with both hands and hurled him to the ground. He stood over the supine boys a long, silent minute while they whined and sniveled. Satisfied that the incident had ended, Bobby turned away and started off to clean up his cut and patch it. Another rock, hurled in defiance, decided Bobby that he would report the situation to Sally after all.

Sally Jensen looked with mounting fury at the rising lump on Bobby's forehead and the court plaster he had stuck on the cut. "That cuts it, damnit!" Although she rarely swore, Sally thought the situation called for it.

Bobby Jensen looked at her with clear, wide eyes. "What are we going to do?"

"You are going to stand back and make the accusation. I am going to take care of what has needed doing for a long time." She crossed to the stove corner and brought out her willow switch, then moved to the door to the hallway and called into the depths of the house. "Mary-Beth, come here right away."

When Mary-Beth arrived, she took one look at the limber willow wand, and her cheeks lost color. A hand flew to the corner of her mouth. "Oh, no. Not again. Not my boys."

"Oh, yes, Mary-Beth, dear. Take a look at Bobby's forehead. Seth attacked him with a rock. Smashed him in the head, then threw another that bruised him between his shoulderblades. You are coming with me right this minute and put an end to it."

Sally took a firm hold on Mary-Beth's left wrist and literally pulled her to the outside kitchen door. With Bobby at her other side, Sally strode to the foaling barn. They rounded the corner in time to see Seth connect with another of the frightened, tormented foals. Sally did not temper her words.

"You will stop that this instant, you little monster."

Impudent defiance shone in the eyes of Seth Gittings. "We don't have to, do we Mother?"

Sammy let escape a revealing statement. "Yeah, you said we could do anything we wanted."

Shocked to the core at last, Mary-Beth stammered a partial denial. "I—I said no such thing. I said you could do anything you wanted, so long as it did no harm to others."

Seth whined in protest of his innocence. "We didn't hurt anyone. All we did was tease the little horsies some."

Bobby could contain his outrage no longer. "Then you turned on me and threw rocks at me. When I pushed Sammy down, you hit me in the head."

Sally advanced on the boys. At the last moment, she whirled to Mary-Beth. "Either you do what is necessary, Mary-Beth, or I will do it for you."

Faced with such determination, Mary-Beth came forward and took the willow switch from Sally. She started after Sammy first. His small face took on an expression of horror, and he tried to back away, arms extended, palms outward to ward off imagined blows.

"No, don't. You can't hit me with that. Poppa wouldn't like that. No, Mother. Please."

Without a word, her lips set in a grim line, Mary-Beth yanked down Sammy's trousers and bent him over one knee. Then she laid on with a dozen good, hard, swift blows. He howled, shrieked and wailed, tears flowed freely from his eyes. When she had finished, she put him on his feet again.

"You, young man, will not leave the house for the next three days. Now, Seth, it's your turn. You are old enough to know better."

"You can't do this! I won't let you," Seth screamed in utter panic. *"No, Momma, please!* You can't, you can't."

A wild light glowed behind golden lashes as Mary-Beth spoke wonderingly, more to Sally and herself than to the boy. "You know, I just discovered that I can indeed."

In a thrice, Seth received the same treatment as Sammy. Only this time his mother delivered fifteen strokes before ending it. A very satisfied Sally Jensen looked on. When Seth again stood before her, still blubbering, she had further admonishment for him. "If you ever, ever again use a weapon on an animal or another person, whether it is a rock or a knife or, God forbid, a gun, I will beat you to within an inch of your life. Now apologize to Bobby this instant."

"Alejandro will round up those among my vaqueros who can shoot the best," Diego Alvarado told Smoke Jensen.

Ten minutes after Wally Gower arrived at Rancho de la Gloria, Smoke Jensen and fifteen vaqueros rode out for town. The boy kept station close beside Smoke, his chest puffed with pride. They soon came upon several disgruntled people who had been turned back from town, and from them learned more details of the roadblocks.

"Beats all hell," one long-faced rancher observed. "There was six of them when we made to enter town. Told me an' the boys to turn about and high-tail it for home. Said that the town was closed 'til further notice. Who can do a thing like that?"

"From what I've heard," said Smoke Jensen, with a nod toward Wally Gower, "it's Whitewater Paddy Quinn."

A glower answered Smoke. "That no-account. Claims to be foreman for some outfit called C.S. Enterprises. Common outlaw, you ask me."

"I think you have the right of it, sir," Smoke agreed.

They rode on, allowing the horses to walk only when they began to retch and grunt from exertion. In that manner, they made it to a point where they could observe the roadblock from a distance. Smoke studied the activity, noting that people no longer queued up to attempt to leave town. Smoke sent Wally back beyond range and turned to the Mexican cowboys.

"First things first," he told them. "We're going to take out these *bandidos,* then move around to each road entering town and do the same."

"Do we kill them, Señor Smoke?" Bernal Sandoval asked.

Smoke eyed him levely. "We're not here to kiss them, Bernal."

"Muy bien." He turned to his companions. *"Adelante, muchachos."*

Smoke led the way as they charged down on the outlaws ahead. With weapons at the ready, they closed in a cloud of red dust. Quinn's men turned at the sound of pounding hooves, and the one in the center of the road shouted a challenge.

"Rein in and turn around. Nobody gets into town today. This is your last chance. Do it now or you'll be hurtin'."

With a firm tug on Cougar's reins, Smoke halted first and took careful aim. He intentionally shot the hard case in charge through the left shoulder. The man grunted and raised his own six-gun. It barked loudly, but without effect. Smoke had given him his chance, and he had not taken it. So the last mountain man put a bullet through the chest of the outlaw. At once the gunman's underlings opened fire.

Not lacking in courage, the vaqueros sent a storm of hot lead into the rank that partitioned the road. Slugs from both sides whipped and cracked through the air. More dust churned up, to mingle with powder smoke and obscure the view. From the midst of the haze, a man screamed. Another called for help. Alejandro silenced him. Two vaqueros cursed in Spanish. Another ragged volley rippled across the hilly ground. Then, on the far side of the melee, a horse sprinted free. Its rider cried out in near hysteria.

"Get out before they kill us all!"

Within five seconds, the roar of gunfire dwindled to silence. The dust blew away on a stiff breeze, and the vaqueros began to slap one another on the back and congratulate themselves for the easy victory. Smoke Jensen gave them a couple of seconds, then called them together.

"We'll go on to the next. Alejandro, you take half our men and come at them at an angle; we'll take them head on. No time to waste until we clean out all of these skunks." He beckoned to Wally and the boy joined him expectantly.

Yank Hastings had been with the Quinn gang for three years. He had seen the scruffy rabble of low-grade highwaymen and rustlers turned into a finely tuned force, not unlike an army. At the constant goading of Paddy Quinn and Garth Thompson, they had cleaned up their collective rag-tag, unwashed appearance. They had practiced with their weapons until they had reached a proficiency unheard of among most common bandits. Every man now took orders without questioning them, obeyed to the letter or died trying. They robbed banks like precision machines; they learned the skills of intimidation to add to their ability to use force; those most skilled at it stole cattle by the whole herd, rather than twenty or thirty had at a time. It made Yank Hastings proud to be among their number.

That was why it shocked him, then, when two of the gang

ran down on their barricade on the Taos-Raton road on froth-
ing horses. Their eyes wide with panic, they shouted that an
attack was imminent.

"A bunch of Mezkin cowboys hit our roadblock jist a
while ago," one blurted out "They shot hell outta Cort an'
Davey and lit out after us toward here."

"Yeah. They'll be here any minute," his companion assured.

Yank had started to calm them and discredit their fears
when a bullet cracked overhead. He looked beyond them
with a stunned expression.

Alejandro Alvarado and seven vaqueros raced toward the
roadblock at an oblique angle to the road. It had been Alejandro who had fired at Yank. Hastings holstered his six-gun and
drew his rifle. He was not about to let this jumped-up Mezkin
get the better of him. He worked the lever to chamber a round
and felt a stunning pain in his hand as a bullet struck the small
of the stock. Fingers numbed, he dropped the weapon as he
stared in disbelief while seven more vaqueros, led by a white
man, stormed toward them along the road. The air filled with
deadly bees as the attackers blazed away at Yank and his men.
He had to do something, and fast.

"Everybody dismount. Josh, take the horses back. The
rest of you get in those rocks. Hold your fire until you have
a sure target."

Quickly the men spread out to take positions of at least
partial cover. Undeterred, the riders came on. Return fire
spurted from the muzzles of guns in the outlaws' hands.
From a peaceful, quiet afternoon, the world had swiftly
changed into a place of noise, fury, and death. The fighting
intensified. Suddenly, a whole swarm of Quinn's hard cases
appeared over a low rise and charged toward the attackers.

Smoke Jensen watched the approach of the reinforce-
ments and made a quick decision. He turned aside and can-

tered back a hundred yards to where Wally Gower had hunkered down in a pile of boulders. He leaned forward and spoke urgently to the boy.

"Wally, I want you to ride like lightning back to where we cleaned out that first roadblock. Then skedaddle into town and go to the sheriff. Tell him what we are doing and to get some men here right now."

"Yes, sir, I can do that."

Wally sprinted off on his pony before Smoke could wish him good luck. Smoke turned back to the battle that had developed in his absence. The vaqueros appeared to hold their own. They kept moving, making difficult targets of themselves. Smoke located one outlaw, who had climbed high on the rocks and now took careful aim with a Winchester at Alejandro Alvarado. Smoke settled Cougar with a pat on the neck and sighted in on the exposed target. When he had what he wanted, he gave a sharp whistle and shouted to the hard case.

"Over here!"

Obligingly the man turned, so that Smoke caught him in the upper left chest with his first round. Quickly Smoke cycled the action of his Express rifle and fired again. A shower of volcanic rock chips formed a plume behind the thug after the bullet exited along the midline of his body. He flopped back down and lay still. Smoke sought another target. He had no lack of them, he soon discovered.

Outlaws milled everywhere. The new arrivals had been slow in taking to the rocks. Diego's vaqueros made a good harvest among them. Bodies sprawled in the grotesque postures of the dead and dying. Smoke saw another man seeking a vantage point high in the rocks. Quickly he raised his Winchester. The discharge of a heavy .44 revolver close by caused Cougar to flinch and side-step at the moment the weapon fired. A torrent of dark, red-brown, porous rock exploded in the face of the gunman.

His sharp cry of pain sounded over the tumult of battle.

Smoke levered a fresh round into the chamber and felt the hot breath of a bullet kiss his cheek. Unflinching, he raised the sights into line and shot the author of that close call through the breast bone. Smoke made a quick count. They had taken a hefty toll of the gang. The advantage of numbers had shifted to their side. Only one vaquero showed signs of having taken a wound. And that, Smoke noted, seemed slight. Smoke was about to call to the Mexican cowboys to rally and storm the rocks when more of the outlaw gang closed in, led by Garth Thompson.

Santan Tossa kneeled at the edge of the sacred sand painting and examined the evidence. Someone had come again to the kiva and stolen several of the religious articles stored there. The footprint of the culprit was distinctive. Much wider than usual, longer also, it served as a signature. Santan Tossa knew to whom the splayed foot belonged. He and several others had been most vocal about raising up the entire male population of the tua pueblo and striking at the outsiders who had invaded their land. And he thought he knew who it was that they worked for.

There was a white man, a round-eye, named Satterlee. This would be the one. He had come to the pueblo to talk the elders into giving him permission to cut trees, a whole lot of trees, on their land. It had been refused, of course. Many of the trees were very old, older than the memories of the Tua. So old as to have shaded the Anasazi, those mysterious dwellers of the time of legends. Santan Tossa had noted the glow of greed in Satterlee's eyes as he had looked upon the sacred amulets, bracelets and necklaces in their niches. Now, fully half of them had disappeared. How much, he wondered, had Dohatsa taken to become a thief?

No matter the reason or the reward, this required help from outside the pueblo. Although he didn't like it, Tossa knew he must take his findings to the white lawman in Taos.

He was powerless to investigate anyone not of the pueblo, but the sheriff would know how to go about it. Thus decided, Santan Tossa made a quick examination of the remainder of the kiva and exited through the hole in the roof. He went directly to the small corral on the southeast side of the compound and caught up one of his ponies.

Tossa rode the short three miles to the low adobe wall that surrounded the outsider town of Taos. There he went directly to the sheriff's office. To his surprise, he found it empty. He would wait. Now that he had committed himself to this course, he might as well see it through. While he bided his time, Tossa reflected on conditions at the pueblo.

Theft of the religious objects had been a shock to those who knew—and not all did—and also a source of much justified anger. As a tribal policeman, he kept his own counsel, but Santan Tossa did not question the rightness of his suspicions. Some of the hot heads among the young warriors had been most vocal in demanding retribution against the whites, who, they felt certain had stolen the object. Particularly Dohatsa, who had called a meeting of his warrior society in the kiva the previous night. After the meeting would have been an ideal time to steal the missing items. Santan Tossa had attended the gathering, although he had not been made to feel welcome. Now he recalled what had happened. . . .

Firelight flickered off the bare, bronze shoulders of Dohatsa as he addressed the Puma Society members. "Brothers, we all know that precious articles of our religion have been stolen. It is clear to me who is responsible. It is white men. Not the Mexicans, not even the Spanish before them, would touch any of our holy relics. They considered them heathen and forbidden. Their lust was for gold not silver. So they discounted even the value of our most treasured works.

"I know that somewhere, our sacred squash blossoms and shells decorate the body of a white woman, maybe more than one. We must ask our mothers and sisters who work in the houses of the whites to look for them. Only they must do this carefully and quietly. And caution them not to say anything of this to anyone."

A young warrior raised a hand in protest. "Our women have never seen the sacred objects. How will they know what to look for?"

Dohatsa produced a wicked smile. "We will describe them, only not tell of their meaning and purpose. When they are found, we will move silently and swiftly. Our knives and lances will taste white blood. Not a one of the guilty shall live."

Santan Tossa could not keep silent. "If you do such a thing, outside the pueblo, you will bring much trouble to us."

Dohatsa turned a scornful sneer to Tossa. "What do you know? A policeman? You have already sold yourself to the whites. This is the best way."

Santan Tossa knew better. He believed it to be wrong that night. . . .

And he believed it today as he awaited the return of Sheriff Hank Banner. More so for knowing now that the thief had been Dohatsa.

Twelve

Another five minutes and they would be as dead as King Sol, Smoke Jensen thought to himself as the fresh wave of bandits rolled toward them. He took time to aim carefully and knocked another outlaw from the saddle. Still they came. Around him, the vaqueros from Rancho de la Gloria made the switch from a near victory to furious defense with smooth unconcern. Their expressions did not change as they pumped round after round into the advancing gang members.

Truth was, Smoke realized, they seemed to enjoy it. With a violent forward surge by the gang, little more than two dozen yards separated the contending forces. Any time now Smoke and the vaqueros would have to break and run or be annihilated. The outlaw leader sensed it also.

With a triumphant whoop, he urged his men on. They closed the gap by five yards. Suddenly a stutter of shots erupted behind them. It rapidly grew to a ragged volley. Confused, fully half of the bandits turned about. Smoke Jensen seized the moment to charge.

"At them! *¡Cuchillos y machettes!*" he yelled, calling for knives and the deadly long blades used for chopping jungle and high grass.

"Yiiiiiiii!" several vaqueros shouted in unison.

With bared blades in one hand, revolvers in the other, reins between their teeth or looped over the large, flat pommels of their saddles, the Mexican cowboys broke clear and thundered down on the astonished Anglo outlaws. The appearance of keen-edged steel unnerved many among the gang. They would gladly face down four or more blazing six-guns, but the thought of deep, gaping wounds, of severed limbs, or decapitation filled them with dread. Pressed from both sides, they abandoned all effort at resistance and fled in panicked disarray.

In no time, the posse led by Sheriff Banner and the vaqueros joined up. The field had been abandoned by Quinn's rogues so swiftly that the wounded had been left behind. Smoke and the sheriff rode among them. None of them appeared capable of further fight.

"It's over," the sheriff opined.

Smoke did not share Banner's confidence. "For now."

Back in the sheriff's office, Banner showed surprise to find Santan Tossa waiting. "It is good to see you, Santan. May I ask what brings you to Taos?"

"I wanted to check in. See what is going on in town."

Banner sensed the young Tua policeman's hesitation and decided to change the subject. "Oh, by the way, this is a very famous man among my people. His name is Smoke Jensen. Smoke, Santan Tossa, one of the Tua tribal police."

A smile bloomed on the dark copper face of Santan Tossa. To Smoke's surprise, he spoke excellent English. "Smoke Jensen. I have heard much about you. You have fought our brothers among the Kiowa, the Cheyenne, the Sioux, Blackfeet and Shoshone. But you were always fair. You've had a lot of run-ins with white men also. I had some of your exploits read to me by one of our people who understands English better than I do."

Smoke gave him a deprecating grin. "All lies, Santan. If I had shot at, let alone killed, as many men as the dime novels say, there would be an ammunition shortage in the country to this day."

They laughed together. When the sheriff joined them, the tension eased some. Banner decided to get to the point. "Now, what is it that brought you here?"

"We have had some thefts at the pueblo. Religious articles." He went on to explain about the stolen objects, and the desecration. He did not reveal the possibility of an uprising.

"Do you have any suspects?"

Tossa shook his head, looking unhappy. "Yes, I do. It had to be one of our own who entered the kiva. No Mexican or white man could get away with it. The one I think took the relics is Dohatsa. I think he stole them for a man named Clifton Satterlee."

"But why?"

"To cause trouble between our two people. I think he wants us to do something that will result in our being driven out. Satterlee wants the land. The trees most of all."

Smoke, who had listened with intense concentration to the conversation, looked up then and spoke what was on his mind. "I suggest that it might be time for me and this young man to pay a visit to Satterlee's hacienda in Santa Fe. Who knows what we might spook him into doing?"

Sheriff Banner snorted and shook his head. "That's it exactly. Who knows? I don't like it. There's too much can go wrong. But, I suppose there's no other choice. Be careful, Smoke."

Smoke gave him a curt nod. "Now that I will do."

Rapid, strident notes shivered brassily from the bell of a sliver-plated trumpet. The short, thin, dapper mariachi who played it had a pencil line of mustache that writhed above the mouthpiece as he articulated each tone. To his right, a big man with a huge bass guitar plucked the strings with gusto, rhythmic vibrations that directly strummed the heart. To the trumpeter's left, a standard guitar and two violins played out the melody. Under their wide-brimmed *charro* sombreros, three of the quartet sang lustily. The song was "Sonora Querrida." Clifton Satterlee looked with pride over the milling guests at his hacienda outside Santa Fe. Seated at the table on the palm frond shaded dais with him, his three partners and several of his eastern connections ate and drank to their hearts' content.

Across the patio, on which some of the guests danced to the music, two small, barefoot boys, dressed in loosely fitted white cotton shirts and knee-length pants, turned a spit over a large bed of oak and piñon coals. Their eyes shone with the excitement generated by the fiesta that swirled around them. Steam and smoke rose from the fat and juices that dripped off the split side of beef the youngsters tended. The aroma of the roasting flesh kept everyone in a constant state of hunger. Large, glazed clay bowls of beans were emptied and promptly refilled. Others of delicate saffron rice, mixed with onions, green peas and tomatoes, suffered deep inroads. Mountains of freshly made tortillas, both flour and corn, disappeared with regularity. Beer, tequila and bourbon flowed freely. The happy laughter of women tinkled from every quarter.

Obviously enjoying all of this, one huge-bellied, over-dressed man with pink pate showing through thinning hair leaned toward Satterlee and patted him on the forearm. "I have to hand it to you, Cliff, you know how to throw a party. All of this must cost a fortune."

"Not at all, Findley. Labor is cheap. Back when the Spanish, then the Mexicans, ruled this land, the law had it that when a man owned the ground, he owned everything on it. That included villages and the people in them. Of course, he was required to provide a livelihood for the peons, see that they had a roof over their heads, food to eat, even paid a small amount of money. The patron had responsibility for their well-being, but to all intent and purpose, they were his property. When I took over, they had nowhere else to go, so they stayed. I provide and maintain their houses in the village, employ them to run the stores and the cantina. I even support their church, although it is the Popish Roman rite."

"Rather like slavery," Findley Ashbrook said with a chuckle.

Satterlee affected shock and abhorrence. "Heaven forbid, Findley. They are nothing of the sort. After all, they get paid. Ten dollars a month is tops."

"You crafty devil," burbled Quinton Damerest, a burly man with a hang-dog face seated beside Findley Ashbrook. "You've gotten around that demagog Lincoln and his emancipation, damned if you haven't. I admire you for it. Is that how you intend to log out lumber way out here, ship it all the way back east and sell at a profit?"

Satterlee nodded, sipping from a clay mug of beer. "Precisely, Quinton. Once we have the workers living in company houses, buying only from the company store, getting their work clothes from the company commissary, just like my peons here at Santa Fe, then we wait until they are deeply in debt to the company and cut their wages by half, then half again. Before long, they'll also be making only ten-dollars a month, like these Mexican peons."

Findley Ashbrook spoke up next. "What says they have to stay here?"

"The law, Ashbrook my friend, the law. We'll be their employer, and also the local law. If they try to get away from here, we'll take them in front of our tame justice of the peace, get an easy conviction for some trumped-up charge, then slap them and their whole family into jail. A little of that and they'll see the light, have no fear."

"What about the unions?" Findley asked darkly.

Satterlee smirked. "They'll never get a start here. If they try, or if they organize a strike, we have Paddy Quinn and his men to take care of such annoyances." He nodded to a slender, young, boyish-faced individual at one of the trestle tables, helping himself to another plate of *carnitas de puerco*, *carne de res barbacóa* and all the fixings. "You see that one over there? He is a prime example of what I'm talking about. He looks like a baby, but Patrick Quinn assures me he is one of the fastest, most accurate gunhands he has ever witnessed."

Eyes wide, his cheeks gone pale, Quinton Damerest spoke in an awed tone. "Is that William Bonney?"

Satterlee chuckled indulgently. "Not at all, Quinton. He calls himself Mac. A Texas boy named MacGreggor. But he's hell-fire with a six-gun. I've seen him in action."

Unaware that he had become the topic of conversation on the dais, Ian MacGreggor went about filling his plate. He had grown up on the spicy foods of the Southwest. The barbecued beef, with its hot, sweet, red sauce and the carnitas with the wide variety of condiments were among his favorites. He had consumed two plates so far. He could eat at least that much more.

"A growing boy," his mother had often said in mock irritation.

Well, it was true. For the last two years he had always felt hungry. At least being with the Quinn gang had that advantage. The food was good and plentiful. It had surprised Ian when he had been told he would be going along with a part of the gang to act as bodyguards at a fancy do put on by the Big Boss, Clifton Satterlee. The prospect excited him. He would get a chance for a close-up study of the man. He might also overhear something useful to Smoke Jensen. His plate loaded, Mac picked up a squatty clay pot of *jugo de tamarindo,* the savory extract of tamarind pods sweetened with honey and cut with water.

He could have had all the beer he wanted. No one would have questioned him. But he felt it wiser to remain alert and sober. His wisdom proved itself fifteen minutes later when Cole Granger rode in on a lathered, foaming-mouthed horse.

Granger knocked the dust from his clothing and came directly to where Mac sat chewing industriously at his meal.

"Where's the boss?"

"Mr. Quinn? He's over there with the 'important' people on that platform," Ian responded between bites.

Granger was abrupt. "Thanks."

Mac sensed something important came with Granger. "Hey, what's up?"

Cole Granger made an all-encompassing gesture. "Big trouble. You'll find out soon enough."

With a sigh and a regretful backward glance at his abandoned plate, Ian MacGreggor drifted along behind Cole Granger. The latter stopped at the bottom of the three steps that led to the dais. There he waited to catch the eye of Paddy Quinn. Mac held back and turned away to avoid recognition. At last Paddy looked up and saw the agitated Granger standing on the edge of the tile patio.

"Sure an' what is it ye are lookin' so exercised over, Cole, me lad?"

"We've got some big trouble up in Taos, Paddy."

"Ouch, now, that's such fresh news, it is." Paddy had been hitting the tequila heavily. It showed clearly to an attentive Mac.

"No, really. We had the roadblocks busted up by a posse and some vaqueros who work for Diego Alvarado. About nine of the guys dead, some others near to death. Shot all to doll rags. An' I—well, I recognized someone fighting with the Mezkin cowboys."

"An' who might that be?"

"Maybe we ought to move away a bit before I tell you?" Cole Granger suggested, as he cut his eyes nervously to Clifton Satterlee and his partners.

Grumbling under his breath, Paddy Quinn grabbed a fresh shot of tequila and a lime wedge from the tray of a waiter and climbed from the platform. Ian MacGreggor had moved off, though not out of hearing. Granger led Paddy over by a palo verde. There he spoke in a low tone.

"It was none other than Smoke Jensen."

Shock and surprise registered on the face of Paddy Quinn. "Th' hell. I thought him to be dead and buried long ago."

"Not so. He's taken a hand in what's goin' on in Taos."

Quinn looked grim. "I'll have to tell Mr. Satterlee."

He went at once to where Satterlee sat and asked to speak alone with him. Off the dais, the head of C.S. Enterprises listened while Quinn explained. From the thunderous expression that shaped Satterlee's face, Mac could tell he liked the news even less. At last, Satterlee spoke in a low tone.

"The presence of Smoke Jensen could prove a major threat. Quinn, I want you to select some men and do something about Jensen. And do it fast."

Riding side by side, Smoke Jensen and Santan Tossa felt the warm sun on their right cheeks and shoulders. Santa Fe remained a full thirty-five miles away. They would not reach the bustling territorial capital until the next morning. As they neared a steep saddle, Smoke noted a large red-tailed hawk, its wings extended, tips down-curved, riding stationary on the strong breeze that blew through the opening.

Abruptly a shrill squeal came from a small, young rabbit crouched on the ground. Frightened beyond endurance by the hawk that hovered above it, it broke cover and sent spurts of red dust from under its hind feet. Instantly, the hawk folded its wings and dived like an arrow. Legs suddenly extended, claws flexed, the red-tail snatched the tiny creature from the earth and soared away toward its lair. The pitiful cry of its victim faded as it gained distance. Smoke Jensen watched unperturbed. He never forgot that nature was indeed a harsh mistress.

Santan Tossa nodded toward the dwindling silhouette of the hawk. "The young of the red-tail will eat well today."

"That is so," Smoke allowed. "Tell me, Santan, how long have you been a policeman?"

Tossa smiled, his chin lifted somewhat in pride. "Four years now. Although I will admit that this is the first real crime I have had to investigate. Most of the time I deal with a few drunks, or a dispute over ownership of a horse. What about yourself?"

Smoke had no need to search memory. "I've worn a badge, off and on, for well over fifteen years. I've fought outlaws and cleaned the riffraff out of towns, protected people in the government, even looked into the murder of friends and a few strangers."

Tossa looked expectant of Smoke's answer. "Do you like it?"

Smoke gave a snort of laughter. "A whole lot better than bein' on the other side of the law. I've not run into many Indian policemen. The Sioux and Cheyenne don't have them."

Tossa shrugged. "They are still controlled by the soldiers and the Indian agents. We are on our own. We're . . . pacified." The word sounded bitter to his mouth.

That decided Smoke to change the subject. "Do you have a woman? A family?"

"I am too young to raise children. At least that is the way we Tua believe. The padres of the *iglesia católica* want us to marry young and have many children."

"But that is not the Tua way."

A broad grin spread across Tossa's face. "No. And in that way, we mystify them. A Tua man usually takes a wife when he has twenty-six summers—er—years. He is through with war and breaking wild horses by then. Ready to settle down, hunt and plant and provide for a family. It is a good way."

"I agree," Smoke conceded.

They rode along making infrequent and idle conversation. They came down out of the Sangre de Cristo at Española and rode on a ways. The sun slanted far to the west and highlighted red plumes to their backs. Smoke Jensen had kept notice of them for some five miles when he reigned up.

"Someone is following us."

Tossa nodded. "I noticed it, too."

Smoke cut his level, gold-flecked gaze to Tossa. "What do you think we should do about it?"

The Tua shrugged. "Find out who they are."

Cole Granger and the four men Paddy Quinn sent with him rode hard and fast out of Santa Fe, in an effort to reach the halfway point between the Satterlee hacienda and Taos before nightfall. As it happened, they arrived in Española only minutes before Smoke Jensen and Santan Tossa passed through. Granger, who had been the one to recognize Smoke in the first place, spotted the tall, broad-shouldered, firmly erect figure as Smoke walked his mount down the main street. In spite of three hundred years of settlement, roads remained sparse in this part of New Mexico. It did not require great genius for Cole Granger to figure out where Smoke Jensen might be headed.

"Him an' that Injun are on the way to Satterlee's."

Pete Stringer eyed him dubiously. "How you know?"

"Where else would he be going? He's in a dust-up with us and right off, he heads south. He's goin' to call out the big boss."

Stringer eagerly went for the obvious solution. "Then, let's take him out right here an' now."

Granger shook his head. "Not likely. The marshal here's hell on killings in his town. Even if we let Jensen draw first—which would be a terrible mistake—we'd wind up in jail, most likely charged with murder. We're gonna follow along. Pick our spot, then jump the two of them."

"What does the Injun have to do with it?" another of the hard cases asked.

With a squint-eyed stare, Granger spat on the ground. "Who cares? He'll be only another dead Injun."

At Granger's suggestion, they gave Smoke and Tossa time enough to cover five miles, then rode out, retracing their hurried route to the small mountain town. The outlaws pulled into sight twenty minutes later. To their right, the sun floated over the western arm of the Sangre de Cristo range. Long shafts of orange and magenta light cast their features in unnatural colors. Dark, elongated shadows of horses and riders kept pace with them. Their quarry dipped below the horizon, where the road descended yet another three hundred feet to the more open desert land that stretched to Santa Fe.

When Granger and his henchmen reached the grade, the outlaw leader immediately discovered that the men they hunted had disappeared. The first cold, portentous inklings of extreme danger clutched the spine of Cole Granger.

Thirteen

Fat, dumb and inattentive, four of the five hard cases who followed Smoke Jensen rode into a nasty surprise. Only Cole Granger hung back, acutely conscious that the missing men represented a threat that could not be ignored. Yet, had he warned the others, taken some sort of defensive position, Smoke Jensen and the Indian could have simply ridden off some unexpected direction and disappeared for good. Jensen was slippery as a greased eel. Somehow, Granger knew, he had to allow them to spring any trap they had planned. That happened far sooner than he had expected.

His underlings had ridden on ahead, and only now became aware that their intended targets could no longer be seen. "Hey," Pete Stringer called out. "Where 'n hell did they go?"

"I'm right here." The voice of Smoke Jensen came from beyond a jumble of rocks that masked the right side of the trail from the view of Granger and the others.

"And I am here," Tossa answered from the opposite side.

Four astonished saddle trash cut their eyes from one side of the trail to the other. On their left they saw the squat figure of a Pueblo Indian, powerful shoulder muscles bunched as he drew the string of a thick, stubby bow back to his cheek, an arrow nocked and ready. In the other direction, a hard-faced white man held a six-gun on them in a competent, steady grip. All at once a terrible reality had caught up with them.

Given the alternatives, they decided to do what, to them, seemed the only thing to do. All four went for their guns. The arrow made a ripping cloth sound as it left its perch, propelled by a seventy-pound pull. It made an eerie moan through the air before it penetrated the chest wall of one thug and buried half its length in his lungs and other vital organs. He didn't even scream before he fell from the saddle.

From the other side, a .45 Colt Peacemaker barked with authority, and a hot slug smacked solidly into the gut of Pete Stringer. Pete's arm jerked, and his one shot went wild, to scream off the rocks. Another bullet brought an immense darkness to shroud him until a tiny, bright pinpoint of light began to swell and Pete Stringer rushed off to eternity. Pete didn't hear the next shot, which clipped Handy Manson in one shoulder and sent him in wild flight down the trail toward Santa Fe. The third, stiff-legged jounce threw Manson from the back of his horse. He hit the ground hard, folded into a ball to moan and writhe in misery.

On the opposite side of the trail, the close quarters left no time to string another arrow. Santan Tossa leaped from the back of his pony and dragged the remaining outlaw clear of his horse. They landed with a thud, the Tua Indian on top. Brigand ribs cracked like brittle sticks under the impact of Tossa's knees. Orange sunlight flashed on the keen edge of the knife Tossa whipped out and pressed to the throat of the winded thug.

So much for making a plan based on Jensen's expected attack, Cole Granger thought quickly. The only *plan* that made sense was to get the hell out of here. He reined his mount around and put spurs to its flanks. Smoke Jensen rode into sight then and threw a shot at the departing Granger with little hope of it hitting meat.

At the forefeet of Cougar, the youthful desperado had eyes only for the knife that threatened him. After a cautious, though nervous, shudder, he raised his gaze to the white man who calmly sat his horse, looking down with apparent dispassionate interest. That sight caused him to lose it entirely. He began to shriek and utter great sobs. Only gradually did Smoke manage to interpret what the sniveling thug tried to say.

"Please . . . puh-leeeze! Save me from this savage. Drag him off me. You're a white man. You can't let him kill me."

Laughing nastily, Smoke Jensen bent down and spoke softly. "I'll let Tossa skin you alive if you don't cooperate. You and your friend down there." He gestured toward the fallen Handy Manson.

"What do you want to know? What? What?"

"Who do you ride for?"

"I can't—I can't tell you. He'll—kill me if I do."

Coldly, Smoke taunted him. "And you don't think Tossa there will kill you if you don't?"

Face ashen, he cut his eyes away from both of his captors. "Oh, Jesus."

Iron tipped Smoke's words. "He can't help you. I might. If you tell me what I want to know. Who do you ride for?"

"Whi—Whitewater Paddy Quinn."

Relentless, Smoke pressed on. "And who does he work for?"

Shaking with terror born of the impossibility of his situation, certain he would die no matter what he said, the craven rascal gulped himself into a fit of hiccoughs. His eyes squinted tightly shut, and great tears squeezed out. "C-C-Clif—Clifton Sa-Sa-Satterlee."

Smoke Jensen cut his eyes to Santan Tossa and asked rhetorically, "Why am I not surprised?" He made a curt gesture, and Tossa released the captive. "Get the other one. We'll patch them up and take them along with us while we go have a talk with Satterlee. Then, on the way back, we can drop them off in Española. The law can lock them up for us there."

* * *

Seth and Sammy Gittings intermittently wiped at the tears that streamed down their dirt-grimed faces with the backs of their hands as they saddled two small Morgan horses they had decided to take for their escape from the Sugarloaf. Horror and a terrible sensation of rejection burned in their minds. She had done it again. Their rumps still stung from the hard, swift swipes from the willow switch.

Seth sniffled loudly and smeared his upper lip with the mucous that ran from his nose. Then he spoke both their thoughts. "It ain't right. What did it matter if that dumb ol' pig got squashed. It was fun rollin' rocks downhill into the pig pen and watchin' the mud splash up."

"Yeah, Seth. It wasn't our fault that baby pig was stuck in the muck and couldn't get away in time. Mother had no right to spank us. She's never ever done it before."

Seth nodded energetically. "Poppa wouldn't let her. Now she's done it twice. It ain't fair," he whined. "We'll show her. She'll be sorry when we're gone."

Abruptly a rooster bugled his welcome to the pending dawn. Both boys jumped and looked at each other with the shock of fear reflected in their eyes. The cock crowed again, and a fit of giggles erupted from Seth and Sammy.

Through his sniggers, Sammy admitted, "That cock-a-doodle scared me. I about peed my pants."

"What's new about that?"

"Liar! I ain't done it in a year now."

"Shut up an' let's finish."

Seth completed the fold-over tie-off of his cinch strap, grateful that his older brother's friendship with Bobby Jensen had allowed him to learn how to master the tricks of saddling a horse, and he had in turn taught them. He went to check on his little brother. Sammy, as usual, had made a mess of it. He began to undo the bulky knot.

"Not like that, stupid. Here, watch."

Quickly Seth adjusted the cinch strap, slipped the leather end through the crosspiece and jerked it down. Next he hung a canteen over the saddle horn and added a cloth bag that contained some biscuits, split and smeared with apple butter, two pieces of cold, fried chicken and a hunk of cheese. An identical bundle already waited on his saddle. Through the barn window he saw a thin, gray line on the eastern horizon. It was time they left. Any more delay and they might get caught.

"Miz Jensen will be awake any time," he observed to his brother. "So'll the hands. We gotta go now and fast."

"Mother won't get up for hours," Sammy remarked.

"So what? We've gotta be way gone from here by then."

Both boys led their stolen horses from the barn and mounted up. Walking the animals to make the least amount of noise, they angled across the ranch yard and into the near pasture. Only then did Sammy notice the smooth, dark wood of a rifle stock in the scabbard on Seth's saddle.

"Gosh, what's that, Sethie?"

"Bobby's rifle."

"Why'd you take that; you don't like guns, do you?"

Seth had a wild gleam in his eyes. "Really, I think they're keen. Besides, we might need it. Mother says it is dangerous and wild out there." He put heels to the little Morgan and moved the beast into a trot.

Neither youngster had the slightest smidgen of horsemanship. Their thin legs bounced out from the sides of their mounts while their rumps banged up and down without even a hint about posting. By the time they had left the cleared fields of the Sugarloaf their thighs ached and their behinds knew more agony than any from the spanking. Tall fir, hemlock and pine closed around them, and the sky disappeared above a thick mat of branches. Stunted aspens reduced visibility to twenty feet on either side. Sammy grew round-eyed with apprehension. It did not decrease when they picked up a game trail.

Seth pointed it out. "Look, there's a trail. I bet it leads to that dismal little town, you know the one?"

"Big Rock?"

"That's it, Sammy. We'll follow it, okay?"

"Sure."

Seth took the lead on the narrow trace, with Sammy close behind. They remained totally unaware that they were going in the exact opposite direction from Big Rock. Or that they grew more lost with each step their mounts took. They also continued into the vastness, ignorant of the cool, amber eyes that watched them.

Slowly the muscular, tawny body roused itself, lifted its blunt, white muzzle and sniffed the air. With a surge of new interest, the wily old cougar smelled a fresh meal.

Diamonds of moisture sparked on the leaves of Spanish bayonet and tufts of saw grass as Smoke Jensen and Santan Tossa reigned in behind a low, sandy knoll outside the hacienda of Clifton Satterlee. Smoke nodded to their captives.

"We'll put them down and tie them to those mesquite bushes. Gag 'em, too."

Handy Manson had regained some of his former bravado. "You go in there after Clifton Satterlee an' you ain't comin' out alive."

Smoke gave him an amused expression. "You had better hope we do. Because no one is going to know where you are. Dying of thirst and hunger is a bad way to go, I'm told. So, hold a good thought for us, eh?"

"You—you ain't gonna leave us some water? Something to eat?"

Smoke appeared downright jovial. "Nope. You won't be able to make use of it anyway, what with a gag in your mouth and hands tied behind a tree."

After securing the prisoners, Smoke and Santan rode on into the warmth of mid-morning. Once out of hearing, Tossa asked of Smoke, "Do you think they will try to escape?"

"I imagine so."

"You do not seem concerned, Smoke."

"I'm not. The way I tied those knots, the harder they struggle, the tighter they'll become. Those two will still be there when we return."

"Don't they know a man can live five or six days without food and nearly as long without water, even in this desert?"

"I doubt it. Even if they do, it will take them some time to remember it. By then we should be back. In a case like theirs, fear can kill more likely than the doin' without."

Worry rode firm in the saddle on the back of Ian MacGreggor. A full day had passed since he had overheard the conversation between Cole Granger and Paddy Quinn. Four men had ridden out with Granger to "take care of Jensen," as Satterlee had put it. What had happened to Smoke? Pushing his concern to the back of his mind, he went about his assigned task of scanning the distant horizon. Motion caught his attention. He stared at the spot, and the dark silhouettes disappeared. He blinked and rubbed his eyes.

There they were. Two figures, clearly on horseback, headed toward the hacienda at a fast trot. Ian MacGreggor soon got the knack of looking slightly to the side of what he wanted to see, instead of dead-bang on. It let him decide that they were definitely both men. As they drew nearer, he determined that they did not resemble any of the gang he knew. What would strangers be coming here for? Mac turned aside and called down from the rampart that spanned the inner side of the high outer wall.

"Riders coming. I don't recognize them yet."

Another member of the gang repeated his announcement. Mac went back to a study of the approaching men. He could make out the color of their clothing now, and the style. Another dozen strides from the powerful shoulder muscles of their horses and Mac could make out their features. One of them appeared to be an Indian. And the other . . . the other rider Mac suddenly recognized as Smoke Jensen. It struck Mac like a fist in the stomach: *Smoke Jensen.* In a flash he recalled Smoke's admonition that if they saw each other, they would not give any sign of recognition. He shouted down to the cobblestone courtyard again.

"They're both strangers. One of them is an Injun. The other is a white man."

"Will ye come on down now, lad, will ye?" Whitewater Paddy Quinn called to him.

"Yes, sir, Mr. Quinn."

Hoofbeats rang loud in his ears as the horsemen grew nearer. Mac clattered down the rickety ladder that gave access to the parapet and joined a cluster of other outlaws who had formed up between the main gate and the house. Mac heard Smoke and his companion rein in. After a pause, the large iron ring that served as a knocker struck the portal with a hollow bang.

Old Jorge Banderes shuffled to the small, human-sized door in the thick wooden gates and opened the viewing port. "¿Sí, señores?"

"We're here to see Señor Satterlee."

"Lo siento, señores, Señor Satterlee is not receiving anyone at this hour," the grizzled Mexican retainer replied.

"Tell him that Smoke Jensen is here. He'll see us, I'm sure."

Jorge scuttled off to deliver the message. While they waited, Smoke exchanged an amused glance with Tossa. Despite the age of the doorman, it took only three minutes. Jorge Banderes threw the bolt on the door and swung it wide.

"Come in, señores. Don Clifton will admit you to his salon now."

Smoke Jensen took a purposeful stride through the opening and cut his eyes to the gathering of hard cases. At once he saw Ian MacGreggor, then his gaze slid on without the slightest sign of recognition. Mac turned slightly as though to keep eyes on the Indian.

"We may regret this," Santan Tossa spoke in a whisper.

Mary-Beth Gittings entered the large living room of the Sugarloaf headquarters in a state of high agitation. Sally Jensen knelt on the hearth, removing ashes from the fireplace. Mary-Beth wrung her hands, and her face showed a puffiness unusual to herself. Sally noted her friend's perplexity at once.

"Mary-Beth, what is the matter?"

"I can't find them. No one has seen them this whole day.

"Who is it you cannot find, Mary-Beth?"

"Seth and Samuel. Your son says he knows nothing about them, only that his rifle is missing. Though I doubt his word on both counts."

Sally fought unsuccessfully to hold back a scowl. "That is entirely uncalled for. I resent the implication that Bobby would lie. It reflects on us as parents, and that is insulting."

Mary-Beth's face crumpled. "I'm sorry, Sally, dear. It's only . . . I am so worried. None of the hands have seen them. The boys are not at the corral, not in any of the barns, not in their room. I've been everywhere."

"Have you asked Billy about his brothers?"

"Yes, and he knows nothing either."

She could be mean, Sally considered, and ask if Mary Beth doubted her son's word also. No, that would hardly do. "Ike Mitchell has a good eye for reading sign. I'll have him take a good look around and see what he can come up with."

"Would you? I'd be so grateful. I worry so whenever they are out of my sight."

Sally found that unsettling. "Even when they go to school?"

"Of course not, Sally. I'm not an over-protective mother."

Oh, no, not by half, Sally opined silently.

Sally left her task for later and, with Mary-Beth trailing along, went in search of the foreman, Ike Mitchell. She found him in the smithy, pounding on a newly forged iron hinge. He looked up as they approached and wiped sweat from his brow with the back of one forearm.

"Ike, have you seen the younger two Gittings boys today?"

"No, ma'am. That I haven't. Told the missus that not two hours ago."

"Well, Ike, they've gone missing. Would you please take a good look around and see if you can come up with anything that might indicate where they got off to?"

"Sure, Miz Sally. Glad to be of help."

Ike completed leveling the hinge, doused it in a tub of water and laid it aside to cool. Then he plunged both hands into another container of clean water and washed the charcoal smudges from his face. He rolled down his sleeves and started off to examine various parts of the headquarters ranch yard. Sally put a hand on Mary-Beth's arm.

"This is likely to take some time. Come back to the house and I'll make us some tea. We can let Ike work at his own pace."

Three-quarters of an hour later, a stern-faced Ike Mitchell presented himself at the kitchen door. Hat in hand, he knocked briskly. Although clearly uncomfortable, he presented his findings in a crisp flow.

"I reckon they done lit a shuck outta here, Miz Sally. I cut their sign west of the big corral. Tracks led northwest across the pastures. I followed them to the edge of tall timber. They kept goin'. Then I came back here and went over the stock. It appears they took two of the young Morgans, blankets and saddles, and high-tailed it early this morning. Don't look like they reckon to come back. We'd best get some of the boys together an' go after them."

"I should say so," Mary-Beth blurted. Then the realization of the danger her children might face struck her. "My babies!" she wailed.

Blunt as usual, Ike had the last word. "They ain't babies anymore, ma'am. They're horse thieves."

Fourteen

Jorge Banderes escorted Smoke Jensen and Santan Tossa into the high, curved-ceiling passageway that separated the main entrance of the house from the gardenlike atrium at the center. Smoke found it to be cool and dark. Everyone blinked when they stepped out into the bright sunlight that washed the tiled central courtyard. A burly man stood beside the central fountain, his face a square mask that failed to conceal the boiling anger beneath the surface. Although Smoke had not seen him before, he surmised this to be Patrick Quinn. Leave it to a two-bit, gunslinging thug to choose as pretentious a moniker as *Whitewater,* Smoke thought.

Smoke Jensen had seen real whitewater on the Rogue River and sincerely doubted that Quinn had the stuffing to ride on it under any conditions. Paddy Quinn took a single step forward and extended both arms, palms up. "The guns. I'll take them now."

Smoke scowled, and his eyes went cold and flat, narrowed slightly. "That'll be the day," he growled.

Quinn proved himself no fool to Smoke's reckoning when he did not choose to press the matter. "Suit yerselves. An', sure ye'd not mind if me an' a couple of the boys stood close at hand while ye have yer little talk with Mr. Satterlee, would ye?"

Smoke could not resist the opportunity to tweek his enemy. "Not at all, a-tall."

For a flash, Quinn's expression grew even more furious.

His eyes widened and revealed black centers that glittered malevolently. With obvious effort he reined in his emotion. "Come this way, then."

Framed by lush vegetation, an attractive young woman took her ease on a white-painted, wrought-iron settee near one side of the patio. Her silver-blond hair and fair, peaches-and-cream complexion glowed in the leaf-filtered sunbeams. She smiled warmly at the visitors and greeted them in a musical contralto. "Welcome to Hacienda Colina del Sol. I am Martha Estes, another guest of Clifton's. I trust we will be together for dinner tonight?"

Always appreciative of a good-looking woman, Smoke spoke his regrets with sincerity. "I doubt that such a pleasure will be possible. We must meet with Mr. Satterlee and then attend to other urgent matters.

Now *here* was a man who could make her knees weak. Martha breathed deeply, expanding her firm, medium-sized bosom, and gave him a melting smile. "What a pity. I—ah—don't believe I caught your name?"

"It's Jensen, Miss Martha. Smoke Jensen."

Martha raised an ivory Spanish fan to her lips and spread it in an agitated motion. "Oh, my. A regular celebrity where I come from. An honor, Mr. Jensen."

"Thank you. Now, if you will excuse us?"

No such warm welcome awaited Smoke Jensen and Santan Tossa when they entered the presence of Clifton Satterlee. The master of the house turned from his affected pose of gazing out the tall windows of his library and spoke with a petulant, condescending tone. "Don't you find it a bit presumptuous to be calling on me like this?"

Although not entirely certain of the meaning of the word, Smoke considered 'presumptuous' to be insulting. So he accepted that the best defense would be a good offense. "Not at all. But I do consider it presumptuous of you to have sent men to follow us and attempt to kill us. Likewise to put up roadblocks to cut off all commerce and other traffic into or out of the town of Taos. And I am sure my friend here, a tribal policeman from the Taos Pueblo, sees it as presumptuous of you to inveigle someone among his people to steal certain religious articles from their kiva."

Clifton Satterlee affected a hurt expression, colored somewhat by indignation, and undertook to talk down to them like foolish boys who had been caught in some school yard prank. "Oh, come now. That's all quite preposterous. You can't possibly believe I would deign to stoop to such brigandish endeavors? I am a man of influence and substance in the territory. What flightiness could bring you to believe that anyone in my employ might be responsible for the difficulties in and around Taos. Dismiss the thought, gentlemen."

With that, Satterlee took Tossa by one elbow and began to steer the both of them toward the door to his library. Smoke Jensen set his boots and did not move. "One minute, if you please, Mr. Satterlee. You have not heard the full extent of our complaints, let alone our opinion of your condescending, self-serving response."

Satterlee stopped, rolled his eyes heavenward and sighed heavily. "Then, I suppose I must."

"You may have influence, and this layout proves your substance," Smoke told him levelly. "But in my book, you are just a grasping, greedy, lying son of a bitch. If you continue to send your third-rate gunfighters to enforce your will and to harm the people around Taos, I will have no choice but to keep on putting them in the *campo santo. ¿Comprende?*"

With that, Smoke allowed himself and Tossa to be escorted from the presence of the great man. In the garden, Martha Estes gave them a light-hearted wave as they passed by on their way to the outside. At the tall, double doors of the main entrance, Paddy Quinn drew closer to Smoke Jensen and spoke heatedly, though softly, through a sneer.

"You're dead meat, Jensen."

Smoke gave Quinn a bleak, thousand-mile, gunfighter stare. "I'll remember that. I trust that you will?"

Riding away from Hacienda Colina del Sol, in the direction of Santa Fe, the two lawmen who had become friends on the ride south remained silent until well away from Satterlee's lair. Then Santan Tossa spoke what was on his heart.

"You really aren't afraid of Satterlee and his gunmen, are you, Smoke?"

Smoke held a moment before replying. "As a matter of fact, I am. Any man who faces death from so many enemies and says he is not afraid is a fool or a liar. But, knowing that, you can use that healthy fear to help you decide which enemy you are going to knock down first. Say you are facing three armed men. One is good, cool under fire and fast with a gun. Another is a common thug with a gun. The third is edgy and unsure of himself. Which one do you go against first?"

Tossa rubbed his lantern jaw, absorbed in thought. "You take the easiest one first, right?"

"You might think that, but it is absolutely necessary to get rid of the greatest threat first. So you go for the best gun. Take him out while you are fresh and unharmed. Then go after the weakest one, because he's likely to do something cowardly. Save the average feller for last."

Santan Tossa stared at his companion. "I would never have thought of that."

Smoke Jensen gave Tossa a smile that reached all the way to the crinkle lines at the corners of his eyes. "No one does, first time out."

"All right, I'll accept that. Now, I have one for you. Did you see that squash blossom necklace that Miss Estes was wearing?"

Smoke nodded. "Yes, I did. It's the most beautiful piece of its kind I've ever seen."

"It should be. It is one of the stolen sacred objects."

"You are sure?"

"Positive, Smoke. I have worn it in ceremonies a dozen times."

Smoke gave that only a second's reflection. "I think we ought to return later tonight and have a private talk with that young woman."

Santan Tossa stared in astonishment as they entered the outskirts of the territorial capital. Tiny Taos was the largest community he had ever seen. By the time they reached the business district of Santa Fe, which extended two blocks in all four directions from the Plaza de Armas, his head swam.

"So many outsiders," he gasped, then recovered himself. "Sorry. It is how we think of those who are not of the Pueblo people. And I have come to not think of you as an outsider, Smoke."

"I'm flattered," responded Smoke dryly. "We'll find a saloon and start to ask around about Satterlee."

"I cannot enter any place that sells the white man's crazy water—uh—liquor."

"That's right, you can't. What do you reckon to do?"

"There are signs in Spanish on the walls that tell of a *Charrida* ring. There I will find others of my Pueblo people. I will ask questions among them about Satterlee."

"Good idea. We'll meet—ah—there." Smoke pointed to a small restaurant on a corner at right angles to the cathedral. "Say, two hours before sundown?"

Tossa nodded and rode off. Smoke turned the other way and reined in outside an arcade formed of plastered adobe arches. From the cool shade crated by the sidewalk overhang, the door of a cantina invited him. Smoke dismounted and handed Cougar's reins to a small, brown-skinned boy with big, shiny, black eyes.

"The livery stable, señor?"

"No. Take him into the Plaza *jardín* and get him watered.

Then bring him back and tie him off here." He handed the boy a coin.

Eying the silver U.S. quarter dollar, the lad's face glowed. "Gracias, señor."

Smoke touched him on a thin shoulder. "That is to insure he is here when I come out. You understand?"

"Comprendo, señor. Muchas gracias."

Inside the cantina, Smoke stood at the bar, beside two white cowboys, and ordered a beer. He nodded to the men and their nearly empty *tubos*. "Buy you a refill?"

The older ranch hand smiled under a well-groomed walrus mustache. "Don't mind if you do. Thank you kindly. I'm Eric, this is Rob."

"Jensen," Smoke said shortly, then observed, "You two have the look of working stockmen."

Eric found that grimly amusing. "Working ain't the half of it. You must be new in these parts not to know that graze is so sparse we've gotta keep the cattle on the move all the time or they'll starve. Weren't half this bad in Texas. Used to be I could sit all night and play poker. Now I've got so many calluses on my butt I stand up to eat."

Smoke affected to consider that a moment, then put on a sorrowful expression. "Maybe I came out here on a snipe hunt?"

"How's that?" Eric asked.

"I got let out by the last outfit I worked for. There was this posting in our local paper about someone hiring out here. All sorts of jobs, including cattle work."

"What newspaper was that?"

"The Amarillo *Star,*" Smoke replied, using the name of Mac's source.

Eric nodded. "Don't want to pry, but what's the name of this man who can spend so much money to get hands?"

"Didn't give a man's name. Some outfit called C.S. Enterprises."

"Cliff Satterlee." Eric spat the name as though it had a

foul taste. Then he turned fully to Smoke and gave him a long, cool study from head to boot toe. "You look to be a straight shooter. I figger you're on the right side of the law. So, if you don't mind, I'll give you some good advice. Were I you, Jensen, I'd steer as far clear of Satterlee, an' any of those around him, as I could."

Pleased with what he had heard, Smoke pressed his luck. "He's crossed horns with the law, has he?"

Eric nodded. "More'n once. Nothin' ever proved, of course. Money talks. Though it's said by more than one that Satterlee's drovers throw wide loops."

Smoke knew what that meant. In cowmen talk, throwing a wide loop implied that a man rustled most of his stock, or at the least, claimed more than his share of unbranded cattle. "There's more?"

"Some fellers have died of a sudden," Eric confided. "Satterlee has him a so-called foreman, name o' Paddy Quinn, who's prone to be quick to use his Colts. The rest of them that rides for the brand are jist as proddy."

"What brand is that?"

Rob added his bit. "C-Bar-S. There's some say it stands for his ranch, Colina del Sol. But it's for Clifton Satterlee and his C.S. Enterprises, you can be damn sure. Leastwise, it's an easy brand to use to blot another one with a runnin' iron."

"Thank you, Eric, Rob. I'll sure keep distance between me and Satterlee." Smoke downed the last of his beer and strode to the bead-curtained doorway.

Outside, Cougar waited for him, the reins in the patient hands of the small boy. Smoke looked left and right and located another saloon only three doors down. He spoke to the boy. "You keep him here. I'm going to walk down to the Cinco de Mayo."

Surprise raised black eyebrows. "Walk? You are not a vaquero, señor, ¿es verdad?"

"That's right, son. I guess you could call me un *ranchero,* un *hacendado.*"

"*¡Por Dios!* It is an honor to serve you, señor."

Smoke ruffled the lad's thatch of black hair and started off to continue his information gathering mission.

Santan Tossa sat on the top of the low, plastered adobe wall that separated the *callejón* from the performance ring at the *Charrida* plaza. Elongated, like a hippodrome or the Circus Maximus, the Mexican rodeo ground lacked the circular symmetry of a Plaza de Toros. To one side and in front of Tossa, a young vaquero from the San Vincente Pueblo leaned his back against the wall, one leg elevated, knee cocked, boot resting against the inner surface of the barrier. The youth longed to be a recognized *Charro*, but knew of the prejudice harbored by the Spanish-blooded Mexicans against anyone of pure Indian origins. Tossa understood this and used it to loosen the fellow's tongue.

"You will ride in the *Charrida* this Sunday?"

A glum expression darkened the wide, Indian face. "I will clean stalls, saddle horses, and maybe, just maybe, ride as a header—to set up the bulls for the *Charros* to rope. It is dangerous, but it lets people see what you can do. Another year . . two years, who knows?"

Tossa tried to be encouraging. "Chosteen, you will one day wear the *Sombrero Grande* of a *Charro*. This is part of the land of the White Father in Washington now. He will not let the Mexicans keep our people out of the *Asociacion Nacional de Charros.*"

Chosteen turned to him. "And why not? Its headquarters is in Mexico . . . the old Mexico. The white eyes' laws do not apply there."

With a shrewd expression, Tossa offered his bait. "If you worked for C.S. Enterprises, perhaps the *Charros* would accept you as an Americano."

Suddenly, Chosteen's features clouded. "I would rather work for Soul Eater. At last you expect Him to be evil." His eyes quickly narrowed as he thought of something. "Do you work for Satterlee? Are you here to try to get others to sell their Spirits to that outsider demon?"

"No—no," Tossa hastened to object. "I am interested in him, only. We believe that he, or someone he used, has stolen sacred objects from our kiva."

Chosteen spat on the sand. "Then he is as evil as I have been told."

"You know something of this Satterlee, Chosteen?"

"I do." For the next twenty minutes the two Pueblos spoke earnestly and intensely about Clifton Satterlee.

When they concluded their talk, Santan Tossa made his way to an outdoor barbecue pit where a small calf, which had been crippled in the day's practice, had been dressed out and put on a spit to roast. He watched the small carcass turn for a while, his stomach rumbling, prompted by the aroma. Mostly his people ate sheep, or wild meat. Over the years as a policeman, Tossa's frequent visits to the white man's town had given him a taste for beef. He pushed temptation aside to ask among the Pueblo men about Clifton Satterlee. One lean, young man, not yet in his twenties, gave him confirmation of a suspicion of his own.

"I have heard it said that he wants the land where your pueblo stands. He would cut the trees. All of them. He would lay our Earth Mother bare and let the rains wash gullies and ravines in her breast."

"Is nothing sacred to these pale skins?" another asked.

The first to speak went on. "They care nothing for the land. There is more, always more, to be taken, laid waste and then move on to yet more. Their god is formed of those circles of gold that they treasure so much."

Yet another advised, "Do not speak ill of the white outsider, Satterlee. He is a dangerous man."

Through the afternoon, Tossa heard much the same, and more, from those he questioned. He reached the conclusion that none of them admired or trusted Clifton Satterlee, and that most feared him. He ate some of the roasted veal, wrapped in flat, cornmeal cakes, and seasoned by a thick sauce of chile peppers and garlic. Then he made his farewells and left to join Smoke Jensen.

Smoke Jensen had finished his first swallow of beer in the Cinco de Mayo cantina and had settled down to weighing up the other occupants when Ian MacGreggor pushed aside the strings of glass beads and entered the saloon. Mac ambled to the bar and elbowed a place beside Smoke. He ordered a beer and drank deeply before speaking in a low tone, his lips not moving.

"I have something important. We need to talk soon. And it's getting too hot for me here. There's nothing much for us to do and too much time for the others to ask questions."

Smoke did not look at the young undercover deputy when he replied. "Find some excuse to get away for a while. Ride out from the estancia and join us on the road to Taos. We'll be there early tomorrow.

"I can do it. And, Smoke, you're not going to believe what I found out." Lapsing into silence, Mac finished his beer, then turned away from the bar. Smoke stopped him with a hand on one shoulder.

"There's one thing you can tell me now. Which room is Miss Estes using?"

Mac frowned slightly. "She's not. Not in the main house, anyway. She has a small cabin outside the place, near the north wall. It's the one on the south end of a row of three."

"Thanks." Smoke released Mac and the young man walked out the door.

In every saloon and eating place Smoke Jensen visited, he encountered someone who had heard of either Clifton Satterlee or Paddy Quinn or both. Not until the fourth cantina he looked into, did he run into the first men to have anything good to say. In fact, they took immediate exception to Smoke even asking questions. Thrown from a blind spot, when he least expected it, a fist whistled past Smoke's head.

Smoke dodged it and spun on a boot heel. A hard-knuckled right fist drove up from waist level. Off balance from the missed blow, the pig-faced brawler caught Smoke's punch full in the gut. A loud grunt exploded from his lips. Eyes bulging, he bent double in time to take Smoke's swiftly upraised knee in the nose. Bright lights flashed in his eyes, to be swiftly followed by a blanket of blackness. He keeled over and struck his bloodied chin on the tile floor. At once, two others grabbed Smoke from behind and sought to yank him around.

Smoke Jensen set his powerful legs and twisted at the waist. One of the thugs went flying. The other hung on. *This shouldn't be happening,* Smoke thought. All he had asked was, "Anyone here know a feller named Satterlee? I hear he's hiring."

The others said nothing. Instead, they started swinging. They still remained silent as another one jumped into the brawl. Smoke rolled a punch off his shoulder and popped the hard case who held him under the chin. His eyes rolled up, he blinked and tried to kick Smoke in the crotch. Smoke turned slightly and hit him again. He gave a shudder and let go of Smoke to sprawl with his face in the urinal trough that fronted the bar in most Mexican saloons.

Right then the fight took on a far more serious tone as two of the Quinn gang went for their six-guns.

Fifteen

Smoke Jensen saw their moves from the corner of one eye. He filled his own hand with a .45 Peacemaker in a blur of speed. One cut-rate gunfighter had time to gasp in astonishment before a 230 grain slug smashed into his left shoulder and he went flailing into a table, which collapsed under his weight. His six-gun, only partly out of the holster, fell to the floor at his side. Already, Smoke had swung his Colt to bear on the second gunman.

That unfortunate fellow had time enough to pull his barrel clear of leather and began to level the muzzle on the mid-section of Smoke Jensen. His misfortune came from that fact which caused Smoke to put a bullet through his heart rather than shoot to wound. The gunhawk slammed back against the bar and slid to a sitting position. It had all happened so fast that only now did the bartender react with a shout to his other customers as he ducked below the bar.

"Tengan cuidado! Los pistoleros."

A third gang member unlimbered his six-gun as Smoke swung his Colt that direction. He stopped the move instantly when Smoke raised his point of aim and the man could look down the black tunnel of the barrel. A thin curl of powder smoke rose from the muzzle. Smoke remained motionless while bar patrons dived for cover and the rest of the Satterlee partisans showed open, empty hands. A tense three minutes went by in which the only sound to be heard came from the wounded hard case. Smoke lowered his revolver only when the law arrived.

Face a fierce mask, the town marshal entered the saloon with drawn six-gun. He cut his eyes from the downed men to the bartender, and then to Smoke. "All right, who started all of this?"

No one seemed eager to reply, so Smoke Jensen holstered his Colt and stepped into the breach. "They did." He indicated the wounded gunman and the dead one. "First off, three of those fellers over at the bar took offense to something I said and threw punches at me. When I knocked a couple of them flat, those two drew on me."

A skeptical raise of eyebrow projected the lawman's mood. "And you just happened to be faster."

"That's right. I was . . . or should I say am?"

"Do you have a name to go with all that speed?"

"I do. Could we talk about it at your office, Marshal?"

"You'll get there soon enough, I'd say. What's wrong with here?"

Smoke nodded at the gang members. "There are—other ears. What I have to say is for you alone."

With a shrug, and another dubious look, the marshal turned to one of his subordinates. "Nate, take care of things here. You, mister, come with me."

The marshal marched Smoke Jensen cattycorner across the Plaza de Armas to his office. Inside, the lawman took a seat behind a scarred, water-stained desk. "If it hadn't been some of Clifton Satterlee's hirelings, you'd be answering questions from inside a cell. So, speak your piece."

Smoke dug into his vest pocket and produced his badge. "I'm glad to hear that, marshal. My name's Smoke Jensen. I'm a deputy U.S. marshal. At the request of a friend, I am here to look into Satterlee and his dealings."

"Who is this friend?"

"Don Diego Alvarado, of Rancho de la Gloria, outside Taos."

"It's about time," the marshal snapped. "Governor Lew Wallace will be glad to hear that Satterlee is being investigated. By the way, I know your friend, Alvarado, and m'name's Ambrose . . . Dave Ambrose."

Smoke Jensen appeared more amused than relieved. "Well, Marshal Ambrose, I'm not here to investigate Satterlee. My job is to eliminate him."

Marshal Ambrose had a sudden change of mood. He snorted with contempt. "Another hired gun hidin' behind a badge."

Smoke immediately put him straight. "Nothing of the sort. What I should have said is that Satterlee has broken several federal laws, or at least arranged for others to break some for him. I'm here to bring down his business and put him away for a good long time."

Ambrose shot Smoke a disgusted look. "What if he chooses not to cooperate? Hell, man, he owns the judges."

Smoke gave the marshal a cold, hard smile. "Then I'll just have to eliminate him."

A bloated, red-orange ball hung over the snow-capped peaks to the west. Cold air rising off the white mantle distorted it into the wavy shape of an egg. Dark, purple shadows lay across the ground. Sammy Gittings sat on a fallen tree trunk, tears sliding silently down his chubby, round cheeks. They were lost. They had wandered off the Sugarloaf and no one would ever find them. He knew it, no matter what Seth said.

Seth looked up now from the pile of dry wood he had gathered. "Don't just sit there. Help me. We need to get a fire started."

"What good will that do?" Sammy pouted. "We don't have anything to cook."

Seth stood, grubby hands on his hips. "You come down here and build a fire and I'll get us something to eat."

"How? You can't hit anything you shoot at."

"Shut up! Jist shut up. I'll get something this time."

A squirrel chattered alarmingly as it suddenly darted away through the tree limbs above. Seth looked up. "Maybe a squirrel."

Sammy made a face. "Ugh! They look like rats when they're skinned."

"Are you hungry or not?"

Sammy paused before replying to his brother. "Not that hungry."

"Then don't eat. I'll have it all."

Lower lip protruded in a pout, Sammy challenged Seth. "Won't either. I get my share. It's only right."

Seth started to laugh at his little brother only to have it cut off by a harsh primordial cough. His face went chalk white. "What was that?"

Right then, the wily old cougar that had been stalking them uttered another hoarse hack, flexed its powerful hind legs, and with a strident snarl, launched itself. Sammy screamed at the sight of the tawny blur and fell backward off the tree trunk. Seth let go a yowl and scampered backward. He tripped over an exposed root and landed on his round bottom. His arm stretched out as he desperately searched the ground. His fingers found the cold steel of a rifle barrel, and he closed around it in desperation. The mountain lion missed Sammy by a foot when the boy toppled away from its spring and now whirled in the small clearing under large, overgrown branches. It lunged again at the terrified, smaller lad.

In that split second, Seth brought up Bobby Jensen's little .32-20 rifle and fired at point-blank range. By sheer chance, the slug hit the cougar in the right ear and plowed a ragged furrow through its brain. It leaped into the air and fell back dead. One needle-clawed paw twitched three inches from the soft belly of Sammy Gittings.

"You got him! You got him, Seth," Sammy shouted.

Unfortunately for the boys, the ferocious charge and odor of the puma thoroughly frightened the horses. Neighing in terror, both animals slipped their insecure tie offs and ran away. Only a haze of dust and pine needles marked their course as their rumps disappeared down the trail.

Seth stared after them in consternation. Sammy came to him then, wailing between great sobs. "What—are—we gonna—do? What are we—gonna do? We'll die out here all alone."

The moon would not rise until after midnight. It provided ideal conditions for Smoke Jensen and Santan Tossa to penetrate the security around the hacienda of Clifton Satterlee. Thanks to the information he had received from Ian MacGreggor, Smoke could pick the right place to scale the wall and be the least exposed to any of the watchers. The cabana occupied by Martha Estes was located close to the east wall of the compound, well away from the main house. Smoke had not come prepared to scale a high wall. Particularly he had not planned for the rows of jagged-edged, broken bottles that lined the top.

With gloves in place, moccasins on his feet, Smoke Jensen balanced himself on the shoulders of Santan Tossa. Cautiously, he reached up and felt his way between the blue ranks of dragon's teeth and found purchase. Smoke flexed his knees, then launched himself. He swung one leg upward to nudge against the outer row of bottle shoulders. He held onto the inside of the wall until his balance returned, then dropped the bite end of the rope around his neck to Tossa Levering himself upward, Smoke went over the wall and dropped to the ground below.

Quickly he secured the loop of the rope to a post and gave the line a little tug. At once, it tightened and began to vibrate. On the far side, Tossa literally walked up the adobe palisade. In brief seconds he joined the last mountain man on the ground. Smoke pointed to a low, square adobe cabin to one side. A yellow square picked out a window, and indicated that someone occupied the premises. Silently, the two men moved in that direction.

Smoke eased to the corner of the building and peered around to take in the outer courtyard. Nothing moved, and he saw no sign of sentries. He beckoned to Tossa, and they went directly to the only door. Smoke put his ear to the panel and listened for ten long seconds, then grasped the latch, threw it and swung the portal inward.

Startled, Martha Estes looked up from the book she had been reading, her expression showing her to be a bit frightened. "Wha—what are you doing here, Mr. Jensen?"

"I've come to see you, ask a few questions, Miss Estes."

Martha took a deep breath, reaching up with her hand. "This is—rather irregular."

Smoke made a pacifying gesture. "I apologize for that, but I have learned something of importance that I want you to explain for me."

Martha gathered herself "I—I'll try to help if I can."

"Good. What it is . . ." Smoke hesitated, then went on. "That squash blossom necklace you were wearing this morning. Where did you get it?"

"Why, Cliff—er—Clifton gave it to me. He has some other lovely pieces in the safe in the library."

Smoke eyed her levelly. "Are you aware that those are stolen property?"

Martha started an immediate protest. "That can't be. Clifton is a respected businessman, an enterprising investor."

Santan Tossa took over then. "Miss Estes, that necklace and the other items are religious objects, stolen from my people at the Taos pueblo. They are sacred to our kiva."

Martha's face twisted in a war between disbelief and outrage. "Why, that's—that's terrible. However could Clifton have gotten ahold of them? Perhaps he purchased them, not knowing their origin?"

Smoke Jensen shook his head. "I'm afraid not, Miss Estes. Santan Tossa here is a tribal policeman, investigating the theft. All of his leads have taken him to Clifton Satterlee. For all his mighty reputation around Santa Fe, Miss Estes, Satterlee is not what he appears to be."

"But . . . my father is a business associate. Surely he cannot be involved in such nefarious schemes."

Deciding to ease her mind, at last for the moment, Smoke offered a suggestion. "To get away with what he is planning, Satterlee needs the cover of honorable, legitimate businessmen. By reflection, you see, it makes him seem the same. Your father is most likely one of those."

Martha became more agitated. "No matter how he acquired the jewelry, it is simply unforgivable that your sacred items not be returned."

She rose and crossed to a large, walnut armoire against one wall. There she kneeled and slid open a drawer. From it, she took the necklace. A look of anger had replaced her earlier confusion and shock. "Here, take this back and put it where it rightfully belongs."

A thought occurred to Smoke Jensen. "What will you tell Satterlee if he notices it is gone?"

"I'll think of something. We women have our ways." Martha smiled for the first time since they had entered the room.

Tossa accepted the silver and turquoise work of art and folded it into a strip of purple velvet. "Thank you, Miss Estes. I will keep it secret for a while that the necklace has been recovered."

"I thank you, too," Smoke added. "Now we'll say good night. It would be prudent if you did not let anyone know we have been here."

"Of course. Good night, Mr. Jensen."

Smoke built her a smile. "Call me Smoke."

* * *

Clifton Satterlee had stayed up late also. He paced the confines of his library, hands clasped behind his back. Thick, rich velvet drapes covered the leaded glass windows so that not a hint of light escaped. A small fire crackled in the beehive fireplace set into one wall. These early spring nights remained chill. Seated in a large, wing chair, his long legs sprawled carelessly across the Kermint oriental rug, Paddy Quinn sipped appreciatively at the Irish whiskey his employer had thoughtfully provided for him. At last, Satterlee stopped his measured tread, poured himself an inch of cognac in a snifter and sighed heavily as he turned back to his guest.

"Obviously the men I sent to deal with Jensen failed in their task. He knew too much when he came here to warn me. *Warn me!* What impudence."

Quinn waggled a finger at his boss. "Every rooster likes to make his cock-a-doodle-doo before he gets his head lopped off for the stew pot, he does. Ye ask me, Mr. Satterlee, this Smoke Jensen is runnin' scared. He was flexin' muscles he don't have. He's tryin' to buy hisself some time."

Satterlee sipped the liquor and breathed out its aroma. "Somehow I don't quite believe that. There's more to the man than we saw in this room today. Are you familiar with his reputation?"

Quinn dismissed that with a curt gesture. "Reputations amongst the gunfighting brotherhood are gen'rally tall tales blown out of all proportions, they are."

"Even your own?"

For a long moment Quinn studied Satterlee until he decided the remark had been made in jest. He responded then with joviality. "Far be it from me to disabuse anyone of my ferocious nature."

Satterlee smiled tightly. "The same applies to Smoke Jensen. He is dangerous. I want you to send more men, enough this time to get the job done."

"An' what is it ye have in mind?"

"I want them to follow and finish off that inquisitive Smoke Jensen and the savage he had with him this morning. Then they are to continue on to Taos and join in the blockade Garth Thompson is conducting."

Quinn looked uncomfortable with the news he had to impart. "It might be more of a task than you think. Some of the boys had a brush with Smoke Jensen in town this afternoon. They came out the losers. Two dead."

"Damn that man. Neither you nor I can afford his arrogance. Too much of it will make us look bad. Perhaps I will have to take care of this personally."

Sheriff Hank Banner thoroughly enjoyed getting together with Doc Walters and several of the Taos businessmen once a week for a few hands of poker. This particular night had been especially satisfying, considering the step-up in pressure from the Quinn gang. To top it off, Banner had played only with other men's money after the third hand. Matter of fact, he had come away from the table about twenty dollars to the good. Not bad for a dime ante, quarter limit game. His boot heels echoed hollowly on the red tile sidewalk as he turned the corner and started to cross the Plaza de Armas to his office. Two men suddenly stepped out of the well-tended shrubs to block his path.

One of them worked his mouth in a nasty sneer under a poorly kept mustache. "Goin' somewhere, Law—man?"

"If it's any of your business, I'm headed back to my office."

"Unh-uh. Oh, no."

"Nope, you ain't," the second man added.

So far, neither man had done anything serious enough to justify drawing a weapon, but Sheriff Banner sensed the very real menace they exuded. His hand twitched to close on the butt of his Colt. Right then, two more hard cases stepped onto the crushed rock path behind the sheriff.

"No, you're not goin' to your office," the first one said again. "We're gonna go have us a nice little talk."

He recognized them then. The one doing the talking was named Islip; the one with him they called Funk. Drawing a deep breath, Banner mustered his nerve. "Were I you, I'd go have a nice talk with a bed, Islip. You're drunk. If you don't want to face a charge of disorderly conduct, clear out of my way and let me pass."

Grinning like an imbecile, Funk, the second gunhand, shook his head and tapped a forefinger on the center of the badge worn by Hank Banner. "Can't do that. We got our orders. You an' us is gonna have that talk, an' we're gonna reach an understanding."

At once, the two thugs at his back grabbed the sheriff and pinned his arms to his sides. With a smooth move, they lifted him off his feet and carried him toward the mouth of a dark alley that led off of the plaza on the north side. Once within its shadowy confines, they put Banner's boots on the ground and kept hold while the first pair caught up. Without preamble, Islip and Funk began to take turns, driving hard fists into the chest and stomach of Sheriff Banner.

After a little preliminary softening up, Abner Islip started speaking in a low, insistent tone. "You're gonna forget all about what's happenin' in Taos. No more backin' those who get crosswise of Mr. Satterlee. In fact, you're gonna take a nice little vacation. Go off and visit relatives somewhere, why not? Or go fishin'. I hear they've got some bodacious critters down in the Gulf of Mexico. A feller ought to try for 'em onest in his life, don't you think? Maybe you can take up lawin' in Georgia or Mississippi.

"Any way you want it, Sheriff, yer gonna shake the dust of Taos offen yer boots and clear the hell an' gone outta here by tomorrow morning."

Through the haze of pain, Sheriff Banner maintained his defiance. "You'll be in hell long before I do that, you and Funk, too."

Funk shoved his sweaty face in close to that of the lawman. "In that case, we've got other orders. We ain't to leave enough of you to do any fightin'."

With that, all four began to pound on the sheriff. Islip, his hands growing sore, switched to the use of his pistol barrel. He viciously pistol-whipped Banner until he drove the sheriff to the ground. Then all four formed a circle and began to kick him. Mercifully, blackness swarmed over Hank Banner, and he did not feel the last dozen gouges to his ribs, belly and back.

Bare soles made hardly a sound as Wally Dower scampered along outside the closed and unlighted business fronts on the north side of the Plaza de Armas. In another five minutes he would have completed his final rounds. Only the cantinas remained open. He still had to go back and escort old Laro Hurtado to his house. He would be drunk of course. If he had any money at all, or could cage drinks from some of the vaqueros, he would be falling down, piss-his-pants drunk. Oh, well, his wife always gave Wally a big, silver Mexican dollar for his mission of mercy. It was only worth about a dime American, but it felt nice in his pocket. When he neared the alley entrance, he heard the soft thuds and grunts that forewarned him that someone was in a fight. Wisely, Wally held back.

After what seemed forever to the boy, the noises ended, and Wally heard the thump of boot heels fading in the distance, toward the opposite end of the alley. He edged closer and risked a quick peek down the alley. Nothing. No, that wasn't right. He saw a darker lump in the blackness of the passageway. Wally watched for a long while, then hazarded to step into the opening. Five paces down the path, he came upon the huddled form of a body. Wally bent and rolled the man by his shoulder.

At once his eyes went wide. It was Sheriff Banner. A low groan escaped from bloodied lips. Wally did not need prompting to know what to do. He came upright and sprinted from the alley, then settled into a dead run toward the office of Doctor Walters.

Sixteen

Their wounded captives in tow, neither the better for wear and tear, Smoke Jensen and Santan Tossa cantered along the wide, well-defined road between Santa Fe and Taos. The sun, slightly over the median, warmed their backs and chewed away at the last of a low ground fog that had given dawn a hazy, closed-in quality. They would reach Española by mid-afternoon. With the prisoners off their hands, they could make even better time. Smoke wanted to meet soon with Sheriff Banner and Diego Alvarado. The encounter with Clifton Satterlee had awakened several questions. He felt certain the lawman and the rancher could provide answers. Always conscious of his back trail, Smoke cast another glance that direction as they crested a low swell.

Immediately, he saw dust where none had been before. His eyes narrowed in concentration. It could be two, three or even more riders. No doubt men sent by Satterlee or Quinn to carry out the threats of yesterday. Smoke turned back and made a gesture to Tossa.

"Behind us. We have company."

Santan Tossa's thoughts traveled the same trail. "You think they are men sent by Satterlee?"

"It wouldn't surprise me." Smoke thought a moment, eyes searching the surrounding terrain. "See that bend up there? I think we should wait for our friends around there, out of sight."

Tossa flashed a wide, white smile. "Who surprises who—er—whom?"

Smoke nodded and laughed. *A very bright young man, this Santan Tossa,* he thought. *He's improving his English by simple exposure.* "It's the best way to be in an ambush . . . be the ambushers."

The dust plumes had grown noticeably closer by the time Smoke and Santan rounded the curve in the road. Shielded by the swell of a sandy mound, they reined in and walked their mounts off the road to either side. In moments, the faint thud of hooves could be heard. Smoke slid his .45 Peacemaker from the right-hand holster. Santan readied his stout bow, a triangular, obsidian point bright in the midday sun. Closer now, the hoofbeats became a regular drum roll.

When the heads of the horses came into sight, the gunfighter and the Indian policeman made ready to fire. Immediately, Smoke Jensen checked himself. "Hold it!" he barked to Santan Tossa.

Much to his surprise, Smoke had recognized the pretty face of Martha Estes over his gun sights. His command had the effect of halting her as well. She blinked in astonishment at sight of the drawn weapons. Beside her rode her maid, a young Zuni woman, whose carriage indicated that she would be capable of taking care of the both of them. On her other side rode Ian MacGreggor.

Hand to her mouth, Martha reacted explosively. "Oh, I . . . you startled me, Mr. Jensen. This nice young man thought it might be you. We were trying to catch up."

"You caught us, all right. Well, Mac, what do you have to say for yourself?"

"I was riding out to meet you like we arranged. She came to the barn while I was saddling. Said she wanted to go with me. That's what delayed me."

Smoke gave Mac a sidelong squint "All night?"

"I couldn't get away last night. Ten of the gang rode out on Quinn's orders. From what I overheard, they were to find you and kill you. The watch was doubled all around the hacienda. As it was, she—the lady helped me leave this morning."

"Yes," Martha verified. "I told the men at the gate that he was accompanying me on my morning ride."

Smoke nodded to the maid. "What about her?"

"Lupe always comes with me, unless I'm riding with Clifton."

"Humm. You're here now, you might as well ride along."

Martha put a bite in her words. "You're too, too kind."

Smoke removed his hat in a sweeping gesture and bowed low. "My pleasure entirely, madam." Then to Mac, "Let's you and me ride up ahead and you can tell me this news you have."

Martha leaned forward in the saddle to press her case. "Let me make something clear, Mr. Jensen. I gave a lot of thought to what the two of you told me, and I've decided to leave Clifton Satterlee. There isn't any way he could have obtained that jewelry lawfully, is there?"

"Not that I can see."

"I only wish I could have taken the rest."

Smoke smiled fleetingly. "We know where it is. We can come for it later. And . . . you are a welcome sight."

"Thank you. And I mean it, this time."

Smoke and Mac trotted on ahead while Tossa escorted the women. Mac's jaunty expression changed as the distance between the parties widened. "Smoke, Quinn is bringing all of the gang north to Taos. Mr. Satterlee has ordered him to blockade the town until the people give in and turn over everything to him. Quinn will leave later today, and Satterlee will come along after. Wants to be there to gloat, I suppose."

A frown creased Jensen's high forehead. "That don't sound good. Any talk of burning down buildings, killing people?"

"No. From what some of the gang said, I believe that Satterlee wants it to look all legal and proper. At least on paper. There were a lot of really important people at a party I was sent there to bodyguard for. Everyone but the governor, and he did send a representative. When things started calming down, they all went inside for a meeting. They seemed mighty pleased to be in Satterlee's company. I got the feeling, when I heard about the siege at Taos, that if Satterlee had the papers all signed and in order, his friends in government would not ask any questions about how he went about getting folks to turn over their land and businesses."

Smoke nodded, well pleased. "You've got a good head on you, Mac. You'll not be able to go back now, of course. Just sort of stay out of sight when we reach Taos."

"Hey, I'm not worried. I can out-shoot near all of them. And, you'll need all the guns you can get on your side."

With a curt nod, Smoke sought to delay the inevitable. "We'll talk about it later."

Leaned back against rocks that reflected the heat of a hat-sized fire, Smoke Jensen listened while Martha Estes talked about her father. He was partners with Clifton Satterlee in a large firm that built houses back in the crowded East. Satterlee became involved because he had, or was going to get, large sources of timber. The lumber that came from the trees would be used to build houses. Some of them would be tenements, three or four stories, half a block deep, with limestone fronts.

Smoke didn't think there would be much of a demand for such expensive structures and said so. Martha informed him to the contrary. "Boats loaded with immigrants arrive at least three days of every week. Wealthy men will buy the tenements and rent apartments in them to the newcomers. With three or four to a floor, the profit will be enormous. The buyers won't mind paying twenty or thirty thousand for the buildings. Clifton—Mr. Satterlee and my father will keep ownership of the land and receive a percentage for the use of it."

Considering that, Smoke scratched at an earlobe. When he spoke, his voice reflected the mystery. "Something seems out of kilter about that, but I can't put my finger on it. It's sort of like having one's cake and eatin' it, too."

Martha's eyes shined. "Exactly. Any time Cliff—er—C.S. Enterprises wants to raise the percentage, they can. After all, the owners can't move their buildings off the ground." The image gave her a new thought. "That does sound a little crooked—no—unethical, doesn't it?"

"I liked your first choice of words. That's what bothered me before. Those rabbit hutches could be held up for ransom. And, from what I've gathered about Clifton Satterlee, he'd be likely to do it."

Martha gave him a puzzled look. "Is he really as awful as you make him sound?"

"Worse, no doubt, Miss Martha. I've just learned that he plans to force everyone out of Taos and take over the whole town for himself. That don't sound like someone who would refuse to squeeze the suckers who bought those houses."

"But, my father . . ." Martha started to protest when a muzzle flash bloomed brightly and a shot crashed out of the darkness.

Orin Lassiter smirked, unseen in the darkness. They'd had some difficulty finding the camp. The small fire, shielded all around by large boulders, gave off little light. He and the others had ridden through Española without finding the men they sought. Lassiter did learn that Jensen and the Indian had come through town about three in the afternoon. They now had three people with them. Two women and another man. One woman appeared to be that sweet thing the big boss was sporting with. How could that be? he asked himself.

Then he put that behind him when he remembered that two of the gang now languished in the jail at Española. He had immediately tried to see them. The sheriff had refused. Angry, he had stomped from the office to be given the only good news for the day. One of his men had informed him that they were only two hours behind their quarry. They had set out at once. Even so, it had taken them until two hours after full darkness to locate this place. The time of month favored them, Orin noted as he moved closer to the camp. The moon would not rise for at least four more hours. Conscious of the men to either side of him, he motioned them to greater silence when reflected firelight made their faces visible.

Then they were in position. Orin Lassiter raised his six-gun and fired at the figure of a man seated beside a woman at the base of a large, volcanic boulder. Dark, red-brown rock turned to powder six inches above the head of the man when the slug struck stone. Orin Lassiter watched as Smoke Jensen dived forward and took the woman with him. What he did not see, because it went too fast, was the big .45 Colt clear leather on the man's hip and snap in his direction.

He saw the muzzle bloom a split second before intense pain exploded in his left biceps as the bullet shattered his humerus. Dimly he was aware of the other boys opening up. The shock of his injury slowly numbed, and he remembered to move before another slug could find him. To his right, Baxter Young screamed horribly and clutched at a feathered shaft that protruded from his belly. Distantly, Orin heard the shouts as five of his men rushed the far side of the camp.

"Stay down," the man Orin Lassiter now believed to be Smoke Jensen shouted to the woman. A fraction of a second later, Jensen sprinted away from his exposed position by the fire.

Biting back his agony, Orin fired again.

* * *

"Stay down," Smoke Jensen commanded as he gave Martha Estes a shove on one shoulder. Before she could reply, he came to his boots and sprinted into the shadows away from the fire.

A revolver blasted from a few feet away, and suddenly another man loomed over her. Martha Estes looked up and stiffened when she recognized Orin Lassiter. He reached down to her. "Come on, you're going with me," he growled.

"No! Leave me alone."

Shock and pain ran through Martha as Lassiter slapped her with a solid, open palm. Her skin burned and tingled, and she could not prevent the sudden flow of tears that washed down her cheeks. Lassiter growled at her again. "Dry that up and do as I say."

Defeated, Martha raised a hand to be assisted upright. Automatically, Lassiter extended his left arm and immediately groaned at the new rush of agony. He spoke through gritted teeth as he holstered his six-gun. "Take my right arm."

She complied and hoisted herself to her high, black, narrow boots. At once, she heard the rustle of a full skirt that came from the darkness to her right. Lupe rushed at Lassiter with a knobby chunk of mesquite root held above her head with both hands. Hampered by Martha clinging to him, Lassiter could not completely dodge the blow. The hunk of wood slammed into his left shoulder, and he could not prevent the howl of agony that burst from his lips. Still aching, he pulled his good arm free of Martha's grasp and dropped the Indian woman with a hard right to the jaw.

Martha noticed the bloodstained shirtsleeve then, which evened the score somewhat for the slap. "He shot you— good."

Mustering his waning resources, Lassiter snarled at her. "Shut up, bitch."

Her courage nearly fully recovered, Martha risked a further taunt. "Or you'll what? Kill me? Clifton wouldn't like that."

Her barb found its mark, and Lassiter only grumbled under his breath as he dragged Martha off into the night. He found another of his henchmen and jerked his head in the direction of the camp. "Go get that Injun woman and bring her along."

A flurry of gunshots alerted him to the fierce resistance his other men had met, and Lassiter let go a shrill whistle. The signal was picked up by someone nearer the conflict and repeated. A third man echoed the call. Heeding the signal, the outlaws broke off their fight and faded into the darkness. Lassiter led the way to the horses and saw to securing Martha and Lupe on dead men's mounts. Then they rode off into the darkness.

Ian MacGreggor counted the muzzle flashes and made note of their positions. Then he raised his .44 Marlin and pumped a round toward the black smear to the right of one red-orange blossom. The burning gasses ceased. To his left he heard the twang of a bow string, followed by the hideous shriek of the target. An outlaw staggered into the firelight, his hands clawing at the wooden shaft of an arrow that had sunk deep into his upper right chest. The Tua bow sang again, and he went down with a shaft through his heart.

Three men tried to rush at that point, overconfident that no bowman could launch arrows quickly enough to hit them all. How quickly they forgot about him, Mac thought as he took aim and began to fire as rapidly as he could cycle the Marlin and take aim. Smoke Jensen's .45 Colt opened up from Mac's right, and another hard case left the earth. Then Mac heard a piercing whistle, repeated twice more close at hand, and the enemy fire ceased. Mac fired once more and then listened to the fading sound of boots thudding in retreat. It was all over. At least for now.

* * *

Yellow fingers of light reached through the second-floor window of the infirmary maintained by Dr. Adam Walters. They brushed invisibly on the eyelids of Sheriff Hank Banner. The lawman blinked and then abruptly opened his eyes. For the first moments everything registered as a blurred mass. Gradually individual objects came into focus. His head ached abominably. After three minutes of silent effort, he discovered that he could not see clearly out of his left eye. Only impressions of light and dark, all of it fuzzy. At last, he tried to move his arms.

A loud groan, brought on by that effort, summoned Dr. Walters from his office and treatment room. "What do we have here?" he asked with forced joviality.

His old friend and poker adversary looked like hell. His left eye was swollen nearly closed by a huge purple-yellow-green mouse. His left arm was immobile in a splint, in hopes the fracture would mend properly. Another device, created out of necessity by the good doctor, tried to give some semblance of the original shape to a broken—no, mashed would be more apt—nose. It consisted of rolls of cotton batting shoved into the nostrils, with court plaster holding in place two pieces of broken-off tongue depressor. A white sea of bandage held broken ribs immobile. Both lips were split, made three times normal size by puffiness. Without consciously thinking about it, Dr. Walters spoke his thoughts bluntly.

"You look like hell, Hank. How many of them were there?"

"Four I'm certain of. Maybe five."

"And I oughtta get a look at them, eh?"

Banner tried a grimace and flinched at the result. "Horse manure. Adam, they done tom turkey tromped the crap out of me."

Dr. Walters winced and spoke ruefully. "No kidding. I

had to get you out of your trousers to treat your injuries, so I know for a fact." A loud groan came from his patient. "Did I embarrass you? If so, I'm sorry."

"No, Doc, it's just your winning bedside manner. What brought that sorrowful noise on was that I just added up the score. It left me with one tail-biting question. What in hell's gonna happen to Taos with me bunged up like this. And, worse, with Smoke Jensen off sniffing around Clifton Satterlee? Those hard cases are going to be back, you can count on it, and who's to stop them from shuttin' down this town right permanent?"

From the bed opposite him came the voice of Pedro Alvarado. Pedro had come in to have the stitches and drain tube removed from his belly wound and stay for overnight observation. "My father will send as many vaqueros as you need."

"That's mighty kind of you, son. But the way I see it, they got us all outnumbered at least three to one."

"You just lie back and rest, Hank. I'll have my girl"—he referred to Dorothy Frye, his sometimes nurse and record keeper as *my girl*—"bring you some broth. Though with the shame your mouth is in, I reckon you'll have to take it through a pipette."

"You're so full of encouragement and good news, Adam."

"Thank you," Dr. Walters said with more humor than he felt. Pedro might be encouraging, but for the life of him, the doctor did not have an answer.

Kyle Curtis, one of the Sugarloaf hands, reined in and raised up on his stirrups. He waved a gloved hand to draw attention from the searchers close at hand. "They're over this way. I can see 'em down in a draw about two hundred yards below me."

At once, the rider closest to Kyle drew his six-gun and fired three fast rounds into the air to summon the remainder of the search party. Faintly he heard cries of alarm when the last shot echoed away among the mountain peaks. Fully a dozen ranch hands, drawn by the sound, closed in on the shooter. Kyle Curtis then pointed the way to the missing Gittings boys.

When the youngsters saw them coming, they were overjoyed. Then a terrible thought struck Seth. They had taken horses without permission, and then lost them when the cougar attacked. No doubt they would be in for it now. And a worse paddling it would be than one that came from their mother. The idea of having their britches yanked down in front of all those men humiliated and shamed Seth beyond anything so far in his young life. Then a black lance of pure, boyish hatred thrust through him.

He was there with them. Bobby Jensen. How he'd sneer and make life miserable for them from now on. He swallowed back his outrage and looked up at Ike Mitchell, who led the search party.

"How—how did you find us?"

"Easy," Ike informed him as he bent forward and down from the height of his sixteen-hand 'Palouse horse. "We just backtracked those horses that got away from you."

Seth's eyes widened when he recalled how they had lost their mounts. "It was a mountain lion. He come at us and scared off the horses."

Ike narrowed his eyes and rubbed at his chin. "Somehow I doubt that. If he had much interest in comin' at you, you would be in his belly 'fore now."

"Nope." Pride swelled Seth's shallow chest. "I shot him dead. One bullet, right in his ear."

Bobby Jensen chose that moment to erupt. "You're a liar as well as a thief, Seth."

Seth shot out his lower lip in a pout. "I didn' lie, an' I'm not a thief."

"You took my rifle and those Morgans without permission. That's stealin'. Horse thievin' is still a hanging offense out here in the High Lonesome. An' I brought along a good rope."

Real terror gripped both boys. His legs trembling, Seth dropped to his knees. Sammy flopped on his belly and bawled like a colicky baby. Seth turned to Ike Mitchell and beseeched him. "You can't do that. We're jist little kids. They don't hang children."

Bobby Jensen stung him with harsh words. "Like hell they don't. They tie a big sack of sand around your ankles so's to get the job done proper-like."

Ike had the last word. "Before we go back I want you two to show me this cougar. If it's like you say, I might put in a good word for you."

Face alabaster, the grime overlaying it became more pronounced as fat, salty tears began to stream down the face of Seth Gittings. Both brats had been thoroughly cowed by this revelation. All sign of rebellion was instantly banished. Heads hanging, they submitted without protest to riding behind two ranch hands, it being deemed that they did not deserve mounts of their own. Sammy cried and sniveled all the way back to the Sugarloaf. His butt made even more painful by the lack of support from stirrups, Seth regained some of his spitefulness.

He lost that quickly enough when the small party reined in outside the main house. Instead of rushing to them, wretched with worry over their disappearance, their mother remained in place on the porch, her face rigid with anger and affront. Slowly she raised an arm and commanded them.

"Come up here this instant."

Ike Mitchell dismounted and handed down the boys, one at a time. With dragging feet, they approached the steps to the porch. Mary-Beth Gittings gazed beyond them and met the eyes of Ike Mitchell. "We know that they took horses without permission, and that Seth, for some insane reason, took a rifle belonging to Sally's son. What else have they done?"

"They left the ranch, ma'am. By a good twelve miles. What I reckon is that they was fixin' to run away for good an' all. Now, about that rifle, ma'am. If they didn't have it along, they would have been cougar meat long before now. Before we started back here, I had them take me to where the cougar jumped them. He was there, all right. Dead with one shot to the brain. Seth, here, saved his brother's life and his own."

Sally's face remained fixed in stern disapproval. "But that does not excuse the terrible things they have done."

By then, Seth had preceded his little brother up to the second step. He gulped involuntarily when he looked up at her rigid features. His mother darted out one hand and closed her fingers tightly around his upper arm, so tightly he squealed from the pain it caused. Then she yanked him off his feet and stood him on the porch. She reached with the other hand for the willow switch Sally Jensen held, puffed down his pats and bent him over.

Seth got twenty-five lashes this time, and every one of them hurt more than he could stand. He was bawling by the fourth one, hoping to wring his mother's heart. He did not, and his humiliation grew greater when he heard some of the hands snigger.

Seventeen

Wally Gower took the reins of the horse ridden by Smoke Jensen. The moment the tall, rangy man stepped down from the saddle on Cougar, the boy piped up with the news he had been bursting to convey. "Did you hear that the sheriff got beaten up the other night?"

Smoke gazed down at the boy. "No, Wally—Wally is it?" The lad nodded and Smoke went on. "Tell me about it, Wally."

Wally went on to describe what he had seen of the attack, mainly the results. He concluded with an unhappy expression. "I didn't see any of them, so I can't say who it was. But Doc Walters and the sheriff say it was some of the Quinn gang."

"Where is the sheriff now?"

"Over at Doc's, Mr. Jensen."

"Then I suppose the thing to do is pay him a visit."

Wally trailed along, hopeful of being allowed inside. At the foot of the stairs, Smoke turned to him. "You'd best wait here, Wally. If the sheriff has any message for you, I'll bring it to you."

Disappointment clouded Wally's face. "Awh, I wanted to talk to him."

"Maybe later."

Up in the office, Dr. Walters took Smoke in to Sheriff Banner. The man looked terrible, Smoke noted at once. "You look like you've been run down by a buffalo stampede," Smoke advised the lawman.

Banner made a sour face as best he could. "I feel like it, too."

"Tell me what happened?"

"First off, that stray, Wally Gower, saved my life right enough. I sure want to see him and thank him in person."

Smoke grinned. "He's downstairs, waitin' on word on your condition."

Hank Banner actually managed a smile. "Bring him up, bring him up. That boy's got him a double eagle waitin' for what he did. He come here right away and brought Doc to me. Hell, we'd jist finished playin' poker half an hour before. Next thing I know, I'm wakin' up in this bed, hurtin' like damn all. But I know who did it. Recognized two of em." Then he went on to identify the men and describe the beating he took before he lost consciousness.

Smoke Jensen listened with growing anger while the sheriff outlined the boot stomp he had received. When the lawman finished, Smoke spoke softly. "I'll go get Wally now. I don't think he needed to hear what you just told me."

Wally nearly wept when he saw the condition of the sheriff. But he manly fought back the huge tears that welled in his gray-green eyes. "I'm sorry this happened to you, Sheriff. You're—you're the best man I know. *Please* get well."

"C'm'ere, Wally."

Obediently, Wally scuffed bare, callused soles across the wooden floor as he approached the bed. Hank Banner reached with his good hand and took a hinge-clasp leather purse from the table. He snapped it open and dug inside with thumb and forefinger. He withdrew a twenty-dollar gold piece.

"Here. This is yours. It's for saving my life."

Eyes huge with awe, the eleven-year-old gulped as he stammered out, "Twen—twenty dollars? I can't—can't take that much."

"You've got to, Wally. It's a reward. That's right, ain't it, Smoke? No one can refuse a reward."

Smoke reached out and tousled the lad's sandy brown hair. "That's right, Wally. Buy your mother a new dress with some of it, if you want."

"Really? I can do that? Oh, boy!"

Doc Walters cleared his throat. "Time's up, Wally. You'd best scoot on and do something like that. You're gettin' Sheriff Banner all exercised."

"Thank you, Sheriff. Thank you, thank you." With that, Wally scampered from the room and thundered down the outside staircase.

"Now, I have some news for you, Sheriff," Smoke Jensen announced.

"Give it."

"Don't tax him too much," warned the doctor.

Quickly Smoke related what he had learned from Mac and told the peace officer that he had proof Satterlee had the stolen Tua religious paraphernalia. Finally he added the abduction of Martha Estes. The sheriff digested it a moment, then spoke brusquely. "That does it, then. Smoke, considerin' the shape I'm in, I want you to become undersheriff. Take over for me. And, you can have a free hand dealing with Satterlee."

Smoke hesitated only a second. "I'll agree to it, Sheriff. Provided I can make Santan Tossa a deputy."

Distress displaced the pain etched on the lawman's face. "But, he's an Injun. Oh, I know, they've been peaceable for more'n a hundred years and the Pueblos are civilized and organized. But . . . he'd have to carry a gun."

"Have any of your deputies been effective against Quinn so far? Tossa has killed at least five of them, and with a bow and arrow."

Banner frowned. "You've got a point. If the governor gets wind of this, he'll have a fit. Armin' an Injun is serious business. There's some places it's still against the law to provide a firearm to any Injun."

"But not here, I gather?"

Banner nodded. "That's right. Okay, go ahead and fit him out from the rack in my office. Then I'll swear the both of you in."

"Not today you won't," Doc Walters interjected.

Banner scowled. "C'mon, Doc. I'm feelin' fitter every hour. If this town is gonna get besieged, we've gotta move fast."

Smoke agreed with that. "Just so. First thing, I'm going to send to Diego Alvarado for all the gunhands he can spare. Then, can you give me names of men in town who are loyal to the local government and willing to fight?" At the sheriff's nod, Smoke went on. "I think it would be a good idea for Tossa to try to recruit some help from among his tribal police."

Banner's good eye widened. "You really like to flirt with wrath from above, don't you, Smoke? All right, Smoke. You're undersheriff, so it's your ball game, as that feller Abner Doubleday would say. Now, you can start by askin' Ezekial Crowder, Marshal Gates, Warren Engals . . ." He went on to name two dozen more.

Sighing heavily, Sheriff Banner lay back on the bed as Smoke Jensen left the room. Within seconds he lapsed into a deep, though troubled, sleep. Even with help from the Tuas and Diego Alvarado, he knew Smoke faced a terrible dilemma.

A small drum tapped a staccato rhythm, and smoke rose from the square opening in the roof of the Tua kiva. Santan Tossa handed the reins of his pony to his younger brother, who looked up at the tribal policeman with an expression of hero worship. He climbed the single rail ladder and washed his hands and face before taking the descending steps to the floor of the religious center. He saw immediately that a dozen young men had gathered, seated on the circular, shelflike ledges that ringed the domed, circular structure. At the altar, sweet grass, pine needles and sage gave off their pleasant aroma as they smoldered on a small bed of coals.

Using an eagle-wing fan, the gray-haired shaman wafted the thin, gray tendrils of pungent smoke over the empty altar. Silently, Santan Tossa approached and kneeled before the medicine man. From his sash he produced the folds of velvet cloth and opened them.

"Grandfather, I have recovered one part of our stolen sacred heritage." Quickly he revealed the necklace.

For the first time since the theft, Whispering Leaves smiled. "You have done well, my son. Have you any idea where the . . ." Hope flared a moment in the old man's eyes. "The others might be?"

Torn nodded. "Yes. It is known to me."

"If he knows that, it is he who stole them," came the grating voice of Dohatsa from behind and to one side of Tossa.

Tossa whirled as he bounded to his moccasins. The muscles of his neck and arms corded. "You should guard your tongue, traitor."

Aware from childhood, as with all of them, that this was no place for anger or violence, Dohatsa did not respond to the challenge, merely shrugged and turned away. Inwardly, a striking sensation gripped his heart. Exactly how much did Santan know? He relaxed some as the soft words of the shaman came to his ears.

"This is not the place for hot hearts, Santan," he gently chided the younger man.

Santan Tossa lowered his eyes and nodded. "That is a true thing. I have come for another reason also." He turned to take in his fellow Tuas. "You all know of the gang of white outsiders who have tried to take our land. They work for a man named Satterlee. While I recovered the necklace from the house of Satterlee, I learned that the white gang is going to ring Taos, like the Spanish did our Pueblo in the first days of their coming. The gringos call it a siege. The purpose is to prevent anyone from entering or leaving, and to starve the people inside into surrender. The star man, the sheriff, has asked us for help. I am made a dep—u—ty of the star men. I want any who will join me to gather outside the kiva with their ponies. We must ride swiftly back to Taos."

His precarious situation forgotten in a flush of anger over this outrageous suggestion, Dohatsa snarled his challenge and contempt. "You are a fool, Santan Tossa. The white outsiders are using you. You will get no thanks from those people. And it is shameful that you ask we give any help to them."

"In other circumstances I would agree with you, Dohatsa. But this is different. These outlaw whites will only come here next. They want all the land, and they can take it if we do not fight."

Goaded by this, Dohatsa lost his composure and his reason. "You lie! Satterlee and his first warrior, Quinn, are our friends. I have spoken with them. To stop you, I will fight you."

Automatically, Santan Tossa's hand went to the unfamiliar butt of the six-gun at his hip. "Have you now? That is interesting. But, as Whispering Leaves says, this is no place for anger, or fighting. If I must fight you, I will. Wait for me outside this sacred place." He turned to the others. "Now, who will join me?"

Several among the young men of the Pueblo made as though to come over, among them three of his tribal policemen. They hesitated, though, at a scowl from Dohatsa, who had begun to climb the ladder to the outside. Santan Tossa turned back to the shaman.

"Be patient, and hopeful, Grandfather. I will soon bring the rest of the sacred objects. With enough men, the white outsiders can be defeated, and I can go with my friends to get the holy dolls and the masks."

"Yes, Santan Tossa, but which outsiders are the real enemy?"

Tossa paused at the foot of the ladder. "Why, the gang led by the one called Quinn, of course."

With a mocking smile almost identical to the one worn by Dohatsa, Whispering Leaves nodded once. Santan Tossa continued out of the kiva. In a steady line behind him, the other young men followed. Tossa found Dohatsa waiting for him on the ground below.

"I will kill you if I have to," Dohatsa stated flatly.

"It is forbidden, you know that."

Dohatsa shrugged. "It does not matter. Take off that white man's weapon."

"Naturally."

While the other occupants of the kiva formed a loose circle around them, more men and a number of small boys of the pueblo gathered to watch. Santan Tossa untied the pegging string of his holster and slipped the buckle. He let the six-gun drop as he instantly launched himself at Dohatsa. The renegade had expected that and easily side-stepped Tossa. Dohatsa drove an elbow into the small of Tossa's back smashing him to the ground, his strength robbed by the burst of pain in his kidneys. Some among the onlookers cheered. At once, Dohatsa whirled and kicked Tossa in the stomach. Renewed agony exploded in the tender parts of Tossa's body. He gasped for air and fought to get purchase.

Failing that, he scooped up a handful of dirt and hurled it in the face of Dohatsa.

"There is no honor in that," shouted two of Dohatsa's partisans.

Fire erupted behind the eyelids of the traitor, and he clawed at his face. Tossa fought back the debilitating effects of the blows he had absorbed and came unsteadily upright. He took two shaky steps forward and engulfed Dohatsa in a bear hug. Flexing his knees, Tossa tried to throw his opponent.

Heavier by far, Dohatsa did not move at first. Then, slowly, his moccasins rose into the air. Tossa swiveled his hips and threw his enemy to the ground. Dohatsa did not land flat. He hit his head first and his shoulders next as Tossa landed on top of him. Now Tossa dimly heard men cheering him. A spectacular nighttime shower of stars filled Dohatsa's head. He fought to suck air into his restricted lungs. When his chest moved, he dimly heard the brittle snap of three ribs. Fiery torment seared his chest cavity. Tossa had greater strength than he had expected. If he did not break this soon, he would not fight on this day, let alone win. As though from a distance, he commanded his legs to rise.

When the soles of his moccasins rested flat on the ground, he flexed powerful thighs and heaved upward. Although the burden of weight upon him shot up into the air, Dohatsa failed to dislodge Tossa. When the wiry young tribal policeman came down, he buried one knee in the slightly paunchy gut of Dohatsa.

Sour bile and the remains of his morning meal erupted from Dohatsa's mouth, preceded by a heavy gust of air. His head swam and his limbs went slack. In desperation, Dohatsa rallied his flagging resources and went for the knife in his bright orange sash. When it came free, he made a swift slash at Tossa.

Nimbly, the young Tua avoided the blade and sprang to his feet. A quick kick sent the knife spinning brightly in the sunlight. Then Tossa had the arm pinned. He rolled the offending hand of Dohatsa over, palm down, and stamped on it with a moccasined foot until he heard bones crack. Howling, Dohatsa doubled up, nursing his injured extremity. Tossa stepped behind him and knelt. He took a large hank of black hair and yanked back the head of his enemy.

"I could, I should, cut your throat. Instead, what I want

from you is the truth. Tell me all about our stolen sacred articles."

Dohatsa surrendered all of his arrogance, along with his resistance. He had been in the pay of Satterlee for nearly a month. He knew that his confession would mean certain exile, if not death, under tribal law. Shamefacedly, he turned his head to look at the man who had bested him. "What you accused me of before is true. I have taken money from the white outsiders, Satterlee and Quinn, for a moon now. It is I who stole the religious objects and gave them to Quinn. What he did with them I do not know."

Disgust at such betrayal twisted the face of Santan Tossa. He came upright and turned to address the gathering of Tua men. "You heard what this disgraced one said. Confine him somewhere until the Council can attend to his crimes. Now, who will join me? Come, it is a thing of honor. Without the help of the white lawman I would never have found the necklace."

Two young Tua men stepped forward. Three more joined them. Then half a dozen. One spoke for the others. "If you will have us, Santan Tossa, we will fight with you for the white men."

Before he left for Taos, Santan Tossa had acquired a force of twenty-eight.

Shortly before nightfall, Deputy Sheriff Sammy Jennings cantered up to the *case grande* at Rancho de la Gloria. The major domo greeted him politely and hailed a boy to lead the lathered horse to the stableyard, to be cooled out, watered and rubbed down. He showed the lawman into the central courtyard.

Don Diego Alvarado sat there, on a white-painted, wrought-iron bench, smoking a cigar. He roused himself to welcome his visitor. Jennings made it short and to the point.

"I've come from Smoke Jensen, Don Diego. He is undersheriff in Taos now."

Jennings, an uncomplicated man, missed the sardonic note of irony in the grandee's chuckle and words. "My friend Smoke is coming up in the world. I gather that there is something of importance that I should know?"

"Yes, sir. Smoke sent me to tell you that the Quinn gang intends to lay siege to Taos. Shut off the town and starve out the occupants. He asks that if it is possible you send as many vaqueros as you can."

"I can fill forty saddles within the hour. Will that do?"

Jennings swallowed hard. "Oh, Lordy, sure. Fine as frog's hair, señor."

"Excellent." He raised his voice and called to his eldest son. "Alejandro! Come out here and round up the vaqueros. I want forty of the best."

Alejandro appeared in a doorway of a room on the second floor. "What is it, Father? Have the rustlers returned?"

"No. We ride to Taos. Smoke Jensen has need of our firepower." He turned back to his visitor. "As I say, this will take an hour. You must be in need of refreshment. Come, I'll have Maria prepare food and get you something to drink." Steering the young deputy toward the doorway to the detached kitchen, Don Diego shouted ahead to his cook to fix some meat and cheese and tortillas. Also to have Pepe bring up three beers from the spring house.

After sending off his last messenger, Smoke Jensen settled down in the sheriff's office to a plate of beef stew from the corner eatery. This being Taos, the stew had potatoes right enough, but with tomatoes, onions, garlic and chile peppers instead of turnips, carrots and garden peas. The gravy was rich and thick, which he scooped up with folded flour tortillas. A soupy bowl of beans came with it, and a side dish of some mashed, yellow-green substance. Guaca-

mole, he had been told. Avocado, Wally Gower had informed
him. Again with the ever-present tomato, garlic, onion and
chiles. It had been flavored with some pungent, green herb
and it tasted delightful. Smoke had just finished wrapping
his lips around another bite of it when a loud crash and the
sound of breaking glass summoned him from the office.
From the knot of excited onlookers in the street, he learned
the disturbance came from La Merced, one of the more unsavory saloons in town.

Smoke headed that way at once. He had to shove his way
through a cluster of brown-faced spectators who crowded
the boardwalk and entranceway. Three steps led to a grime-
coated tile floor. Again, Smoke had to grab shoulders and
heave men out of the way. This time, he noted that the faces
wore expressions of anxiety and concern. He soon learned
the reason.

A quartet of white thugs worked systematically at breaking up the place. Their erstwhile leader snarled at the bartender, who cringed in the far corner of the back bar. "You
damn greasers like to have poisoned two of my men last
night. We're takin' over this town, so you might as well get
an idea of what happens to folks who put funny powders in
drinks for the Quinn gang. You understand? *¿Comprende?*"

Bobbing his head frantically, the barkeep, who knew not
the least word of English, and could not understand a thing
being growled at him, covered his eyes as a wrought-iron
legged chair went hurtling toward the mirror behind the bar.
The big plate of glass shattered into a million shards on
impact. The complaining hard case yanked a jug-eared,
slightly built fellow from his chair and flung him after. Two
of his henchmen turned to check out the disturbance between them and the doorway. In the next instant, Smoke
came face-to-face with them. Neither ruffian suffered from
being slow. As one, they balled fists, and the nearer one drove
a hard-knuckled hand toward the face of Smoke Jensen.

Eighteen

Smoke Jensen jerked his head to one side and let the fist whistle past. Then he brought one up from the cellar that connected with the brute's jaw. Teeth clopped shut, and the yellowish whites of his eyes showed as his pupils rolled upward. Smoke closed in and gave him two hard shots to the heart for good measure. Then he felt a sharp jolt as the second thug caught him in the gut. Smoke took a back step and braced himself.

At once, the brawler came on. Smoke let him get in close. Then he flexed his knees, fired his best right cross and put shoulder and hips into it. The outlaw's boots left the floor. Squalling like a cinch-galled horse, he pitched face first across a nearby table. The legs broke and went four directions, as did the stacks of coins and bills. By that time, the first one to assault Smoke had recovered himself enough to launch another attack.

He came in low, intent on taking Smoke off his feet. Smoke stood his ground and, at the last instant, smartly raised his right knee. Face met knee and the face lost. Blood flew in a shower from a mashed nose. Three teeth snapped loudly, and more crimson ribbons streamed from the damaged mouth. The legs stopped churning and the eyes gradually crossed. The would-be tough dropped two feet in front of Smoke Jensen. Which left the other assailant to tend to.

Smoke turned to face him as the member of the Quinn gang put himself back on his boots. He had lost his cocksure smirk. His eyes glazed, he took an unsteady step toward Smoke Jensen. Blindly, he tripped over the broken table and sprawled again on the green baize. One of the men, who'd had his game disrupted and his winnings scattered, boxed the outlaw's ears. Which got him up right smartly. He spat a curse at Smoke Jensen and came on.

Smoke snapped a right-left combination to the head, then lowered his point of aim to work on the chest and gut. His elbows churned back and forth while he delivered short, punishing blows. When the ruffian's guard disappeared entirely, Smoke took a quick back step and launched a solid left jab that rocked his opponent to the toes. He spun half left and shuddered while still erect. Then he wilted like a stalk of grass before a prairie fire and thudded on the floor. Seeing the pair so hastily dispatched, the leader and his remaining henchman went for their guns.

Smoke did not even change stance. His right arm already across his body for counter balance, he simply grabbed at the butt of his second Colt and hauled it from the horizontal leather. He snapped back the hammer and tripped the trigger. By that time, and much to his later regret, the subordinate section leader of the gang had cleared leather. He had not, however, leveled his weapon when a hot poker jabbed him in the belly and his six-gun discharged into the floor. Beside him he heard his underling utter a boast he knew could not be fulfilled.

"I got him! I got him—got him!"

What he *got* was the center of the forehead of a big black bull that hung on the wall behind Smoke Jensen, as the bullet of the last mountain man smacked into his chest and burst his heart. Smoke crossed the short space between him and the dying man and kicked the Colt from his grasp. Then he turned on the gut-shot leader.

Plucking the Merwin and Hulbert from his numb fingers, Smoke observed, "You won't survive that. So, I'll let you go. I have a message for Paddy Quinn. Tell him to keep the hell away from town or I'll bring down a fire storm of hurt on him."

Gasping, the hard case observed, "You've got a mouth on you. Who are you?"

"Smoke Jensen."

"Awh . . . shit, shit, shit." With that, he passed out.

Smoke turned to the customers. "Will four of you bring those two to the jail. *La carcel, ¿comprende?*"

Volunteers nodded their heads eagerly. They roughly grabbed up the unconscious hard cases and dragged them from the saloon. Smoke faced the bartender. "Whatever money you find on those two, I'll add what I get from the others to help offset damages."

One vaquero at the bar translated. It brought a beaming smile from the worried brow. Smoke had earned his gratitude.

On a small mesa to the west of town, Whitewater Paddy Quinn listened to the sound of gunfire in Taos. All of his section leaders sat horses around him. All except Slim Vickers and three of his henchmen. From what he had learned from one of the seven who did report on time, Slim had remained behind to teach a lesson to some greasers who had poisoned some of them the previous night. Now, hearing the gunfire, Paddy Quinn beckoned to one of the hard cases who waited farther away with many of the gang. The man walked his horse up.

"What do you want, boss?"

"Baker, tell me about this poisoning, will ye?"

Baker looked embarrassed. "Awh, well, boss, it wasn't poison for real. Jist some green beer. It was right skunkey. Bunch of us wound up squirting through the eye of a needle at ten paces. Two of the boys got sick. Threw up over everything."

"Where did this happen?"

Baker frowned. "Some place called La Merced. Don't know what it means."

Paddy gave him a patronizing smile. "It means, 'the mercy.' Though I don't reckon ye got much mercy from them, eh, bucko?"

"That's right, boss."

"Sure an' what did Slim have in mind to do about it?"

Surprised that Quinn would take it further, Baker blinked. "Uh—well, ah, he and three of the boys was gonna go back and bust up the place. Kick some greaser butt."

"He say anything about shootin' them?"

That set Baker back. "Uh—no. Jist wanted to cause some damage."

Quinn's face went hard, his eyes narrowed and he gazed at the distant town. "Then it's that damned Smoke Jensen doin' the shootin'. An' I've no doubt that the boys will not be comin' back I don't."

"Rider comin'," called out one of the outlaws.

Slim Vickers came on slowly, slumped in his saddle, one arm supporting him on the neck of his horse. When he drew nearer, Quinn saw that the man's face had turned a ghostly white. A green tinge surrounded his mouth. Then he saw the red stain on Slim's belly.

"Awh, saints above. What's happened to ye, darlin' boy? Where's the rest of the boys?"

"Two's in jail. One's dead. An' Smoke Jensen has done killed me." With that he fell off his horse and into eternity.

"Awh, damn Jensen's black heart." Quinn threw up his hands. "Nothin' for it, then. We'll be leavin' now, we will. Spread out, boys. An' hold back until the rest of the lads arrive. When they do, we'll be takin' our positions. This time it will be a regular siege," he told them. "Ye have your assignments. Ye are to pursue them and show no quarter."

Merchants and townsmen alike turned out to not be so hot for the prospects of standing off a siege. Feeding all of the volunteers became a problem long before Don Diego

Alvarado and his vaqueros reached town. Several other ranchers had brought cowboys in to supplement the defenses. The opposition became even more vociferous when the new undersheriff strode through town with a bundle of posters, which he attached to the door of every cantina and saloon.

"What's the meaning of this?" one unhappy saloon owner demanded. "You can't take the opportunity away from us to make a nice profit."

Smoke Jensen stared at him with disdain. "The last thing we need is a lot of boozed-up men with guns on their hips. We won't have time to round up drunks when Quinn and his gang get here. The flyers mean exactly what they say. You will restrict yourselves to the sale of beer only. Any violators will have their establishments locked and spend the duration in jail. It would be a good idea to limit your customers' intake, also. I've known men to get fallin' down drunk on good, strong beer."

Bristling, the owner offered defiance. "You ain't no dictator. What if we refuse?"

Smoke snorted. "Are you volunteering to be the first to get locked up?"

Short and stout, with the flabby muscles of a man unaccustomed to hard work, the bar owner gauged the look in the eyes of Smoke Jensen and rightly read his expression. "Well—ah—well, no. I reckon I'll do what you say, but I don't have to like it."

"No, you don't." Smoke moved on.

When that task had been completed, Smoke had to hurry to the town hall for a meeting he had scheduled with the women of the community and the restaurant owners. In the public meeting room, Smoke stepped to the lectern and addressed the gathering.

"Ladies, we have a good fifty outsiders in town. None of them have the facilities to feed themselves. And there will be more coming. I have been assured that the eating places in town cannot handle the increase except on a continuous operation basis. What we need to do is set up a cookhouse here at city hall. I'm asking for volunteers to cook and serve."

Abigail Crowder, wife of the Taos fire chief, raised her hand. When Smoke recognized her, she stood to ask her question. "Where will we get the food?"

"I have spoken with Mr. Hubbard at the general store. The city will purchase all supplies from him. There will be no charge for the meals. If you give of your time, it won't empty the city treasury, what there is of it."

Another woman stood. "How long will this go on?"

Smoke frowned, scratched at his jaw. "Hard to say. At least two or three days. The mayor and I have sent a message to Santa Fe. We're asking the governor to call out the militia. But, politicians move slowly. Troops under arms move even slower. We'll be on our own for a goodly while."

She had another question. "Will there be enough to eat?"

Smoke nodded reassurance. "I reckon so. For the volunteer fighting men, I suggest you concentrate on fixin' what there's the most of. Such as corn bread, biscuits, potatoes, rice and beans. Hubbard has dozens of barrels of those. Plenty of pickles, too. If you can come up with some chickens from home, it would help. Now, if you'll step over here, Mr. Dougherty, the town clerk, will sign you up, put down the times of day you want to work."

Small columns of outlaws streamed down off the mesa. They spread out, and those tasked to the detail made ready to close off the roads. Others waited two miles from Taos to set up roving patrols to prevent anyone from sneaking out of town from houses on the outskirts. What Paddy Quinn did not know would soon prove to have fateful consequences for his plans.

Less than ten minutes earlier, twenty-five young Tua warriors, with Santan Tossa in the lead, had ridden into Taos and assembled outside the sheriff's office. Their faces were set, emotionless, the stereotypical Indian visage. At the direction of their tribal police chief, they filed into the office and came out with far more animated expressions. Each of them clutched a rifle or a shotgun. Faces of horror flashed through the Mexican and white residents of Taos when they saw this. Enough so that Santan Tossa went inside and spoke briefly with Smoke Jensen.

Smoke came outside and went among the troubled citizens of Taos. He spoke briefly and earnestly to small groups. "They are here to fight Quinn's gang. They can't do that with bows and arrows. If more of you had volunteered, it would not be necessary."

One indignant, pudgy man in a banker's suit protested hotly. "It's not our fault. You can't blame us. We're not lawmen. It's your job to protect us."

Such whining complaints quickly wore thin Smoke's sparse layer of patience. After the third such outpouring of whining self-justification, he snapped hotly. "And if you had the brains of a gnat, you'd realize that is exactly what I am doing."

"The governor will hear of this," a voice warned darkly. The banker had slunk back to launch another feeble barb.

Smoke laughed in the man's face. "Not until you can get out of town, he won't."

Diego Alvarado, along with two of his sons, Alejandro and Miguel, at the head of thirty-eight vaqueros, thundered up the long slope from the high desert flats where Rancho de la Gloria was located. All of the cowboys had heavily armed themselves. Twin bandoliers of rifle cartridges crisscrossed their chests. Obrigon .45s rode high in holsters on their belts.

Eight of their number cast frequent, nervous glances at

their saddlebags, which had been packed full of crudely made grenades. The hand-thrown bombs were made of wine and tequila bottles, tightly packed with black powder and horseshoe nails, then fused and stoppered. The prospect of using them excited some of the more reckless among the vengeance-hungry vaqueros. Ahead waited the men who had murdered their *compañeros* and stolen their pride when they had stolen the cattle they tended. This would be a day for *El Degüello*. No quarter would be given. In the heads of some of the older ones echoed the brassy refrain of the "Cutthroat Song," which their grandfathers had played outside the defiant walls of the Alamo. That these ladrones they rode to fight were gringos only sweetened the revenge. Five miles from Taos, Diego Alvarado signaled a halt.

"Alejandro, Miguel, here is where we will divide into three groups. Miguel, you will take ten men and ride directly down the road to town. Alejandro, take fourteen and circle a short way to the north. Not more than half a mile, mind. I will take the rest and go to the south. When Miguel and his men open fire, we will sweep down on the bandido scum and kill them all."

Alejandro and Miguel made their selections and drew the men apart. After signaling to their father, Diego stood in his stirrups and waved a gloved hand over his head. *"¡Adelante, muchachos!"*

With an enthusiastic, shouted cheer of encouragement, the indomitable company of vaqueros thundered off to bring the force of destiny to the unsuspecting outlaws.

Three members of the city council came bustling into the sheriff's office while Smoke Jensen was spooning a plateful of beans into his mouth. From the fiery flavor, Smoke judged that the women cooks had found a ready and willing source of chile peppers among the Mexican households. A florid-faced man in a brown suit and matching derby hat spoke for the politicians.

"What is this we hear that you have actually armed the Indians?"

Smoke chewed and swallowed his most recent mouthful and gestured with the spoon. "Yes, I have."

"Why, that's outrageous. And, it is totally unacceptable."

Smoke shook his head. "No, it's not. Think about it, gentlemen."

Agitation darkening the rosy color of his face, the spokesman yapped at Smoke. "We *have* thought about it. We do not intend to be massacred in our beds or our own homes. We demand—"

Smoke raised a hand to silence him. "Let me acquaint you with some very real, although unpleasant facts of life. When the gang and its hangers-on get here, Paddy Quinn will have between forty-five and seventy highly capable gunfighters at his command. The Tua warriors have come here and are willing to defend your town for you. They can hardly do so against such odds with weapons out of the Stone Age. The mayor agreed with me that we should properly arm them, and that has been done."

"Why were we not consulted about this?"

Smoke Jensen smiled coldly. "To save time. Politicians, from the White House on down, believe that they can talk troubles to death. We could be arguing over arming the Tuas until winter came."

The councilman cut his eyes to his associates and fired his last barb. "Banker Elwell tells us that you refused to notify the governor."

Smoke lowered his gaze a moment. "I—ah—stretched the truth a little when I spoke with the banker. In the letter requesting the militia, I informed the governor of our decision. The mayor assured me it was all right to arm the Indians for—how does the territorial constitution put it?—'the purpose of hunting game and for the defense of the common good.' "

Defeated, and hating it, the spokesman snapped at Smoke. "For a man with so low an opinion of politicians, you can sure quote law like one."

Grinning, Smoke affected to preen himself. "A man of many talents, wouldn't you say?"

Shocked at this effrontery, the senior councilman's eyes bulged. "Well, I never!"

"Nope. Reckon you haven't."

Smoke's mockery sent them to the door. Heads held high in indignation, the delegation had only reached the porch when they collided with Wally Gower and three other town moppets of about his age, who surged past them, into the office. "They're comin', Sheriff Jensen. The Quinn gang's closin' in on town. It looks like there's enough of them, they're gonna ring the whole place."

Nineteen

When the news the boys carried got out, it quickly changed a lot of minds. First to scurry into the sheriff's office was the banker, Elwell. "You're the undersheriff. Do something," he bleated. "We need all of the protection we can get."

Smoke Jensen could not resist a final tweak of this whining hypocrite. "You've changed your mind about arming the Tuas with modern weapons?"

"Yes—yes, anything. Just save us from those vandals out there."

"Well, then, I'd suggest you go home, get your rifle, and help us."

Elwell eyed him with suspicion. "Sheriff Jensen, I've not fired a rifle in years."

Smoke gave him a grin. "It's like ridin' a horse, Elwell. You never forget." To Santan Tossa he suggested, "Let's go out and take a look at the new arrivals."

What they found, as they made their rounds, stunned even the usually unflappable Smoke Jensen. Instead of the expected forty-five to seventy outlaws, Smoke counted fully two hundred border trash, drifters and genuine hard cases spread out around the town. All of them seemed to be cold, grim-faced, hardened killers. Smoke turned to a deputy who stood nearby nervously fingering his Winchester.

"Hardly what we counted on, is it? I want you to go back into town and get those volunteers to speed up filling sandbags. Tell them I want stacks built to line the outer walls of all wooden buildings to the height of a kneeling man. Then come back here and take charge."

The lawman gulped and broke his fixed stare at the outlaws. "Right away, Sheriff." Grateful to be away from there, if only for a few minutes, he hurried off.

Then Smoke advised Tossa and all the men within hearing, "Now all we have to do is wait and find out what the enemy has in mind."

Back at the Sugarloaf, Mary-Beth Gittings worked industriously to load the valises they had brought into the fancy carriage. Her sons, red-eyed from yet another switching, dragged their own packed luggage from the house. Her face drawn, and tight-lipped, she remained ominously silent as she walked past Sally Jensen, who stood on the porch and watched. Sally's face revealed a poorly restrained expression of pleasure.

When the last piece had been loaded, Mary-Beth advanced on Sally, fists on hips, her face a study in self-righteous indignation. Her cheeks burned, not only with her umbrage, but from humiliation. She had allowed this woman to dictate to her how she should deal with the minor infractions her darling children committed. She was the first to admit they were not perfect. All children did naughty things from time to time. But to *spank* them? To viciously punish and degrade them—and one's self—in such a barbaric fashion? It would have never occurred to her that when on another person's property, and under their roof, one should abide by their rules. She should have never listened to Sally, her angry thoughts continued. Especially after she learned what she knew now.

It had come out only an hour ago, while she once again reluctantly put the switch to the boys up in the room they shared. Wailing in hurt and fright, their bottoms a cherry red, they had sobbed out how that monstrous creature had threatened their lives. Horrified, Mary-Beth had decided on the spot to leave. Now she let all her outrage boil out.

With a visible effort, she restrained most of her dudgeon as she addressed her hostess for the final time. "I never believed that such a dear old friend would be so shamelessly protective of such an ill-bred child."

Her patience exhausted, Sally glowered back. "What is it this time, Mary-Beth?"

Mary-Beth let it spill out. "Why, it is about murder. My precious sons revealed to me not an hour ago that Bobby threatened to hang Seth and Sammy when they ran away."

That banished the last of Sally's sense of obligation. "Mary-Beth, don't you recall that after all they had stolen horses. Horse thieves are hanged out here."

Sally might as well have smacked Mary-Beth in the middle of her forehead. Shock silenced her to a small squeak. Then she hoisted her skirts and turned away. Briskly she walked to the carriage and boarded the driver's seat. She picked up the reins and snapped them. Without a farewell or a backward look, she and her troublesome children rolled down the long lane. At the last moment, only Billy Gittings turned back and gave a friendly, forlorn wave to Bobby Jensen.

Soberly, Bobby returned the gesture. The next instant, Sally and Bobby fell into one another's arms in relief and joy. "They're gone. They're finally gone," Sally shouted happily.

For the defenders of Taos, the wait to see what Quinn had in mind proved a long one. Both sides restlessly eyed one another from across the separating distance. Tenseness increased among the besiegers when the faint drumming of many horses came from the southwest. Paddy Quinn and a dozen of his immediate subordinates lingered on the far side of a bridge that spanned a narrow creek in a deep, red rock gorge. They conversed quietly there with the men assigned to operate the roadblock. It was toward them that a party of eleven men, dressed as vaqueros, cantered in mid-afternoon.

Quinn trotted forward a few lengths and raised a hand in a gesture to halt. "Turn back. No one enters town without our leave."

Several seconds went by before their identity became clear to Quinn. Then he shouted over his shoulder. "B'God, it's that Diego Alvarado's outfit. Turn about, boys, an' give 'em hell."

Miguel and the vaqueros had anticipated that. At once their weapons blasted in a volley. They fired again, and three of the outlaws left their saddles. Paddy Quinn barely escaped with his life. Bullets cracked past his head, and one grazed the shoulder of his mount. He turned first left, then right, only to see a swarm of more cowboys appear on both sides of the road. Determined to salvage what he could of his subordinate leaders and the men, he put spurs to his horse as he shouted to his underlings.

"Follow me! It ain't worth it; let 'em in." Then he cut off at an oblique angle between the hostile forces.

At once, the vaqueros converged on the road and cantered into town in a column three wide. Diego and Alejandro waited at the side until the last of the cowboys got through. He halted six of them.

"Stay here and keep the road open," Diego commanded.

One of the younger vaqueros looked nervously over his shoulder. "Sí, patron. But you saw what they did when we rode in. There are so many of them."

Diego nodded. "They cannot all come against you. They are here to close the town. When some of them come back, use your rifles. Keep them at a distance."

With that Diego rode on into town. He stopped at the sheriff's office and was greeted by Smoke Jensen. "It's good you're here, Diego. How many men did you bring?"

"Thirty-eight, and two of my sons."

Smoke laughed and wrung Diego's hand. "Make that three. Pedro insists he is healed enough to take part. He wants a rifle."

Diego nodded his understanding. Then he asked the question foremost on his mind, "How many of them are there?"

"By my count, close to two hundred."

Diego frowned. "That is a formidable force."

A smile bloomed on Smoke's face. "We have nearly as many, thanks to you and our Tua friends. Come, I'll show you how we're set up."

Smoke Jensen set off on a tour of town, explaining the defenses to Diego Alvarado. They had covered two sides of town when a flurry of gunshots broke out.

Being run off from the barricade rankled some of the gang. A dozen of the outlaws on the east side received a blistering lecture from their section leader on holding their place at all costs. Being of the criminal class, they saw any orders, especially those couched as criticism, as an affront. It made them restless, and eventually their patience wore out.

One hothead gave his opinion. "I say we can take that town full of sissies just by ourselves."

Another slightly more intelligent one disagreed. "Those Mezkin cowboys are in there now."

"Don't matter. Mezkins is dumb like Injuns. They think it's the noise that knocks a man down, so they don't aim."

A third piece of trash had news that slowed them for a while. "These must; they done knocked two of the boys outten their saddles."

"Lucky shots," the first insisted. He kept on for another ten minutes, until he had them all convinced.

They trotted their horses to the east road and passed through the blockaders without restraint. Then the reckless hard cases spurred their mounts to a gallop and, with six-

guns out and ready, rode like a whirlwind into Taos. They
met immediate opposition. A hail of lead came from the
second-floor windows in buildings near the center of town.
Rifle fire, they soon learned to their regret. Two of the frontier trash left their perches and sprawled in the dirt of the
street. A third gritted teeth and clapped a hand to a hole in
his shoulder.

From closer at hand, more guns sought out the survivors.
Bullets clipped through the air around them. For all that the
defenders had been instructed to take good aim, the fact
remained that there was more air out there than meat. Nine
of the outlaws managed to reach the Plaza de Armas, which
they proceeded to ride around, firing into the building fronts.
They had made half the circuit when Smoke Jensen and
Diego Alvarado arrived on the scene. The situation changed
abruptly.

"That shooting is coming from the Plaza." Diego Alvarado announced something that Smoke Jensen already
knew.

"We'd best get there the fastest way," the last mountain
man opined.

Diego pointed to an alley that cut through several blocks
at a sharp angle "Take this *callejón.*"

They set out at a fast trot, both men with six-guns in
hand. At the far end, Smoke could now see the fountain in
the center of the square. A horseman obscured his view a
moment as he rode by in the Plaza de Armas, firing into
buildings as he went. Another followed, then another. One
block to go. Smoke held his fire as another of the Quinn
gang—he figured it could be none other—rode by the alley
mouth. In another three seconds they came out into the open.

"Here's a couple of 'em," a strange voice brayed from
behind Smoke Jensen.

He crouched and whirled in the same move. The Colt in

his right hand bucked, and the outlaw who had called to his friends took a bullet in the right side of his chest. To Smoke's other side, the Obrigon in the hand of Diego Alvarado belched flame, and a .45 slug struck another bandit in the gut. His eyes bulged, but he kept coming. The odd, foreign-looking revolver—the barrel, cylinder and frame had not been blued—in his hand raised to line up on the chest of Diego Alvarado.

Diego fired again and put his bullet in the brain of the man with the 11mm Mle. '74 Saint Etienne, French-made six-gun. He died before the shock of his first wound faded. The heavy, soft-gray steel weapon fell from his hand. Immediately more of the outlaws came at them. By then, a scattering of defenders had reacted to the sudden appearance of the enemy. The volume of fire raining on the intruders grew rapidly. It soon had an effect.

Three more went down, and Smoke Jensen found himself nearly run over by a riderless horse. He jumped to one side, tripped over the body of a hard case, and fell to the red tile walkway around the base of the fountain.

"I've got you now," a triumphant voice shouted from above Smoke.

Instantly, Smoke Jensen rolled to his left and brought up his Peacemaker. He fired the moment he saw a human form. By the sheer perversity of chance, the slug struck the front of the outlaw's revolver cylinder. The thug screamed and dropped his now useless weapon while Smoke rolled again. This time, Smoke took better aim.

"Dutch!" the dying man screamed, in spite of the hole in his throat. "He got me, Dutch. Did me good." Then he groaned softly and fell across the neck of his mount. The frightened horse carried the corpse away from the plaza.

Smoke rounded the base of the fountain, forced to dodge bullets from both sides. Inexorably the numbers mounted. Suddenly Dutch Volker found himself and only two others cursing and firing defiantly at the defenders. He opened his

mouth and bellowed loudly enough to carry above the tumult
of gunfire.

"Get out of here! We're all that's left."

Swiftly, they clattered away through a low screen of powder smoke. Diego Alvarado, his face grimed with black
smudges, walked over to where Smoke Jensen stood with
the loading gate of his .45 Colt open for reloading. "If they
are all as stupid as those were, we should have an easy time,
¿no, amigo?"

Smoke gazed at the litter of the dead. "I wouldn't count
on it."

Soft shafts of yellow lanced through the wrought-iron
barred windows set high in the outer wall of the second-floor
master bedroom. This side of the Satterlee hacienda outside
Santa Fe faced the south. It provided a slight, though no-
ticeable, temperature advantage during the winter months.
Clifton Satterlee selected articles of clothing from a large
armoire, which he handed to an Indian woman servant, who
diligently folded and packed them into a large carpetbag.

Satterlee spoke aloud to himself as he decided on his
wardrobe. "I think something elegant, perhaps a morning
coat. For the formal capitulation of Taos nothing less would
do." A soft rap sounded on the open door, and he looked
up.

His major domo stood there, a sparkle of expectation in
his ebony eyes. "A rider just in from Taos, señor."

The expression on the face of Satterlee reflected that of
his servant. "Show him up."

In two minutes the official greeter of the house returned
with a smiling Yank Hastings. The young outlaw did not
dwell on formalities. "Ever'thing's goin' fine, Mr. Satterlee.
Paddy Quinn says there's no need for you to hurry up there.
We'll have 'em flushed out by tomorrow morning. That's
his guarantee."

Satterlee stretched his thin lips to even narrower proportions. "Mr. Quinn may well want his hour in the sun, but I have no intention of being denied my triumph. I will be ready within the hour. You will accompany me and my personal retinue to Taos at that time."

Sundown lingered only a quarter hour away. Rich orange light bathed the bowl in which Taos lay. It painted the red, yellow, and brown buttes, mesas and volcanic mountains in muted shadow. Following the ill-thought-out charge of the hotheads, the gang had settled down to strengthen their stranglehold on the town and its occupants. On the three sides not influenced by the creek and its deep gorge, the bandits edged in close enough to be well within range of their weapons. They opened up in a fury.

Windows became the first targets. Every visible pane ceased to exist in a wildfire storm that lasted twelve minutes. By then, the town custodian, whom no one had thought to inform to the contrary, had begun to light the street lamps. They quickly became the objects of punishment for the outlaws.

Glass flew into the street first, followed by thin streams of kerosene. It did not take long for one burning wick to be dislodged from the body of a lamp and fall into a pool of the flammable liquid that formed at the base of the post. Flickering blue at first, to be reduced to yellow-white, the flames swept the length of one block, then a second. At once the alarm sounded at the fire station, and volunteers had to abandon their fighting positions to answer the call. Always a curse, fire could reduce the city as surely as the outlaws who had caused its release.

Chief Ezekial Crowder directed his firemen from the shelter of a doorway. Bullets from the gang continued to be a hazard. One young fire fighter suddenly dropped his length of hose and yowled as he grabbed at his ear. Blood trickled between his fingers.

"At least it ain't like fightin' a structural fire," Crowder observed to Smoke Jensen, who had come at the first alarm. "So far, that is," Barnes amended.

His volunteers quickly spread out to beat down the flames. To Smoke it appeared the very earth burned. Black smoke vaulted the sky above town, and the outlaws cheered and shouted in derision. Gradually, the blazes subsided. After ten hard minutes the last one went out.

Encouraged by the diversion the fires had created, half a dozen scum charged the vaqueros who had been holding the west road. One of the Mexican cowboys reached to the saddlebag at his feet, grabbed up a bottle and used his hand-rolled cigarette to ignite the fuse that protruded from the cork in its mouth. When it began to sputter, he counted to three, stood and threw it out the open window.

It turned end-for-end four full times before it exploded violently at shoulder level in the midst of the gang members. All six screamed piteously and went down in a heap. That quickly changed the minds of those who thought of joining them. The effect on those who had witnessed the grenade became obvious as the fire it had caused began to dwindle. The last shots came from the outlaws only minutes after nightfall.

Half an hour later, Smoke Jensen finished off a piece of pie, sent over by one of the restaurants, and licked his lips. "I think that ends it for today. Diego, I'd keep a few people on the lookout for any effort to test our strength. The rest can get a little sleep, at least until an hour before daylight."

"And you, amigo, what will you be doing?"

Smoke gave him a wicked grin. "I'm going to go out and raise a little hob."

Twenty

Smoke Jensen chose to leave town by way of the road controlled by the vaqueros from Rancho de la Gloria. The ranch hand on watch gave him a silent salute as he crossed the bridge on foot. Thick coatings of burlap muffled the hooves of his stallion, Cougar. They would remain on until Smoke slipped past the pickets of the outlaw army. So skilled was the last mountain man that when the vaquero lookout who watched him depart blinked, Smoke had completely disappeared.

It did not take long after that for Smoke to find targets for his night's mischief. Silently he wormed his way in among the outlaws at one camp fire. One look at his gunfighter rig and they accepted him as one of their own. He was offered coffee, which Smoke accepted.

"Thanks, I needed that. Maybe it'll settle my nerves."

"What are you gittin' at—er . . . ?"

Smoke dropped into the loose grammar and dialect of his mentor, the old mountain man called Preacher. "They call me Jagger. An' what I'm gettin' at is that there's Injuns in among the folks in town."

"Naw," another hard case disputed. "They're Mezkins, Jagger. You've jist caught a case of the spooks."

Smoke played the trump in his rumor hand. "Mezkins wearin' moccasins, loincloths and floppy shirts? Hair down to their shoulders? Believe it. I've seen 'em myself. They're all sharpenin' scalpin' knives."

A shiver passed over his audience. Smoke added more to their unease. "There must be as many fightin' men in thar as out here."

The doubtful one again challenged his statement. "Not accordin' to Whitewater Paddy."

Smoke cracked a grin. "Mr. Quinn don't know ever'thing. I've seed 'em. There's Injuns, an' Mezkin cowboys, and a whole lot of townies."

Smoke answered a string of troubled questions with inventions calculated to fan the blaze of fear he had introduced. After ten minutes of yarn spinning, Smoke drank off his coffee, came to his boots and drifted on.

"I'm makin' the rounds, checkin' if anyone needs anything," Smoke explained at the next fire. Using the names he had acquired at the first gathering, he deepened his cover. "Are you Zeke? Well, Rupe told me to tell you howdy for him. He's holdin' his own. 'Cept for what he found out about the Injuns in Taos."

Zeke eyed Smoke. "What's this about Injuns?"

Smoke launched into his tall tale about scalping. Then he added another log to the overloaded wagon. "That's not all. A feller who's been in close to town tells me that this Smoke Jensen has put up a hundred-dollar bounty on every one of us who gets killed."

Zeke denied that at once. "I don't believe it. Nobody, especially a rovin' gunfighter, has that kind of money."

Smoke ignored him. "Somethin' more about those Injuns. Jensen's armed them with rifles and shotguns."

"No!" Agitated, Zeke came to his boots. "Ain't no way them townies would stand for that. It's fools' work givin' guns to Injuns."

"Makes no never-mind. That's what I saw with my own eyes. Injuns runnin' around with Winchesters. An' that's not all of it. Not by half." Smoke went on to add yet another burden to the worried outlaws. Then he quietly left the uneasy souls to these imaginings.

After three more such visits, Smoke decided that his rumors would take sprout and grow with satisfactory speed. Crouched low, he worked his way in among the horses of those who ringed the town between roads. With a cautious hand, he reached for the cinch ring of one animal. He kept the other on the nose of the animal to calm it.

Ever so slowly, Smoke eased the leather end free of the ring and loosened the cinch. Next time the owner tried to straddle his mount, he would wind up with a lap full of saddle. Smiling to himself, Smoke completed the task and moved on to another critter to do the same. He repeated the loosening of cinch straps a dozen times, then switched tactics.

Along the west side, he fitted front hooves into black leather hobbles on ten other horses. He started to come upright from the last one when a voice challenged him from the darkness. "What are you doin' here?"

Smoke had a ready explanation. "Cleanin' the frog on the right forehoof of my horse. On the way out here he come up lame. Figgered it wouldn't do for us to jump up a fight and me unable to ride."

"Good thinking." The speaker moved closer. "Say, I don't think I—"

Prepared for that, Smoke had already slid his left-hand Colt from its pocket and gripped it tightly around the cylinder with his left hand. He swung the weapon now and connected the butt with the outlaw's temple. The alert section leader went down without a sound. Smoke bent and checked him, then tied the man's wrists and ankles and dragged him off toward the rear. His night vision in perfect condition, Smoke sought a place to stash his burden.

He found it in the form of a small ravine. He lined up the bandit parallel to the gully and rolled him down, out of sight. During his brief search, Smoke had come upon a secondary ring of camp fires. These had not as yet been ignited. He carefully marked their location for later attention. For now, he moved on to find more who had straggled away from the picket line.

Nate Carver had his mind on a glass of whiskey, a hand of winning cards, and a pretty bit of fluff to sit on his lap. He eased his cartridge belt upward and unbuttoned his fly in order to relieve himself. While he fumbled with one stubborn button, visions of the sort of celebration he would have once this was over danced behind his eyes.

That whiskey would sure taste good. His mouth watered at the thought of it. And a nice big steak, well done, the way he had learned to eat it in Texas. And four of the stupidest fellers to ever hold pasteboards in a poker game to play against. Yeah. And then that tingling feeling that came every time a feller walked up them stairs with a floozy on his arm. The small room, the soft bed, the tender flesh. His self-distraction prevented him from sighting the ghostly movement against the lighter darkness of a star-lit horizon. All too late, he sensed another presence an instant before Smoke Jensen smacked him on the side of the head.

Nate would have rather died than be found by his friends in the condition that resulted from sudden unconsciousness and a full bladder. Smoke Jensen trussed him up and set him in the center of a collection of large, fat, barrel cactus. There were bound to be more, Smoke told himself.

Ten minutes later, Smoke found the reason for the second ring of fire pits. An outlaw wearing a cook's apron gathered dry mesquite branches and stacked them beside a chuck wagon. Well beyond rifle range, this would provide a safe place for breakfast. Smoke quickly thought out a way to spoil the meal for them. Ghosting in on moccasined feet, he closed with the belly robber. Smoke's lips thinned to a grim line of disapproval when he saw the curly gray hair on the head he intended to thump. A feller his age should know better than to run with outlaws.

Smoke's regret was not tempered by mercy. He eased up behind the unsuspecting rascal and put him to sleep with a solid blow from his Colt. Quickly he grabbed the man and eased him to the ground. He pulled another prepared strip of latigo leather from a pocket and bound the bean burner's wrists. Then he pulled off the man's boots and removed a sock. After binding the ankles, he stuffed the dirty, smelly wool stocking into an open mouth, careful to remove a poorly fitted set of dentures first, and used another pigging string to secure it in place.

"Time to get to work," Smoke muttered to himself.

He went directly to the rear of the chuck wagon, where the oversized tailgate/worktable had been lowered into place. He opened the drawer that contained about five pounds of salt. This he poured into a bowl for the time being and refilled the receptacle from the sugar bin. The salt then went in to replace the sugar. A quick search under a rising moon located an ant hill. Using a tin plate, Smoke scooped up a generous number of the busybody insects and delivered them to the flour barrel.

Half a dozen road apples, from the team of mules that pulled the wagon, completed his sabotage when he dropped them into the liquid that covered the corned pork. Then he hoisted the supine cook over one shoulder and carried him off a goodly distance to where he would not be found for some time. Someone else would be fixing breakfast for the Quinn gang. Someone Smoke felt confident would not have the skill to recognize the change in the ingredients. That attended to, he began a round of the prelaid fires.

Into each of ten, he inserted a capped and fused stick of dynamite. Being careful to cover them well with dirt, he replaced the kindling and larger wood, then faded off into the night. He reflected on what he had done and counted it a good night's work.

Clifton Satterlee fumed over the delay. A wheel had broken on his surrey not thirty miles north of Santa Fe. Fortunately there had been a posada close by. One that did not have vermin swarming in the mattresses and climbing the walls of the kitchen, he noted grudgingly. The food had been good, for a change. Not the excellent meals his cook prepared, yet flavorful and generous in quantity. Much against his best instincts, Brice Noble had come with him. They sat now at a small table in the alcovelike cantina off the lobby of the inn. Noble poured for both of them from a green glass bottle of Domeq Don Pedro brandy. Not so good as his preferred cognac, but it would do, Satterlee considered.

Taking a sip, he spoke to Brice Noble. "This delay is inexcusable. A spare wheel should be brought along at all times."

"It's your carriage, Cliff" Noble did not mention that the damage had been done as a result of Satterlee's insistence that they travel at the fastest possible speed.

Satterlee cued on his partner's tone. "Meaning?"

"You are the one who has to order a spare being lashed on the surrey."

With a snort, Satterlee took a long pull on the amber liquid. "I hate people who ooze practicality." Abruptly he changed the subject. "We may have some difficulty with some of the people in Taos. They are a stubborn lot. But our time is running out. Quinn has assured me he has rounded up enough gunfighters and rough types to overcome any objections. We'll have about two hundred men."

Noble winced. "That's going to cost a lot of money."

"Yes, but necessary. We may have to take the town by force." He paused, sighed heavily. "Although I would prefer not to resort to that. It might effect our credibility when it comes to filing for new deeds. No matter what, we will have Taos, and we will log that Indian land. That is all vital to our project. I think I've had enough of this." He nodded to a quartet of mariachis playing to a Mexican couple at a corner table. "I'm going to retire. Hastings has assured me that they will have the wheel fitted by morning. Good night, Brice."

Smoke Jensen returned to Taos, linking up with the route he had used to depart only at the last moment. His keen night vision, augmented now by a hazy full moon, allowed him to pick out the significant differences from when he had left town. Seven darker lumps stood out against a background of twinkling pinpoints of light in a black velvet sky. Slowly they resolved into human figures. All faced inward toward the community they invested. Smoke had already dismounted. Now he clapped a hand over Cougar's muzzle and eased the big 'Palouse off the roadway. He ground reined his horse and slid off into the night once again.

One of those who attempted to reestablish the roadblock under cover of night had taken a position some fifty feet from the verge of the road. He had hunkered down, the stock of his rifle used as a prop. He constantly cut his eyes from side to side and up and down to enable him to better see what lay across the deep gully and its creek that divided him from the outermost houses. He had no way of knowing that Alvarado's vaqueros knew to do the same and had picked out his position to within an inch. Had he known so, it would not have done him any good. He lost consciousness before they could do anything about his presence.

Smoke Jensen eased up behind the gunman and slammed the butt of a Colt Peacemaker into the side of his head. With a soft grunt, the outlaw fell over onto the sandy red soil. Smoke quickly tied him and moved on.

Another of Quinn's ragtag army sat cross-legged with his back against a low paloverde. Smoke Jensen found him and decided upon a little trickery. "Hey," he whispered harshly. "Over here. We've got a problem."

Almost dozed off, the response sounded quarrelsome. "What's the matter. Ground too hard?"

"Come here. An' be quiet."

Roused from his near snooze, the outlaw came to his boots and duck-walked over. "Now, what's this problem?"

"I am," Smoke told him before he clouted him on the temple with the barrel of one .45. The thug went rigid and then dropped face first to the ground.

Smoke moved on in an instant. He suddenly realized that he had allowed himself to grow overconfident when a voice growled at him from the side. "Hold it right there."

Moving slowly, so as not to startle the speaker into shooting, Smoke faced his challenger. "What do you mean? I was only goin' down to bum a smoke offa Hank."

Suspicion thickened in the outlaw's voice. "There ain't no Hank with this outfit, an' I ain't seen you before." He beckoned with the muzzle of his rifle. "Come over here an' let me get a look at you."

Smoke complied, easing his left hand around out of sight. When he got within a long arm's reach, he stopped. The distrustful hard case peered closely at Smoke's face. "Nope. Never saw you with the gang before. Who are you?"

Smoke came out with his Greenriver sheath knife in his left hand and, with a short lunge, drove it horizontally through the costal region between the fifth and sixth ribs on the left side. The pointed tip penetrated the heart and sank the blade deep into the pulsing organ. Then Smoke jerked the haft to rip sideways. The man died without a sound. Smoke maneuvered to hold the dead man between him and any outlaw bullets and called out loudly to the defenders across the way.

"¡Oigan, vaqueros de la Gloria! Ayudenme!"

He got his help right away as the Mexican cowboys opened fire on the hard cases they had previously located. Smoke gave a shrill whistle, and Cougar trotted toward him. Quickly he flung the body away from him and swung into the saddle. With heels drumming into his sides, Cougar jumped to a fast canter and sprinted across the bridge and into the shelter of the buildings on the outskirts of Taos.

Smoke had thoughts only for sleep. But he found a delegation waiting for him at the sheriff's office. The mayor, Fidel Arianas, and Dr. Walters occupied chairs, along with Santan Tossa and Ed Hubbard. All except Tossa wore worried expressions.

Arianas opened the session. "How long do we have to hold them off?"

Smoke studied on that. "Three or four days, however long it takes for the militia to get here."

Arianas turned pale. "*¡Chingada!* There's not maybe fifty hombres in the militia. And that's on a good day. This ladrón has four times that many."

"Not anymore. I took care of a few. And tomorrow's sure to do in more."

Dr. Walters addressed a more serious problem. "We cannot hold out for more than four days. There is not enough food. There are too many mouths to feed."

Smoke frowned. "Make sure the vittles at the town hall get served only to the fighting men. The townspeople will have to fend for themselves."

Horrified at that prospect, the mayor thought first of votes. "The people will not stand for that. They'll blame me."

Smoke Jensen cut hot, angry eyes to the politician. "They'll have to live with it, if they don't want Paddy Quinn campin' on their doorstep." He had not the slightest concern over the mayor's reelection possibilities.

Dr. Walters had another idea. "What about the water supply? If they poison the creek we have only a few cisterns, fewer wells."

Smoke looked to Tossa for a solution. "Can you have some of your warriors slip out of town and make sure Quinn's men do not put anything in the water?"

Satan Tossa smiled. "That will be easy. They will never be seen."

"Then that's settled. Reduce rations all around and guard the water that is in town. No matter how this goes, we'll all have to tighten our belts to survive. And . . . you can expect another attack in the morning. I reckon those scum will be spoilin' for a fight."

Twenty-one

Four o'clock in the morning was entirely too dang early to get up and get around, the swamper for the missing cook complained as he trudged through the darkness toward the chuck wagon. All around him, the tiny flames twinkled as men struck lucifers to ignite their fires. They would boil their own coffee. It was up to him and old Snuffy to turn out the grub. Where was Snuffy? he wondered as he reached the wagon and did not find the belly robber anywhere. By now he usually had a lantern going and the first rollout of biscuit dough ready to cut.

"Snuffy! Where are you? Come on, we're fallin' behind."

Right then, at a fire pit not far away, flame hit the split and frazzled end of a length of fuse. It sputtered and hissed gustily, consumed the powder train that ran down its middle, and reached the detonator cap. A bright flash drew the swamper's eyes as a stick of dynamite let go with a tremendous roar. An instant later a shower of dirt and burning kindling mushroomed over the fire ring nearest the chuck wagon. Concussion knocked men rolling. One, who had leaned over, blowing gently to encourage the flames, died instantly.

Five seconds later another buried stick let go. Then a third. The sound of the eruptions echoed off the walls of buildings in Taos. Reverberations had not died out when a fourth fire ring erupted in a gout of dirt. A fifth followed on its heels. By then, the swamper had dived to the ground and hugged red-brown clots of earth in a forlorn hope that a similar fate would not overtake him. Light the cook fire? Not very damn likely.

Two more blasts shattered the predawn quiet. An eerie silence followed. Then the swamper heard the cries and moans of the injured. Gradually his heartbeat began to slow. Then an anguished shout chilled him anew.

"Don't light that! Nooooo!"

BLAM!

No, there was no way he would light that fire. Two more explosions quickly dotted the *i*'s and crossed the *t*'s of that decision. No matter what Snuffy might say, he would absolutely, positively never even strike a match.

Smoke Jensen stood in a second-floor window, an old pair of brass army field glasses to his eyes. Ignited by the exploding dynamite, tufts of prairie grass had burst into flame, along with mesquite bushes and greasewood. The conflagration illuminated the disordered ranks of the enemy enough to let him clearly see the results of his night's work. It turned out to be better than he had expected.

Those outlaws already awake and not injured took to their horses. Shouts and curses blistered the air when some of them put a boot in a stirrup and wound up flat on their backsides. Several forked their mounts only to pitch face forward to the ground when their hobbled beasts jerked to sudden stops. Some rode off in the direction of Raton without a backward glance. Yet other hard cases ran around in confusion, their horses scattered in fright by the explosions.

More men helplessly stood in place to shout curses and shake their fists. Dust thrown into the air by the dynamite explosions began to settle and obscure the entire scene. Acrid smoke from the explosives hung in undulating waves over the former fire sites. The others who had crowded into the room with him were laughing and slapping one another on the back. Smoke Jensen felt no such elation. Men had died, and others had been maimed by his actions. If it served to break the resolve of the outlaws, well and good.

"What happened to them?" Diego Alvarado asked Smoke.

Smoke lowered the field glasses. "That's what I'm here for anyway, isn't it? I prepared a little wake-up call for them."

Don Diego studied Smoke's handiwork in awe. "It looks . . . devastating."

"Who was it said something about omelets and eggs?" Smoke asked aloud.

He shifted the glasses again as a pearlescent ribbon silhouetted the jagged mountain peaks to the east. There. He had found him. Paddy Quinn stood on a knoll, the reins of his horse in one hand. His expression was one of disbelief. What next? he seemed to be asking himself. If need be, Smoke Jensen decided, he would show Quinn what.

"Begorrah, there's a black-hearted bastard at work here," an enraged Paddy Quinn exclaimed as Garth Thompson approached to report on their condition.

"You'll think it is Old Nick himself when I tell you where we stand right now."

Quinn cut his eyes to Thompson. His black orbs, which usually twinkled in harmony with his perpetual smile, had become flat mirrors. The beaming expression had melted away. "What is it yer sayin', boy-o, what is it?"

Garth had never seen his boss like this. He noted the black smudge of unshaven jaws, the little mouth set in an angry slash, high forehead furrowed, the muscles of his head so rigid that his small ears literally twitched. To Garth, Quinn looked ready to explode like one of their fire pits.

"We've had fifteen men killed. There's another twenty injured. Twenty-five men just plain rode off. I don't reckon they'll be coming back. Old Snuffy, our cook, and his swamper have plain disappeared."

A foul stream of curses gushed from Paddy's mouth. At last he curbed his fury. "By damn, this is the doing of Smoke Jensen. I've got to talk to whoever is in charge in Taos. He's got to curb his mad dog. And, he's got to see reason, he does. Even with our losses, we've enough men to wipe out the entire town. There's other places to live, an' men start over all the time, they do." Paddy went on for a good five minutes, as though rehearsing his presentation to the leader of the defenders. When he wound down, he issued his orders to Garth Thompson.

"Rig a white flag. Then ride down there and tell them I want to meet and talk with whoever is in charge. We'll meet after break—awh, hell, we don't have a cook, ye say. How am I gonna get some breakfast?"

Smoke Jensen and Diego Alvarado rode out to the meeting with Paddy Quinn later that morning. As they swung into their saddles, Smoke offered a word of caution. "I think it would be wise to have some of your vaqueros keep a close eye on every hard case in rifle range of our meeting."

Diego cut a knowing eye to Smoke. "You suspect that Señor Quinn will not honor his own flag of truce?"

"That's putting it mildly. I'll keep watch on Quinn. You do the talking."

Smoke's arrangement worked out excellently. Paddy Quinn knew Diego Alvarado from previous encounters and naturally addressed him as the leader. He chose to ignore Smoke Jensen, whom he also recognized. The snub was wasted on Smoke.

"Don Diego, it's good to see you again, it is."

Diego's black hair and mustache and chiseled features gave him a sardonic appearance. "Somehow I doubt that. What is it you want, Quinn?"

"Ah, no time for pleasantries, is it? A busy man ye are, no doubt. Well, then, we might as well get to it." Quinn paused and drew a deep breath, which he sighed out before he continued. "There's no denyin' that ye hurt me some. An' Mr. Satterlee will be sore distressed over that, an' that's a fact. But, it's also a fact, it is, that we've the strength to wipe out any resistance ye might choose to put up. So, me fine grandee, I've come to discuss the terms of your surrender. Not just the town, but that grand ranch of yers."

Diego Alvarado swallowed the rising anger to request in a cold, grave tone, "In return for what?"

Paddy Quinn leaned back in the saddle, as though considering that question, then produced his usual cherubic smile. "Now, Mr. Satterlee was perfectly willing to pay fair market price for all the property he desires. But . . ." His expression changed to the mask of deadly fury witnessed earlier by Garth Thompson. He nodded toward Smoke Jensen. "Then the devilment wrought overnight by this hired cur of yours changed all that, it did. So, Señor Alvarado, here's what we'll be havin'. All hostilities will end immediately. We will be allowed into town at once, without hindrance, to select which properties Mr. Satterlee desires."

To Paddy Quinn's surprise, it was Smoke Jensen who answered. "You'll be dancing with the devil before that happens."

Quinn masked his reaction and raised an arm to make a curt gesture. Two of his henchmen appeared over a low rise. Between them they held Martha Estes. They brought her forward until Smoke could plainly see the fear in her eyes. Quinn openly gloated over his prize, his voice a velvet purr.

"So, then, unless we are allowed into Taos, and the people are lined up eager and ready to sign over their property to C.S. Development Company, a division of C.S. Enterprises, Miss Martha here will be slowly killed right out here before your eyes."

Smoke Jensen's face took on a rock-hard stillness, his

amber eyes and expression thunderous. "I sincerely doubt that's true. Clifton Satterlee would not be at all pleased."

Quinn appeared not at all affected by that judgment. To further prove he did not bluff, he made another signal. Four houses on the edge of town, which belonged to some of the poorer Mexican farmers, suddenly burst into flames. The dry thatch of their roofs burned rapidly. Women and small children ran screaming from their fiery homes. In the distance, the fire bell began to clang. Smoke and Diego looked on, unable to do anything.

Paddy Quinn watched with them for a while, then turned his horse and spoke over his shoulder. "You have one hour." Then he posed a question for Smoke Jensen. "Tell me, Smoke Jensen? How does it feel to at last meet your better?"

Smoke Jensen's flat, level gaze pierced Paddy Quinn and fixed him in place. "I don't think I have."

For a long, tense moment Paddy Quinn did nothing. Then he turned about and rode swiftly away without another word.

Smoke Jensen looked up from the lists of preparations that had so far been completed. A delegation of some eight local merchants stood in the sheriff's office. He clearly read the fear on their faces. Smoke erased the frown that had creased his brow and forced a smile.

"Something bothering you gentlemen?"

He noted that they were among those he had rated as the most timid among the businessmen of Taos. They fidgeted now, like schoolboys caught in some naughty act. One ran an index finger around the interior of his celluloid collar. Two shifted their feet in an uneasy manner. All eight clearly wished to be elsewhere.

"Come on, no need to hold back."

Charlie Lang, the haberdasher, cleared his throat and bobbed his Adam's apple. "Well, ah . . . we—that is, it's gotten around that we have an hour before those brigands just come in and take what they want. Is that true?"

Smoke shook his head. "No. We have an hour before they supposedly murder a young woman before our eyes and then come in and take what they want."

"Oh. That—ah—that makes a difference."

Smoke's face registered his discontent. "Mr. Lang, I was trying to be sarcastic. I chose the wrong words. The facts are that they cannot take this town no matter how hard they try. A lot of them are along out of curiosity. They have no real loyalty to Paddy Quinn or Clifton Satterlee. When they get a taste of our firepower, a lot of them will drift away. More than twenty of them ran out this morning before sunup."

"What about the young woman?"

Again, Smoke made a negative gesture. "Quinn will never kill her, not even hurt her in a serious way. He believes she is still the lady friend of his boss. With all the gunfighters he commands, Quinn would never buck Satterlee."

Lang persisted. "Why is that?"

"Mr. Lang, do you pay your employees at the start of the week or at the end?"

Charlie Lang frowned. The question puzzled him. "Why, at the end of the week, for all that it matters."

"My point. You don't pay them until they have performed the work for which they are being compensated. I firmly doubt that Satterlee has paid Quinn, and won't until the job is done. If Quinn and Satterlee got at odds, and Quinn didn't get paid, he'd have a whole lot of angry, broke gunhawks to contend with."

Lang thought on that awhile. "That makes sense. Even so, we've been talking about the danger we're in, what those outlaws can do to us. We have families, investments, roots in the community. We don't want to risk harm to our wives and children and lose everything we have. This Clifton Satterlee has offered to compensate us fairly for our property. It seems wise for us to accept what he is proposing."

"Not anymore. Quinn says our resistance has changed all that. Satterlee is going to take what he wants, and that's all of Taos. As to protecting what you have at stake, I suggest that all of you grow a pair of stones and fight for what's yours."

Lang and three others began jabbering as one. "But some of us will get injured." "We'll be killed." "We have a right to be protected."

Smoke Jensen's disgust spilled over. "Listen to me you yellow-bellied rabbits," he thundered. "You are going to have to fight for your rights; we'll be too busy protecting the town as a whole. Here's my final word. Not a one of you will give in to such cheap intimidation. If I need to, I'll put a Tua warrior in every store, eatery and saloon to prevent your surrender. Now, get out of here."

Paddy Quinn rode to the abandoned adobe farmhouse where Martha Estes had been imprisoned. Following his instructions, his underlings had lashed her arms to a chair and left her sitting at a table, with only a crumbling wall to stare at. Quinn entered and stood between her and that unpromising vista. At once, Martha's gorge rose, and she began to unload onto him all her disgust and loathing.

"You are the most disgusting, foul, misbegotten piece of human refuse I have ever laid eyes upon. Your every act shames your mother and father."

She stopped for a breath, and Paddy seized the opportunity to get in a word of his own. "My mother, God rest her soul, is dead these twenty long years. An' me father is a drunk, who would not feel insult if someone crapped in his hat."

Eyes narrowed in her rage, Martha spat, "When Clifton

discovers how you have treated me, he'll have you horse whipped."

"Ye've got the right of it, lass. He's not got the balls to do it hisself." Realization that Jensen's taunt had struck home made her reminder even more unwelcome. "It's well an' good, it is, that ye know I'll never be for carryin' out me threats against you. That was for those dogs from town. Let them be worryin' over it. But, between you an' me—ah, an' Lord, there's somethin' I'd love to have between you an' me, there is—before this is over, I intend to get to know you better. *Intimately* better, if ye catch me meanin'?"

Martha twisted her face into an expression of disgust. "I'll see you in hell before that happens."

His smile bright as ever, so disarming it did not lend credibility to his words, Paddy Quinn spoke lightly as he started for her. "Will ye now? An' what's to stop me? All I need do is hoist them skirts and have at you with a will."

A sudden clatter from a carriage outside halted Quinn. He stopped, then took two hasty back steps. The next moment, Clifton Satterlee stormed through the askew doorway. His face flushed, Satterlee pointed a glove-covered forefinger at Quinn.

"That lout of yours out there tells me that you have Martha Estes in here as a prisoner, trussed up like a Christmas goose."

Paddy gestured to his prisoner. As though jerked by a string, Satterlee took two steps toward the young woman, then turned on Quinn. "Release her. *At once!*" Then to Martha, "My dear, this is inexcusable. I'll have you freed in a moment. And I promise you nothing like this will ever happen again. Where is Lupe?"

Martha turned her cobalt gaze on Clifton. "She's . . . being held someplace else."

Ice formed around the words of Clifton Satterlee. "Quinn, you will finish untying this young lady; then you will go and fetch her maid. And be certain that she has with her everything needed to restore Miss Martha to her usual loveliness."

Paddy Quinn had recovered himself enough to bark back. "She ran away from you, did you know that? I didn't send men to take her, I didn't. She went of with none other than Smoke Jensen."

Satterlee cut his eyes from Quinn to Martha. "Is that true?"

"Yes and no. I left on my own. I encountered Mr. Jensen on the road, and he was to escort me here to Taos." Hurrying to get it out before her nerve failed, Martha added, "I felt so terrible when I learned that the jewelry you gave me had been stolen. And that they were sacred objects to the Indians here. I wanted to do what I could to make amends."

Satterlee's anger found a new source. "Lies. Jensen must have told you that. It is not true. Trust me in that."

Martha clenched her jaw a moment, then braved it out. "I talked with a young Indian policeman who identified the necklace I wore . . . when they visited in Santa Fe."

"A copy perhaps," Satterlee suggested.

Martha held her own. "They do not make copies."

Satterlee took another tack. "Come, my dear. Let's put all that behind us. I am so relieved to find you safe and sound."

"Not so safe, nor so sound, if that one had his way," Martha challenged.

Clifton Satterlee rounded on Quinn again. "I thought I gave you an order. Now do it."

"You may regret this, Mr. Satterlee," Quinn muttered softly while he undid Martha's bonds.

Satterlee winced as though the threat had hit home. In that instant, after her release, Martha bounded upright and made a break for the door. Before Satterlee could react, Quinn passed him in a flash and snagged Martha by one arm.

"Not so fast, me fine colleen."

Martha did not resign herself so easily. She clawed at Paddy Quinn, scratched his cheek and neck, kicked him in the shins and pounded one small fist on his chest. While she struggled, Clifton Satterlee took it in with an astonished, bemused expression. Martha tried to knee Paddy in the crotch, and he hurled her against a wall.

All fight left her as she slammed painfully into the adobe blocks. Shoulders slumped, she faced the two men like an animal at bay. Her chest heaved from her exertion, and her face had turned a pale white. Clifton Satterlee studied her with new eyes.

At last he spoke. "Perhaps I have been hasty. I may have misjudged you, Mr. Quinn. Yes, I think I far underrated Martha's spirit. It seems that for the time being, you will have to detain her forcibly if she persists in such unbecoming activity."

Paddy Quinn touched fingers to his cheek. They came away bloody. Then he saluted his employer with a tap to the brim of his hat. "I'll see to it right away, that I will." Before departing, he added, "When that is done, there are some changes I want to discuss with you as to the taking of the town of Taos."

Twenty-two

Shortly before the hour deadline, Smoke Jensen came to Santan Tossa with a suggestion. "I want you to gather your warriors. Have them start to drum and sing, do a war dance out in plain view of Quinn's gang."

A huge grin spread on the mahogany face of the Tua. "We haven't done a war dance in fifty years. This will be a true pleasure. We'll make it look very bloodthirsty indeed. Lots of howls, leaping in the air, swinging war clubs and knives." He went off, gleefully listing loudly the terrorizing features they would use.

Twenty minutes later, a drum began to throb in the outskirts of Taos. Tua warriors started to prance and stomp in a circle around a large fire. High, thin voices chanted the challenge to fight and die to all who could hear. Knife blades flashed in the sunlight. The drum beat louder. Some among the outlaws became visibly uncomfortable. Several exchanged knowing glances. They had heard the rumors about scalping.

Some few did not want to test it further. Two drifters, who had joined up for the fun the siege promised, went for their horses. They rode off five minutes later. Five minutes later, three more, who were not part of the gang, held a whispered conference, nodded agreement and left for other parts.

A grinning Santan Tossa waved a lighthearted farewell to Smoke Jensen as Smoke eased himself into the gorge that contained the streambed and set off to locate Martha Estes and her maid.

Smoke followed the creek upstream to the southwest until well past the ring of outlaws. Then he led Cougar up out of the ravine and mounted. Carefully he worked his way back toward the siege lines. He left Cougar behind a screen of young palo verdes and proceeded afoot. Bent double, he presented a far diminished profile to any eyes that might look outward, instead of toward town. There would be few places where Martha might be kept, he reasoned. With silent determination, he set about eliminating those.

Ten minutes went by. Smoke found himself on a small produce farm. No doubt the Mexican owner sold to the general store in Taos, and to others who happened by. Yes, there, beyond the work sheds, barn and house, a palapa had been erected over a stairstepped set of shelves. Baskets of peppers and fresh vegetables lined them. Two small boys, under the age of thirteen or so, kept watch and called out to passersby.

Making little sound in his moccasins, Smoke eased his way up to the side of one shed. The sound of splashing water came from within. Women's voices came from inside, chattering in Spanish over the latest gossip. Smoke's command of the language, slight at best, had not improved over years of non-use. Even so, he made out a number of juicy items.

"Raquel is going to have a baby," one woman revealed as she energetically sloshed a bowl of red and green jalapeno peppers in a tub of water to remove the red-brown dust.

"How can that be?" asked a much younger, more innocent voice. "She is not even married."

"*Sí, esto es verdad.* She has no husband, but she has a baby."

"Padre Domingo says that is a sin." Smoke could almost see the blush her words produced.

"That is true, little one. And you will promise your

mother that you will never, ever do what it takes to make a baby . . . until you are safely married."

Another woman brought a change of subject. "I hear that Juanita Sanchez is going to marry that Guerrero boy."

"Which one?" several asked.

"Mateo, I think. Or is it Raul? No, it is Enrique."

"Carlos Guerrero has nine sons. How can you tell which one?"

A titter came from the youngest. "It's not Ricardo. He's only ten."

A superior sounding voice discounted that. "What difference does that make? My sister, Esperanza, was married at twelve."

A snippy voice followed a nasty laugh. "Everyone knows she had to. It was that Dominquez boy, although she married Sancho Valdez."

A wounded squeal came from the defender of early weddings. "Cow."

"Pig."

"¡Bruja!" her target spat, then repeated, "Witch!"

"Ladies, please," a matronly woman commanded. "We are here to work, is that not true? Someone hand me some of those squash."

Grinning, Smoke moved on. Small wonder that men who owned businesses preferred not to hire women. The metallic screech of metal against stone directed Smoke to another shack. The farmer sat under a thatch palapa, working a peddle-power whetstone to sharpen a machete. Smoke coughed softly to attract the man's attention.

"¿Sí, señor?"

"Have any of the ladrónes around Taos come around here?" Smoke asked. When the man shook his head in the negative, Smoke tried another. "Have you seen any of them taking a young woman somewhere?"

Another shake of his head, then, "¡Ay, sí! Early this morning, I was turning water into my corn. Two men rode over toward the old Olivera place. They had a woman with them. She did not look happy."

Smoke nodded in satisfaction. "That's the one. Thank you, señor."

Then Smoke asked for and was given directions to the Olivera farm. He headed that way on foot. He had covered half a mile when he came upon the first of several layers of lookouts. Smoke skirted the man easily and continued on. The second one proved not so simple to evade.

He sat his mount, alertly searching the surrounding terrain. From time to time, he stood in his stirrups and peered beyond low obstructions. Smoke, clad in buckskin, hugged the ground. The man's diligence and regularity became his undoing. After carefully timing the outlaw's routine, Smoke was ready when a missed gaze beyond the low brow behind which Smoke waited signaled a change. He came up and moved out in a split second.

Habit had outweighed diligence. The man had his head down, intent on rolling a cigarette. Smoke leaped and landed on him like a stone statue. Tobacco flakes flew everywhere. Dragged from the saddle, the outlaw landed heavily with Smoke on top. Rancid breath shot out of his twisted mouth. His lungs empty, it took only a hard right to the jaw by Smoke Jensen to put him asleep. Smoke quickly tied him and hurried on.

Another watcher lounged in the doorway of a partially fallen in adobe house. Smoke froze and sank to the ground. For five long minutes he studied the man who leaned against the doorframe. He looked bored. He also looked sleepy. Another minute passed, and the thug abruptly jerked awake, stepped out of the shade and paced to each corner of the building, Winchester held at the ready. He looked around the wall and returned to his position. Once more he slouched.

Such kind were dangerous, Smoke reasoned. If the hunch hit him at the wrong time, he might see someone sneaking up on him. Smoke inched his way behind a rock ridge and circled widely around the crumbling structure. He came at the adobe building from the rear.

Through a small, high window he had a clear view of the interior. Across the single room, he saw a large loft, obviously where the family slept when they lived here. In the middle of the room he noted a small table. Seated at two sides of it were Martha and her maid. They had been tied tightly to their chairs. To one side, Smoke observed Paddy Quinn and two of his men in the room conferring quietly. The bad news became immediately obvious.

There wouldn't be time enough to take out Quinn and his fast guns and free both women. This small farm lay too close to the ring of outlaws. Any exchange of gunfire would draw two dozen gunmen in seconds. He could not free them, yet he had a firm belief that Satterlee would not want her harmed. What happened next reinforced that attitude. Quinn's voice raised suddenly, and Smoke listened carefully to each word.

"You're right, Huber. These two are poison. I think we can get away with it if we do it that way, I do. We just take 'em out in the desert and lose them somewhere."

At once, Martha snapped hotly at him. "Clifton will have you gelded if you actually go through with killing me. You heard what he said when he had you bring my maid here."

That was news to Smoke. The criminal overlord was here now. That gave him some fresh ideas. Quietly he slipped away, headed back for Cougar and a ride to town.

Never one to take strict notice of exact time, Smoke Jensen found himself eying the big, octagonal face of the Regulator wall clock that hung on the wall of the sheriff's office. When the hour deadline arrived, he strode out to where Quinn had confronted them earlier. It did not surprise Smoke when he found none of the outlaws present. Particularly, Smoke noted, no torturers and no Martha Estes. In the next instant, he learned why.

Rifle fire broke out on two sides of town. With shouts and curses, the outlaw gang opened an attack on Taos in earnest. Smoke could not understand why the entire force that ringed the defenders did not press the engagement. He needn't have speculated. Smoke had no sooner than reached the line of houses that defined the city limits than riders thundered down the slope where he and Diego had met with Quinn. They opened fire as the range closed.

Immediately, Smoke ducked behind a low adobe wall and drew a .45 Colt. Two .44 slugs slammed into the outer face of the brown mud bricks, which sent a plume of dust upward to obscure Smoke's vision. He triggered a round, and a hard case cried out in pain, his right arm limp and useless. That concentrated more fire on Smoke's position. He could not stay in such an exposed place for long, Smoke reasoned.

Sheriff Hank Banner sat propped up in bed by rolled blankets and plump pillows. At his insistence, Dr. Walters had rolled the bed over close to a window. Now he stood in exasperation at his patient's request.

"I'll do no such a thing, Hank Banner," the physician snapped, his well-scrubbed hands clasped in front of him.

"Awh, come on, Adam. We've got the fight of our lives goin' on out there, and I ain't in it. Hell, man, even you've got a six-gun strapped on."

"That's to protect my patients and my medical equipment," Dr. Walters responded testily.

"You gave Pedro Alvarado a rifle. All I'm askin' is you get me one, too."

Unmoved by the argument, Adam Walters answered primly. "Pedro is thirty years younger than you, Hank, and he's ambulatory. Besides, how are you going to operate a Winchester from that bed?"

Bushy eyebrows knit over his nose, Banner grumped at the doctor. "Easy if you'll give me a rifle and open the damned window. I mean it now, Adam. I can see out of both eyes now, and things ain't so fuzzy I'd shoot one of the town folks. I'm the sheriff, and by damn, it's my duty to help defend the people out there."

Dr. Walters knew that Hank was right. But he was his friend, and Adam Walters did not want to see Hank Banner taking unnecessary risks in his weakened condition. While his thoughts roamed over that little dilemma, Dr. Walters heard a light smack and the musical tinkle of falling glass. The bullet cracked loudly when it struck the wall opposite the window.

"Goldag it, Adam. That does it. If they're shootin' at me, I've got the right to shoot back."

Sighing, Dr. Walters turned from the infirmary and entered his treatment room. From there he proceeded to the office, where he picked up a Winchester and a box of cartridges. He returned to the room where the sheriff continued to fume at the attackers. Adam's face wore a sheepish expression.

"Here. And try not to shoot yourself in the leg." The doctor busied himself with opening the sash. From the end window, which faced the alley behind the building, a rifle barked in the hands of Pedro Alvarado.

For all the fury of their resistance, small groups of Quinn's outlaw band penetrated the defenders' barricades. Six of them from the west side of town headed directly for the center. They made their approach by way of one of the radiating alleys that formed an X based on the Plaza de Armas. To reach their goal, they had to go past the window where young Pedro Alvarado waited with a ready Winchester. The moment one of them came into view, he immediately regretted his hastiness.

Fiery agony spread in his leg as Pedro put a round into his hip. The outlaw fell at once and painfully crawled, crablike, toward the shelter of a doorway. Pedro fired again, ending the thug's movement forever. As his life ebbed from him, the hard case faintly heard the voices of his comrades.

"Up there."

"Yeah, I see him. In that window."

Funny, the dying rogue thought, *I didn't hear any shots.* He did not hear the return fire as his fellow outlaws opened up and darkness engulfed him.

Up in the infirmary, Pedro Alvarado flattened himself on the floor as a rat-a-tat of slugs punched through the thin wall. Glass shattered in the window above him. The moment a lull came, Pedro popped up and sighted on one of the five. The .44 Winchester recoiled smoothly, and the target clutched his chest and slammed back against a wall. Pedro got off another round before he had to dive for the floor again.

Ian MacGreggor held his own from his second-floor room in the hotel. He had been on town patrol duty during the night and had returned to grab a few hours' sleep only to have the attack break out after only forty minutes' rest. Over his sights, he saw one hard case, who appeared to be directing the actions of a dozen others in a push to breach the defenses to the south of town. A long shot for a rifle, but Mac retained the confidence of youth.

He elevated his aim to the maximum and fired. After what seemed a terribly long time, the section leader jerked in his saddle, then slowly folded forward at the waist. He clung to his horse for a moment, then dropped away to land in a puff of dust on the hard ground. Mac levered another round into his Winchester and sought another target. He found one much closer than he would have liked.

Two hard cases ran out of the mouth of an alley and

randomly discharged their weapons upward toward second-floor windows. Mac pulled a quick bead and let fly another .44 slug. One of the outlaws continued to run forward while the other did a crazy little jig and crashed blindly into a rain barrel. He died before he hit the tile walk.

Mac charged his rifle again and sighted on the remaining gunman. The Winchester bucked, and Mac remembered this time to shove three fresh cartridges through the loading gate. He ejected the empty and chambered a loaded one. If this kept up, they could easily reduce the enemy by half, he speculated.

Someone else had figured out the same thing. Shouts to pull back went from one outlaw to the next. Slowly they began to withdraw from town, yet they continued to pour a withering fire on the defenders from a distance outside Taos. Whitewater Paddy Quinn sought out his second in command.

"We'll give it a little time, then go back again. I want to get that bastid Smoke Jensen in me sights, an' that's a fact."

Garth Thompson did not sound so eager. "I've heard he is hard to kill. So far, I have no reason to doubt that. How many did we lose?"

Quinn raised a hand and swept the hillside. "That's what I want you to find out, boy-o. Didn't seem to me that half the lads what went in there came back. With losses like that, we can't keep this up for long. Whether Mr. Satterlee likes it or not, we may have to use fire to drive those stubborn folk out."

"He'll have a fit if we do. But, I agree with you. We can't let them whittle us down like that much longer. When do we go back?"

Quinn rubbed a powder-grimed hand across his brow. "Find out where we stand an' we'll give it an hour."

* * *

Ezekial Crowder and Ed Hubbard had taken positions on the south side of town, close to Smoke Jensen. They looked first to the sky when they heard a distant rumble. When they found it to be clear and bright, they lowered their gaze to observe the ominous approach of a large body of outlaws. They exchanged a worried glance and tightened the grip on their weapons. Over the growing thunder of hooves, they could hear the voice of Smoke Jensen, low and calm.

"Steady . . . hold it . . . let 'em come in real close. Make every shot count."

Smoke knew it would not happen that way. Excitement or fear would make the inexperienced men fire carelessly. They would rush their aim and no doubt jerk the trigger. It would only get worse when the outlaws opened fire. Some, though, he knew would make good account of themselves. Like young Mac, who had shouted to him during the brief respite.

"Hey, Smoke, I got three of them. Those two down there and another on his horse outside town."

"Good shootin'," Smoke praised. He continued on his way to check the other defenses. His inspection gave him the impression that some twenty outlaws had gotten inside the town. Perimeter defenses had to be shored up. He had arranged for that, though only just in time.

They were going to have to keep the gang from entering town this time, Smoke thought as he watched the outlaws close once again. A few seconds later, Ed Hubbard proved a better gunhand than expected when he cleared two saddles in rapid succession.

"Did ya see that?" Hubbard called out, surprised by his own success. He took aim again.

With a loud crash, the hard cases opened up. It drowned out Ed's third shot, which hit Dutch Volker in the side. It was a severe enough wound to put him out of the action. With a blistering backward look and a hot curse, Dutch steered his mount away from the conflict. He would get patched up and come back, Dutch thought.

Smoke Jensen had other ideas for him. Careful aim with his .45-70-500 Winchester Express paid a dividend to Smoke. For enough time to make it count, the head of Dutch Volker sat like a hairy ball on the top of the front blade sight. The upright post rested in the notch of the rear, buckhorn sight. Smoke squeezed the trigger. Volker's head snapped forward and back as the bullet bore through his brain and exited the front, taking with it his entire forehead. A fountain of gore splashed on his horse. Without a controlling hand, it went berserk.

Crow hopping and squealing in fright over the smell of blood and brain tissue, the animal cut crossways to the advance, scattered several other riders and at last dislodged its odious burden in a thicket of mesquite. Already, Smoke Jensen tracked another outlaw. The volume of defending fire increased from other points as Smoke concentrated on his aim. He discharged a round that missed one hard case by a finger's width and drove into the shoulder of the man behind him. Smoke risked a quick glance toward Hubbard and Crowder while he cycled his lever action.

Both men so far remained calm. They took time to aim, worked the action of their rifles in a controlled manner and shoved fresh cartridges into the magazine between shots. Hubbard spoke up loudly enough for Smoke to hear him above the rattle of gunfire.

"You're doin' all right for a fireman."

Crowder grinned. "So are you . . . shopkeeper. I'd sell my soul for a shot of whiskey and a cool beer."

"If I was the devil, I'd take you up on that." Hubbard broke off to fire his Winchester again. "Got another one," he commented.

"The way they're comin', this could last until sundown," opined Zeke Crowder.

Hubbard blinked and swallowed hard. "It had better not."

* * *

Sheriff Banner thought much the same as Chief Crowder. From his vantage point he watched the huge gang swirl around Taos. Here and there, one would slump in the saddle or fall to the ground. Not nearly enough, though, the lawman concluded. He watched as three of them charged a barricade made of two overturned wagons.

Their mounts easily cleared the obstacle, and he had one of the men in his sights before the hooves touched ground. An easy squeeze and the sheriff's rifle fired. His bullet drilled the outlaw through the chest. Quickly Banner worked the action and sighted in on another. Before he could fire, one of Diego Alvarado's vaqueros dashed into the street. He carried a large yellow and magenta cape. Swiftly he unfurled it and billowed it out into a fat curve; the skirt flapped in the breeze his motion created.

At once the horses sat back on their haunches and reared. One rider fell off; the second barely hung on. And then not for long. Another rippling pass put the animal in a walleyed frenzy. The rider had all he could do to regain control. While thus occupied, Sheriff Banner shot the hard case through the heart.

Fierce fighting continued through the afternoon. Smoke Jensen made periodic visits to the defenders positioned on the outer edges of Taos. He always had a word of encouragement and usually replacement ammunition. Braving the chance of a bullet, the older boys of the town, organized by Wally Gower, brought food and water to the fighting men. The fury promised to go on forever.

When night fell, the gag withdrew, much to the relief of everyone. To their immediate discomfort, the defenders of Taos soon discovered that the enemy had not gone far enough so that anyone could escape.

Smoke Jensen's words were not greeted with enthusiasm when he made his dark prediction. "They'll be back tomorrow."

Twenty-three

"They're comin' back!"

Early the next morning the shouts of the lookouts roused the wearied protectors of Taos from uneasy sleep. Too many of the townspeople moved with a lethargy that they would soon regret. Caught between their homes and fighting stations, most looked on in numbed horror as the outlaws easily penetrated the thin defenses and streamed into town.

"We ain't got a chance this time," one less courageous townie wailed.

"We're gonners for sure," the faint-hearted barber took up the cry.

Smoke Jensen would hear none of it. He seemed to be everywhere at once as he worked to rally the resistance of the battle-tired people. "Quit your whining," he growled at the timid souls. "Take your weapons and form up in the streets. We can stop them easier when they don't have room to maneuver."

"Say, that's right," one of the more imaginative townies declared. "We can trap them between the buildings. It'll be like shootin' fish in a water trough."

Smoke moved on, praising the idea over his shoulder. "That's the idea. Get to it." Smoke's confidence rose more when he came upon the more reliant among the defenders.

Those Tua warriors not on water watch were the first to respond. Santan Tossa stood on one side of the Plaza de Armas and directed his fighting men to vantage points on the roofs of buildings. Unaccustomed to the Spanish tile roofing material, one of the Tua men put a moccasin on a loose one and all but fell.

"Be careful," Tossa cautioned. Then he produced a fleeting smile at that choice of words in the face of an all-out assault by men determined to kill them all.

On two sides of town, Don Diego's vaqueros labored valiantly to keep more of the trash from entering Taos. The dapper senior Alvarado shouted encouragement to his cowboys. *"Buena suerte, compañeros.* Shoot their eyes out."

Gradually, men caught by surprise on the west side of town began to calm and take better stock of their situation. Smoke Jensen quickly exhorted them. "This isn't the end of it. Not unless you want to go belly-up. Get some backbone, dammit. All of you there, quit milling around and form up to drive and trap those who got past the barricades in the center of town."

Slowly they began to respond. As the first remotivated men spread out, more joined them. Before long they had enough to ring the business district and began to close in. From the moment of the first encounter, the fighting grew more fierce with each passing minute.

Smoke Jensen soon saw that the outer defenses had been completely breached. The vaqueros fought valiantly as they retreated street by street from the pressure put on them by the Quinn gang. Here and there they managed to rally as those facing them turned out to be drifting bits of frontier trash with no deep-set loyalties. That sort crumbled rapidly, especially when confronted with a revival cry from the Mexican cowboys.

"Con nuestra Señora, Santa Maria de Guadalupe! Matenlos maten!"

Even Smoke Jensen developed chills down his spine the first time he heard it and translated the words. *With our lady, Holy Mother of Guadalupe! Kill them, kill!* He had to admit it had a galvanizing effect. The vaqueros swarmed back down the street, a wall of death with six-gun, rifle and knife. At one point, a saddle tramp who had become overwhelmed by their ferocity dropped to his knees and began to howl like a dog. It did him little good. He got his throat slit anyway.

On the next street over, the vaqueros put a full dozen to flight. Horses surged into one another and spilled two riders to face the advancing fury of the Mexican cowboys. They screamed a long time as they died.

Paddy Quinn shoved his way into a cantina to catch his breath and reload. He found Garth Thompson there ahead of him. Whitewater Paddy flashed a big grin. "We're doin' fine. Another half hour and the town will be ours."

Thompson looked at him in consternation. "Are you kidding? We have men dying out there by the handful. It doesn't make sense. These townies are fighting back like mad men."

"Awh, Garth me bucko, yer not seein' clear, yer not. Most of those who are being killed are not part of the gang. What that trash is here for is to soak up bullets for us, it is. Let's go upstairs where we can better see what's really happenin'. Ye'll be surprised how good it's goin', ye will."

Two blocks down, in a narrow alley, three of Quinn's men found the situation more like Garth Thompson saw it than their boss. Seven Tua warriors rounded the corner and started toward them. Clearly they had heard the rumors started by Smoke Jensen. The trio cut their eyes to the Indians and began to run in the opposite direction. Not a one made an effort to fire a weapon.

"Lou, Lou, we gotta get out of here. They're gonna scalp us."

Lou looked ahead and paled. The rear of a building closed off their escape route from the narrow alley. "We're trapped," he wailed.

The others saw it, too. Unnerved by his belief in the scalping story, one of the outlaws turned his gun on himself. His body had hardly hit the ground when Santan Tossa and his brother Tuas opened fire. One of Quinn's men jerked spastically, staggered two paces to his left and keeled over. The other got off a shot before Tossa put a bullet through his screaming mouth.

"They were cowards," the Tua policeman pronounced over the cooling corpses.

Gradually the tide turned. The shock of their earlier failure began to wear off, and the men of Taos ceased in their headlong flight from the threat of the gunmen. They turned back in twos and threes in one place, half a dozen in two others. Instead of two men fighting a desperate rear guard, while the others fled, the mass of harried men turned about and lashed out at their enemy.

At first it did not look like much. Then an angry growl raced through the defenders, until it became one voice. Five of the gang rounded a corner, laughing and firing blindly. Halfway down the block a solid mass of growling, snarling men began to run toward them. A high, clear cry raised above the roar of their discontent.

"Fire! Open fire!"

A ragged volley crackled from the weapons in the hands of shop keepers and clerks, bank tellers and wheelwrights. A stream of lead scythed into the startled outlaws and they began to die. Two of the gunhawks wisely opted to flee. One made it to the corner they had rounded half a minute before. The other one took two faltering steps along his escape route before he fell over dead.

Throughout town the spirit of defeat disappeared as he

died. Shouting, the defenders charged in a massive counter-attack. Determined men soon swept the byways of Taos of the dregs of humanity who had attacked them. The only resistance that remained centered around the saloon named Cantina del Sol. Smoke Jensen reached that strong point in the vanguard of the revived defenders.

Curly Lasher and eight relatively capable gunfighters had been stationed outside the cantina to protect their leaders. He and his underlings listened to the shift in mood among the defenders with growing apprehension. When four of them rounded the corner with a determined stride, the outlaws realized that the seeming ease of their capture of the town was an illusion. Weapons already in hand, the townsfolk had the advantage when the hard cases reached for their six-guns.

Curly had time to shout only brief advice. "Spread out!"

Gunfire roared in the confines between two-story buildings. Two of the outlaws went down. Curly Lasher took cover behind a watering trough and traded shots with the aroused residents of Taos. That lasted until Smoke Jensen and six vaqueros rounded the other corner and closed in on them.

"Make for the saloon," Curly yelled to his surviving men.

Curly backed up the steps to the portico over the entrance to the cantina. A quick check showed that the others had preceded him. He had almost disappeared through the glass-bead curtain that screened the doorway when Smoke Jensen stepped out into the center of the street and pointed his left index finger at the outlaw leader.

"Curly Lasher, you yellow-bellied piss ant, come out and face me like a man."

Smoke Jensen had recognized Curly Lasher the moment the man came to his boots and started for the cantina. Although quite young, Lasher had a respectable reputation as a gunfighter. He was reputed to have killed ten men in face-downs in Texas and New Mexico. Rumor had it his total number of kills included three for-hire assassinations and a dozen ambush shootings. At the age of twenty-three, he was about as good as they came these days. But not in Smoke Jensen's book.

The way Smoke saw it, it was time to cancel Curly's pay book. After issuing his challenge, Smoke waited now, ignoring the random bullets, fired by Lasher's henchmen, that cracked into the ground near him. A second stretched interminably long, then another. Smoke counted to five before Curly waved a grubby, rumpled bit of cloth out the opening to La Cantina del Sol.

"You make those others stop shootin' at me an' I'll face you, Jensen. Hell, you're an old man. You can't be much good anymore."

There it was again, *old man*. Smoke's expression grew grim. "We'll see, won't we? And have those back-shooting gun trash with you holster their irons."

Another second went by. "You heard him, boys. Put 'em up." A nervous giggle escaped Curly. "This is between Smoke Jensen an' me."

With that, Curly Lasher stepped out into the street. He looked formidable enough, except for the muscle tic that twitched his left eye. Smoke Jensen side-stepped to line up with Curly Lasher. Curly's hand hovered over the butt-grip of his Smith and Wesson .44 American. He nodded evenly to Smoke.

"Your play, Jensen."

"No, you go first. I want this to be fair."

Another giggle burst from Curly's throat. "Fair? Hell, Jensen, you better be pickin' out your coffin right now."

"You reckon to jaw me to death? If so, it'll be like ol' Samson, eh? Killed with the jawbone of an ass."

That tripped Curly's hair-trigger temper. "Goddamn you, Smoke Jensen, kiss your tail goodbye."

Curly Lasher drew then, confident that he had beaten Smoke Jensen by a good half second. Not until a stunning force slammed into his chest did he realize how terribly mistaken he had been. His lips formed a perfect *O*, and his legs went rubbery. Enormous pain spread through his body, followed instantly by a frightening numbness. Try as his brain might to send signals to his heart, they never arrived. A fat, 230 grain .45 slug had destroyed that vital organ.

His eyes rolled up in their sockets, Curly discharged a round into the street and fell in a crumpled heap. In the moment after he fired, Smoke Jensen moved. He waved at the astonished townies to follow him.

"Come on, let's get in that saloon."

"B'God, that was fast," Warren Engals muttered. "I never seen his hand move."

"Neither did that cocky gunhawk," Buel Spencer snorted in satisfaction.

Mid-morning came and went. Still the fighting lingered, as Smoke Jensen and five of the men from town entered La Cantina del Sol. Theirs could hardly be called a conventional means of entry. Smoke sent four vaqueros around to the rear to make a show of breaking in through the service door. He gave them enough time to be convincing, then dived low through the front doorway. Smoke hit the floor and did a roll, to come up with his Colt blazing. He got immediate results.

One hard case slammed into the bar, his back arched to the point of breaking his spine. Smoke fired again and the bones cracked. The outlaw dropped to flop on the floor like a headless chicken. A townsman and one of Diego's vaqueros entered behind the last mountain man. Flame gushed from the muzzles of their six-guns.

Another hard case died in their hail of lead. A third had dived for cover behind the bar when Smoke first entered. He popped up now and shot Ransom Clover between the eyes. The feed store proprietor died on his feet. But not before Smoke Jensen sent the killer off to eternity with a similar wound. Terrible discordance came from the upright piano in one corner as another thug hastily fired a bullet at Smoke's back.

Smoke ducked and spun on one boot heel. The muzzle of his Peacemaker tracked with him, and he squeezed off a round the moment the back shooter came into view. Hot lead punched through thick leather and then did awful damage to the hip bone of the man. By then, Smoke had cocked his .45 and put a second slug into the chest of his assailant. Restricted by the muslin safeguards suspended below the ceiling, viscous layers of powder smoke undulated in the room, obscuring the whereabouts of other enemies.

Ears ringing from the enclosed gunfire, Smoke made for the stairway. There had to be some reason why a fairly reliable gunfighter like Curly Lasher and eight men had been guarding this place. He had reached the first riser with a boot toe when another of the gunmen appeared at the top of the stairs. Smoke acted at once.

So close to the wall, the force of his gun blast nearly ruptured Jensen's eardrum. Yet he did not even flinch as he recocked his six-gun and sent another .45 round winging upward to seal the fate of the hard case who menaced him. Hit twice in less than half a minute, the outlaw staggered back and rammed slack shoulders into the wall of the upper hallway. Smoke paused at the landing and called back to the ground floor to one of the vaqueros.

"Juaquin, come up here with me." When the slender, boyish-faced cowboy reached the top of the stairs, Smoke gave terse instructions. "Stay here. Watch my back."

Smoke set off to search the rooms in the rear portion of the second floor. Someone of importance had to be up here, his gut feeling told him. He readied himself at the first door, cocked his leg and plated a boot beside the doorknob. A loud crack followed and the panel flew inward. Following his six-gun, Smoke entered the room in a crouch.

Empty. He turned on one heel and started for the next. His explosive entry caught two outlaws with their backs to him, taking shots at Taos residents in the street below. The slam of the door against the inner wall brought one around in a blur of movement. His eyes went wide as he gazed at Death with a outstretched hand. The six-gun in that hand fired a second later, and reflex drove the bandit backward to crash through the window, taking both sashes with him as he fell to the ground. The second hard case wisely released his revolver and threw up his hands. Smoke Jensen stepped up close and rapped him on the skull with the barrel of a Colt. That left three more rooms to check.

The next proved even more empty than the first. It did not even have furniture. Smoke moved on to the next in line.

His vicious kick surprised Garth Thompson and Paddy Quinn in the act of reloading. Thompson swung his six-gun up first and fired at Smoke. The man from the Sugarloaf had already fired a round which ripped into the body of Garth Thompson a fraction of an instant before the outlaw's bullet punched a neat hole in the left side of Smoke Jensen's waist. It burned like hell fire, but it did not even stagger him. Thompson tried to fire again, not realizing he looked at his target with a dead man's eyes.

His bullet cut air beside Smoke Jensen's left ear as the legs of Garth Thompson gave way. Smoke gave him a safety round and turned his attention to Paddy Quinn.

Stunned by the swiftness of action by Smoke Jensen, Paddy Quinn only belatedly closed the loading gate of his Colt Peacemaker. Instinctively, he knew he did not have time for a shot. Not if he wanted to continue living. Instead, he diverted his energy to his legs and sprinted past the wounded

Jensen out into the hall. Smoke bit back the pain that burned in his side and turned in pursuit.

Out in the hall, Paddy Quinn raced toward the far end of the building. A window in the center of the corridor there bore a sign above it that read *Escalera de Incendios*. Fire Escape for those who could read Spanish. Smoke Jensen pounded down the bare board floor behind Quinn. The outlaw leader made better time.

Without a break in his stride, Paddy Quinn threw his arms up to cover his face and hurtled through the glass partition. Fragments of the sashes clung to him as he hit the small, square projection that served as a platform for a ladder. Legs still churning, Paddy cleared the railing in a single bound and dropped out of sight before Smoke reached the shattered window casement.

Quinn landed flat-footed and hard on the packed earth below. Pain shot up his leg from a broken heel bone. His horse, and those of Thompson and another hard case, had been tied off at the rear door earlier in the day. So unexpected and precipitous had been his arrival from above that the vaqueros sent to break in the rear stood in immobile surprise while Paddy limped to his mount, retrieved the reins and swung into the saddle.

Smoke Jensen sent a bullet after Paddy Quinn as the latter called out to his men. "Pull back. Get clear of town. We've lost it for now."

Twenty-four

His face twisted in anger and contempt, Clifton Satterlee rounded on Paddy Quinn. "What do you mean you had the town taken, and then got pushed out? How can that happen?"

Whitewater Paddy's answer came low and meek. "Smoke Jensen. That's how it happened. He killed Garth, he did, an' he near to finished me in the bargain. He found out somehow where we were and came after us with some of those Mezkins."

Satterlee paced the confined space in the ruined adobe farmhouse. "Better that you and a dozen like you die than that I lose Taos."

Stung by the insult, Paddy's eyes narrowed. "Pardon me, Mr. Satterlee, sir. There's no denyin' yer smart an' all that. But, truth to tell, your chances of takin' Taos without me are somewhere between slim an' none, they are."

Face florid with his fury, Clifton Satterlee raised a fist as though to strike the gang leader and bellowed up close in Quinn's face. "Then get out there, gather up what men you have left and go back. And keep on going back until their resistance crumbles. Brice, you're going with them."

Brice Noble gaped at his partner. He knew himself to be good with his guns, better than most of the petty criminals in Quinn's gang. Yet, he realized he was not any sort of gunfighter like Smoke Jensen. The man was entirely too good. "You're not serious. What could I possibly do?"

Sarcasm dripped from Satterlee's words. "You could be like a famous general. An inspiration to the men."

"That's uncalled for. There's simply no reason for me to go there."

Satterlee turned even nastier. "But there is . . . because I insist. Now, get going, Quinn, and bring me back a town on its knees."

Shortly after noon, the gang came back to Taos. Those in the lead met with a shower of wine-bottle grenades. The black-powder bombs exploded with sharp cracks and bright flashes. The shards of their containers, and the scraps of metal within, whizzed through the air. Many pieces bit into vulnerable flesh, both equine and human. One went off so close to two hard cases that both of them and their horses were disemboweled. Their shrieks of agony engendered pity even among those they attacked.

Soon their distressed wailing faded under the tumult as the fighting rose toward a crescendo. Paddy Quinn had centered nearly all of his men on one side of town. Only a few snipers and riders kept the defenders on the other three sides occupied. As the volume of fire increased at the center of the offensive, a voice rose from the assailants.

"They broke! They broke! They're running."

It was quickly picked up. The shouts merged into a roar as the allies could no longer withstand the onslaught. Outlaws poured into the gap in the line and spread out through the streets of Taos. Pushed to the forefront of the vanguard, Brice Noble found himself the first to enter the small town. When the resistance melted away his confidence soared. This might be easier than he had expected. His horse trotted down the narrow avenue toward the center of town.

At the Plaza de Armas, Noble found a tall, broad-shouldered man directing the fight. He forcefully snatched demoralized residents off their feet and shoved them into a position from which they could engage the invaders. His calm demeanor told Brice Noble that if they were to succeed, this man must be eliminated. He edged closer and formed the words of a challenge as he raised his revolver to accomplish that. Off to the side, someone yelled the gunfighter's name.

"Smoke! Smoke Jensen. I've got ten men here ready to fight." Then, sighting Noble, he pointed out the menace, "Look out, Smoke!"

Smoke Jensen turned his cold gaze on the man who sought to kill him. He backed it up with the muzzle of a .45 Colt. Instantly, fear eroded his guts, and Brice Noble swallowed his provocation. He lowered his right arm and released the six-gun. It dropped to the grass with a thud while Noble raised his hands over his head.

"I surrender. I've not fired my weapon. Don't shoot me, Mr. Jensen."

"Get down." Smoke's command moved Noble with alacrity. He swung a leg over and dismounted while Smoke walked up to him "Who are you?"

"I—I'm Brice Noble, a business associate of Clifton Satterlee."

"Umm." Smoke swung from the belt line. His hard fist connected with the lantern jaw of Brice Noble. When the arch criminal crumbled, Smoke reached out and caught a townsman by one arm. "Drag this piece of dog dung to the jail."

Diego Alvarado sought a single man among the outlaws. His wide experience in fighting a variety of enemies told him that the majority of these vermin would flee if they lost their leader. Smoke Jensen had killed Garth Thompson that morning. That left only Paddy Quinn. He left Alejandro and Miguel in charge of the vaqueros and started off to locate the gang boss. Mayor Arianas, an old friend, approached him as Diego crossed the Plaza de Armas.

"Diego, I am astonished at the valor of the Tua warriors. They fight for us as though this was their town."

Alvarado gave him a wry smile. "They know that if Taos falls, their pueblo will be right behind. Satterlee wants everything around here. I, for one, am grateful for their aid."

"As am I, amigo." Arianas paused a moment, uncertain of the propriety of his question. "May I ask, where are you going? Most of your men are on the east side."

"Don't worry, my friend. I am looking for Paddy Quinn. When I find him, I am going to kill him and end this madness."

Arianas clapped Diego on one shoulder. *"Buena suerte,* then."

"Gracias. I can use all the good luck I can manage."

Diego Alvarado strode off, headed north. As he went by the flight of granite steps that fronted the church on the plaza, he automatically crossed himself and cast a reverent glance at the impressive structure. Suddenly the bells began to toll. Padre Luis threw wide the tall, oak doors and stepped out onto the wide flagstones at the top of the stairs.

"Men of Taos, rally your strength. Fight for your freedom," he exhorted the confused and demoralized defenders who huddled in the plaza. "Remember your women and children. Drive out the invaders."

A gunshot cracked across the plaza, seemingly louder than all of the others. Father Luis jerked at the impact and swayed, a large red stain spreading on the shoulder of his cassock. Diego Alvarado looked in the direction from which the shot had come. Seated on his horse was the man he sought. Paddy Quinn had a smoking six-gun in his hand and a nasty sneer on his face.

"Easy for you to say, priest. You who hides behind his own skirt," the apostate outlaw snarled. Oblivious to Diego

Alvarado, Paddy Quinn started to raise his revolver for another shot.

Diego Alvarado filled his hand with his Obregon .45 with all the smoothness and almost the speed of Smoke Jensen. He cocked and fired in one even motion. The bullet took Quinn in the belly. He winced, but seemed otherwise unaffected. His icy black eyes turned on Diego.

"So, cowherder, you defy me one last time, is it now? The priest can wait. This is between you an' me, bucko."

Before the last word left his mouth, Quinn fired the Colt in his hand. The slug cut a deep, painful gouge across the top of Diego's left shoulder. Then Alvarado fired the Obrigon again. His aim off because of his wound, he nailed Quinn in the right thigh. That proved enough to unhorse the gang leader. He fell and sprawled on the cobbles that paved the street in front of the church. Immediately Paddy Quinn learned how mistaken he had been in shooting the priest.

Rather than demoralizing the residents of Taos, his blasphemous act served to electrify the defenders. A great roar of outrage filled the plaza from Protestant, Catholic and pagan alike. Suddenly the peons, who did not possess firearms, swarmed over the fallen outlaw. Sunlight glinted off the well-honed edges of their machetes. Their arms rose and fell in a steady rhythm while Paddy Quinn shrieked and screamed his way into oblivion.

Blood streaming from his own wound, Diego Alvarado hurried to the injured priest. "Padre, you are hurt. I will get the doctor."

Gentle brown eyes settled on Alvarado. "Care for your own wound, Diego. God will tend to my needs."

Diego would not back down so easily. "Dr. Walters can give Him a lot of help. Let me take you inside. Then I will go for the doctor." Diego Alvarado cut his eyes to the mutilated corpse of Paddy Quinn. "He has answered for his crimes here, now I hope he burns in the hottest corner of hell."

* * *

Word quickly spread about the demise of Paddy Quinn. It restored the fighting spirit of those who protected Taos, especially when they learned how and why he had died. It proved to have the opposite affect on the outlaws. Leaderless, and with no assurance of being paid, the hangers-on deserted in droves. Harried by the emboldened townsmen, they streamed out of the city and made tracks toward Raton. The first two dozen to desert opened the flood gates.

Fighting continued for another twenty minutes while the headlong flight reduced the number of outlaws by more than half. Three of Quinn's subordinate leaders held a hasty meeting in the shelter of an adobe house on the west edge of town.

Yank Hastings came right to the point. "We have to get out of here. Those gutless cowards have left us in a fine fix.

Vic Tyson nodded, his face a grim mask. "Tell us something we don't know."

Hastings faced the sarcasm without a reaction. "The boss was right about puttin' all our force on one place. We got in, didn't we? I say we can do the same to get back out."

"Then what?"

"We run like hell for someplace else, Vic."

"What about our share of the loot?"

"There ain't gonna be anything to share. We can rob a couple of banks if we need money. Only I ain't stayin' around here any longer. You with me?"

"We'll do it," the other two agreed.

It did not take long. Hungry for revenge, the guardians of Taos roamed from building to building, street to street. Those outlaws who offered resistance they gunned down. The wiser ones they drove ahead of them. Smoke Jensen and Diego Alvarado led two thirds of them, Santan Tossa the remainder. Within half an hour the streets had been cleared.

"Now what?" a tired, powder-grimed Diego Alvarado asked over the top of a tubo of beer. A thick bandage bulged under his coat.

"Do you think they will be back?" Alejandro Alvarado queried.

Smoke Jensen had been thinking along those lines. "There's always the chance that they will. Though I hope not. We've lost fifteen men killed, and twice that wounded. If there's none of them left except the original gang, they can overwhelm us, given the right leader. To keep that from happening, I reckon to go out late tonight and cut off the head of the snake. That'll end it once and for all."

Alejandro looked eagerly at the big man. "I want to go along."

A smile spread on Smoke's face. "Welcome you'll be, Alejandro. Now, let's drink up and get something to eat. We need to rest before going out there."

⌁

Vic Tyson's concern over losing their pay proved baseless. While the remains of the gang fought its way out of Taos, Clifton Satterlee and his bodyguard, Cole Granger, rounded them up and persuaded them to listen. Reluctantly, others joined the gathering.

"Listen to me, men. We have to control Taos in order for our development scheme to succeed. You will all be rewarded. And most generously, I might add. In fact, I will offer you a bonus of one half your original share if you will agree to do what must be done. You will remain here, deny the people in town any contact with the outside. Cut off their food supply. Shoot any armed man you see on the streets. In short, maintain the siege until more men can be recruited and sent here to make the final push." Satterlee paused and let his gaze sweep over the assembled outlaws.

"Do you understand what I'm saying? The whole project now depends upon you. You have good leaders in Yank Hastings, Vic Tyson and Coop Ellis."

Coopersmith Ellis flushed slightly at that praise. Satterlee continued his harangue. "What I want is for you to do this. Return to positions well out of rifle range, and encircle the town again. Concentrate on the roads. Roving patrols can take care of anyone who tries to slip away across the fields. That's simple, isn't it? When enough men reach here for another attack, go at it with a will. Don't let anything stop you."

His stirring words brought a ragged cheer. But not enough to change Satterlee's mind on a matter of some considerable importance. When the remotivated gunmen started out to take their new positions, Clifton Satterlee huddled with Cole Granger and explained what he had in mind.

Darkness had covered Taos three hours earlier when Smoke Jensen and Alejandro Alvarado left town to spy out the enemy. It had taken that long for the gang to settle down. Some of them still had strong reservations about staying there. Several voiced their opinions loudly while Smoke and Alejandro slipped quietly through their line, headed for the adobe ruin where Smoke had earlier seen Martha.

"I think this is damn foolishness," one tough spared no effort in informing those near the fire where they prepared a meal and a pot of coffee.

"Biggs is right," another put in. "Without Whitewater Paddy, we've got no one to stand up to this Satterlee. Who says he'll for real pay us when it's over?"

"I'm glad you agree," Biggs included the man. "I say we walk our horses out of here right now, hit the high road to Santa Fe and don't look back."

"Hell yes. Those Injuns could be out there, sneakin' around with their scalpin' knifes right this minute."

"Don't even mention that," a third hard case replied. "It gives me cold chills."

Smoke and Alejandro crept on in the moonless night. When they reached the spot where Smoke thought the building should be, they found nothing. Smoke motioned for Alejandro to separate from him and look for the adobe. Quietly, both men went about finding the place.

Smoke located it first and saw that the farmhouse was unlighted. Had everyone gone to sleep? Somehow he doubted that. Moments later, Alejandro joined him, having made a wide, half circle. Smoke leaned close and whispered in the young ranchero's ear.

"I want to get a look inside. But if you were to ask me, I'd say the place is deserted. No light, no guards."

Smoke's speculation proved correct. He cautiously entered the structure through a crumbled rear wall. There he quickly discovered that Martha and Lupe no longer occupied the chairs. The table where they had sat had been overturned. He saw no sign of Clifton Satterlee either. Back outside, Smoke suggested they check along the line of fires where the watchers remained at the roadblocks.

A careful search among them revealed no sign of Martha Estes, her maid, or Clifton Satterlee. When they approached the last of the barricades, Smoke suddenly realized that Alejandro's appearance would give them away. Smoke made an abrupt signal that told the youthful *caballero* to wait outside the firelight and cover him while he went in to talk with the outlaws. Alejandro disappeared into the night, and Smoke continued to the fireside.

"Quiet as a graveyard," Smoke observed as he walked up.

"You coulda picked something better to say about it," grumbled one of the saddle trash. "What you doin' here?"

"You've got coffee goin', I smelled it. So, here I am."

His earlier jitters forgotten in light of no forays from town, the outlaw chuckled. "Pour yourself a cup."

Smoke took a blue granite tin cup and filled it. "Where's the big boss? He was so hot for us stayin' here," Smoke probed casually.

A low curse answered him. "Didn't have the grit to stay here himself. A little while after that pep talk, he took the women an' Granger and they high-tailed it outta here. Off to Santa Fe, I reckon."

One of his companions spoke up in support of Satterlee. "He's goin' to get more men. Remember what he said about sending us some fresh blood?"

"Yeah. And blood is what it'll be, you ask me."

Smoke let them talk for a while, then drained his coffee and handed back the cup. "Thanks for the brew. I'd best get back to rovin' from place to place or someone will have a hissy."

"Yeah, that's right. So, you're with Vic Tyson's crew, eh?"

"Yep. For better or for worse. See you fellers."

Reunited with Alejandro Alvarado, Smoke Jensen and the ranchero made a rapid return to town. On the way, Smoke weighed the alternatives facing him. Not unusual, he did not like any of them. Back in the sheriff's office, he sent loungers to summon a war council. This would be a long night, Smoke knew.

"There's nothing for it but that I go after them," Smoke announced after relaying what he had learned beyond the town.

Mayor Fidel Arianas nodded thoughtfully. "I can understand that. But how are you going to go about it?"

Smoke Jensen had his answers ready. "First we have to break this siege. They are mighty spooked over two defeats in one day. And we've not attacked them at night before. What we are going to do is organize an assault force from the local volunteers and Diego's vaqueros and wipe out their roadblocks, scatter the patrols around the town and plain raise a lot of hell."

Diego Alvarado's eyes glowed. *"Muy bien, amigo.* Naturally, all of my men will volunteer."

Smoke shook his head. "We only need half of them. Someone has to hold the fort. Gather five groups of ten each, and meet me in the Plaza de Armas in half an hour. One bunch will take each road out of town. The fifth will make a sweep of the roving patrols. Tonight we're going to kick hell out of these scum."

Thirty minutes later, grim-faced men gathered in the plaza. All were heavily armed. Every man had a horse. Smoke quietly gave them their assignments and moved out himself with those going after the mobile pickets. When everyone had gotten into position, they watched the hands on one of the clocks located on the four sides of the church steeple. The minute hand closed on 10:45, and the deadly bands moved out.

Three hundred yards from the roadblocks they urged their mounts to a gallop. Weapons out and ready, they opened fire at seventy-five yards.

With Quinn and Thompson dead and Satterlee gone, the attack quickly became a rout. Already demoralized by the turn of the day's events, the outlaw trash had little heart for a fight. Muzzle flashes in the night, followed by the crack of bullets and roar of weapons, undid even the most courageous among them. Men seemed to be shooting at them from all directions. Riderless horses ran past, and those securely picketed whinnied in the mad desire to join their fellows.

"To hell with this, I'm gettin' outta here," the hard case known as Rucker spat as he ankled over the ground to his horse.

He slipped on a bridle and swung up bareback. No time

for the niceties. Too many guns out there. He drummed his heels into the flanks of his horse and broke clear of the melee behind him. His mount nearly ran into the chest of a big, gray, spotted-rump 'Palouse. Veering at the last instant, he caught a glimpse of the rider.

"Oh, God, Smoke Jensen," he wailed aloud.

Then Smoke shot him.

In twenty minutes the last of the vermin had been exterminated or surrendered. Diego's vaqueros herded them back toward town. At the jail, Smoke confronted the leaders of the resistance. "Thank you all for what you've done. You've saved your town. The end of this is up to me. I'm going after Clifton Satterlee. Mac, Alejandro, I'd like you to come with me. We'll take about twenty-five men to handle any opposition Satterlee can muster. Even with them, it's gonna be mighty hard to end this."

Twenty-five

Smoke, Alejandro and Mac rode out of Taos at the head of a twenty-three-man force. Even pushing to the limit, they would not reach Santa Fe until early morning of the next day. Smoke used the time to review how they should go about cornering Satterlee. His options were limited; that he accepted. He had no way of knowing how many gunhands Satterlee might have at the large estancia outside the territorial capital. Whatever the count, he wanted to keep the number of injuries and deaths small among his volunteers. Most of all he wanted to give Mac a chance at building a satisfying life for himself. All such considerations aside, he wanted to end it quickly. Could he count on the sheriff in Santa Fe?

That question remained with him as they rode through Española. False dawn caught them still two miles from Satterlee's lair. To Smoke that answered his preoccupation with the sheriff. They simply did not have time to ride past the road that led to the ranch and into Santa Fe. They would have to do it on their own.

Half a mile from the estancia, Smoke halted his small force and informed them of what they would do. "Mac, I want you to take charge of everyone but Alejandro and myself. Take on any gunhands Satterlee has at the ranch and keep them busy. Alejandro and I will go in to find Martha. Also to get Satterlee." Then he added with a crooked smile,

"If something happens to let us open the gates for you, we will."

"I want to go with you, Smoke," Mac protested.

"Not this time. Keep in mind, youngster, that you are only fifteen years old. I'm not going to coddle you, but I want you in a responsible position, doing something that has to be done. Something that keeps you out of the center of most danger."

Mac blurted his objection. "But I want to be there, to help."

"Hell, boy, you're gonna get shot at anyway. Why make it worse?"

Grudgingly, Mac saw his point. "I'll do my best, Smoke. Count on it."

Alejandro nodded silent approval. He couldn't help but like this boy/man. "I think my father will find it impossible to continue his food production without you, young Mac. We want you around to make our gardens more productive."

Mac flushed and put on a foolish grin to hide his elation at this praise. "Yes, sir—uh—Alejandro. Do they—ah—ever call you Alex?"

Alejandro flashed white teeth in his olive face. "Only my gringo friends. So, I suppose you can, too."

Smoke concluded his strategy session. "Let's get to it, then. Mac, circle wide around and hit the place from the rear. Once you have their attention, we'll come at 'em from the front."

A short while later, Mac and his mixed force invested the walls around three sides of the hacienda. Under cover of darkness, Smoke and Alejandro approached the front gate in the twelve-foot wall that surrounded the compound. Smoke had a little surprise that he had not mentioned to the others. With the battle raging around them, he quickly went to work sheltered by the inset of the massive portals.

"Alejandro, gather up all the big rocks you can find. Bring them here."

Diego's eldest son went to work with a twinkle in his eyes from sight of the cylindrical sticks in Smoke's hands. By the time Alejandro returned for the sixth time, Smoke had attached a bundle of five sticks of dynamite to the center of the gate, where the crossbar would be.

"Mix some mud," Smoke commanded as he bent to place more dynamite against one of the hinges.

Alejandro found water in a horse trough and plenty of desert soil right where they needed it. He carried the liquid in his hat to make a quagmire under the sheltering lip above them. When he thought he had it right, he stopped to watch Smoke packing rocks against the charge on the hinge.

"Smoke, it is ready."

Studying the consistency of the mud, Smoke passed judgment. "Thicker. Make it sticky."

When it reached the desired texture, Smoke began to pack it around the explosives in the middle of the gate, then poured more over the rocks. That completed, he cut his eyes to Alejandro. "We'll let that dry awhile."

The volume of gunfire rose and fell as the outlaws traded shots with the men from Taos. It served well to keep attention off Smoke and Alejandro. After ten minutes, the surface had returned to its natural color, and cracks began to appear in the mud. Smoke nodded approvingly and bent with a lucifer in his hand.

"You light that one and I'll get this. Then we get out of here . . . fast."

With the fuses sputtering, Smoke and Alejandro ran from the gateway and flattened their backs against the wall to either side. Three minutes went by, and then a tremendous roar shattered the sporadic gunfire from within the hacienda. Dirt and acrid smoke billowed out of the arched opening. Splinters of flaming wood mingled with them. The ground shook, and Alejandro smelled the nauseous fumes of the burned dynamite. In the numbing silence that followed, Smoke and Alejandro heard a shrill shriek, followed by an enormous crash.

"Let's go," said Smoke tautly.

Quickly they rounded the corners that had sheltered them. Alejandro's jaw sagged at sight of the damage the explosives had wrought. One side of the thick gate hung askew. The other lay flat on the ground, blown out from the bottom. Smoke jumped on top of it and ran into the courtyard. They met with no resistance until they reached the main entrance to the hacienda. Two dumbfounded thugs with bestubbled jaws stood inside. They gaped at the damage until the figures of Smoke Jensen and Alejandro Alvarado filled the range of their vision.

"Lutie, it's him. It's Smoke Jensen," babbled one.

"Then git him, Frank, git him."

Each man made the fateful mistake of reaching for his six-gun. Smoke beat them both, with Alejandro not far behind. The Colt in Smoke's hand bellowed, and Lutie doubled over, shot through the liver. Frank fired a round before Alejandro ended his life with a bullet in the head. Side-stepping the dying men, Smoke and Alejandro pushed on into the house. Cole Granger and three men waited for them in the inner courtyard.

"There they are," shouted one piece of human debris as Smoke became visible at the inner opening of the corridor.

Smoke, the .45 still in his hand, shot him through the heart. Two others dived for cover behind the cheerily splashing fountain. Granger dropped behind a huge clay olla that held a stunted banana tree. From there he triggered a round that ripped along the left ribs of Alejandro Alvarado.

Face grimaced in agony, the young grandee spun to one side and leaned back against the wall of the arched corridor that connected the front door to the patio. "Go on, Smoke. I'll be all right."

Alejadro extended his right arm along the wall and took

aim at a pale face that appeared above the lip of the fountain. Biting his lip, he squeezed his trigger. The slug slammed into the edge of the marble basin. Water and stone chips showered into the air. The face disappeared, an irregular hole in the center of its forehead. At once, Smoke was on the move.

He bounded to his left and dropped behind a long, earth-filled planter. Three slugs pounded into the opposite surface. Smoke inched along to the end and hazarded a quick look. Granger had come to his boots, peering across the open garden in a attempt to get a sight on Smoke. It would be all too easy.

Smoke raised his arm and fired at the center line of Granger's body. The bullet smashed into Granger's belly, and he staggered backward. Smoke came to his boots and jinked off another direction. He learned that he had miscalculated Granger's strength a moment later when Alejadro shouted from behind him.

"Smoke, look out!"

Cole Granger fired his six-gun with less than acceptable accuracy. A hot tunnel opened in Jensen's left arm an instant before he discharged his Colt and put another bullet in Cole Granger's chest. To his surprise Granger absorbed the punishment and turned his gun on Alejandro.

This time he wavered unsteadily so that the slug struck the stucco-plastered, adobe wall before it plowed into the chest of Alejandro Alvarado. Cursing his bad luck, Smoke raised his point of aim. He fired at Granger's face and blasted the life out of his assailant. Quickly he bound his arm and changed his empty Colt for the fresh one. Then Smoke began to search for the final hard case.

Sagged to his knees, Alejandro called out to Smoke. "He's gone. Ran out on the others."

"What about you?" Concern rang in Smoke's voice.

"It's . . . not bad. Go on. Find Satterlee and get the girl to safety."

Smoke Jensen started for the stairway that led to the second floor. Behind him a door flew open. Smoke spun on one heel and snapped off a shot. Another of Satterlee's henchmen died. Halfway up the stairs, he paused to look back. Alejandro sat spread-legged against the wall, his face pale, but his breathing regular. The bullet must not have reached his lung, Smoke speculated.

He took time then to reload, then ascended to the open-sided hallway that ran around the upper story. Now the search turned serious. Smoke stepped to the first door and kicked it in. A startled hard case turned from the window where he had been exchanging rounds with Mac and the attackers, who had swarmed into the compound through the damaged gate. Smoke shot him in the shoulder, took his weapons and locked the door behind as he left. The next two rooms were empty. Smoke worked his way out into the open.

From below, Alejandro spoke to Smoke, his words light and breathy. "I can cover you from here."

Smoke nodded and went on. The next door he found locked from the inside. His .45 Peacemaker at the ready, Smoke lined up and kicked the center panel beside the lock case. It hurt like hell. Made of stout manzanita, the door did not yield. Smoke kicked again, with the other foot. Wood splintered in the frame. Dimly, from behind and below, Smoke noted the arrival of Mac and some of the vaqueros. They swarmed through the courtyard as Smoke lashed out with his boot a third time. The door flew open to reveal a frightened and startled Lupe and a bulldog-faced hard case.

"Down," Smoke shouted to the maid.

She dropped without hesitation. Smoke popped a cap on the outlaw at close range. The slug pierced a forearm and entered a vulnerable chest. Smoke shot him again, and the thug's six-gun flew upward out of his hand. It discharged when it struck the ceiling. The bullet went through the thin plaster and exited the building by way of the tin roof. A stunned expression washed over the dying gunman's features, and he fell face-first to the floor.

Smoke pointed to Lupe. "Stay here."

Footsteps pounded in the stairwell as Smoke faced the next door. It was also locked. Smoke reared back for a good blow with his boot as Mac and three of Diego's cowboys ran toward him.

"We got 'em all, Smoke. Most just gave up."

"Stay back," Smoke cautioned. Then he slammed his boot sole against the door.

It happened in a blur. Smoke saw a thick-shouldered gunman facing the door and fired instinctively. The lout dropped his revolver and clasped his belly with both hands. Smoke shot him again. At once he looked to his left.

With a long-legged stride, Clifton Satterlee moved across the carpet toward a wide-eyed, visibly shaken Martha Estes. He had a .44 Colt Lightning in his left hand. Too late, and knowing it, Smoke swung his Peacemaker toward Satterlee and fought to gain time with his voice.

"Don't move!"

"Stop where you are." Mac's voice broke as he stormed into the room, eyes fixed on Satterlee.

Satterlee swung his Lightning away from Martha and fired double-action. His bullet hit Mac in the notch at the bottom of his throat. Quickly, Satterlee shot again. This .44 slug punched through Mac's right lung and ripped out his back. Instantly, Clifton Satterlee grabbed Martha Estes and pulled her in front of him. Driven backward by the agony of his wounds, Ian MacGreggor stumbled into the corridor. He teetered on the banister for a precarious moment. Then his legs went out from under him, and he caught himself with his elbows.

Smoke did not have time to check the youngster and knew it. He faced Satterlee, who now held the muzzle of his Colt Lightning to Martha's temple. "I'll kill her. So help me, I will. Holster your iron and get out of my way. Let me go and she won't be harmed."

Reluctantly, Smoke complied. Then he heard a miserable groan from Mac, and his eyes narrowed to furious slits. "You're a dead man, Satterlee. There's no way you are getting out of here."

Satterlee cut his eyes to a large carpetbag on the floor. It bulged with his portable wealth. Two finely wrought pieces of Tua jewelry spilled from the open top. "I'm taking that and her and leaving.

Smoke eyed the loot and returned his attention to Satterlee. "You killed that boy for nothing, Satterlee. More than for any other reason, I'm going to kill you for that."

Clifton Satterlee forced a nasty chuckle. "Not likely, Jensen. I've worked too hard for that." Again his eyes shifted to his ill-gotten gains. "You make a try and the girl dies."

Suddenly, Martha Estes moaned and uttered a huge sigh. She went limp in the arms of Clifton Satterlee. The instant her head fell away from the gun barrel, Smoke Jensen drew with blinding speed and triggered a round. The slug hit Satterlee at the top of his nose and pulped the empire builder's brain. He did not have time to send a signal to his trigger finger. He flew away from Martha Estes and sprawled across the bed.

At once, Martha straightened and opened her eyes. A big smile adorned her face. "I thought you might do that," she told Smoke a moment before she rushed to him and gave him a big hug.

Gently Smoke disengaged her. "You're safe now, Miss Martha. I'll arrange for passage to your home. Now, if you'll excuse me."

Smoke stepped out into the hall and gazed down at the bloody, sweating, pale-faced Mac. Ian MacGreggor worked his throat, and his lips moved. He spoke in a low, wheezy voice. "I—I guess I'll not be needing that gardening job."

Something stung Smoke's eyes, and he blinked rapidly.

"That was a fool thing to do, Mac. But you did save a girl's life. I'm proud of you." No reason to hide the obvious from the boy. "I'll see that your family gets your pay."

"Th—thank you, Smoke. It was—was an honor to fight at . . . your side." That said, Mac heaved a mighty sigh and died.

Eyes wet and burning, Smoke Jensen turned away to discover that Don Diego Alvarado and his remaining vaqueros had arrived. Smoke went to his friend. "Alejandro took a couple of bad ones."

"Yes. I saw. What about you?"

"I'll live. But . . . Mac didn't make it. I'll have to see that the Marshal's Office sends his pay to his parents."

"It's a beautiful day," Martha Estes opined as she joined the two men.

Still deeply moved by the death of Ian MacGreggor, Smoke looked across the early morning vista. The rising sun cast a pink hue on the white caps of the Sangre de Cristo range. No matter the cost, peace could return to Taos and the Tua pueblo. He nodded to Martha.

"Yes, it is a right nice day." *She's right, it's beautiful,* Smoke mused. *Almost as beautiful as the Sugarloaf.*

Sally and Bobby Jensen greeted Smoke's triumphant return to the Sugarloaf with unbounded joy. After a long, energetic embrace, Smoke looked around and then kissed Sally on one cheek.

"It doesn't look like anything has changed. What did you do while I was gone?"

Sally pursed her lips, fought to banish her sour memories, then answered. "I had a visit from an old school friend."

"That's nice. Did you have a good time?"

"Like heck," Bobby put in. "Her kids sure are a bunch of brats." In spite of Sally's sharp look, Bobby went on. "It's the truth. And you're always after me to tell the truth, Smoke. An' to be man enough to stand up for it."

Smoke put an arm around each of his family and started for the porch, hugging them tightly. "So, tell me about this friend of yours, Sally. And don't forget the brats."

THE MOUNTAIN MAN SERIES BY
WILLIAM W. JOHNSTONE

Available Wherever Books Are Sold!

Visit our website at **www.kensingtonbooks.com**